THE SOUL OF THE CITY

THE SOUL OF THE CITY

JOHN MCMILLAN

iUniverse LLC
Bloomington

THE SOUL OF THE CITY

iUniverse books may be ordered through booksellers or by contacting:

iUniverse LLC
1663 Liberty Drive
Bloomington, IN 47403
www.iuniverse.com
1-800-Authors (1-800-288-4677)

ISBN: 978-1-4917-1438-6 (sc)
ISBN: 978-1-4917-1439-3 (e)

Printed in the United States of America.

iUniverse rev. date: 02/20/2014

To Fiona

CONTENTS

PART ONE

Native Ground

PART TWO

A Stranger On The Earth

PART ONE

NATIVE GROUND

Where Lagan stream sings lullaby
There blows a lily fair
The twilight gleam is in her eye
The night is on her hair . . .
(Irish trad.)

CHAPTER 1

The Girl from the Jazz Club

I got back from summer work in Guernsey at the end of August 1965 and began looking for a full-time job in Belfast. I had left school in June with the requisite certificates for a career in "business"; I would be eighteen in February. My one real ambition in life, however, was to be a writer; I thought that in the meantime and to that end I might like a job in the city library where I could read my way through its massive book stock. I duly submitted an application form to the Corporation for the post of Clerical Officer/Library Assistant, as advertised in the *Belfast News Letter*. I got a haircut and bought my first ever suit, a charcoal grey worsted three-piece from John Collier's in Royal Avenue.

The interview took place in the marbled, echoey Edwardian edifice of City Hall, up the grand staircase and into an oak-panelled room where I faced a daunting panel of the important kind of middle-aged men I dubbed "Jimmies".

"Well, Mr Mitchell," said the big Jimmy in the middle, "I see you have obtained a great number of passes—and fails—in your Certificates of Education. Tell us now what you can bring to the Corporation that might be useful enough for us to consider having you in our employ." He looked over his reading glasses at me; he was a shrewd Jimmy.

But I was young and cocky; I even imagined the Corporation would be lucky to get me.

"My love of English," I replied rather grandly. "Of books, language, words." You'd think I was going for resident poet.

The head Jimmy seemed impressed, however. Maybe he thought I was raising the status of the post of Clerical Officer/ Library Assistant with my literary ideals.

"Very well, Mr Mitchell," he pronounced, "I can assure you we have plenty of those—plenty of words here at the Corporation; we do all our business through them."

The letter came a few weeks later offering me a position, to commence on the 5th of October. There was a bit of a hiatus till then; I had a lie-in every morning and spent the afternoons in town, meeting up with friends for lunch or coffee then moseying around the book and record shops. It would be the last of the carefree lazy days of my youth.

I was the last child at home, my brother and sister, both much older than me, working in England now. My father, sixty-five that year, had officially retired from the railway after some years on the sick.

We inhabited a 1950s' terraced estate house in the "dormitory" village of Loughside, eight miles north of Belfast. In the failing light of an autumn evening the ships' foghorns blew mournfully out on Belfast Lough. Inside 5 Coolmore Green you were met by the homely smells of polish and dinner cooking; a big coal fire blazed a welcome. My artist brother Ned's framed oil paintings of Belfast street scenes adorned the walls and there were good books in the bookcase, the Brontes and George Eliot, Dostoyevsky and Faulkner. From the farther corner of the living room came the flickering black and white images and companionable gabble of the 17-inch television set.

After the evening meal I was off to town again on the five-past-seven train to meet up with the gang, usually at Isibeal's restaurant for coffee, with forays out to a club or the cinema, or someone's house if their parents had gone out. When I got back home off the last train my parents were in bed. In the TV-less silence I sat by the fireside exulting in my own company at the day's end. In the richly satisfying midnight stillness of the house

I read a novel or scribbled in a journal I kept, illustrating my entries with little sketches of faces or places I'd encountered. Then putting my book aside I would sit there looking into the red cave of the fire and luxuriate in the protracted sense of the living moment.

My thoughts turned in on myself. Who was I anyway, this life named James Mitchell? What was to be my destiny in this world? My ego bubbled up warmly and I felt famous in my own eyes. Simply to be alive was an ongoing work of art, a novel writing itself, the story of your life; every day a blank page to be filled with more wonders. And here I was now at this critical juncture in my years, at seventeen, poised between youth and adulthood. Funny to think of the autumn term at school already well under way without me, the falling leaves blowing across the old quad, gimlet-eyed Quelch on the warpath. Suddenly those schooldays seemed very distant. My old school pals had already started work, Hugh in the family printing firm, Stuarty in insurance, Howie in the bank, Malcolm in a quantity surveyor's. They all seemed to slot effortlessly into the adult world with their sensible concrete ambitions.

It wasn't so easy for me. In Guernsey that summer I had toyed with the idea of the bohemian life, a dream of mine since reading the novels of Jack Kerouac. A crowd of friendly "beats" inhabited the ground floor of the gaunt tenement where we stayed in Pedvin Street, high above St Peter's Port harbour. Peering down from the dormer window of the tiny attic room I shared with Hugh and Malcolm, I could see, in the scrap of dirty backyard far below, a pair of well-worn jeans dancing on the washing line in the wind, like a flag of anarchy and freedom. The Pedvin Street beats were moving on to casual labour in the Canaries for the winter and had invited us to join them. I had finished school and there was nothing to stop me going with them, and Hugh might have been persuaded to come along too. We were young with the whole world at our feet and anything was possible.

Through July we worked in the greenhouses across Guernsey, then in August we got jobs living in at the Royal Hotel on the sea front; I was kitchen porter. However, by summer's end I'd had enough of the hard graft and squalor of the hotel kitchen that left you fit for nothing at the day's end but the pub, to swallow pints of the local Pony Ale over games of shove-halfpenny. I realised it would be the same story in the Canaries or anywhere else you went roughing it, the mindless dirty jobs and sordid digs, a half-animal existence.

The notion of respectability, a career of some sort back home, didn't seem so bad after all. At least there would be the home comforts and maybe enough energy left you at the end of the working day to think straight. Anyway the age of bohemianism seemed played out; it was better that the writer these days should not cut himself off from the mainstream of society; that was where real life happened. John Braine had been a library assistant; that sounded good enough for me.

I met Julie Martin shortly after I got back from Guernsey, soon after Katie Burns and I had split up. A crowd of us went to the Jazz Club for Them's return to Belfast after their first tour. The group was warming up with *Green Onions* with Van on saxophone as we came in. The club on the top floor of the tall building at the heart of town was by no means packed for the occasion. Solemn devotees of the blues, the small crowd eschewed dancing and closed around the stage to give our full attention to the music.

In the interval a striking-looking girl with her chopped, angular black hair and pinafore dress, came up to me and said, "Hi, for a minute there I thought you were Donovan!"

I'd had the Celtic minstrel's name shouted after me on the harbour front at St Peter's Port all summer.

"But I am!" I said; I'd almost come to believe it. "Who are you—Mary Quant?"

"Wish I was!" she said. "She's my hero. Afraid I'm just Julie!"

"I'm just Jim really. Would you like something to drink? It's soft drinks only."

"Okay, I'll have a Coke, please."

We watched the second half of the show together. The group was in full swing now, the music tremendous like it had taken on a life of its own, building breathlessly in astonishing protracted passages. When it seemed at one point that the girl and I might get separated in the excited press of bodies about the stage, she gripped my hand and we held hands for the rest of the evening. There was no need to speak; tonight the music said it all.

Afterwards I walked her to her bus stop.

"Van and Billy and the boys were in great form tonight!" she enthused in her warm little voice, nestling close under my arm in her leather coat with the small clacking steps of her high heels.

"Aye, Van gives it his all," I said. "Like he really means it, with nothing held back. I suppose that's the definition of a soul singer."

"He kind of opens himself up completely and becomes a channel for all that emotion," she said.

"It must take it out of him," I said. "Where's your bus stop?"

"Here we are, the Athletic Stores. I live in Duncairn Gardens."

"Oh, I go your way to the station!"

We sat upstairs on the Cavehill bus. Julie told me she was a hairdresser, Belle's salon back of the City Hall. There was an aura of fashion and glamour about her that elevated the dingy bus ride and the dark back streets as we left the city centre behind. It was funny how a girl could do that, like the touch of a magic wand on her surroundings.

"Do you like living in the country?" she asked me. Her manner was ingenuous and direct, with a homely quality you wouldn't expect looking at her; it was a winning combination.

"I hate it," I said. "It's not even proper country, just a big new estate stuck down in the middle of some fields. They call it a dormitory development, somewhere you just sleep. If I miss the last train it's an eight-mile hike."

We got down on North Queen Street and I walked her up the Gardens, past the Duncairn Cinema.

"I came this way to school every day for six years," I said. "To the Royal School."

"I went to the Girls' Model," she said.

"Oh, it's a good school, isn't it? Did you know Katie Burns and Miriam Gold?" I asked, my tell-tale heart beating a little faster at the memory.

"Aye, they were in the year above me. Both boy mad. Tubby Burns was great craic, a pretty girl too. Her pal Miriam, wee Jewess, she was a bit wild. How do you know them?"

"Tubby" Burns! I had to smile at the schoolgirl nickname; it helped put an old flame into perspective.

I said, "We used to hang about together, a gang of us lads and girls, after we met in Portrush one Easter."

We came to the door of a tall Victorian terraced house, its tiny front garden enclosed by a low street-wall. There in the dark of the porch and the half-cover of some shrubbery, we kissed goodnight. It was a meaningful first kiss, full and warm and lingering, her arms closing around my neck.

"I'll ring you!" I gulped, heart pounding as we drew apart. I had her business card safe in my wallet. She opened her front door and stood framed in the hall light, waving me goodbye in a little-girl fashion that touched me profoundly.

I knew all the short cuts in this neck of the woods; I slipped along North Queen Street and dropped down Lower Canning Street, over the cobbles, floating on a dream of my new girl. The lit face of the station clock hove into view: ten-past-eleven, just ten minutes to the last train.

"Julie—Julie—" I loved that name, repeating it aloud as if to convince myself its owner wasn't a figment of my imagination.

Waiting to cross at the traffic lights to the station, I felt the old childhood squeal of joy well up in my throat and had to struggle not to let it out. That kind of behaviour on York Street late at night could get you certified.

CHAPTER 2

"There must be a mistake"

"There must be a mistake; I'm supposed to be working in the library!"

"Mr James Girvan Mitchell?"

"Aye, that's me."

"No, Mr Mitchell, it states quite categorically *Accounts Department*. There were no suitable vacancies for you at the library."

In the stubborn fit of a naturally timid person, I insisted that I had stated specifically at my interview that English was my best subject and I wanted to work with words not figures.

The City Hall Jimmy eyed me coldly now. "I said there's been no mistake, Mr Mitchell. But let me assure you, all the Corporation's business is conducted through the English language and the Accounts Department is no exception."

End of argument, a Jimmy always knew best. I felt flustered and foolish. A job was a job after all and here I was in my new suit, all set to go.

"Okay then," I agreed, retreating to timidity. Better not push my luck and end up with nothing, my Da would kill me.

"Miss Saunders here is starting at the Accounts Department with you," said the Jimmy. "You can go together. There is a bus from Chichester Street or if the rain has stopped it's only a ten minute walk, out the back here and left along May Street. Keep going on through Cromac Square and out past the market, and you'll see the green dome, it's a large building standing on its own along the river, you can't miss it."

Outside the rain had stopped. Miss Saunders said, "Shall we walk it?"

"Yeah, let's, it'll be quicker and cheaper!" I said.

She was a tallish, gentle-looking girl, dark hair to her shoulders and a pleasant face, soft brown eyes that smiled and flirted, or at least it was nice to think so. Well, it was something anyway to be out walking the busy morning streets of the city with a nice girl who seemed to appreciate your company; I'd had enough of lying in bed half the day.

"I've never worked in my life before," Miss Saunders confided in me. "I haven't a clue what I'm supposed to be doing!"

"I've had summer holiday jobs," I said. "Just do what they ask you, as quick as you can and you can't go far wrong." I was reassuring myself really, all the time thinking oh my godfathers, me of all people to be working in the Accounts Department, who flunked his O-level maths twice!

"I heard you arguing with your man," said the girl with her indulgent wee smile.

"Aye, that was a waste of time. Oh well, I suppose it'll be alright where we're going, it's a job. Maybe I can get a transfer later. It's just that I love books and reading and the library would have been ideal for me."

"At least you've got a foot in the door of the Corporation now," she said.

In a few minutes we turned a corner and suddenly we'd put the bright bustle of the city centre behind us. We were the only pedestrians now in an unfamiliar bleak sort of no man's land. The roar of accelerating traffic, the lumbering lorries, drowned our voices.

"There's the green dome!" I cried, as if the girl and I were characters in a fairy tale.

It stood up in the grey October sky, a quarter-mile or so ahead of us, at the summit of the long, straight, hammering road. We lowered our heads into the gritty, cold autumn wind that, unobstructed by buildings, blew down it like a tunnel.

Over a chest-high old stone wall, the kind you saw out in the country, there was a long drop to the deserted market-place below. The road sloped up with a view over the market-place to rusty scrapyards, the railway embankment, the roof of the bus depot and the docks beyond. Past halfway up on the other side of the road, a side street led to the long, low, dark brick building of the abattoir. Beyond it were the wet slate roofs and smoking chimneys of the close terraced streets with the rusty round hulk of the gasworks rising out of them.

The Accounts Department loomed out before us; its municipal pale green dome mounted on Grecian pillars above the entrance seemed to float in the blowy sky.

"It's like Count Dracula's castle!" exclaimed the girl.

"Drawbridge and all!" I said.

A footbridge connected the street to the public entrance on the first floor. The ground floor was set below the street, level with the market-place. The building rose in three storeys, a ponderous mill-like edifice with its dark red glazed brick walls and rows of blind windows, sprawling like a recumbent giant along the west bank of the River Lagan.

A discreet old polished brass plaque on a pillar bore the legend *Belfast Corporation Accounts Department*. Over the balustrade of the footbridge you could see down in through the big windows of a ground floor office, lights burning there in the shadow of the elevated road, with girls, girls, girls, seated, standing, walking to and fro, working at the desks and filing cabinets.

Revolving half-glass doors propelled us into a butterscotch-coloured, polished reception area, wood-panelled, with long, burnished counters. A grizzled, navy-uniformed porter checked our names on his list.

"Righto, Fred will show yous the way." There was no one else visible behind the counter but the flap shot up and a wee hunchback porter emerged. The long, bony face with its red-veined cheeks, under a tumbled quiff of oiled black hair, was a shut dutiful mask.

Fred took off ahead of us fast, low to the ground and determined like a spider. We followed him through tall, half-glass swing doors down a khaki and cream corridor. At the second door on the left, *Consumer Accounts*, he bade me follow him while Miss Saunders waited there.

She saw the look of something like terror blanch my face and murmured a sympathetic, "Best of luck," blinking her soft brown eyes at me in empathy. She was going to Wages and I scarcely ever saw her again, one of those momentary nice girls that disappear into the crowd but you always remember them and wonder about what might have been—. And with all the enthusiasm of a prisoner beginning a life sentence, I followed Fred into the busy office.

"Mr Mitchell for ye, sor," Fred introduced me to the office boss and slid away soundlessly.

Mr Faris, "Wee Cecil" as I would come to know him, sprang up behind his large desk, neat in his tonic-coloured suit, flustered and jumpy but gripping my hand with an unexpected manly vigour and looking me straight in the eye, earnest and democratic. He was gnome-like, with a grizzled round head, the toothbrush moustache and small round glasses left over from the wartime.

Cecil took me straight across the office to meet Owen, a middle-aged, dark, nice-looking man in a light-coloured sports jacket and brown twills, who bounced to his surprisingly small feet and shook my hand warmly.

One of the first things Owen said to me was, "You don't want to wear that good suit in here, you'll ruin it."

He pulled up a chair for me and was explaining the bought ledger system, his hairy paws, small and strong, moving on the long pages of calculations like a gentle bear's. He had a warm, tweedy, wholesome smell, like a favourite schoolteacher. I warmed to Owen straight away, but I was only pretending interest in his words; all I could think was *this is a terrible mistake, what am I doing here and how soon can I escape?*

There were maybe twenty clerks in this office, heads bowed over the high, sloping desks while they laboured in a continuous muted, dreary hub-bub of dry work-talk, shuffle of papers and ringing of phones. You could see how important and all-consuming their work was to them. They believed in it, the files and ledgers, the long columns of debit and credit that had to balance up at the bottom. They were married folk, with the responsibility of families to keep their noses to the grindstone. I could see only one other young fellow besides myself in the office, Pat, and he a few years older than me and wearing a wedding ring. My heart sank deeper. I very soon decided that I could not possibly stay here working in this place. I would slip away in the lunch break and not come back.

At twelve-thirty I came out over the "drawbridge" under the green dome and turned down Bridge Street in the teeth of the wind. Ten minutes later I entered White's restaurant in Donegall Square. Julie, on her lunch hour, waited for me at a table over by the big plate glass window.

"Oh Jim, are you alright?" she said, seeing my face.

"Guess what," I blurted, "I'm not even working at the library! They've put me in the bloody Accounts Department, away out by the market, stuck with a lot of fogeys in a kind of converted spinning mill!"

Over lunch Julie said, "That's what working in an office is like. That's why I couldn't stick the Moon Insurance, my first job after leaving school; I was only fifteen. Hairdressing's hard work but at least I feel alive, there's a bit of craic with other young people and one day I'll be my own boss running my own salon."

"I'm not going back there," I said.

"You have to go back," she said with her disarming girl's groundedness. "You can't just walk out after one morning like that. Look, you've still got time to enrol at the Tech for A-levels."

"The Tech! Oh, I wish I'd thought of that before! It'd be grown up, not like going to school in a uniform, that's what I couldn't take for another year. I can be a proper college student!"

"You'd even get a grant. Once you've been accepted at college you can pack in the job, tell them you're sorry but it wasn't the job you applied for and you've decided to go and finish your education first."

"Julie, you're a genius!"

But I was sinking again by the time we kissed goodbye at the foot of the steps to Belle's salon in May Street. The flooding autumn sunshine, ancient as sadness, lit up Julie's helmet of perfect straight black hair, her creamy skin and black eyes. The glowing beauty of a girl took on a terrible poignancy in the cold business-like reality of the working day, the murderous rush of the traffic round City Hall, the bleak ugly road back to the Accounts Department. Tears welled in my eyes, like a child torn from his mother on his first day at school.

"Och, m' poor wee boy!" said Julie, kissing away the tears. "Everythin' ll be alright, don't you worry!"

As I turned up Bridge Street and caught sight of Dracula's castle waiting for me at the top, I felt my stomach lurch and leaning on the coping of the old stone wall above the market-place, I brought my luncheon of cheese roll and frothy coffee back up, on to the pavement. I had a momentary out-of-body experience, looking down from a height on the pitiful figure doubled over boking on the lonely stretch of pavement as the traffic swept past indifferently.

I got through that afternoon in the office by constantly reassuring myself that this was only a temporary crisis in my young life and I'd go home that evening and inform my parents of the change of plan, that I couldn't work in the library so I was going to be a student now. My words made perfect sense, yet another doubting, realistic part of my brain told me it wasn't going to be that easy.

I emerged from the building at five with the worker-horde, out from the yellow office lighting into the autumn twilight, down Bridge Street under the foggy lamppost lights, past the going-home traffic stuck in long queues. In rush hour Donegall Place between the big department stores I queued for the bus and squeezed on board upstairs with the other blank, jaded faces and dank overcoats, sweaty socks coagulating on cold feet.

I sat in the stuffy packed compartment of the diesel train rattling out along the black Lough and in through the darkened fields to Whiteabbey. Endlessly I rehearsed the speech I would make to my parents at tea. The lights of Kenbane Crescent sprang up below the railway embankment and the diesel train braked for Loughside station.

The hall light of 5 Coolmore Green shone its welcome through the frosted pane in the door. A paraffin heater warmed the hall, its cosy smell commingling with the tea cooking. The living room shone with a big fire. The bowl of boiled jacket potatoes steamed at the centre of the table under the window. Everything signalled a sort of celebration of the man of the house home from work and it struck me guiltily now that with Dad retired I had taken over that role. It was not going to be easy to tell them after one day that I didn't want it.

For a few minutes we ate in silence, liver and onions in thick dark gravy, with mashed turnip and glasses of cold milk to wash it down. The TV was on at my back, Dad half-watching the evening news over my shoulder. At a lull in the usual reports of economic problems and foul crimes in the UK, famine and war abroad, Dad said, "And tell us, Jim, how was your first day at the Corporation?"

So I took a deep breath and told them. There was no library assistant post available and they'd put me in the Accounts Department where it was all working with figures and I hated it and couldn't stay there, I'd be no good at it anyway. I wanted to go to the Tech instead now, to continue my studies with a view to becoming an English teacher.

I had chosen my words carefully and thought they sounded reasonable. I was already dreaming of the student bohemian life, attending lectures and coffee bars, the books and essays and intellectual discussions. I could see myself in a leather jacket and blue jeans, with Julie looking great on my arm.

But in the deafening silence that greeted my neat little speech I had the sensation of falling down a mine shaft. Dad got up and turned off the TV. Then they started in on me, their individual responses to my proposal blending into one reproving voice:

"Indeed and ye're not giving up your good new job like that, Jim. Sure ye'd the chance to stay on in the sixth form and sit your A-levels but you were adamant, you couldn't wait to get out of the school and into a job like your mates. And now ye're telling us ye've changed your mind again after your first day at work. You want to do A-levels after all? Sure how is the Tech better than the Belfast Royal School? Divil the much grant ye'd get either, two pounds a week max, and here's us managing on your father's pension now.

"We can't afford to keep you or Dorothy or Ned any longer. We thought your brother was never going to work again and then he was three years at the College of Art and now he's labouring in a brewery in Birmingham and says he feels sick going into work there every morning. He's twenty-nine years of age.

"Dorothy walked out of the sixth form then she hated her job we got her in the Ministry of Finance through Uncle Bob Dixon and couldn't wait to get out of that either, and it was four years at Stranmiilis getting her teaching certificate and now she's serving in a toy shop in London still waiting for a school to teach in.

"So I'm afraid the money's run out and you may just content yourself now, Jim, with the Corporation. You can sit at a desk and add up and subtract figures the best. You'll get a monthly salary, paid holidays and a pension. Not bad for a young fellow just out of school. There's always a night class at the Tech if you're that keen to take more exams. If you liked you could study part-time for the Chartered Institute of Secretaries like Uncle Eric, it's a seven year course, if you want to acquire a good professional qualification and get on in the Corporation—"

I'd really not expected this barrage of opposition and had to sit there swallowing my pride with the rubbery lumps of pig's liver, head down, crushed by their rigid incontrovertible parental logic.

In truth they'd had enough of my brother and sister messing about and acting superior and it was third time unlucky for me. Enough was enough. I had a good job and I could darn well stay in it. Well okay then, I supposed it was the price I had to pay now for my dreamy adolescence, preoccupied with mates and girlfriends and my own extracurricular reading. And behind all that had been the heady conviction that I was born to be a writer and the dusty grinds of examinations were irrelevant to my destiny.

Grim reality focused my mind now like a clamp applied to the head. Once you had no real choice any more life was simpler, easier in a way. So I would put up with the ghastly office job somehow for the time being and enrol at night school, get the certificates I needed then apply for teacher training on the full grant so I'd be independent of my parents—

I headed back up Station Road to the train and my date with Julie. Courting in the plushy crimson back stalls' tobacco-scented dark of the ABC Ritz cinema, the latest comedy with Doris Day and Rock Hudson up on the screen in larger than life Technicolor Superama, everything else could be forgotten for a couple of hours.

It was only later as we cuddled and kissed goodnight on the doorstep on Duncairn Gardens that the reality hit me again: *work in the morning!*

"What's the matter, love?" said Julie, feeling me stiffen in her arms.

"I'm a number now," I announced bleakly. "1-3-8 on the clock we have to punch in and out on every day. That's my life now."

"Aw, Jimmy!" she soothed, taking my face between her cool, soft hands and looking deeply into my eyes brimming again with self-pity. "You'll be alright, love, honest, it won't be half as bad as you think. Just get yourself in there every day and things have a momentum of their own that takes over and carries you along on it. You're not going to be there for ever, are you?"

She kissed away a little fugitive tear. But in a funny way having such a nice girlfriend made it all the harder to bear. It emphasised the split between aspiration and reality, the real me and the social me, that had come into my life now with the hateful job.

CHAPTER 3

The Department of Life

Of course the lovely Julie was right. In no time at all I was over the initial cold water shock of starting work and had settled into the lukewarmth of its routine. My confidence grew as I got the hang of the simple repetitive figure-work Owen allotted me. I was okay at mental arithmetic and liked playing with the calculator. I learnt to meet head on the terror of a ringing phone and deal calmly with the enquiring voice on the other end of the line.

I could draft a good business letter, signing off,

> *"I remain your humble and obedient servant,*
> *James G. Mitchell"*

I liked the Dickensian touch of the language as I penned it painstakingly, my starchy cuffs protruding from the sleeves of my jacket, the enamel inkwell in the top of the high desk, the lights burning overhead through the winter's day. There was the sense of an old established security and comfort, a white-collar dignity in the work.

I dressed for the part, immaculately at first, alternating my dark suit with a tan sports jacket and grey flannels, with tab-collared white or checked shirts and knitted ties. I enjoyed the crisp comfort of tailored cloth across my shoulders, against my elbows and knees as I sat there at my desk. Outside autumn deepened into winter, rain rattled on the tall narrow windows, but there in the office it was purposeful and cosy and I had to admit to myself that I couldn't think of anywhere else I'd rather be at that exact moment in time.

We worked in sub-section groups of five clerks of different grades. I was grateful to be working under Owen, a dead decent fatherly man, in his early forties with four children. He was dark and handsome in a kind way, delicate features, soft brown eyes, blue-shadowed dark complexion; a hairy man, bushy greying black hair sprouting thickly from a widow's peak above the smooth olive forehead.

Des Mullen was thirtyish, slim and pale with a prominent Adam's apple, light blue eyes that crinkled sweetly when he smiled, with a sort of star quality. He was a singer in the Sinatra mould and had performed on Ulster Television.

George Lennon was forty-five. As we were introduced he said of me, "Hey, he looks like Paul McCartney!" He spoke in a rapid, wisecracking, Scouse comedian's sort of voice. "My band was going strong back in Liverpool when that lot were still in nappies. You're looking at the first Beatle, mate: me!"

There was an arty touch about George, his brown corduroy jacket and one day beard, the lank floppy hair swept back from the tall bony forehead. He had a long, ravaged-looking face, deeply lined, pitted and pocked, but paradoxically boyish and innocent, with zany humour never far below the surface. He lounged back low in his chair, his legs stretched out under the desk as he busily ticked long columns of figures, sometimes glancing up risibly over his hornrims.

Isobel was late twenties, married, fair, with wing-framed glasses that gave her a glazed, dotty blonde look. She'd been to my grammar school, so we had that much in common.

"And this is Frank!" She pointed to a grey photo of the Aussie crooner Frank Ifield pinned up on a column next her desk. "What singer do you like best, Jim?"

"Bob Dylan."

Isobel pulled a face. "I saw him on the News coming off the plane. He just looks so *dirty!*"

"Good songs though."

"Do you sing yourself?" she asked. "You look as if you're in a group."

"Yes, we've just started up. I sing and play the guitar."

"You're in the right place here then," she said, "with Des and George."

Owen was the one I felt drawn to most, sensing a sincerity and depth there that I wanted to connect with. He worked steadily, quietly at his book-keeping but he opened up in conversation at our morning tea break.

"Cuppa tea?" Owen's warm, homely words fell like a blessing on my head. It was good to down pens, walk together to the end of the corridor and climb the steep stairs to the canteen. Owen engaged me all the while in his thoughtful opinions on society, politics and religion. I enjoyed the attention of this older man. Upstairs we queued for tea and biscuits, Owen treating me in my first days there and leading me down the long, narrow, noisy room to one of the crowded tables. There he introduced me to some clerical officers from the other sub-sections, who had come up earlier and were just drinking up. They were more my age group, intelligent, attractive girls. Then the whole place emptied suddenly, leaving the air in the room vibrating with the phantoms of frantic, half-shouted conversations around the wreckage of emptied cups and plates.

Now Owen and I were left alone at the table by the high window that looked across the market-place below to the tall city-centre buildings crowded around the dome of City Hall. The tea and chocolate digestives tasted delicious and I had the satisfying sense of having arrived here in Belfast city, no longer a schoolboy but an officer of the Corporation no less.

It was market day and the big market square under our window was noisily alive with men and beasts in an interval of autumn sunshine. There were cattle pens directly below where we sat; the animals were herded from here under the elevated road to the abattoir on its far side.

"We get the flies in the summer," said Owen. Then he asked me, "Did you ever hear tell of Silver McKee?"

"A-ye, famous fighter, wasn't he?" Silver was one of those legendary Belfast hard man names.

"He was a great boxer in his time. A drover by day, dance hall bouncer by night. Anyway, we were looking out the window here one day and we saw Silver in action. This bull that was tethered by itself had broken loose from its rope and was strolling round and round the pen. There were twelve to fifteen drovers looking on, sitting on the fence watching it. Then Silver appeared, looking over the fence at the bull and climbed straight into the pen with it.

"He'd only a short stick with him, about two feet long. He held the bull back with this stick pressed against its neck, grabbed the rope and shoved it through the ring in the bull's nose. The other drovers gave a big cheer. Silver was fearless!"

Owen laughed. "Aye, those were the days. I recall other characters that used to hang round the market and Cromac Square. There was Alec the Duck; he had this pet duck that led the farmers into the *Black Bull* to ply the creature with Guinness.

"Andy Ireland was another one. He'd get drunk and start shouting at the police. It would take half a dozen of them to arrest Andy and march him up to Musgrave Barracks. There were no police cars in those days. I never knew if Ireland was his real name or they called him that because of his nationalist fervour."

We were up standing by the window. Owen pointed to the railway embankment and recalled the days of summer holiday excursion trains to Bangor. "Terry McKeemin in the Costs office at the back spent a lot of time talking on the phone and looking out the window. As the holiday season came round, 'First one!' he'd shout, and wave just to see the whole train waving back."

I liked the cosy, intensely local feeling of these little tales, the Belfast craic. I could see that Owen enjoyed a yarn and I deliberately kept him talking there, postponing our return to the office. He told me he had started at the Department out of the Tech in 1942. I admired the sense of his rootedness and belonging in one place in an ever-changing world, though there seemed to be no love lost between him and the Corporation bosses.

"What are your plans, Jim?" he asked me.

"I'd like to travel and write," I heard myself say. I'd got that long ago from the biographies of writers I liked on the back of Penguin paperbacks.

"Learn book-keeping here," he said, "and you'll be able to find work anywhere you go in the world."

Back in the office in the later morning the boredom set in as the fountain pen-shaped hands of the big wall-clock crept round to midday. At half-past-twelve Owen cleared a space on his desk, got out his packed lunch and flask and the *Irish News*. I lunched up in the canteen to begin with.

"Are you a Cyathlick?" Mrs "Gooky" McGookin would enquire bluntly if you requested the fish option on Fridays. Having to declare your religious denomination publicly like that in Nor'n Ireland seemed insensitive to me but fish supplies were limited so discrimination against Protestants (for once) was the order of the day!

I bolted the stodgy dinner in the busy, clattering room with its steamed-up windows and hurried out afterwards down the town. The buildings grew taller, engulfing me. It was a long lunch break, an hour and twenty minutes. I visited the artists' shop in Corn Market for materials for the Art evening class I'd begun. Then I had a browse round the bookshops, the record shops and the art gallery. Killing time, I eyed up the Carnaby Street fashions in the windows of the Mod boutiques that had sprung up around the centre. You could be a walking work of art yourself now. But I didn't care much for shopping really and had little to spend anyway; rail and bus fares, fags and cinema tickets consumed my small salary, *"No more than a charlady earns,"* I'd heard Tom our union man comment on the remuneration of young Clerical Officers.

The city centre crowds soon overwhelmed you. What was it all about anyway, this ceaseless milling commerce? I felt crushed by it. I missed my old school friends badly. Julie couldn't always get away to see me for lunch. I hadn't a real friend at work. I ran out of steam wandering around on my own. A dreadful dark feeling of pointlessness took hold of me and I started to imagine everybody was looking at me, as if I were walking along with no clothes on.

I stayed in the office instead in the lunch break, reading. I brought a good novel in with me; I needed to go on developing my mind. I felt better indoors where it was small and safe and you belonged. Out in the city streets you were exposed, you felt like nothing, a nobody.

Back to work again at two and I dragged myself through the afternoon, spinning out my tasks to occupy the long hours till five o'clock. Time was the great oppressor at work at seventeen years of age. When I grew restless at my desk I would take off under the pretext of some "query" round the rambling complex of the dusty old building. In one direction a narrow staircase leading down to a circuitous draughty subterranean passageway took me to Comptometers and Filing. These two rooms were exclusively female realms where I could be guaranteed a time-killing natter with some pretty face.

I felt at ease with these girls who were mostly a bit older than me, big-sisterly young women who wouldn't think you were trying to chat them up and you could have a decent conversation with them. Their indulgent smiles told me they thought I was just a "nice wee boy". Hurrying through the Comp room once, I heard one of the girls tell the girl next her, "See that wee boy, he's awful brainy, so he is!" Maybe it was my glasses gave that impression as I'd never spoken to that girl. But I enjoyed the compliment.

Eileen, perky and fun and easy to talk to, was my best pal in the Comp room. Small and slim, pretty in a pale way, with fashionably short, layered fairish hair, she would tell me all about herself and her fiancé as I leant over her desk, listening hard above the racket of the other girls bashing away on the comptometers. When she mentioned one day that it was her birthday I thought I should buy her some chocolates. In the lunch hour I called at the sweetie shop in Cromac Square for a quarter of *Roses,* loose from the jar, in a small paper bag—nothing romantic-looking, I only wanted to appear thoughtful with this modest token of appreciation for our friendly chats together.

Mistake!

"Happy birthday, Eileen!" I slipped her the plain little white paper bag neatly twirled at the top.

And in horror I watched her cringe, her cheeks blazing up as if I'd struck her. Then she said in her wee babyish voice, "Och Jim, you've embarrassed me now!"

I backed off desperately, like a spurned suitor. It was a complete misunderstanding. The bag of sweeties sat there on her desk between us looking grubby and wrinkled from its short transit in my pocket, the chocolates sweating inside it, a sad little offering.

I turned away abruptly and exited the room in a huff, my small gesture of pure platonic friendship thrown back in my face. I supposed I was naïve to imagine you could be just good friends with a girl. Or to not have fully appreciated the romantic symbolism of chocolates, even loose ones in a humble paper bag. Anyway my great adolescent pride had been punctured and I never spoke to Eileen again. Passing through the Comp room on my travels, I swept past her desk, keeping my eyes fixed arrogantly straight ahead.

I was able to amuse myself just sitting at my own desk people-watching, sometimes surreptitiously sketching my colleagues on scrap paper. There was the novelty of being out in the adult working world, the whole gamut of types around me. I was often struck by their resemblance to the animal kingdom: Noel was a solemn big grizzly, Cecil a burrowing mole, Chris a wily fox, Margaret a purry pussy, and so on. The effect was endearing.

I had an eye for the girls, the mysterious shy beauty of the young ones, like wild flowers in a wood; they hid behind the shining curtain-fall of their hair—shy or just moody, it was impossible to tell. I was instantly infatuated with some of them— Alison with her pale skin and frank cold blue siren eyes; Deirdre with her blushing, delicate sweetness—lovely Catholic girls. It was infatuation with a face, that was all, an ideal of femininity I projected on to them. It could never go beyond goddess worship, an impossible, spiritualised delicacy and refinement of feeling. There was no proper sense of a flesh and blood female. I had that with Julie anyway.

The mature women were something else, the married ones with their self-confidence and natural grace; they looked you straight in the eye as if they could read your mind and smiled in amusement at your wee-boy innocence.

And then there were the older young men, late twenties, early thirties, who you looked up to and it made your day if they grinned or winked at you or spoke to you. I hero-worshiped Sean Hughes in particular.

"You all right, Mr Mitchell?" Sean would enquire pleasantly and looking me over he'd comment, "You're looking very smart and fashionable as usual!"

I felt very drawn to some quality in Sean. Kindness, yes, and depth of character. Yet he was a simple, uncomplicated man; perhaps I liked that most about him.

He sat directly opposite me at the next row of desks, near wee Cecil the boss. Sean was twenty-eight, not long married—they had saved up a long time for a honeymoon in Rome. He had come into the Corporation out of school at fifteen as a Clerical Assistant, which, without O-levels, he remained, one rung below Clerical Officer. I was impressed somehow by his apparent indifference to promotion and position. Sean was himself and that was enough, with no sense of inferiority, always his very own man.

He was medium height like me, but thickset; he had a well-shaped head, black hair and beard. It was the beard that got me, uncommon then except on folk singers; it added to a dark Gaelic quality about Sean that I liked. At his desk he was seated with his back to me; I could see him without being seen and be rewarded with views of the noble bearded head in profile and occasional full face. A kind of brooding severity around the eyebrows, the sharp blue eyes and sculpted features emphasised by the full dark beard, suggested the head of a warrior chieftain hero. Sean wore his feelings, every subtle intimation of mood, naked on his face; his colour would surge to an even brick-red in suppressed irritation—but never rudeness—then just as impulsively a smile would spread, banishing the dark battle clouds and he'd be all gentle strength and powerful humility, Christlike to my young hero-worshipping eyes.

Even the clothes Sean wore held a hypnotic fascination for me. They were the styles you saw in the windows of Belfast's small local draper's shops, traditional gent's outfitters. The green tweed jacket of a suit, an orange heavy-knit pullover, brown worsted slacks, solid laced black shoes with round toecaps. His garments had a worn, baggy, comfortable look, lived-in, invested with Sean's solid physical presence and character and the Belfast weather, the streets he moved in, the Falls Road, the Catholic church, the Belfast Corporation. There was the complete sense of a deep-rooted, grounded belonging about him, an Irishness. I felt here is a man who is completely of himself and his community and has no need to pretend anything else. I could only envy that.

Sean was also known as John, the Christian given name on his birth certificate. Like Owen he sported two small badges on his lapels, the Pioneer pin of the Catholic total abstinence league and the gold Fainne of the fluent Irish Gaelic speaker. The two men would converse naturally and quietly in the native tongue. I had schoolteacher uncles, Protestants, in the South, who spoke Irish and I understood there was nothing sectarian about it and liked the idea of it, the roots and romance and poetry in it. Sean saw me watching him and Owen talking Irish one day and asked me, "D'you understand?"

I smiled and shook my head and said, "No, but I'd like to."

I knew they'd welcome a Protestant taking an interest in Irish culture. Sean and I drew closer after that. He was a a plain-spoken, down-to-earth man, but with a considered, thoughtful quality and a natural curiosity that made things interesting. I was grateful for the way in which Owen and Sean bothered to take such an interest in a young Protestant fellow like myself.

I went along with Owen to one of the Irish language classes he organised at Divis Street below the Falls. We entered a big hall filled with Irish music and teenage girls in Irish costumes performing a kind of running, weaving, interpretative style of traditional dance, like something out of Yeats, I thought. The language classes were held in a couple of small rooms at the back. Owen put me with the other teacher, Joe, an older man. The method was teaching through Irish language conversation to begin with, no textbooks or note taking. There were half a dozen of us in this beginners' class, all men, seated in a circle around Joe. There was another Protestant there, Harry, a workingman type who'd come with a Catholic workmate. That was good.

It was cosy and matey in there on a freezing winter's night, acquiring knowledge and culture sociably, with tea and biscuits at half-time. I went home afterwards repeating the handful of words I'd memorized, ready to try them out on Sean the next day and impress my hero.

I'd have liked to have persevered and become an Irish speaker; I dreamt that one day I might, but turning out to night classes in winter after work is heavy going at seventeen or eighteen, it was a leisure class and my A-level Art had to come first; I was thinking of applying to the College of Art now.

The morning tea breaks with Owen continued to be the social highlight of the working day. There was often quite a crowd from the sections gathered around a couple of tables pushed together under the window in the sky. Mary and Margaret were Clerical Officers around my age, who'd come from school with good O-levels; they were both of an intellectual bent and liked to compete with each other.

"No, Margaret! You cannot talk about a novel being *futuristic* in that way," opined Mary with a proud toss of her black mane. "Not whenever the narrative has its sole existence and meaning in a putative *present*."

Dissecting literature in this nit-picking pedantic fashion made me yawn; it was the *life* in books that I loved. I just sat back and observed the girls in amusement.

Mary was a West Belfast beauty with a lovely little heart-shaped olive face and chocolate eyes. I liked to think of her as the descendant of some old dispossessed Spanish-Irish aristocracy. There was a faded look about her clothing but she had a soft, expressive voice, honed by a convent school education.

Mary had the intellectual edge perhaps but Margaret was sleek and glossy, the genuine Malone Road article, educated at Princess Gardens. Her jaw dropped a little at Mary's cerebral onslaught and she blinked defensively behind her owlish glasses.

"Well now, Mary," she retorted, "I think thet's a metter of opinion, surely? The term *futuristic* derives from *futurism,* in fect an artistic movement dating from nineteen-o-nine, which sought to express growth and change—"

"Exactly, Margaret!" Mary's fine dark eyes widened critically and fixed the victim as she moved in for the kill. "You are confusing the idea of looking like the future with the futurist movement. There's a subtle difference, Margaret!"

But who cared anyway? Margaret had a fiancé, Norman, she talked about; they had a joint building society account. They liked to eat out in proper restaurants. It struck me as the most sophisticated thing I'd ever heard when she mentioned how they'd "called for a cheeseboard" after their dessert. Most of all it was the idea of *calling* for it, *"Cheeseboard!"* and the daft image that rose in my mind's eye of the cheeseboard running on legs to their table.

Once I mentioned the possibility that I might live in England in the future.

"Eoh neoh!" was Margaret's unexpected response. "Over there they think we Irish are all stevedores!"

Of course she wasn't far wrong. The Margarets of this world knew a thing or two about the class system.

CHAPTER 4

The Look of Love

I soon became a regular visitor to the house on Duncairn Gardens. Julie's parents ran a sweetie shop a few doors down. Her dad Cyril was a quiet, boyish man, shy-witty, a tall, porky figure with gold-coloured wavy hair and a pink, blushing face. Her mum Myrna, a beautician, was young-looking and attractive, with a chatty, easy way about her; Julie had inherited her glamorous dark looks.

For all the intensity of first, or was it second or third love, I'd known with Katie Burns, I'd never been able to picture us married at some future point in time. The essential homeliness required for that was lacking in her nature and you couldn't imagine her having children, ever. Maybe it was a consequence of growing up in the shadow of her parents' unhappy marriage. She had never once told me the magic words, *"I love you"*, she was far too cynical for that. She used to sneer whenever we passed a girl linking her fellow's arm in the street; she found that pathetic and laughable for some perverse reason, while holding hands was okay. The underlying sense that our relationship was going nowhere ultimately made it easy for me to forget her now.

Julie was altogether different; it wasn't just about having a laugh and a court. A few weeks in from our first meeting at the Jazz Club, I got *the look* from Julie. We were alone in her front parlour, on the couch before the open fire, listening to the record player. We'd been talking quietly when suddenly we ran out of words and our eyes met, hers dilated and shining in the firelight as she held me in her gaze. A happy smile spread across her face and she came in my arms.

"I love you," she said quietly, almost matter of fact.

"I love you too," I said awkwardly though I really meant it.

"I can tell!" she said. "I can see it in your eyes."

"Would you marry me?" I asked her, half-jokingly. "I mean one day in the future if we were ready for it?"

"Mm, lemme think: Mrs Mitchell? Not too bad, I suppose. Oh alright then!"

"We could put our names down for a prefab on the Shore Road!"

"Sure they're knocking them down now," she said. "But Daddy might let us move into the box room at the back of the wee shop. We could live on Tayto crisps and Aero bars and minerals."

"Only we'd hear *ding! 'Shop!'* all the time!"

"I'm hungry," she said. "Fancy a fish supper tonight?"

The Moyola Fish Salon was just along North Queen Street on the corner with Upper Canning Street. I'd passed it on my way to school every day for six years. I'd never imagined eating there; I was wary of the shadowy proletarians who inhabited the back streets around it.

Now Julie led the way in confidently, straight down to a table at the back. We were the only eating-in customers. Posh. The waitress came to take our order.

"Two fish suppers and two Cokes, please." Julie ordered with assurance; she'd been coming to the Moyola all her life.

It was cosy with the plate glass window between us and dark, cold North Queen Street. With Julie the simple, satisfying meal in the warm yellow light of the chip shop took on a special intimacy. We'd gone a bit quiet and serious after our parlour professions of love for one another, as if we'd suddenly grown up a few more years. She looked up into my eyes between forkfuls, but unlike Katie, Julie didn't feel the need to talk all the time; she was grounded and purposeful, with a quiet, strong inner focus that made sense of life. And even just sitting there in a back streets' chip shop she looked a perfect fashion plate, everything about her fresh and crisp and beautiful. She rose naturally and easily above circumstance and place, the mistress of her own destiny.

One weekend afternoon when her parents had gone out for the day we half-undressed and got into her bed. The sheets were like a cold bath but as we warmed up the kissing and petting grew feverish, till she had to calm me down:

"Wait! We don't want the baby yet!"

I drifted off to sleep in her arms feeling like a baby myself, mindless and secure against her bosom. It was dark in the bedroom when I opened my eyes, late in the December afternoon. Julie was warm beside me in the single bed, sharing the pillow with me, and it felt so natural, as if we were married already. Wouldn't that be nice!

She opened her eyes and said, "I'm hungry! Fancy a fry?"

Down in the kitchen she got the pan going, bacon and egg and fried leftover boiled potatoes. The kitchen table was laid for two, complete with the Daddies OK sauce. Our winter love was all cosy cuddles and comfort food. This is what it's really all about, I told myself. Life was simple really: with the love of your girl everything else fell into place, it was all of secondary importance.

"How many babies would you want when we get married?" It gave me a thrill to ask her this and I watched her cute face closely as she thought about it.

"A girl for you, a boy for me?"

"Yes. I'd like two."

"Or maybe three or four!"

" Or more? Why stop?" I was getting over-excited.

We'd have to wait though; we both earned very little. She'd not achieved much at school, she was more the practical type, though artistic too. She showed an interest in the paperbacks I carried in my coat pocket to read on the train.

"What's it about?"

It was Stan Barstow, *A Kind of Loving.* "Oh, a young couple in Yorkshire getting married." I didn't tell her it was an unhappy little tale.

"When are you going to write your book?"

"Once I've had a bit more experience of life, when I'm in my twenties."

"What will you write about?"

"Oh, I can think of a good story, all about a young Belfast couple just like us. I'll call it *The Book of Love*. Like that old song, remember?"

"Don't know if I'd want Mammy to read that!"

"Don't worry; it'll be a novel with all 'the names changed to protect the innocent'. It'll be all about life in Belfast, like the way Barstow and Braine and Storey and Waterhouse have written about Yorkshire."

"Well, I'll buy a copy of your book, that's for sure!" she perked up bravely.

"It'll be dedicated to you, pretty baby. Who would you like to play your character in the book when they make it into a film?"

"Ah, lemme think— Natalie Wood!"

"An American? Not Shirley Anne Field then? It'd be more of a Woodfalls film, kitchen sink drama kind of thing. Not really Hollywood."

"American accents sound more like Belfast. Who would play you?"

"If I can't have Tom Courtenay, if it has to be Hollywood then—with James Dean dead, it'll have to be John Kerr!"

"Oh Jim, just imagine our lives up on the screen at the ABC Ritz!"

"Aw, you're gettin' all excited like a wee girl, Julie!"

"Well, I'll be famous! I mean even if people don't know my real name—if that makes sense!"

*

Our rock group got going that autumn. We had planned it all in the sixth form, at the back of the Art class. Steve White was the driving force and real talent behind *The Fringe* as we now called ourselves. We practised Monday nights and some Saturday mornings at the big house where Steve lived with his father, next to Jordanstown station. Cancer had taken his mother a year before and his older brother had joined the Royal Navy. They were a Birmingham English family originally.

We practised in Steve's bedroom usually, taping ourselves on a reel-to-reel recorder. Steve, Stuarty and I sang and played acoustic guitars, Malcolm was on a basic drum kit he'd bought off Hugh who'd retired from the music scene and tagged along with us now just to listen, together with Howie, Ronnie and a few other friends who'd drop by. It was a crowded, noisy little bedroom.

We played back and re-recorded until we had something fairly polished to listen to. It was exciting to hear ourselves taped, like a record. Steve had resisted the original idea of a blues group and we did a variety of classy pop: Billy J. Kramer, *I'll Keep You Satisfied*, The Kinks' *You Really Got Me*, the Beatles' *Day Tripper*, the Stones' *Come On* and the Buddy Holly classics Steve loved— *Well All Right* was a favourite.

Then there were the songs Steve wrote, a mix of wistful love songs and upbeat rockers; he'd composed over forty of them. Steve looked and sounded like a fair-haired Cliff Richard, a light, smooth tenor voice, accompanying himself with a driving rhythm guitar while Stuarty picked out the lead and I struggled with bass lines they showed me—all on our acoustic guitars. I sang baritone and the three of us harmonised rather effectively.

The tape recordings began to sound good and we got our first gig, courtesy of Steve's dad, at Carrick Golf Club's Christmas party. We began serious rehearsals down in the spacious living room at Steve's with a mike borrowed from the club. Steve got agitated and bossy now knocking our little bedroom band into shape for our first public performance.

The Saturday night in mid-December came round. Steve went ahead to the club with his dad; the rest of us piled into Malcolm's Minivan, drums, guitars, girlfriends, getting lost in Carrick town centre before we found the club. I felt nervous because I would be singing one of our numbers solo, but I was elated also because this was the fulfilment of a long-held dream and who could tell, our first step on the road to stardom?!

Inside the club hall we had a table reserved next the stage. We were first on: I stood in the middle between Steve and Stuarty. We kicked off with *Satisfaction*, an easy Stones' rocker that went down well, then I did my folksy *Where Have All the Flowers Gone?*—our own tasteful folk-rock arrangement that I fondly imagined sounded like the Byrds. It was disorientating hearing my voice coming over the p.a. system instead of out of my mouth and I felt my face flaring the bright pink that I hated and the hipster trousers my sister had sent me from Carnaby Street slipping, slipping down my snake-hips till they threatened to end up round my ankles.

I gave them a good hitch before our next number, one of Steve's compositions, *Something Tearing Us In Two,* a strong, mournful ballad that seemed to turn into a lament and lose itself tragically in the acoustics of the hall. We proceeded into the Kinks' wistful *Set Me Free, Little Girl* , Steve and I alternating effectively on verse and chorus. Then we finished brightly with the Beatles' *I Feel Fine,* Stuarty struggling on the fiddly guitar breaks but our three-part vocal harmonies laid down lush and powerful in a fairish imitation of the Fab Four!

We seemed to be a hit with the golfers anyway, bowing out to sustained applause. Down at our table Julie was jumping around, clapping and cheering us on, creating the impression of a whole crowd of eager girl fans. Stuarty had his latest pretty girl, Marie Kelly, tagging along. Steve's girl Jennifer—never "Jennie"—was there too, a more restrained female presence. Steve and Jennifer were a serious couple who'd gone steady since the fourth form; they were still at school together doing A-levels now. She was blonde, slender and pretty in a pale, serious way, with level, candid blue eyes. I'd asked her out once before she was Steve's—"Would you like to come and see a film with me?"—and got a blunt "No" for an answer.

Steve kept Jennifer to himself in a joined at the hip relationship, spending all their time together, at school and each other's houses. I'd slept on his bedroom floor after one lads' poker night and heard him call out her name deliriously in his sleep. It seemed an awfully intense relationship, the kind that doesn't last, I felt, because you're too young for that intensity. You could hear it in Steve's melancholy song lyrics, the inevitable tragedy of young love: *"You love me, I love you/But something's tearing us in two/Doesn't matter what we do/Something's tearing us in two."*

Banal pop lyric maybe but in its sheer simplicity so true to the consequences of adolescent infatuation. I'd felt it with Katie, the fun leeching away as it went hurtful and sad. It was so different, so easy now with Julie, the love was there but it was so natural and light and free, it stayed so fresh and uncomplicated. There was no bitterness or carping cynicism in Julie; she was just the dear good girl who loved me for who I was and asked nothing more of me. I blessed her wee heart for that and loved her back twice over. I saw no reason why we shouldn't go on forever like this, the two of us, just naturally, one day at a time, no pain and no tragedy—

CHAPTER 5

Swingin' London

In the summer of 1966 I had a week in London with the lads. We stayed at my sister Dorothy's flat in Fulham; she and her flatmate Freda, both teachers, were off on holiday, travelling on the Continent. It was a first trip to the metropolis for all of us, Stuarty, Hugh, Malcolm and me. We flew from Belfast, enthusiastic; London was at its swingin' sixties' peak.

It was August, overcast, grey and muggy when we arrived. We got a taxi from the air terminal; you felt the bustle and excitement of a great city, the long hammering roads delivering you between the big square buildings, a heady sense of liberation from your own small provincial world. The address was up a quiet aide street in Fulham, tall old houses of faded yellow brick. The keys were under the bin; we entered the dusty communal hall and climbed the threadbare-carpeted stairs with our cases, up through the gloomy silent house to the top floor flat. It waited for us, lifeless, shabby but tidy, filled with the quiet grey afternoon light, feeling remote from the street far below. Out the back there was an overgrown garden and big trees heavy with their dark green summer foliage; a view of the dingy tall backs of houses that seemed sunk in time like the trees. The district had a seedy, rotting quality, suspended in the humid stillness of the August afternoon.

Later Al Price showed up. Freda's older brother, he occupied a tiny bedsit on the half-landing below us. He was one of those famous names from Dorothy and Ned's Belfast student days, so I felt I already knew him.

"Dot asked me to look in on you. Is everything okay?" he grinned round at us, good white teeth, dancing blue eyes, fair with a look of Albert Finney.

We sat round chatting. Al was a bright, energising presence. He told us he was thirty-three, the "eternal student", working on his Master's in Education now. He seemed glad of our company in the big silent house; it was nice for us to find a friendly face and listen to a voice from home here in the strangeness of the metropolis. We were to see a lot of Al during our stay. There was a boyish, light-hearted quality about him; we could have sat happily there talking all week in that high room and left the sights of London down below to the tourists.

"So where are we heading tonight?" We'd come all this way and it was our duty to see the sights.

"West End!"

"Something to eat, a drink and a dander round."

"Londoners don't dander," said Al. "They race round mad-arsed." Then he issued a serious warning: "Just one thing, lads: don't let the coppers catch you pishing in the street. It's not like home; it's an offence they take seriously over here and they'll prosecute you, no excuses."

"Imagine a criminal record for life with that on it!" I shuddered.

We travelled on the tube for the first time. I liked the streaming people on the long, steep, rumbling escalators, the sweetish, warm underground smell, the sexy advertising posters that covered the concave walls, the thrilling rush of the tube train out of the tunnel, the automatic doors swallowing you up and the strange enigmatic, waxwork types sitting in the carriage: a City business type, a half-tramp, a pretty secretary, an Arab sheikh, each one locked in silent self-absorption. Here was the drama of Londoners.

We emerged among the evening crowds on Oxford Street. We found the Wimpy Bar to eat in and afterwards the German

Bier Keller for a drink, down steps to the dim cellar; it promised something different but inside it was plastic and empty, and we sat over our pints in a gloomy corner with a jaded feeling. We were too tired to even think much that first evening. We walked down to Piccadilly Circus to see it lit up in all its garish frenetic splendour before taking the tube back to Fulham.

It was a relief to retreat to the flat in Ongar Road. Al came up to see how we'd got on and we sat round talking till late, one topic leading spontaneously to the next, so much to say. This was how I'd imagined the real London to be, not the sights so much but the spaciousness of the anonymous city with your own flat and the company of other free spirits who had landed up here like yourself.

In the morning Al took us round the corner to the smart little café where he breakfasted. Today the London summer sun shone hotly out of a blue sky, the sizzling green pavement-trees afforded a sensuous shade; the feeling was Continental. Al, clean-shaven and crisp-shirted, in a powder blue mohair suit, the *Racing Standard* tucked under his arm, seemed to crackle with the brisk, energetic purpose and promise of the London morning. He symbolised London to me with his air of independence and optimism. We sat in a booth in the clean, sunny space of the little café, drinking fresh orange juice, Espresso coffee and eating toast and butter and jam. Al studied the racing form for that day and we planned our sightseeing. After breakfast Al disappeared across London to his fiancée's via the bookie's and we took the tube to the West End.

As the day progressed it grew humid and the blue sky faded to a pallid haze, while the diffuse foggy blob of the sun continued to beat down mercilessly. The temperature made the sightseeing heavy going. Dazed and lost, we trudged the glaring boulevards between the lofty buildings till our aching feet seemed to scream for mercy.

The August days went by in a blur of museums and art galleries, the Thames and the Tower. We visited the East End and Sidney Street—the anarchist siege with the young Home Secretary Churchill in attendance, depicted in a boys' comic years ago, had caught my imagination and stayed with me. We saw an unremarkable play in the West End, a murder-mystery with Honor Blackman, I think, playing a blind woman.

Sharp-eyed, with-it Stuarty spotted various celebrities around the West End: the singer Wayne Fontana in Regent Street; actress Geraldine Chaplin sitting on a wall at Trafalgar Square. Then we got tickets for the TV pop show *Ready Steady Go*. Dorothy had arranged it with the girls in the basement flat of her house, who worked for Rediffusion. It was exciting going down into their feminine quarters; there were three of them, London lionesses, superbly long-haired creatures in the fullness of young womanhood, a few years older than us, busy making up costumes for TV. But there wasn't a spark of real human contact with them, just their unsmiling air of preoccupation and the tickets located and handed over with all the impersonality of a box office.

It was a long run out to Wembley on the tube, with a race from the station down industrial streets to the warehouse-like TV studio building for the seven o'clock start. The crowd of youngsters waiting in the lobby for the double doors to open eyed us up critically—we were on Mod territory here. It was exciting then to be shut into the big studio as the cameras rolled and the familiar introductory music, *5-4-3-2-1*, rocked out.

And there was Cathy McGowan in the flesh, long dark hair framing a pudgy little face, skinny legs hanging from a miniskirt, perched on her stool in front of the camera, telling you the weekend started here and everything was "Super!"

Manfred Mann, one of my favourite bands, performed *Just Like A Woman*. The singer Mike d'Abo, long fair hair, very good-looking, had just replaced Paul Jones. We were standing very close to them and I was sure Manfred Mann himself, the hornrimmed, bearded keyboardist, was staring incredulously at my new polka-dot kipper tie, big white spots on navy, which I'd purchased from Carnaby Street that day.

The Gojos girl dancers came frisking out gorgeously to do their piece, all smooth, tanned, leggy litheness and tossing manes, golden wonder girls, the cameramen stumbling after them in close-up as they pranced away. The other performances that night of the 19th of August 1966 were The Who, *I'm A Boy*, Salena Jones *I Am Yours* and Cliff Bennett *Got to get you into my life*. It was all very fast, spontaneity verging on the chaotic, the half-hour programme gone in a flash of immediacy and excitement.

Then we were turned out into the blank evening streets, the oblique sunshine firing factory and warehouse walls.

*

Wandering through Soho on another sticky afternoon under the dull heat-haze we found ourselves in a street of strip clubs. A cockney tout persuaded us inside with the offer of half-price tickets. It was down steps to a cellar. Inside we got charged extra for "membership" but having come this far it was easier to pay up and go ahead now. With the heart's tremor and sick dread that accompanies sin, we passed through the heavy curtains into the dark, tiny theatre, just a few rows of hard chairs facing a small stage. There were a few other customers, older men sitting on their own. It was creepy, sleazy, *all wrong*; you wanted to *not be there* but you were trapped now.

It was as anonymous as you could get there in the dark under the London pavement. Once the performance got going you forgot everything else. It was reassuring that the strippers were ordinary young women who gave a convincing impression that they might be enjoying themselves too.

Of course I had seen paintings of female nudes in art books and galleries, a photograph in a magazine and odd glimpses of a girlfriend's body, but none of that prepared me for the stark reality framed in the brightly-lit box of the stage as all the clothes came off exposing the lavishness of soft, waxen, sensual female flesh, the full curves of breasts and hips—the shocking animal fact of a naked woman, that affected you like a kick in the stomach. The finale came with the removal of the G-string and the stripper posed there immobile while the curtains closed on her, as required by the Censor.

The sign outside the club boasted *Non-stop Striptease*. Each stripper did a 15-minute performance, each with her own recorded music, costume and dance routine, though this was rather predictable with similar gyrations and high kicks and straddling or bending over a hard chair. One stripper sported tassels on her nipples that she swung in a sustained perfect circular motion, first one direction then the other.

A walking cane provided the prop for a stripper who mimed to a charming little ditty that went *"Johnny's got a little pogo stick—"*

Some of the strippers just went through the motions, while others made more of an effort to please. We soon had our favourites. It was a drug and we sat there for hours, hooked. We gathered that the strippers worked a circuit of the whole row of clubs and if you waited they all came round again. Time was suspended; it was perpetual night there under the street. You completely forgot about the rest of the world.

Our favourite was a fun-loving little blonde who couldn't have been any older than ourselves (eighteen) and we moved boldly into the front row to get closer to her second time round. She connected easily with her small audience: there was a city gent, a soldier in uniform and us nice middle class Belfast boys. Altogether a respectable little group. Blondie seemed to be enjoying it as much as we were. You could easily imagine her as your very own Cockney bird pleasing you. She swayed to the edge of the stage over us, then singling me out, to the amusement of the other lads, did a belly-dance right in my upturned baby face. As I squirmed there the mates gave a mighty cheer at my ritual humiliation.

Here we were in London, at the heart of western civilisation, all that culture at our disposal, yet it stood for nothing against this ritual in the dark, the procession of pallid flesh under the artificial lights in the cramped cellar. The worst thing was coming out afterwards, surfacing on the street again with a grubby, zombified feeling, blinking in the daylight in the unreality of the evening rush hour. Tantalising images of the naked women were seared on your brain; the lust clung about you still like a dirty mac. If the blank faces on the crowded tube could have read your mind—!

A Belfast girl sitting next us in the Oxford Street Wimpy Bar heard our accents and invited us to a party at her flat. The address was the opposite side of London but we thought it'd be worth the journey. Maybe this would be a taste of the swingin' London scene, at least we'd get a chance to meet some girls other than strippers in a club.

Lowering his voice confidentially, Al Price counselled us thrillingly, "If one of these London birds fancies you, she'll go all the way. It's not like back home, waiting for a ring on her finger first."

A long journey across London, carefully charted on our London Transport maps, brought us to another faded street of tall houses and another top flat.

"Och, did you not bring any girls with you?" moaned the girl from the Wimpy Bar.

"We only came over a week ago, don't know anyone."

The four of us lads made the party number up to nine. We sat round on threadbare chairs in a cramped room, swallowing beer from the cans we'd brought. The two girls had their boyfriends there and the Belfast girl's brother. He slouched morosely in the lumpy armchair spilling horsehair, squeezing his beer can. "Ye went to the Belfast Royal School, ye say? Aye, yous look it and all!" he sneered, a sleekit skitter.

The English fiancée of the other Belfastman got tiddly quickly. "All these Irish accents, Aw don't know! We're outnumbered tonight!" she exclaimed. "Not that I'm compl'ining, Aw could listen to them awrl night! Aw lav the expressions Frank uses, he teaches me them!" She planked herself down clumsily on Frank's knee; I saw him wince with pain but then he sat there under her, shy but pleased with himself for bagging this game London bird. "S'y some of them to the boys here, Frank!" she urged him. "'*Ack, yer head's a marley, wee doll!*' he tells me sometimes!"

She staggered up to the table and poured herself another gin, missing the glass.

"Aoh Gawrd, Aw'm pished!" she cried as her knees buckled woozily. Frank jumped up and caught her, scooping her in his arms. She clutched at the hem of her sack-like dress to cover her knickers as he whisked her off to tuck her into bed. That was the end of the liveliest person at the party.

Nobody else came. We stayed on drinking pointlessly; there was no craic but we'd come a long way to be here. We left too late for public transport and had to get a taxi all the way back to Fulham, belting along the dark and deserted, interminable streets of the London night.

In the morning it was onto the plane home with hangovers; I was duly sick into my sick-bag. In a shorter time than the taxi ride of the night before, the plane was tilting in over misty green fields with toy cows. It was raining in the north of Ireland.

CHAPTER 6

In Dreams

I had been at the Department a year. I went in and out to work every day letting the mindless routine carry me along while all the time quietly planning my escape. Sometimes Department business took me out of the office, round the south Belfast district my section covered. I felt a wonderful sense of liberation just walking the streets around the university on cold, bright autumn afternoons, seeing the students drift past fresh-faced, wrapped in their long college scarves. I'd drop in at Smokey Joe's University Café and drink a coffee down the back, watching the students' comings and goings and dreaming of the day when I would number myself among them.

The student life promised lighter days. a brighter future. It was the dream of freedom and privilege. The only problem was gaining the entrance qualifications. My attendance at the A-level Art night class had lasted to the previous Christmas when, after a term, I'd realised I would never be another Jack Yeats and suddenly lost interest in painting.

In June I'd gone for an interview for teacher training at Stranmillis College where my sister had qualified. I got the morning off work, turning through the big gate in the high wall, up the long drive to the ivy-clad old manor house. An expanse of lawn stretched away in the sunshine; blossomy fragrances drugged the senses, new life erupting all around. It would be new life for me too. The students were on vacation now but I had no problem picturing myself here with them in the summer term, lolling over our books in chummy little groups, boys and girls, on the warm grass.

The interview went wonderfully. I knew this course was right for me and my enthusiasm and confidence communicated itself to the amiable interview panel with their friendly, enlightened approach. They were my kind of people, idealists, and my eager talk of the literature I'd read under my own steam impressed them. The chairman shook my hand warmly at the end and told me how much they looked forward to welcoming me to the college in a year's time when I had met the entrance qualification by acquiring just one more O-level certificate: Maths or Geography or a scientific subject. I'd floated away from Stranmillis—*"where the sweet water flows"*—feeling like one of the little white clouds high in the blue sky overarching Belfast that fine June morning; a sensation that stayed with me through the remainder of the office day, knowing now I would soon be free. One more year, that was all!

In September I started the Geography night class that would secure my entrance to teacher training. It was a comedown from the Art class the previous year, so I signed up for A-level English Literature as well, for my own interest. So that was two nights a week of tech classes, Tuesday and Thursday, plus homework. Julie had come out in sympathy with me and started a Tuesday night Fashion and Design class.

"Och, you inspired me!" she said. "Hairdressing is slave labour. Maybe I'll be the next Mary Quant instead!"

"Belfast's answer to her, with your own boutique: *'Julie Martin'*, yeah!"

"I think you need to go to London to really make it in fashion," she said.

"Would you move to London?"

"Sure!" she proclaimed. "What about you?"

"Well, my brother and sister are over there; I was planning to follow them sooner or later—move into a basement in West 11 and write my novel."

"Great minds think alike then!" she said happily and we darted meaningful glances at each other. A new shared dream was taking seed: moving to London! It held out all the promise of the wide world, unlimited opportunity, sophistication—fame!

There is the dream and then there is reality, and that is the problem. My Tuesday night geography class was at seven on the south side of town so I went on there from work, stopping off en route at the nice little café in Montgomery Street for a bowl of soup and a ham sandwich. Sometimes I was the only person eating there in its discreet gingham splendour.

"Careful with the salt, the cook's got a salty taste," the refined middle-aged waitress would advise me without fail each week as she brought the soup of the day to my table.

I sat on a while, trying to read a little from my geography book but tired and unable to concentrate much. Then I'd set out with a measured tread to kill time on the long, straight walk through Donegall Square and out the Grosvenor Road which was fresh territory to me. The class was in a dark stone Victorian primary school where we sat cramped into the small desks like overgrown kids, just a half-dozen of us doing penance for the time we'd wasted at school.

The teacher was a nice kind man, I recall, but I found no more inspiration in geography here than I had in six years of it at secondary school. As the dark freezing nights drew in I could no longer face the dispiriting trudge out through the barren brick channels to the Dickensian school, squashing into my little desk, my little brain doing battle with the contour lines on ordnance survey maps. I lasted there till Halloween; I told myself I had the book and could just as well study for the exam at home.

The A-level English Literature class was at the Jaffe further education college in the same road as my old school. The vivacious young Englishwoman who taught it did her best to wring some response out of the large inhibited class who preferred to sit there silent as statues, to listen carefully and note down uncritically every word that came out of her mouth. I didn't encounter any other would-be writers or literary types there but got friendly with Philip who sat next me, a sandy-haired, soap-smelling, mild, good-livin' boy, a civil service clerk who like me hoped to escape into teaching. The shared aspiration united us in a sort of conspiracy and after class, in the bar of the *Phoenix*, Philip would drink a shandy to my pint of bitter while we talked of a better life to come.

You cannot live in the future anyway. It might never happen and every day has to be got through in the meantime without wishing your life away. The office life drifted on, five days a week, 8.40 to 5; in truth you grew attached to the secure routine of it, the important small comforts of the tea breaks and little chats, the familiar homely faces around you. Sometimes I thought how easy it would be to forget college or moving away to London and just stay on at the Department and make a life for myself here, the same as all my colleagues were doing. There were much worse fates. There was a promotion ladder right up to the top if you were ambitious enough. Also these people I worked with were far from dull or unimaginative; they did a lot of other interesting creative things in their free time: they were singers and musicians, actors and Irish speakers, dancers and poets and philosophers.

The Department was a little world unto itself, a small planet stuck out on a limb between the market and the river.

"Herbie's kingdom," someone had called it. Herbie Gill was the Chief, his office situated directly off the reception. Occasionally I had to take some figures there for Owen. I tapped on the important-looking door and entered meekly. Sometimes the office was empty and I'd have a good nose around this little pocket of privilege and power with its dark panelled walls and glass-fronted bookcase containing fat reference volumes on the public services, engineering, law and accountancy. I'd kill a few minutes and have a bit of fun, squaring my shoulders like Herbie and strutting on the red carpet, looming importantly at the deep sash window overlooking the market-place, rocking on my heels. Maybe I could be Chief one day, if I were to take Dad's advice and complete the part-time seven year Institute of Chartered Secretaries course, like his clever younger brother, my Uncle Eric, who was high up on the railway.

Whenever I found Herbie there at his desk he scarcely acknowledged my humanity. A hand was stuck out, starched cuffs and gold links protruding from a blue suit, to receive the figures while he kept the otter-sleek oiled dark head with its shiny pate lowered to his work, not as much as a "Thank you" out of him. I worried he might ask me for some kind of explanation of the figures and I'd be exposed as the innumerate dunce and impostor I really was.

"Whadderyadoin' working in an accounts department, sonny?" The hectoring voice of Cheyenne, an old hated maths teacher, rang in my head.

Herbie had never married. Nor, unusually for a middle-aged man in his position, had he ever learnt to drive. I'd see him stepping out ahead of me up Bridge Street of a morning with his rapid domineering stride, swinging his arms like a general.

Although Herbie appeared not to see me I'd heard him call out to our office boss in the foyer one morning, "Cecil, what are we going to do about all these young fellows with long hair?"

Herbie had taken exception to George Lennon bringing his guitar into the office Christmas party. "A grown man playing a guitar!"he scoffed as if it were a child's toy rather than a complicated musical instrument.

Nobody liked Herbie and wee Cecil refused to be party to his purges. "A man's got a right to grow a beard," Cecil told Sean Hughes after Herbie had complained about Sean's beaver.

Cecil's small stature lent him a boyish quality and everyone spoke affectionately of him as "Wee Cecil". He was a democrat all right; some mornings he'd catch me up on Bridge Street in the wind and rain, scuttling along beside me, addressing me as an equal.

"I have a friend who runs an engineering company," he said, "and he tells me the long-haired lads are the best workers he has. After all, they had a name for short-haired men once, didn't they: Roundheads!"

Another older senior man was Robin the accountant. He was a bachelor, late middle age and lived with his aged mother. A thin, bony, balding, delicate-looking man, he dressed impeccably in navy pinstripe three-piece suits. He had a gentle manner with a fluting warm voice and a ready bright laugh. There was a simple childlike quality about Robin, but also a touch of the old maid, owlish gold-rimmed specs perched on the long, pointed, cold-looking neb projecting from his flat round face with its rosy apple cheeks and long teeth, Adam's apple bobbing rawly over the starched collar. A man-woman-child. I liked him.

There was a big to-do when Robin started bringing flowers in to the girls at work. He'd single out a different girl every week to present with his bouquet first thing in the morning, flashing his horse-teeth at her in a doting smile, the round light blue eyes magnified childlike behind his spectacle lenses, while the object of his appreciation gulped for words, roasting bright red to the roots of her hair.

After he'd gone the other girls would rally supportively round the victim and try to just have a quiet laugh about it. But the question was whose turn would it be next? They'd all be squirming, praying when they saw Robin coming with the bouquet, *"Please not me, Lord!"* The ill-conceived well-meaning gesture continued for some time till it had gone well beyond a joke and some of the girls were in tears and afraid to come into work. In the end Herbie had to speak to Robin and the flowers stopped at last.

I sat next to George Lennon, another sad sort of man, whose main topic of conversation was "Me trouble wi' me nerves." He'd suffered a nervous breakdown a few years back. "Ah didn't know what the hell was happenin'. Ah thought Ah was havin' a heart attack. Then Ah just started cryin' me eyes out and couldn't stop and they came and took me away."

George believed it was a consequence of the hectic double life he was leading, a grade 3 senior clerk by day and dance band leader in a nightclub, "Burnin' the candle at both ends for too many years."

At Purdysburn Asylum they administered electric shock therapy. "A terrible thing!" George recalled in wide-eyed horror. At least he was able in time to resume a normal life after a fashion. He still played with the band one or two nights a week. A lot of the clerks who were married men had evening jobs, mostly as barmen, to help make ends meet. Now George needed tranquillisers to keep going and it sometimes seemed like part of his brain had gone missing. Kind, decent Owen, protecting him, corrected the numerous minor errors in his work. Others plotted to get rid of George. His forgetfulness and constant obsessional talk of his condition annoyed them. I noticed the general lack of sympathy for mental illness, a notion that it was self-indulgent.

George often looked scruffy, unshaven, with greasy lank hair. He'd knock himself out at night with a sleeping pill, "Aye and do a meditation, feel the tension runnin' down me forehead and off the end o' me nose." He'd rise groggily and stumble out to work in the morning. He lived with a wife and children who put up with him the best they could.

"You could write your book all about the crazy characters in that place," said Julie.

"And I thought working at the Department was going to be boring!"

It was a Saturday afternoon in November and just for a change she'd come to me in Loughside. We had a cup of tea with my parents then I said, "C'mon, we'll walk to the shore. I've not been down that way for years."

We went down through the housing estate and into the old country loanen past the big house.

"I used to come this way with Davy or Matt every day all summer, to swim at the tide."

"Gosh, it's real country here!" Julie exclaimed in the fresh-faced wonder of a city girl on a Sunday school excursion as we strolled hand in hand down the unmade lane between the high, bare winter hedges.

Further down, the lane wound between stables and a paddock, then you passed a sunken, overgrown waste-ground next before the main road.

"We used to play Tarzan in there," I told Julie. "See those creepers hanging down from the trees? We pretended they were lianas and I was swinging from one of them—you know, *oh-owoh-owoh*!—and it snapped and I fell in a pile of rubbish and cut the palm of my hand on a broken whisky bottle, vicious. Look, I still bear the scar, across an earlier one I got in Ormagh."

"You were alwaysa bit wild, Jimmy!"

"Fancy a go now, wee-doll? Me Tarzan, you Jane!"

"D'ye think I look a bit like her, Maureen O'Sullivan?"

"Now you mention it, aye! Dead ringer, I'd say!"

"Thanks but no thanks anyway, wee-lad!"

We crossed the Shore Road to the little wooden gate into the Villiers-Stuarts' vegetable garden.

"Och look, they've padlocked it! The ones in these big houses were always blocking off the way down to the shore to keep us urchins out. We were only trying to get to the water for a swim."

"To have a wash—sure you'd never seen a bath in your slums!"

"We shoulda told them that."

"Look, we can get through here!" Julie had found a gap in the hedge. "Hold that barbed wire down for me!"

She hiked up her skirt and one elegant, shapely leg in thick maroon tights went over the fence, followed by the other leg.

"Julie, you'll cause a traffic accident doing that!" I said. "Now your turn, hold the barbed wire well down for me—Ah'm a man, yes I am!"

"And you wanna stay one!"

We followed the faint track down the side of the garden that was more a small field. Trees hid us from view of the big house. Past a hedge at the bottom we came to the sea wall. The tide washed calmly into the little sheltered rocky cove.

"It's so peaceful here!" Julie sighed. "Listen, the sea seems to be whispering to you, telling you its secrets!"

"Like voices from long ago. The first time I discovered this spot with Davy Robinson I had an overwhelming sensation of *déjà vu*, I felt sure I had been here in a previous life. It's an enchanted place. It became our secret private bathing spot that summer, 1958."

"It's our secret place now!" said Julie in her little-girl voice.

"Come on and I'll show you the secret beach!"

"This is an exciting adventure, better than the Famous Five!"

Over the sea wall we picked our way across the black rocks above the lapping tide, Julie very tentative, hanging on to my hand for dear life.

"You're Ann rather than George."

"Pardon?"

"The girls from the Famous Five. You're the feminine one."

"Oh!"

We clambered up to where the wall enclosed the spacious lawn of the big grey detached house. A startlingly lifelike statue of a reclining deer watched from under a tall tree. Beneath our feet a cobblestone embankment sloped down to the water; we walked to the end of it and dropped down on to the little run of yellow sandy beach. Beyond, the coastline receded in bays and promontories away past the Green Island to Carrickfergus Castle looming out on its high rock.

"The Shore of Adventure!" I proclaimed. "Davy and I used to come here for Rupert Bear and Algie Pug adventures: foiling a smugglers' plot; getting washed out to sea on a raft we found then swimming back to shore for dear life!"

Now it was a dry, cold November's day; silvery glints of sunshine in the west struggled through the grey cloud-mass. The Lough was a sluggish grey-green. I skimmed a few flat stones across the surface to be a lad again and impress Julie, watching them bounce miraculously, three, four, five, six times!

"Here, have a seat." I spread my car-coat on a nice dry patch of sand and we sat huddled together on it. I hugged Julie's knees sticking up pointed and warm in her maroon tights. The waves curled in smoothly and landed with a dull thump; we sat there mesmerised by the ancient rhythm of it.

"There's something about the winter sea," I said. "Beautiful in a remote, cold, deadly way. Like a woman can be!" I teased.

"Like you daren't look her straight in the face," said Julie, "or she'll put her spell on you."

"Like you do to me."

"Oh aye! *Ah put a spell on you . . . !*"

"Your wee face is all cold," I said and began to warm her cheeks with pecking kisses.

"You're kissin' me like I was your wee baby sister!" she pouted.

"*Li'l sister, doncha!* Here then!" I cupped the oval of her soft, cold little face in my hands, the dark eyes searching mine sweetly, and kissed her fair and square on the lips. I felt the soft, scented warmth of her through her clothing. We closed our eyes, swaying there in an embrace for a minute, in a little ecstasy of oneness, our hearts beating to the rhythm of the sea.

We stood up and shivered. The bit of sun was gone, leaving the shoreline grey, frozen and dead, with the bleak, lonely feeling of evening coming on.

"We're like the last people on earth here," I said, feeling the joy of just a minute ago draining from me like the light from the sky.

Now as we made our way back over the cobblestones and rocks Julie was preoccupied once more with where she was putting her feet down.

"Got the wrong shoes for this but thank God I didn't wear stilettos!"

"You're funny, Julie! But I'm glad you're not the Girl Guides' leader type leppin' over the rocks!"

Back on level ground, still feeling the melancholia descending on my shoulders with the grainy evening light, I asked her childishly, "Am I still your boy, Julie?"

"Yep!"

"Am I your boy forever?" I used to ask Mum and Dad this when I was small; it became a family joke, especially after I'd turned on Dad once with, *"You're not my boy anymore, you cheeky ould brat!"*

I still felt that funny neediness sometimes, a basic insecurity; your girlfriend took the place of your parents.

"You're my boy and I'm your girl, for always," said Julie. I was sure she meant it but I could tell her thoughts had moved on to more practical concerns. She didn't question love, it was always there, a fact of life. But she linked my arm as if silently reassuring me.

Back on the Shore Road we passed the old gatehouse with the Villiers-Stuarts' trees behind it. It looked derelict now.

"They've gone," I said. "Big poor family, lots of raggedy kids, used to live there. It didn't look much better then. The eldest girl was in my class at the primary school, faded clothes hanging on her thin frame, but she was a beautiful girl: high-cheekboned, olive skin, dark hair—romantic gipsy looks. I used to find myself staring at her, though I'd have dropped dead if she or any other girl had spoken to me at that age. She was a nice well-mannered girl too. And what's more, she was one of ten of us that passed the eleven-plus out of a class of forty-five pupils. I don't know what became of her after that. I don't even remember her name."

"It's a mystery what happens to people, isn't it?" said Julie pensively. "A girl like that would be sure to get on in life no matter what. There must have been love in that big poor family; it just shows you money isn't everything."

Julie's words warmed me through and I felt the depression lift. What was depression anyway but a failure to believe in that power of love.

We went in out of the November dusk to light and warmth and a Saturday tea of fried pork chops with my parents. Julie was so right with them, the perfect girlfriend, easy and natural, respectful and charming. I had a warm feeling of her as one of the family now.

After tea Julie and I retired to the front room where a fire had been lit specially for us. This was a room that seemed designed to be uncomfortable and unlived-in with its overcrowded stiff, scratchy furniture. The china cabinet and the piano lived here and a couple of old landscapes of Ned's on the walls, paintings that had survived art college and his switch to social realism: a moonlit snow-covered farm and a view of White Park Bay, all that was left of a bygone Celtic sentimentalism. A low bookcase contained his big art books. The front room was a sort of dusty family museum.

The thin gold and green-striped curtains didn't quite meet across the recess of the square bay window. I told Julie, "I get wee kids gathering outside chanting '*Beatle!*' when I practise my guitar here."

"Beatlemania hits Loughside, eh?"

"Aye and one day coming from the station a gang of wee boys chased me. It was scary!"

Now the tall concrete electric standards dimly lighted the empty rectangle of streets around the big dark central green of the estate. Turning away from the dismal scene with a shiver, I plugged in the record player and put on some jazz, Tatum and Webster, for the right atmosphere of sophistication and intimacy. I turned off the light and we sat in the flickering firelight courting on the old red couch pulled up close to the flames.

We were deep in a clinch later when the door swung open and Dad appeared with our own supper tray of tea and sandwiches, cake and biscuits. After we'd eaten it was time for Julie to put on her coat and stick her head round the living room door to say, "Goodnight now, Mr and Mrs Mitchell!"

"Goodnight now, Julie dear!"

I walked her to the station, through the queer heavy silence and desolation that was Loughside by night.

"Well, that was different anyway," I said. "Saturday night at Coolmore Green."

"I like your mum and dad," said Julie. "There's a very relaxed atmosphere in your house."

"No phone, no car. No rush. And look at Loughside: no pub, no chip shop. Four churches. The mountain and the shore. Everybody in watching the box. Life in a dormitory village."

"Just somewhere to sleep."

"That's mostly what my old man does; you were lucky to see him stay awake so long. Mind you, he likes to meet a nice wee girl!"

*He's a handsome man still."

"They used to think he was a visiting Hollywood film star up on the North Antrim coast where we went on holiday."

"Your Ma's a bright, well-educated lady."

"Oh very, smarter than my Da probably, though it all got a bit wasted on the selfless grind of housework and kids, nearly drove her mad at times."

"That's the way it was then for women. I'm going to work in a job I like *and* have kids as well."

"That's what I'd want my wife to do," I said and we looked knowingly at each other.

I kissed her goodnight there under the dingy lights on the cold, late platform at Loughside station.

My memories of Julie are of quietly satisfying times like that, the two of us doing nothing much; just being together was enough. We saw increasingly less of my mates, none of whom had a steady girl. The laddish pubs where they drank didn't attract Julie and me. We scarcely drank alcohol, preferring *Isibeal's* coffee bar which stayed open late. We went to the cinema a lot, two or three times a week; on Saturdays to the early house and then on to the Chinese restaurant in Donegall Square, sweet and sour pork our favourite. We went to concerts: Bob Dylan, Joan Baez, Peter, Paul and Mary, the Walker Brothers and Freddie and the Dreamers; they all came to Belfast. And there was the James Young Show; not the English crooner but a very local man, a comedian and raconteur whose one man show touching on thorny issues like "mixed marriages" (Protestant-Catholic) held Belfast audiences spellbound and tearful.

We spent a lot of time back at the Martin house on Duncairn Gardens, often having it to ourselves, with the parents involved in various activities at the Presbyterian church. There was an older brother, Wesley, an amiable, red-haired student, who was in the Young Liberals at Queen's University, "plotting the overthrow of the Unionist government," he said.

With the house empty Julie and I enjoyed a comfortable court under the eiderdown on her bed. Afterwards, back in the parlour I'd watch her at her dressmaking. With her patterns and material pinned and spread out over the entire floor, kneeling down she snipped away with the chunky scissors with a determined, deadeye precision. Then she ran the garment up on the antique Singer sewing machine. Unself-conscious with me, standing in her underwear before the fire, she'd try a dress on before putting the finishing stitches to it.

I was happy to sit there and watch her at her work, the two of us close and warm in the cosy room, the outside world forgotten. In a college sketchbook she drew with an easy deft accuracy female figures in various styles of clothing. She asked my opinion on details of style and colour and I amazed myself as I began to develop an eye for the aesthetics of women's fashion. I loved the look and feel of the materials, like an extension of her. Men's fashion bored me frankly but women's style was something else, a real art form celebrating the God-given grace and mystery of the female form.

"You're good at this," Julie complimented me and I felt pleased with myself, clothes meant so much to her. Then there were the trips round the shops with her on her Saturday afternoons off, her new pay packet in her handbag, round the big department stores and down old, narrow passages of Victorian Belfast where the little fashion boutiques were tucked away. Every last penny she had went on her back.

"Well, I don't smoke or drink," she justified it. "You can't be a fashion student and go round looking like an ould bag."

I was happy to tag along; it was a relaxing kind of show for me watching Julie try things on. She was my girl, my fantasy. "What do you think?" she'd ask me; she truly valued my opinion. I was glad it wasn't me having to buy clothes, that was a form of torture to me. Sometimes she'd present me with something new to wear, like a pink shirt with a long pointy collar, or maroon hipster trousers with a thick belt, something to jolt me out of my instinctive male conservatism.

"And let your hair grow longer," she instructed me. "Like the *Pretty Things*."

"My hair's too long already for the Department. Herbie would have me sent over the road to the slaughterhouse for the chop."

"Wait'll you see in a few years' time, even Herbie will have collar-length hair."

"Make up for him going bald on top."

Winter, dark and bitter or cosy and self-contained, opened out at last to spring, chilly and gusting, snowdrifts of pink and white petals along the gutters, an unnerving sense of time and space in the lengthening daylight hours, culminating in the annual heat wave for the exams at the end of May. I wasn't at all prepared for the exams, I'd missed too many classes and done no homework, but I went through the motions on a wing and a prayer, in and out of the cavernous public examinations hall on Chichester Street, on the off-chance that Lady Luck might carry me through. Julie had stuck at her Fashion and Design course and I was sure she'd do well in the exam. She had applied for full-time courses in Belfast and London.

We had a nice summer with some weekends away together, one with all the old gang at Hugh's cottage on Copeland Island, another with Julie's parents in their caravan at Groomsport. A lot of drinking was done in the caravans and at the pub down the road with football matches on the TV. Julie and I didn't care for the crowds and slipped away together after a few drinks.

Across a large sun-bleached meadow we came to where the tide washed in from a golden evening sea. There wasn't another soul in sight; rays of lowering sun flooded the lonely, gull-calling coastline. We lay on my jacket on a grassy spot above the water's edge. As we started kissing the wild, romantic spirit of the place took hold of us.

"Oh Jim!" she cried helplessly, clinging to me.

We got our exam results in August. I'd failed Geography again, by a few marks again, and only got an O-level pass in the A-level English—even that was an achievement, considering how little preparation I had put into any of it. But it was goodbye to the dream of Stranmillis for another year.

Julie had passed her course with a distinction. "I've been offered a place at Chelsea to study Fashion and Design," she said quietly. "Or Belfast wants me too." Her round black eyes searched my face.

"Oh Julie, that's fabulous! You must go to Chelsea!" I didn't even have to think about it. "London is the fashion centre of the world right now, the only place for you to be with your talent!"

"What'll you do?" she asked. "I mean, how am I going to go without you?"

"I could get into teacher training college in England with the O-levels I've got. Goldsmith's looks good, not far from where you'll be. I'll wait till you're settled in first then apply for next year."

"Why wait? They might take you this year. Anyway, you'd get an office job over there, no problem, until you start college." I could only envy that directness of hers: you saw what you wanted and you went for it, simple as that; no beating about the bush. You could have it all right now: college, London, Julie. It was thrilling. But getting what you wanted just like that was scary too.

My cautious instincts told me I wasn't ready for it yet. Even the Department seemed dear to me suddenly, now I had the chance to escape it.

I was torn in two. It was possible I might feel differently in a year's time; I'd be twenty then. We agreed that Julie would take up the place at Chelsea and I would join her in London at some point in the near future.

CHAPTER 7

Night Life

Julie had gone and I was left with the sadness of autumn, the rattle of dead leaves in the gutters down Station Road, the evenings closing in like death. I wrote my girl long letters almost every day at first, addressed to her flat in Kensington. At first she wrote and told me how homesick she felt, how terribly she missed me, she felt lost in the big city and was going to have to come back. But once she'd settled in at college there was no stopping her: she loved the course, her tutors were great, and the other girls just her type and really friendly, they were mostly new to London like her and they could all just live and breathe fashion together.

That enthusiasm coming off the page of her neat uniform handwriting got to me now; I felt the freedom and energy of London in her words, the glamour of Chelsea, and I could have kicked myself for being such a stick-in-the-mud in Belfast. Maybe I would make the move there early in the new year. In the meantime I just went through the motions, in and out of work each day. There was a lot of overtime going at the office and we'd have one of Mrs McGookin's chip teas at half-four up in the canteen: fat chips, bread and butter, pot of tea. It tasted utterly delicious somehow.

"Chip butties!" Margaret exclaimed; it was an English delicacy. We all fairly tucked in, sat round the table for four high in the old building like a castle, looking out on the darkening

Belfast evening, the headlamps of cars along Bridge Street, the dome of City Hall lit up beyond. It was dark and cold, nasty and impersonal out there in the rush hour; inside it was cosy and homely. I felt I could stay here at work for ever, safe and secure. You belonged here, you had a purpose. Looking at Owen and Margaret sharing my table, I felt a kind of love for them both, like a family to me.

We went downstairs at five as the crowds poured towards the exits. With the others gone from the office the atmosphere was relaxed and intimate, we chatted a bit or worked in a satisfying timeless, companionable sort of silence. The big black pen-nib hands of the wall clock seemed stuck; it was a very long time to six, an age till seven or half-past when we began to clear up for the day. But you didn't mind; there was no rush, nowhere else you wanted to be. Rain streaked the black window panes overlooking the desolate market-place. It was a timeless, secure, contented feeling, encompassed by the dark fortress of the old night-time building.

The overtime pay would be there boosting your salary cheque at the end of the month; that added to the sense of well-being. Owen had five children to support; Margaret was saving up to marry Norman. I—well, who knew?—might be moving to London and anyway i liked the reassurance of the fat wallet next my heart.

Sadder still, I took to hanging out with George Lennon in the working day. He provided companionship on the long lunch break. We started with brisk keep-fit walks out round Ormeau Park, George swinging his arms and stepping out purposefully— he was ex-army. Soon it eased into pub lunches down by the docks; we took books to read in our corner of the lounge bar, close to the electric fire, while we dined on steak and kidney pies and cups of tea. We were usually the only customers there in the lounge at the back of the pub. George knew the manager and the women who came through sometimes, greeting him familiarly in broad Belfast.

"They're on the game," he confided to me. "Great girls, got the heart of gold," he said in his kindly Liverpool accent. I was impressed.

We went on a fishing trip to Lough Neagh one Saturday, a works' outing organised by Sean Hughes. I travelled in George's car with his young son in the back seat nagging him all through the journey, "Daddy, your indicator's still on!"

George was a great advocate of fishing as a form of meditation and relaxation. I was interested to try it, especially with my hero Sean, but it turned out a day of boredom and cold in the flat, bushy, wintry wilderness, the expanse of Lough water mirroring the big grey sky.

I felt sorry for George; I guessed his family wasn't that sympathetic to the self-preoccupation that went with his condition. His good-looking grown-up daughter was in the car when he stopped in Chichester Street to give me a lift to work one morning. Laura: big tumbling dark brown hair and large hazel eyes that didn't care about much except Laura. He dropped her off at the gas department where she worked.

"You have a very nice daughter, George!" I declared jauntily as I took her place in the front passenger seat. She was round about my age too.

"She's goin' steady, Jim," he informed me. "The doctor's son," he added with a touch of fatherly pride.

I had to smile sometimes at people's pretensions. But not long afterwards the bombshell struck.

"Laura's pregnant," George confided in me. It was a chilling misfortune in those days, the fear of it keeping most of us virgins, boys and girls alike, until we were safely married. "She told me in the car coming to work the other day. I had to pull into the side; I just sat there behind the driving wheel cryin' me eyes out. I've told Owen."

You had to feel sorry for poor old George, and admire the way he let his emotions out into the open and talked about his feelings. It came from the therapy he'd had for his breakdown, I supposed.

"The doctor's son?" I had to ask.

"No, it's Dan, he's a motor mechanic. They're getting married now." It sounded more like a funeral.

It seemed nothing went right for George. One afternoon he came limping in the office door, red in the face with vexation.

"That little bitch Sonia kicked me!" he moaned. "All I did was pat her on the bottom goin' up the back stairs in front of me! Aoh, me shin bloody hurts! Nasty little cow, she is!"

One lunch hour we drove to a garden centre outside town. The owner had offered George a good discount on bedding plants. He was a client of the Ambassador Club where George and his band played. He came to help George select his plants; it was difficult to square the respectable middle-aged business man with someone who used prostitutes. I imagined a darkness around him; I viewed him as a tainted character.

"We get a lot of business men like him," George told me going back in the car afterwards. "Senior policemen too. You must come up the club and see me play one night, Jim."

I really wanted to see the Ambassador Club, the pros; it was the kind of scene you could put in a novel one day. I persuaded my mates it'd be an interesting experience at least. The club didn't open till eleven, so we had a drink down the road at *Hannegan's* first for Dutch courage. We had no intention of using prostitutes; we just wanted to witness this den of iniquity in the heart of our good-livin' town. And the club served alcohol till two in the morning.

We were among the first customers that night. The club was in Fountain Street, off Donegall Square in the city centre. An insignificant sign on the street door announced *Ambassador Club–Members Only.* The door opened on to a badly-lit flight of wide dingy stairs that climbed steep and straight a long way up to a black door at the top. There was a doorbell and a notice, *Please ring and wait.* I pressed the bell, grinned round at the lads for moral support. It was just the way it should have been, a cliché really, *Hernando's hideaway.*

The door opened; an incredibly wide figure in a dinner jacket and bow tie, with Brylcreemed Teddy boy hair, filled the doorway.

"We're George Lennon's guests," I announced, my cocky self emerging with the drink taken. We were motioned sullenly inside.

George was sent for while we waited awkwardly under the baleful stares of the bouncers standing round. The glittering bar was right there opposite the entrance.

George appeared, impressive in a red quilted dinner jacket, like Jack Hilton. He was reassuring with his jaunty, proprietorial air and the warm Scouse voice, "How are you, boys? Glad you could come. Get yourselves a drink and come on through."

The bottled beer and whiskey shots served by the surly barman were overpriced. We took the drinks through to the cavernous dance hall with tables lined round the walls. George and the band in their red jackets were setting up on the stage at the far end of the hall. We sat at a table near the entrance, uneasily, sipping our drinks.

"There they are!" Stuarty whispered. The women were sitting round drinking and smoking further down the line of tables. They were all pros; there was a certain look about them, hair and clothes styles out of the 1950s, but then they weren't that young. Seeing them gave us lads a sordid little thrill: they were waiting there for the express purpose of *that!* Yet they looked so normal in a way, just like any group of women in a dance hall.

George's band got going, George leading on his red electric guitar, the tinkly piano breaking in, the plodding double bass, drag of the drummer's brushes, churning out *Begin the Beguine*, George on vocals; a laboured, lacklustre sound echoing around the half-empty hall. Some of the pros got up and jived smoothly together to get things moving. The hall began to fill up a bit, well set-up middle-aged men who sat and had drinks with the girls in sociable little groups, all surprisingly civilised really.

We observed the group of punters and pros next us, gathered round two or three tables pushed together, talking easily, regulars it seemed.

"The young one's nice," said Howie. She was slender and pretty with Gina Lollobrigida piled-up brown hair and a busty, bunchy frock. She had personality besides, tossing her dark fringe out of her eyes and showing teeth and gums attractively as she laughed, or making her eyes wide and round in fascination as she listened to some yarn around the table. We caught her name: Rita.

Later dark Rita and the peroxide blonde Jeannie, coming back together from the loo, paused at our table to enquire in a pleasant, friendly fashion, "Are yous students?"

"I work with George," I explained..

"Och, he's an awful nice fellah, George!" said Rita.

"Sure he shoulda been in the Beatles," said Jeannie, "if he'd been younger."

"George Lennon, " said Rita. "Sure isn't he yer mon's Da? John Lennon's Da?"

"He looks more like Ringo," said Jeannie.

"Annyway, nice spakin' to yous, boys!"

When they'd gone back to their table we agreed, "They're really nice girls!"

As we sat on over a few more drinks the floor began to fill up a bit, the paunchy balding men and the ladies of the night shuffling around in clinches, painted long fingernails resting on a bulge of shaved neck over a collar, and I could see George was in his element as he crooned a more recent hit song, *Strangers in the Night*.

"*—Exchangin' pant-ees!*" he crooned comically.

Some of the women whooped. I'd heard this take of George's on the lyric before; he'd come out with it frequently in the office. Nobody there laughed of course, it was a bit blue. But what did it mean anyway, *"exchanging panties"*? Mutual cross-dressing? Confusion in the dark? No, it made no sense at all. Yet the sheer silliness of it stuck in my head like a neurosis; it was George all over, incomprehensible!

Between numbers George would adjust his hornrims on his long nose, look round blankly at the crowd with a setter-like movement of his head and crack tired old jokes that no one laughed at.

We sat on in a sort of trance for some time. We had nothing better to do. It was half-twelve when we exited into the strange dead of the Belfast night. The traffic lights kept on changing on the forlorn empty streets around the City Hall. The only figures to be seen were the mannequins in Robinson and Cleaver's window. Malcolm drove steadily down the long, dark, deserted roads, dropping us all home safely to our mammies and daddies.

"Hi, imagine your Ma tomorrow morning asking, 'Where were you last night, son?'" said Hugh.

"In a brothel, Mammy!" we chorused in the flying after-midnight Minivan.

CHAPTER 8

Runaway

There was always something going on at the Department to liven up the working day. Noreen Batt from downstairs came to work beside me on our section when Isobel was promoted to another office. Noreen was all drive and efficiency with her quick birdlike head and angular, forward-leaning scurrying body that quivered and twitched with nervous energy whenever she was stationary. She was only a couple of years older than me but seemed middle-aged already; it was doubtful that she had ever been young.

"Shtupid!" was her favourite word, meaning anything that wasn't strictly down to earth and logical, as she saw it. She focused on something practical—ledgers, vegetable shopping, family matters—and went flat out for it, her face closed in concentration. Her bulgy pale blue eyes, magnified a little crazily by her glasses, stared you down if you got in the way.

So there she was, slotted between George and me on the line of high desks. George acted like a kindly joking uncle towards her but she treated him with barely disguised contempt. Everything about him spelt incompetence and failure and was an irritant to her. As for the nervous problems he claimed to suffer from, well, he should pull himself together, it was simple as that. Knowing I had nothing whatsoever in common with her, I made a special effort to get along with her; to be openly at odds with her, stuck there cheek by jowl, day in, day out, would be unbearable. Every single person comprises a little world that is of interest to the writer in me. Noreen's world consisted of the Department and her family; she was the older sister who takes on part of the mother's responsibilities for the house and younger siblings. She was spiritually active in the Legion of Mary.

It was civil rights time in the North and I let drop some comment about the possible existence of institutional anti-Catholic discrimination.

"What? Discrimination? What discrimination? No, it never happened! That kind of talk annoys me, Jim, it's a loady ould rubbish! Shtupid, so it is!"

"But—but—" Politics never was my forte, though I cared about people, "look at the statistics—housing, jobs, the vote. Ask Owen, he'll tell you," I concluded ineffectually.

"Owen is the youngest senior clerk, at forty-two, in this Department !"

"Owen says that's as far as he'll ever get; they told him as much to his face."

"Ach, not at all!""

Well, if she wanted to think that then good luck to her; I wasn't going to make her a victim against her will.

Noreen Batt was not the kind of woman you'd expect to fall victim to a mad hopeless passion. She was clearly fond of Owen, but then so was everyone who came into contact with this thoughtful, kindly man. Only there was perhaps a touch of hysteria about Noreen's dizzy smiles and hysterical laughter as she fluttered around him in her Girl Friday fashion. An older man was so much more appreciative of a young woman. Also Owen just happened to be very handsome, though he was not a ladies' man; rather, he represented the ideal of a good Catholic family man, Noreen's ideal man, and there was the rub, the paradox, the problem: Noreen and Owen, it could never be!

Noreen began to suffer mood swings, turning sulky and tearful. Then one day she threw a sort of fit. Both of us were working away, side by side, when she slumped over her paperwork, burying her face in her folded arms. Her shoulders and blonde head were shaking with emotion. I pretended not to notice.

Then she rose suddenly, scraping back her chair, moving on her quick bandy legs, hen-toed. She flitted across the room and dropped on to a vacant seat behind Owen. Then the tears rolled and she shook her head despairingly. "He doesn't care!" she bawled. "He just doesn't care!"

Owen never once looked up from his work. The rest of us put on a similar pretence, until Molly, a genteel middle-aged lady, went over to Noreen and took her by the arm, "Come along now, dear," off to the Ladies'.

The office went straight back to normal afterwards; the incident was filed away in a communal mental drawer labelled "*Too embarrassing for words*". Noreen quickly regained her sanity; now she spoke of becoming a nun. I heard Sean Hughes dissuading her, knitting his thick black eyebrows in disapproval. "You don't have to be a Holy Joe to practise your religion," he counselled her. "A woman like you needs a man; a man needs a woman like you."

Not long afterwards she sourced some poor fellow at the church who'd been drifting contentedly into middle-aged bachelordom and soon they were engaged.

I would visit the filing office downstairs under the least pretext. It was a legs-stretcher: down the narrow back staircase, along a draughty concrete passageway, past the glass-walled computer room offering a pleasing glimpse of Alison there, slim legs in a short black flared skirt; on past the stores— And there it was, the filing girls all seated in a row facing the big windows on to the corridor; behind them the olive metal filing cabinets under the tall windows that looked out on the dark groins under Bridge Street.

It was the liveliest room in the Department, a young female domain of clerical assistants that was a magnet to the younger male clerks like me with its promise of light-hearted flirtation and craic. Only you had to be on the lookout for Rosa Klebb, the girls' supervisor who had her own little office along the corridor. Rosa Klebb, aptly nicknamed after the spy in James Bond, would come out on the prowl, a thin stick of an old spinster in tweeds, heavy denier and brogues. Once she struck as I was chatting up our filing clerk Sonia by the cabinets.

"Have you two got nothing better to do than stand there gossiping all day?" Her tongue stabbed the air like the flick-knife Rosa Klebb kept concealed in her toecap. Her face shoved up close to mine was a wrinkly, powdered, hateful monkey-mask.

Sonia was a pale, slender girl, a little white face peeping out of a mass of wavy brown hair. I had difficulty telling her age at first, there was a slight hardness around the eyes, but it turned out she was just a year older than me.

"Are you Protestant or Catholic?" she asked me boldly straight out the first time we were on our own.

"Agnostic," I replied evasively, but then warming to her cheeky grin and a refreshing sort of candour about the question, I confessed, "A Protestant agnostic, if you like!"

"I'm Catholic," she said. "I could have sworn you were one of us!"

This was good fun. "You mean you can tell by looking?" I laughed, though I knew some people believed this.

"I could just picture you counting your Rosary beads!" she joked, and then she asked, "Isn't Mitchell a Catholic name?"

I nodded. "I think so." A part of me rather liked the idea.

"My daddy's Protestant," she said. "Mixed marriage. My boyfriend David is too, a Methodist. He works in Larry's office; do you know him?"

"I've seen you together in the canteen." David was a very dark, ruddy-cheeked, very quiet boy. They appeared besotted with one another and I'd heard wee Billy Morney, one of the older clerks, an attercop with big glasses, complaining about them "canoodlin'" at work. He also complained about Owen and Sean talking Irish in the office; he was one of life's complainers.

Sonia liked boys. I'd stand there for ages talking with her, the two of us flirting harmlessly; she was joined at the hip to David and I was still in love with Julie, so it wasn't intended to go beyond words between us, which lent a sort of license to our exchanges. The conversation always came back to sex somehow, and why not? It is after all the reason we are here. As I got to know her she liked to tease me with frank sensual talk that brought the blood rushing to my cheeks, and I could see how she enjoyed wielding this power over the male of the species.

She liked to recount how David would come to her after football practice with injuries he'd sustained to "Percy", and Sonia would be obliged to bathe his wounds. As the explicit details emerged her face shone and set in a doting little fixed grin. There was her gloating amusement over the absurdity of the male anatomy, but an indulgent fondness there too with its "nice baby smell," she said. Then her voice hardened obsessionally as she praised its tumescent power. "Of course I always keep a box of tissues handy!" she concluded jocularly, her blue eyes dancing with wicked merriment again.

I would egg her on with a leading question; it was a mind game we played together.

"What do you think about the testicles?" I employed a researcher's voice, a flat, objective, medical enquiry, the Kinsey Report, masking the turmoil she awoke inside me.

"Oh, I like them!" she smiled, light-hearted and wholesome as a games mistress. "I play with David's, I bounce them: *'one-two-three-a-leery!'* "

These shared fantasies discreetly whispered in the cover of the filing cabinets left me hot and bothered for the rest of the office day. The Department never felt so flat and pointless as after a fever-inducing dose of Sonia's erotic reveries.

"David and I are running away together to London," she informed me quietly one day.

Sonia explained the situation. When the couple had announced their intention of getting engaged both sets of parents had united in opposition to the prospect of a "mixed marriage".

"But your parents are a mixed marriage," I said.

"That's the trouble. They say they couldn't stand seeing us go through what they've had to suffer. I've argued with them but Mummy just goes to pieces, she says I'll give her a nervous breakdown over it all and I believe her. It's left us with no choice. David's got a job in a bank in London, he's going over first then I'll follow."

The day of Sonia's departure arrived. She was flying out from Aldergrove that evening while her parents were at Bingo. She'd be safely in London with David by the time they got back and found her note.

I went downstairs to the filing room the next morning to see if she'd really done it and sure enough, there was the shocking drama of her empty desk with the chair tucked under it. Her father came into the reception "Cryin' he's eyes out," said Dick the porter. "He kept askin' for 'the mon—Ah wanna see the mon!' I got Owen to him."

Owen told me, "I think everybody knew about Sonia running away except her own parents." I was a bit shocked by his words, having fondly imagined she'd confided specially in me. Owen blamed the parents, "Out at their Bingo every night leaving the poor girl at home on her own!"

Two weeks later Sonia was back at her desk looking like death warmed up. The Department had agreed to take her back.

"I feel so sorry for her," Sheila from the typing pool whispered to me. "It must be awful for her!"

Sonia didn't speak for another two weeks. The cold, angry eyes in the downcast, bitter little face warned you off. Much as I liked her, she could be a right bitch anyway, I knew.

But eventually she came round, greeting me one day in the old friendly way again and telling me everything that had happened. Her parents had turned up at the door of David's bedsitter in Ealing. There were no unpleasant scenes. The two couples had enjoyed an impromptu holiday together, sightseeing in London, and Sonia had returned to Belfast with her parents. End of story.

I felt Sonia was putting a good face on things. In the end she had accepted it was the right thing to come home; she was an only child and couldn't go against her parents' wishes like that. She didn't say what, if any, were her and David's plans for the future. But soon there was little talk of David out of her and then no mention of him any more.

The wee drama had taken place in the last dregs of winter. Spring came thrusting in with the light evenings that always came as a surprise. I walked Sonia home one day after work, down Corporation Street, on my way to the station. She lived in Sailortown; we passed the Seamen's Institute—"I go to the dances there, the men are all over you," she said—and turned down the long redbrick terraced street where she lived: Fleet Street; every street in dockside Sailortown was named after ships.

I saw her right to her door. As we stood there chatting a minute in the clear evening light, I felt the peculiar romance of the Victorian industrial streets with their sense of vibrant teeming lives. Sonia was smiling at me in her knowing way but soft and kindly now; there'd been a mellowing in her. She was an attractive young woman with her full dark hair and elegant figure and we'd chatted easily, like warm, close friends, all the way along Laganbank Road and Corporation Street.

"How's Julie getting on in London?" she enquired.

"Doing well, I think. We've kind of drifted apart."

"You're not going together any more?"

I shook my head sorrowfully. The letters had fizzled out; she was too absorbed in her college life in London and anyway tired of waiting forever for me to make the move there.

"I'll be your girl if you like," said Sonia in her direct, appealing way.

I was moved by her brave, good words but not sure how to respond and then she said, "Oh, here's Dad coming from work!"

I turned my head to view the figure of the docker striding up Fleet Street, a fair, youngish man in a donkey jacket. It seemed the right moment for me to bid Sonia goodbye and walk the other way to York Street and the station.

I'm not sure why I didn't take Sonia up on her generous offer to be my girl. She was a forthright, passionate young woman, it seemed, qualities that attracted me for I needed someone like that to bring me out of myself. We were in the same boat, Sonia and I, stuck in Belfast with our love interests living in London. Clearly Sonia was ready to move on now but I still felt the attachment to Julie. I'd sit up late on my own listening to my record of Richard Harris *MacArthur's Park,* my eyes filling with tears, all the sweet green icing flowing down and I'd never have that recipe again, *Oh no!*

In truth I wasn't ready for a serious relationship. I was immature, in a word, unable to commit myself, a hopeless proposition for any good woman. I guessed that going with Sonia would be an intense grown-up affair. And same as with her and David, there'd be all that crap from society about "mixed marriages" to contend with.

CHAPTER 9

The Island

Summertime brought the respite of the island, an escape from the city. We went straight from work on Friday evenings, my weekend clothes packed in a Smithfield market army satchel, catching the bus from Oxford Street to Donaghadee. We sat in our office clothes at the front top deck of the green country bus, heading out the Newtownards Road. Putting the Dundonald suburbs behind us, we smelt the country air coming in the open windows. The patchwork quilt of County Down spread itself around us. This was the best moment of the week, with work behind you and the whole weekend ahead of you, a non-stop celebration of youth and leisure.

The last leg of the bus ride was butting down rough lanes through green drumlin hills, bouncing over potholes while the branches of hedgerow trees flailed the roof. Then the thrill as we emerged on the coastline with our island stretched along the horizon like a sleeping dog, waiting there for us, faithful. Climbing down from the bus at Donaghadee harbour with the round white tower of the lighthouse at the end of the jetty, the wild, romantic clamour of the gulls filled your ears and you breathed the glamour and adventure of the salt sea air.

We drank our first bottle of the weekend in the quiet gloom of the little harbour bar that supplied us with crates of Harp lager and Red Heart Guinness for the island. We carried the booze over to the cobbled quayside along with our other provisions from the Spar grocer's: tea, coffee and sugar, bacon and eggs, baked beans, spuds, bread and butter and lard, Fray Bentos steak and kidney pie in a big round tin, washing up liquid and paraffin oil, ready to go on Trimble's boat.

Throughout the summer season there'd be a crowd making the Friday night crossing, those like us with a holiday home on the greater island and the bird-watchers bound for the sanctuary on the smaller Lighthouse Island. We soon put the harbour, the small town and the Down coast behind us. We watched the island draw closer, the long, low grey shape rising very slowly out of the water, serpent-like. As it filled the horizon we could see the scattered cottages and hedged green fields dotted with sheep, a piece of the countryside stuck down improbably between the typically grey sky and sea. Two families had lived on and farmed the island until 1948, the year I was born; now only the sheep remained and the weekenders who inhabited the houses.

At the old crumbling landing stage there was the precarious business of disembarking with our provisions, then the labour of humping them over the spine of the hill to our place. Loaded up like mules, strung out in a line, we followed the faint track past a weather-beaten wooden bungalow and a little way along the shoreline where the waves plunged at the shiny brown banks of sea-rods. The gulls circled overhead with their harsh predatory cries.

Turning inland through a gap in the high, ragged hawthorn hedge we began the ascent of the big green field, startling the peaceful sheep. Rabbits flickered away through the tufty grass. Labouring up the broad windy back of the field under flying tatters of clouds, you felt small and exposed. The alarmed cacophonous bleating of the sheep blowing on the wind filled your head like madness.

Ould Wully Mejorum's rose into view on the crest of the hill, a long, low old farmhouse with derelict outbuildings, standing in the meagre hilltop shelter of a sparse clump of tall ash trees. It was the highest point of the island here with the green fields dropping away on every side to the encircling water that foamed thickly about the jagged black rocks at the island's extremities. The other old farmhouse stood a few fields away at the south end. It seemed incredible now that anybody could have lived here permanently; it was an inhuman bleak, desolate little world of sky and sea and wind and grass, rocks and birds and sheep and rabbits.

Over the hill past Mejorum's a smaller field dropped away steeply to the headland at the back of the island. We had sight of Trimble's boat butting through the waves, trailing its V of wake over to Lighthouse Island. We let our own momentum carry us downhill at a run, cradling our boxes and crates, sending the frightened sheep stampeding. We came down to the rim of the headland overlooking the sheltered cove with the green wooden bungalow tucked into one corner of it. The building had been floated over in pieces and constructed by Hugh's dad, Billy Boyd and his friends in the 1930s.

A footpath to it wound down the steep grassy hillside, past the well. The bungalow and a square of grass in front of it were fenced in from the small field beside the water. The Boyds' green rowing boat was pulled up on the grass above the little sandy beach between the rocks. It was the perfect spot, secluded from the rest of the island and the world. Up wooden steps to a veranda, the front door opened straight into the living room. Three windows let in the daylight. It was homely with an open fire, comfortable old armchairs and sofa, a table and chairs, pictures on the wall. There was a single bed in one corner of the chimney breast. A door opened into a narrow bunk-room with a washstand under the window. At the back of the living room a doorway, no door, gave on to the wee dark scullery equipped with a sink and an old black oil cooker. It was on this relic that most of us learnt to cook: fried breakfasts and dinners of boiled potatoes with meat and vegetables out of tins. There was drinking water from the well on the hill and rainwater from the butt under the gable-end to wash the dishes. Paraffin lamps and candles supplied the lighting. There was no lavatory; you went down the rocks below the tideline. Hunkering there, trousers down, on the slimy rocks, I was heart-in-mouth afeard of pincered crabs that could creep and leap and swing—! There were all kinds of savage little details to frighten you on the island; it was a primitive place.

One of our first chores upon our arrival was to gather driftwood along the shoreline, to burn on the fire. There were plentiful supplies of wood, especially after a ship had been launched from Haarland and Woolf's, bringing a bonanza of timber off the slips.

The fire we'd lit crackled and spat and roared up the short, windy chimney flu. The wooden walls of the bungalow trembled in the wind. You could hear the rhythmical breathing of the tide in the little bay below. We sat round the table by candlelight, each of us with a forefinger resting on the upturned tumbler at the centre of the table. Around the perimeter of the table were arranged the letters of the alphabet written on little squares of paper.

"Are you there? What's your name?" we called up the spirit of the glass.

"Declare yourself!"

We caught our breath as the glass began to slide towards the letters.

"Boyd's pushin' it, so he is!"

"Ah'm not! Look: T—!"

With one voice we spelled out each letter the glass moved to: "... a—l—l—o—w. Tallow!"

"Aye, it's sayin' we've lit a tallow candle!" said Malcolm.

"No, it's not!" Hugh shook his blond head gravely. His rather gaunt face was white and his blue eyes bulged glassily in the candlelight. "It's the Tallow Men, or at least one of them! They were island men long, long ago, bad ones that lured a ship with a valuable cargo of tallow on to the rocks out there in a storm, pretending they were guiding it to safety with their torches. Anyone on that boat who didn't drown was slain the minute he set foot on shore, cut down with reaping hooks and the bodies chucked back in the tide to feed the fishes!"

"Aye and my uncle's Frankenstein! Ye're havin' us on, Boydo!" said Howie. "Look at the wee sleekit grin he's hidin'! It's him pushin' the glass!"

"Ah'm tellin' ye, Ah didn't!" Hugh protested. " It's one of those murderers' ghosts, the bloody Tallow Men!"

I can't have been the only one around the table who felt the hairs stand on the back of my neck. This was too real to be acting. We all shut up a minute.

"Hi, it's gone cold in here!" Stuarty spoke in a hoarse whisper; he shivered. "The fire's blastin' away there like a furnace but the room's gone chill as a cave!"

"What's your name?" Hugh asked the glass. "We won't tell the rozzers, honest!"

The glass moved, intelligent and quick.

"A—e—n—e—a—s! Aeneas! It's a name out of the Bible."

I put it straight to him then, in a Jack Hawkins kind of voice, straight out of a bad English black and white B-movie: "Did you kill those poor sailors out there, Aeneas? Tell the truth now!"

Nothing then. Candlelight and silence. Then a rumble of wind in the chimney and a slow, tentative circling of the glass under our fingers.

"Come on, Aeneas, tell the truth!"

"Own up to yeer crimes!"

And the glass was circling faster, with a horrible scoring sound on the varnished table, round and round, not spelling anything, spinning angrily till it crashed over on its side and rolled to a stop.

After that you were scared to venture outside in the dark for a pee. Later in your sleeping bag on the floor around the dying embers of the fire you lay awake a long time hearing banshee wails on the wind and the cries of the doomed sailors in the waves jabbling over the rocks in the moonlight.

The island had been something of a male preserve when we first went there: poker schools and huntin', shootin' and fishin'. Fancying myself as a bit of a young Hemingway, I took the twelve-bore shotgun from the bungalow and followed the high cliff path to the south end of the island. Dense brambles and gorse grew along the edge of the cliffs which dropped away to deep, lonely hidden coves that echoed with the susurration of the tide and the plaintive calling of the gulls. The lovely remote island peace of a golden summer's evening up on those breezy headlands was intensified by the primal tension of the hunt. I dreaded the horse's kick of the gun butt against my shoulder as

I fired off a cartridge at a fleeing rabbit or bird, hit or miss, the blind destruction of the double barrel unleashed on nature, but I wouldn't have missed it for anything either. You had to look twice before you fired; there were a lot of pathetic old "maxi" rabbits on the island, enduring the blinding, slow death of myxomatosis.

The cliff path sloped down to the southern extremity of the island, opening out to jagged black rocks seething with nesting birds, a chilling wilderness and desolation here, edged with pounding surf and dark, dangerous currents. Here was the realm of the feathered ones; as we jumped across the rocks, amongst them, their harsh chorus sounded the alarm, rising to a deafening pitch, a sheer wall of maddening screams and soon the air was thick with angry wheeling birds, and they were dive-bombing us, swooping viciously at our heads with their machine gun stutter.

It was a relief to turn inland, past the lower farm facing the Down coast. The long grass blades gilded by the evening sun ran in windblown waves beneath our feet. The nervous bleating of the sheep was a music old as time. A joyful, magical sense of nature took hold of me in the streaming oblique luminous rays of the setting sun as we gained the hilltop; we moved in a shimmer of faery.

There was the long drop down to our house waiting in the shadow of the little cove and the thrilling comfort going indoors to light the oil lamps and the wood fire and draw the curtains on the encroaching wild darkness of the fields and sea. We felt like trappers in our cabin in the wilds as we opened bottles of beer and got the playing cards out on the table. If we'd killed a rabbit worth eating, Hugh would skin it for dinner on the morrow, that we ate picking the shot out of our teeth.

In those early island days Wully Mejorum still held court at the farm on the hilltop, with a crowd of young fellows who stayed weekends with him. Through the half-door, across the stone flags of the kitchen floor, Wully, benign, grizzled and leathery, clad in a big woolly jumper, would be ensconced in his armchair next the huge open fireplace with its crane and blackened cooking pots. Wully's beer-gut rested contentedly on his lap, a Gallaher's Blues smouldered between his thick fingers stained orange with nicotine, sixty a day man, a tumbler of neat Scotch in the other fist.

Wully had a wooden leg; behind it there lay a tale of lost love and the drink-driving accident that followed it, the amputation and his retreat to the island. Wully was an old bachelor now who welcomed the company of young fellows drawn by the promise of the island craic. Warming to the drink on these evenings, he'd look up, twinkly blue eyes in the creased, homely Ulster face, and recite:

> *"Twas on the good ship Venus,*
> *Be God ye shoulda seen us!"*

It was the cue for Rugby rhymes and songs with indecent lyrics, all of us joining in lustily, fired up with the booze and male company, our wind-polished, booze-flushed faces shining in the lamplight.

Orange songs would be sung too, though not with any conviction, only because, God help us, we all knew the words. One Saturday night Wully and Tommy, the leader of the young fellows over from Donaghadee, warned, "No Orange songs tonight! There's a Catholic lad coming." We were all agreed it would be real bad form to inflict them on the visitor; there was an etiquette to sectarianism.

No unwarranted attention was paid to the pleasant-looking young fellow who sat there quietly drinking near the fire. But towards the end of the evening, suddenly, he staggered to his feet, fists clenched, eyes blazing round at the company. The room went silent momentarily as he swayed there, lost for the words that might have expressed some inner turmoil. A couple of the lads caught him as he toppled backwards, almost into the fire, and he was carried unconscious through to the bunk-room and put to bed.

We never learned the reason for his strange behaviour, maybe he was just the worse for the drink, but I felt then, and still do, that even with the best will in the world there was something in the atmosphere, something bigger than any of us, a monster that had risen up unbidden that night out of the dark undercurrents of the tragic division of Ireland.

Wully lost his health, they said; his visits to the island stopped and the farmhouse passed to Jackie Lamb. Jackie and his mates Billy and Ernie, all in their early twenties, took over. The three of them soon went native on the island in the summer months, growing their hair and beards, living in big khaki shorts and writing poetry.

It was they opened the rambling old farmhouse up to a weekend crowd of nice teenage girls from Donaghadee. At the same time the Brennans' house was being used more by their student daughter Harriet; she and her art college friend Diana, two tall, blonde, striking-looking girls, would came striding over the hilltop, their figures silhouetted against the sky, long legs in blue jeans, long yellow hair blowing in the wind, guitars strapped to their backs. Suddenly there was a strong female presence on the island.

Saturday night on the island was the highlight of our week. After dinner and before the party, we took the rowing boat out on the water in the magical calm and beauty of the long, clear summer's evening. The July weather was lovely, mellow and heavenly, the calm sea a mirror holding the clear blue sky. The boat sat low in the water with the half-dozen or so of us lads on board. As we slid out across the glassy bay the only sound was the plop of the oars, emphasising the deep tranquillity.

The shoreline receded, our green wooden cabin perched above the rocks, dwindling; we saw the world with new seafaring eyes. Clear of the bays with the headlands above them, the water parting darkly under our prow, we cast our hooks. The silver sinkers flashed like fish down into the murky deep and we waited for the thrill of the tug on the line. We weren't disappointed; soon we were reeling in the mackerel, their wet dark skin gleaming, one on every hook on your line, a miracle, a feast! Unhooked, they flopped in the bucket, frozen little eyes and hurt mouths reproaching us. The big white gulls came swarming after us, brazen with greed, swooping at our catch, screeching and beating their long, powerful wings.

The real satisfaction of the fishing trip, however, was less to do with catching fish and more about the incomparable sense of camaraderie and feeling of timeless pure contentment that came with being good mates together crowded onto the little boat, afloat in the beauty of the evening. The relaxed, witty sound of our Irish voices, punctuated with laughter, carried very clear and amplified in the still, blue-gold air above the calm water.

At last the sun was going down over the green hill. The water around us turned grey and chill, inhospitable. The little coves were filling with dark shadow, the coastline growing indistinct. Quite a lot of water had seeped into the bottom of the boat. We ran the boat hard up on to the sand and jumped out and hauled it clear of the tideline. The empty cabin waited above in the murky failing light.

Indoors we lit the oil lamps and the wood fire, opened bottles of beer, and soon there was the sound of voices coming down the steep grass hill; the door burst open and Jackie and his mates and the girls pressed in, packing the cosy room. The party had begun!

It was a kind of ceilidh without the dancing—there wasn't enough room. Stuarty and I and Harriet and Diana played our guitars and led the singing. There was some traditional folk music but it was much more the contemporary songs of Dylan, Donovan and Joan Baez, the Mamas and the Papas, the Lovin' Spoonful and anything off the radio that took our fancy.

The crowded little room hummed with the music, the chink of bottles and the diverse avid conversations of a boozed-up Saturday night: the eager gossip of the girls sitting together in a tight little circle on the floor; the fireside tales of Jackie Lamb, pressing his bearded hurt-sensitive face close to you with stories of his life on the building sites and the stand-up fist-fights with his estranged wife—he always came out of them worst. Jackie's crazy bleating laughter, his panacea for all ills, rang out above the general hubbub. Billy read out one of his poems. As the alcohol warmed me through I'd take pause to look slowly round the room and think how much I loved everyone there, the grinning, witty lads and the delicate faery faces of the girls in the lamplight glow. The driftwood fire blazed up the chimney, the beer bottles popped; the board walls seemed to vibrate with our revelry.

Later on, after eleven, there'd be some pairing off of boy and girl, kissing in a corner or going out for a walk in the night, a kiss in the dark, holding hands as you negotiated the cliff-top path by the strokes of the lighthouse beam. Over a succession of weekends, I courted in turn Janet, Edna, Norma, Margaret—; there was the excitement of a fresh court each time, the triumph of a fervent first kiss, but it all ended there somehow; nobody wanted to get serious.

Wee Maura, sweet round face and curly dark hair, bubble-cut to match her personality, cuddled in close under my arm as I walked her home one night to the lower farm where she was staying with Jackie's parents. The old farmhouse was in darkness, everyone gone to bed and we crept in and lay on the leather settle in the darkened kitchen. She was a "good court" as we said, giving warmly of herself. Afterwards I walked back across the island knee-deep in a ground mist rolling on the moonlit fields, so romantic with Maura's kisses still fresh on my lips that I told myself, "Ah, dear God, my life has become an enchanted, beautiful thing!"

But Maura had gone next day, back to Donaghadee on an early boat and I would never lay eyes on her again.

That's the way it was until wee Marie ("Mari") came along. The difference was that Marie *loved* me and was always there for me. That was a great feeling.

"I don't know what I'd do without you, Marie!" I'd tell her drunkenly and quote the Beatles: *"Thank you, girl!"*

She was a slender little girl; her fairish hair cut short and boyish in the new Mod style enclosed a pale wee face with slightly prominent lips and grey-blue eyes—a look of Mick Jagger.

She was mute and solemn in my presence.

"Thank you for existing, Marie!" I persisted. I could be all over a girl like this, sentimental with the drink taken; I did mean it at the time. "Thank you for being you, that's all!"

"You're mad," she said at last.

"Do you mind?"

"No. I like it."

Getting all those words out of her was quite a feat; I'd see her nattering away with the girls but alone with me she withdrew into a sad-eyed silence, a sort of inner suffering. There was nothing for it then but to kiss her. Young, drunk and crass, I was unfaithful to her sometimes, with some new face, I knew it hurt her, but she was still there waiting for me afterwards, in her silent, tortured way and I'd be overwhelmed with compassion and love for her.

After most of the Saturday night crowd had gone off to bed a last few of us, die-hard romantics, would sit up chatting round the dying embers of the fire. Typically there'd be Jackie Lamb, Howie, Harriet and me. Jackie, small and wiry, fine-featured, with the full black beard, olive skin and soft brown eyes lending him a biblical look, was still jawing away and laughing, only a little more subdued now because people were asleep in the bunk beds in the next room. He fished out his poems now and read them to us there by the late fire.

> *"A Lancashire lad,*
> *Like George Formby and the Beatles,*
> *He ended up in East Belfast*
> *More Irish than the Irish—"*

"Aye, that's you alright, Jack Lamb, you can knock back the Guinness, you'd talk the hind legs off a donkey and you're a bard to boot!" said Howie and sat back in the rocking chair, rocking away steadily and blowing his perfect smoke-rings, everything done with his effortless style.

There was something so naïve, trusting and open about Jackie Lamb, a vulnerability that drew your sympathy and affection. I'd lose track of his complicated yarns, his voice had a kind of frenetic life of its own, but his presence held me somehow; behind the rough exterior there was a warmth and sensitivity I couldn't resist.

Harriet, long-legged-blue-jeaned art student, with pre-Raphaelite waves of long blonde hair framing a delicate white face, was the only girl who stayed up so late. She had a warm little voice and a large sense of humour.

"Tell me about your chocolate Teddy, Jim!" She liked this story from my early childhood.

"Yeah, it's one of my earliest memories. I got the chocolate Teddy bear for Easter. I loved that Teddy so much I couldn't bear to eat him. He was in his box in my little bedroom, my new friend; I talked to him. But after I'd gone to bed I got really hungry, I couldn't sleep thinking about the chocolate and I got up again, got Teddy out of his box and bit off one of his ears. And once I started eating him I couldn't stop. It was his ears first then his feet, then his arms and legs and torso and finally all that was left, the rest of his head. I was an incorrigibly greedy small boy. When Teddy had gone completely, inside me, I cried my eyes out. I'd eaten my new friend! Then I began to feel very sick—"

"Cannibal!" Jackie bleated.

"A lesson in love maybe?" Harriet suggested with a feminine subtlety of perception.

"The grossness of sheer lust!" was Howie's verdict on the killing.

"You always hurt the one you love," said Harriet.

Although such a striking-looking girl, she never seemed to get a court for some strange reason. Perhaps her refinement scared off the lads. Determined to right this wrong against womankind and being the worse for drink one night, Howie and I grabbed Harriet for a kiss but she screwed up her wee face and fended us off with hard little fists. It was all very matey and of course we'd never heard of sexual harassment in those days.

We talked on through the night of everything and nothing, but anything that the Saturday night fun, the companionship and sense of timelessness should never end. The fire was reduced to cold ashes; the dawn light crept into the room. Stepping outside for a slash there was the shock of the sun coming up, spreading its new-minted gold over the grass and rocks and sheep. It was the signal to crawl into our sleeping bags for a few hours.

There was a run of fine weather weekends in July. Waking late on the Sunday morning you felt the sun grilling the low roof of the bungalow. Somebody handed you a mug of tea. We crawled into our clothes and set to preparing and devouring a big Ulster fry. After breakfast we lazed around in front of the little house.

In due course the girls would come over the crest of the hill, their figures in cardigans and jeans silhouetted against the blue sky, hair streaming in the sea-breeze, before they plunged down the steep sloping path in a long line to join us.

The previous night's courting, the joy or heartache thereof, was forgotten now as we merged into one glorious carefree gang of boys and girls. There was paddling on the little beach, a few brave souls among us like Marie swimming in the freezing tide. A ball was kicked around on the warm grass. A transistor radio tuned to the pirate ship Radio Caroline blared out *Groovin' on a Sunday afternoon* or *Hey,98.6,* songs that would always bring back that serene, perfect time of the sun-warmed calm and sweetness of beautiful young days.

But past mid-afternoon it was time to clear up and pack up and make our way back over the island to the five o'clock boat to Donaghadee. I got home to Loughside around eight. Mum had kept me a plate of the Sunday salad. I felt the glow of the sun and sea air on my skin. My brain was filled with the big blue vacancy of sea and sky. Our house felt luxurious after roughing it on the island; it was wonderful to soak in the bath, shampoo my hair and rinse it till it squeaked with cleanness, slip into clean pyjamas and lay out my freshly laundered clothes ready for the office in the morning.

Work was merely an interruption to island-going and the important questions of life like which girl you would be kissing next Saturday night.

It was still daylight as I closed my bedroom curtains on the backyards of the estate and the tall dark cedars in the churchyard beyond. I burrowed down into the cool, fragrant fresh linen of my bed. The transistor radio on my bedside dresser was tuned to Luxembourg and turned down low. I lay there for a while listening to its records and turning my mind back over the great times of the weekend: fishing for mackerel out on the golden evening bay, singing around the fire, kissing Marie under the moon—

CHAPTER 10

When the kissing had to stop

The island weekends continued into the middle of September. We talked of an atmospheric Halloween trip but it never happened; we weren't that hardy. As it grew wintry into October, Saturday night was hot toddies in Kelly's or Hannegan's and on to the dance at the Astor where Rory Gallagher and Taste was the resident band. In the week you might take a girl to the pictures, someone you'd met at the Saturday dance or some girl from work; though nothing much ever seemed to come of these dates. There was a sense of sterility.

I went out with one very beautiful girl from the Department, Ann Finnegan, long black hair and big soft brown eyes that glowed in her fine-boned, sensitive face. Ann was said to be an all-Ireland Irish dancing champion. She had the small, light, supple frame that lends itself to excellence in dance. I must have been feeling generous on our date, or else the stalls were sold out, for we sat in the balcony of the crowded ABC Ritz cinema. The film must have been a popular one, all the seats were taken, but I don't remember a thing about it for we courted all the way through it, Ann snuggled up close to me in the bedding of our winter coats on the back of our seats, our hot, passionate kisses holding nothing back. I walked her to her bus stop on Castle Street afterwards and we hugged and kissed some more in the doorway of Sawyer's fish shop in the cold. As we broke off she exclaimed in a bell-like voice of wonder and awe tinged with amusement and irony, "Oh, Jim, I can't believe I'm standing here kissing a Protestant boy!"

"Doesn't matter, does it?" I mumbled thickly, weak at the knees.

I waved her off on her bus up the Falls. It had been a wonderful date, a girl with some passion in her soul.

But somehow I never got round to asking her out again. What was wrong with me? I had to ask myself. I could see Ann looking hurt and resentful at work that I'd not come back to her. I thought it must be awful for girls having to wait for the boys to make all the moves; it wasn't good for us either. I disliked myself for being so unresponsive, a cold fish; I felt stuck in a limbo, unable to act, like some creep out of an existentialist novel. I'd let Julie and I just drift apart once she was out of sight in London. I never bothered with Marie when I was away from the island although it'd have been easy enough for us to meet up. I couldn't help myself somehow; I seemed to be constitutionally incapable of sustaining a relationship with a girl any more. I was less than a man.

Gerry McCorley and two others from the Department were emigrating to Canada and having a leaving do at Gerry's sister's flat on the Antrim Road. I had a social-phobic dread of parties and like dances I could only face them drunk. On my way to the party that weekday night, I walked off the train at York Street station straight into the Refreshments buffet and ordered, "Scotch and ginger ale, please."

The place was empty at this time, *Coronation Street* on the TV high in one corner. The large plate glass window faced the toilets' block. The ginger fizz helped the disgusting liquor down my throat tight with nerves; soon the butterflies in my belly were drowning in it. I could have thrown up for a minute. But the anaesthetic effect was kicking in, I felt more confident or at least indifferent to my fate with every sip now. A warmth crept through my arteries; a protective band closed around my temples.

I went to the bar and ordered, "Same again, please!"

While the first drink dulled my social-phobic anxiety, the second one erected a bulletproof glass wall between me and the worst the world might ever care to throw at me. Even the sad, ugly station bar with its lurid décor and Formica had acquired a friendly look.

I drained my glass and made for the door with a newly confident, brisk step; out through the gloomy cavern of the station, through the portals into the spring evening light on York Street. I crossed into Lower Canning Street and cut up the back streets and out on to Duncairn Gardens. Contained in a rosy nimbus of evening sunshine and whisky, I floated under the fresh green foliage on the trees up the avenue.

Turning on to the Antrim Road, I located the small modern block of flats. The dark narrow concrete stairwell to the first floor and the blue door, Flat C, with all those people waiting behind it, didn't faze me one bit. I gave the bell a good ring and Gerry opened it, greeting me in his hospitable Cookstown fashion and ushering me through to the crowded living room. All or most of the office faces were there, Tom and Dan and Enda and Pat and Dennis, mostly older men who'd come in the drab office clothes they seemed to have been born in. They were engaged as usual in their comfortable Jimmyish talk of shop and current affairs.

Yet I was coming to the realisation that being young wasn't everything; I rather envied something about these middle-aged characters. Take a man like Dan McDade, a tall, stooping figure in his glazed brown suit, with his wavy yellow hair and an ugly-lovely face, like a friendly rhinoceros, his pipe-smoking ruminations, long thoughtful nods and slow deliberations on the whole sticky business of living, a come day, go day, God bless Sunday way; a life lived in the plain light of reality and the natural flow of humanity. Dan's world was circumscribed by the Department and family life, a big family to maintain on a modest salary, it can't have been easy, but you never heard a cross word out of him. Only a Catholic could be as grounded and serene as that, I imagined.

I wanted to *be* Dan sometimes as I watched him in fascination and even a kind of awe at the dignity of his sheer ordinariness. "Well, it's like this, you see, boys, there is absolutely no point in fussing and fighting to get somewhere because you are going nowhere in the end, except back to where you came from in the first place—" That at least seemed to be the tenor or subtext of all Dan's speech and actions.

A generous buffet and drinks of every kind were on the table under the window overlooking the Antrim Road. Gerry, teetotal himself, seemed to derive a vicarious pleasure from plying me with whisky, pursuing me through the evening with the whisky bottle, topping up my glass.

A nice wee face stood out of the crowd. I didn't recognise Margaret for a moment without her glasses. She wore her long, shiny chestnut hair loose over her shoulders and a sort of cocktail dress that emphasised her curviness.

"On your own tonight, Margaret?"

"Yes, Norman's revising for his accountancy exams."

I thought what a nice, soft, beaky little face she had, unprotected and vulnerable-looking without her glasses. I knew she liked me, at least as a friend, and suddenly I was kissing her right there in the middle of the party, on the mouth, and she was responding warmly. Just one lingering full-on kiss, that was all it was really. But it was a good kiss. For a half-minute of pure spontaneity and its accompanying mild ecstasy I had forgotten my inhibitions, while she had forgotten her fiancé. There was no sense of shame afterwards; we both looked pleased with ourselves.

But I woke the next morning with a bad hangover and the drunkard's crushing sense of guilt. What was I doing kissing Margaret like that in front of everybody from work? Not that she'd minded but that wasn't the point; it just wasn't supposed to be that kind of a party, she was engaged and I'd made a show of us both in front of all our upright middle-aged colleagues.

I got myself into work somehow, fighting back the waves of crapulence. As I entered the office apprehensively a crowd of the men were standing round talking about how good the party had been the night before. I mingled in with them with a sense of relief that no one was paying me any particular attention. Until wee Billy Morney, the attercop, turned to me, his big hornrims giving him the inimical look of a gnat, and let me have it in the face:

"Here's a boy-lad needs watchin'! Did yous all see the carry-on of him last night, canoodlin' wi' Margaret, atin' the face aff the wee-girl? Aye and she wasn't complainin' neether! Sure the girls is as bad as the fellas these days!"

There was no teasing humour in Billy's words, just cold, angry disapproval. The others took no notice of him, Dan McDade looking away out the window and re-lighting his pipe. I shrank away to my desk with a face like a smacked bottom.

When I saw Margaret she was fine; we both simply acted as if nothing had happened really and we were still just good mates. After all, a kiss was just a kiss. She would still marry Norman. I would go away to England to be regarded as a stevedore. But we'd both have that pleasant little memory for the rest of our lives.

*

Clocking in one morning, I registered the attractive young woman, big dark brown hair and emerald green outfit, waiting at the Wages' window at the end of the corridor. I was aware that she was older than me; it was the face, figure and style of a mature woman in her twenties, but that in no way diminished my manly interest in her. I got a closer look as I passed her on my way to the gent's. Yes, she was really something alright.

Combing my Beatle fringe in the gent's mirror after the windy walk up Bridge Street I wondered what a real woman like that would see when she looked at me? Still a "wee boy"? But I was nineteen now. I was considered good-looking. Sean Hughes joked about how well-dressed I looked coming to work. I was no longer so awfully shy either.

When I walked into the office the woman was there with Owen.

"Jim, Maureen here has come to help us out for a while," he said. "You can show her the ropes this morning."

I could hardly believe my luck; it was like some romantic scenario playing out from the first. A pair of green eyes met mine openly; the luxuriant chestnut brown hair, back-combed and falling heavily to her shoulders, framed a thin oval face that was mature, yes, even a little hardened by the years, yet still a pretty girl's face somehow, smiling and colouring a little as she spoke in a doty-pet kind of little girl voice, "You can make sure I don't get lost here, Jim, it's such a big rambling building!"

The emerald skirt hugged the curves of her hips and flared out to just above the knee, with a matching waistcoat over a black roll-neck top. There was a slightly dishevelled look about her, as if she'd just extricated herself from the housework and kids. She had the earthy glamour of those women in the kitchen sink dramas of the day.

It was wonderful then to have her sitting beside me at the big sloping double desk, like schooldays' sweethearts, while I explained the work we did, enjoying the wee bit of authority it gave me over the attractive new recruit. Noreen Batt had been discreetly transferred away to an office at the far end of the building. Maureen had come in as a temp, "To earn some money," she explained to me, "while my mother-in-law looks after the kids for a bit."

"Nice for you to get out of the house," I said.

"Oh yes, but a bit scary maybe after you've been at home changing nappies for four years."

"This is a nice place to come and work," I told her. "Owen and everybody's dead decent. You'll have nothing to worry about."

A relaxed friendship of colleagues developed quickly between us, yet from the start there was always something more than that, a wordless reaching out to one another. Working together could bring you close together, as I'd experienced with Sonia. And it felt so much easier with an older woman; Maureen was twenty-three to my nineteen but I could seem mature for my years, perhaps from the breadth of my reading, while she could be touchingly girlish; after all, she was only four years older than me. It didn't feel like being her baby brother at all; rather, with her I felt more of a man. Maybe it helped too that although I was attracted to Maureen from the start I had no designs on her. She was, after all, a married woman, a wife and mother. But I could still enjoy being with her in the vital sense of a man and a woman together; we could appreciate one another in a harmless sort of ongoing flirtation, I believed. It suited me to live safely inside my head like that; to be involved with a woman who was unobtainable. It was easier.

That first morning with her I felt all the weight of the working days lift from my shoulders and every moment come alive with vital new meaning. Showing her round the Department, her high heels clicking along faithfully beside me down the endless corridors of my familiar world, I seemed to float in the reflected light of her femininity. She was quiet, not awfully impressed by the old factory-like building and dusty offices, but nevertheless I felt her *with* me all the time, not separate. Back at our shared desk I passed the figures I'd totted up mentally in the ledger to her to check on the adding machine. We were working away in silence when a golden beam of spring sunshine penetrated the window on to our desk and she raised her head to look out at the blue and white sky.

"*I can see for miles,*" she said. "Do you know that song?" She was smiling to herself with a sense of freedom and life's possibilities, like a girl again.

"Yes, *miles and miles*— I like that song," I said, feeling strangely touched, as if she'd quoted from a poem, which of course it was in its own simple direct way. Now I felt we shared a kind of youthful idealism, something reaching-out and lyrical.

We settled into a cosy twosome there at our big desk, working and talking together in a warm contentment as the spring rains beat on the windows and the daylight grew clearer. She soon took me into her confidence with all the fascinating details that women talk around the physical life and relationships. Over-dreamy and isolated in my head as I often was, it was everything I needed and wanted to hear from the real world of men and women that I would ineluctably be drawn into in the not so distant future.

She showed me a creased black and white snap out of her handbag. On holiday with the family at Port Stewart, Maureen in her swimming costume, Peter aged four and Susan, two, and her husband Graham, a good-looking fair man, muscular in his trunks.

She said, "I was five months' gone with Peter when Graham and I got married. After I'd found out I was pregnant we moved to London. We married there at Paddington registry office, no guests, just us two and a man we got hold of to witness the signatures. Not the wedding a girl dreams of. It all seemed to happen in a flash. I was just nineteen, the same age as you are now, Jim, and there I was suddenly, Mrs Jones, with a baby on the way. It wasn't half a shock, I'm telling you."

I felt honoured to be drawn into her story like this. I listened with a total empathy.

"We got a room in Kentish Town. Graham got a job easy over there on a building site though he'd never dirtied his hands in his life before; it was good enough just to speak with an Irish accent. I worked in this super modern office block in Warren Street, really swish and a brill job. I could have stayed on there quite happily.

"We nearly starved for the first few weeks in London till we got paid. I mean it: one night all we had for tea was a tin of sardines on a couple of heels of toast. No shilling for the meter even when the electricity cut out and we were left sitting there in the dark, freezing to death. It was November. We had to go to bed at half-seven; there was nothing else for it.

"By December it was like the North Pole in that room; we kept the electric fire on all the time, eating up the shillings. I was getting near my time with an enormous bump and the landlord didn't allow children, it was the rule in those rented rooms. In the end there was nothing for it but to go back home to Belfast.

"It was Christmas and now Graham's parents put us up while they helped us get our own place. Before we went to London they were going to disown him if he married me, that common girl Maureen who'd led their son astray, tricking him into marrying her! I tell you nothing could have been further from the truth. It was him was mad about me. Of course you grow to love somebody," she added, breaking a little, guiltily.

"But it was his mate I'd fallen for originally: Austin Strang; I'll never forget our summer in the long grass, as I call it, the summer I was eighteen," she said dreamily. "Then Austin went to Canada. He was going to send for me once he got settled in over there, he said. Well, I waited a few months, I heard nothing, so it was frig that for a laugh and I started seeing his best mate Graham for something to do on lonely winter nights. We'd only been going out for a short time when it happened. Graham would come and stay over with me when my dad was away on the boats, he was a merchant seaman. Mammy died when I was thirteen, cancer. I was their only child.

"I couldn't believe it when I tested positive. I was pregnant! Naïve, I know. Graham and I were awful green. Suddenly it was like the end of all my young days; it felt like the end of my life really. An older woman I knew at work gave me a pill to take to bring on a miscarriage. I took it but nothing happened and then I was worried sick all through my pregnancy that there would be something wrong with the baby now, there was all that worry on top of everything else. Thank God Peter was a fine healthy child!

"Anyway, Graham went to work with his father in the family carpet business. Peter was born in March. Then I was pregnant again, with Susan, one year later. We were taking precautions this time too; I think the sheath must have torn." She looked straight into my sympathetic brown eyes; she felt she could tell me anything.

It was summertime. One Friday lunchtime I took the walk across the centre of town and up Divis Street and the Falls Road to the Spanish Rooms for a gallon jar of scrumpy to take to the island that evening. The fine summer weather had brought unemployed-looking men out on to the Falls Road to stand chatting in little groups on the pavement in the sun. Alcoholics were lying around. After the smart city centre it felt like a foreign, underprivileged place, like the New York Bowery.

When I arrived back at the office, sweating, with the flagon under my arm, Maureen said, "I wish I could go to your island with you, Jim!"

I caught the wistful note in her voice, the straining towards a vanished youthful freedom and also the thrilling suggestion that she would like to come away with me. It was a lovely impossible thought.

"Do you love your girl Marie on the island?" she asked me once.

"Love her? Dunno really. Sort of. I'm fond of her, yeah, and kind of grateful that she's always there for me. I thought it was true love with Julie, we talked about getting married and everything, but in the end I just let her slip away. I hadn't the gumption to follow her to London. The truth is I'm not ready for love yet; it's too grown-up for me."

"I had to grow up far too fast," said Maureen. "Got to eighteen and bang, that was it, I was a mum-to-be!" She shook her head sadly. "I mean, I wouldn't give up my kids for the world, but the timing was all wrong. I was just at the right age for having fun in your life, dating different fellas. I mean, I love Graham and everything, but more like a brother really."

I knew I was the non-judgmental, empathetic kind of person that people confide in. I did my best to deny the thrilling possibility that there could be any kind of come on to me in Maureen's wistful words. The idea that I should ever get involved with a married woman was a fantasy out of a novel or play. There was the question of morality also: to *commit adultery,* as the Commandment put it, did not seem a very pretty thing. In short, it was a sin. Not that I was a practising Christian any more but the words of religion, rooted in an ancient wisdom, stayed with you, they meant something.

I valued what I already had with Maureen. I could stay in control of my feelings while both of us continued to enjoy an affair of the mind, a lovely, precious, harmless, perfect thing. I liked to imagine her as my girl. My Maureen. My *woman!* The thought made my heart beat up in ecstasy and a terrible fear. Then I had to remind myself I was still safe, it was still that perfect harmless thing between us.

"You look like whatsisname, on *Top of the Pops,*" she said. "Wears glasses like yours. Peter out of *Peter and Gordon.*"

"Peter Asher. That's a new one for me!"

"I think he's really good-looking . Sort of really sensitive and intelligent."

" *'Please lock me away'. Yes,* that sounds like me!"

"Have you noticed who I look like?" she said cutely, all pleased with herself, seventeen again. "A fil'm actress."

"Umm—lemme think—Not Gina Lollobrigida?"

"Don't think I am quite that bra size, Jim! I'll give you a clue: chased by a dinosaur—"

"While rather scantily clad—yeah, what's her name, *200,000BC.* "

"Raquel Welch!" Maureen smiled triumphantly.

"Why yes, so you do, Maureen, I can see that: the jawline, lips, eyes." I laid it on just to watch the pleased look on her face like a young girl. "And the figure of course!" I felt myself blush as this overfamiliarity popped out of my mouth, giving the game away, then quickly added, "I mean like in your family photo on the sand at Port Stewart."

"Oh yeah?" she laughed, shining-eyed, pleased with my words.

She finished the temporary appointment at the Department shortly before Christmas, inviting a few of us from the office for a farewell drink after work the day before she left.

We went in a pub down the road, the other side of Cromac Square, into the little lounge bar where we occupied its three tables under the window. It was a cold, wet December evening. I drank whisky and ginger to warm me up and put me at ease in the company.

By eight o'clock most of our rather subdued little party had dispersed homeward. Only a few of us unmarried younger ones hung on around Maureen, glad of the excuse for a drink on a Thursday night.

I was sitting on one side of her on the long padded seat under the window. She was talking in a quiet, earnest way to Keith on her other side. He was a nice-looking dark, mild-mannered lad, Mod jacket and layered haircut with big mutton chop sideburns. We'd all had a few drinks by now and Maureen was very relaxed. I saw her holding hands with Keith and I wondered drunkenly if it were he she wanted instead of me. But then she took my hand too. She had a cool, soft hand with long nails that gently impressed on my palm. She sat there between us holding our hands like some dear sister.

But then as we all got up to go she turned to me and said, "Are you walking me to the bus station, Jim?"

Outside the others dispersed into the night; Maureen and I turned along Victoria Street. As soon as we turned the corner into May Street, out of sight of the others, she took my hand again, firmly, naturally, and she was my girl. There was no longer any pretence between us. Now we had come together it felt so right.

The day's rains had stopped for a while, leaving the vacant night streets puddled with the reflections of lampposts. The Law Courts loomed out on our left.

"Oh Jim, it's a pity you haven't got a car now!" she said.

We skirted the lit-up bus station and dived down the steps of the new pedestrian subway. There was no one else in the long, cold tunnel and we had our first swooning kiss there up against the tiled wall under the electric lights. As we drew back to take breath she exclaimed, "Oh Jim, you kiss just like Austin Strang, remember the fella I told you about?"

He was the one she'd really loved, I remembered. It was Katie Burns had taught me to kiss that way, wide-open-mouthed, fluid and moist, like sinking your face into a peach. We pressed into another clinch but were disturbed by the echo of footfalls approaching from the far end of the subway. She jerked my hand and we bolted back up the steps.

Fugitives in the Belfast night, we plunged into the deep darkness down Laganbank Road. With the city lights safely behind us we slowed to a walk, out of breath, hearts pounding, my arm round her shoulders, her arm round my waist. A chill, rank smell came off the inky river. The road dropped away under our marching feet, into a black pit under the viaduct. We paused in the blanketing darkness down there under the railway, by the dripping wall, to steal another kiss. But it was too creepy and squalid there and we quickly moved on, two shadowy figures on the dark and deserted back road.

The high speared railings of the Department yard rose up on our right. To our left, across the river, there shone the dull lights of Short Strand that were reflected in the black Lagan water. They still spoke of the MacMahon family of that Catholic enclave, murdered in the troubles of the 1920s that followed partition, and I never looked that way without thinking of them. It added a gloomy, sinister quality to the scene.

We emerged on the main road by the Albert Bridge and turned back into town, past the entrance of the Department, its dome raised in the night sky, behind it the cumbersome brick sprawl shrouded in darkness.

"The giant asleep on the riverbank!" I said.

"Better tiptoe past, he'd be mad if you woke him up!" said Maureen.

We had come full circle and were following again the old stone wall that ran above the market-place. The wind tunnel bleak inhospitality of Bridge Street emphasised the increasing futility of our romantic little escapade. We held hands tightly as if we might get blown away from each other.

We came down to the lights of Cromac Square and went in a greasy café there, the kind of place that nobody you knew would ever go to. We held hands over cups of tea in a booth, a bit lost for words, looking into each other's eyes, oblivious of the bold, challenging stares of the local yobs congregated there. Maureen's little face was vivid from the cold night air that I could smell on her soft skin and green woollen overcoat and long chestnut hair. Her eyes burned greenly out of her dark eye-shadow; her cheeks were flushed prettily from the kisses and our mad running. She was self-possessed and calm now. I felt completely in love with her, lost in the dream of us.

"I'll have to get home or Graham will be worried," she said at last.

I walked her up Oxford Street to the bus station. As we approached it she disengaged her hand from mine, saying, "Be careful now, someone I know might see us."

But there was no one much about and I kissed her goodnight at the bus stop anyway.

"Jim, what did I tell you?" she protested weakly. I was incorrigible now.

I watched her off on the long green bus, the curtains of her wavy dark hair silhouetted in the lighted window as her face looked back at me, very touching and dear and unforgettable.

Fired up by my brilliant new flame, I struck out on foot for the railway station, down the barren ruled shadowy length of Corporation Street along the docks. The late through-traffic went banging past; there wasn't another sinner out on foot. Vainglorious, I treasured this walking time to marvel and gloat over the momentous events of that evening, re-running them endlessly on the screen of my memory, each scene one by one in careful detail, as if to prove to myself it had all really happened, it wasn't some wild fantasy of my drunken brain. There was the moment she'd held my hand in the little bar; our first kiss in the subway; the circular lovers' walk in the dark and cold; the strangeness of the night café—It was all a shade surreal, with the quality of a dream.

Distance and time dissolved and I found myself sitting in the warm lighted carriage of the diesel train going out along the Lough shore. My thoughts ran on in their whirling ecstasy of recall. I felt my life charmed in some way, that I was the luckiest man alive. When I got home at ten my parents had gone to bed and I went straight up to my room and lay in the dark willing myself to stay awake while I held the image of Maureen's face before me, steady in my mind's eye.

I woke with a hangover in the morning and struggled into work. The bravado and wild joy of the night before had deserted me, I felt nervous and shy of facing Maureen in the cold light of the office day, her last day at the Department. Would she care for me still after our abortive escapade, like a pair of frightened alley cats? But I felt no regret that we had been lovers; my only worry was what would happen now. Was that it? What would I do then?

I was a few minutes' late for work; she was already seated at our shared desk. I slunk to my place beside her, avoiding her eye, afraid of her, but she spoke to me softly then, attentive and kind as a mother, putting me at my ease. Later in the day when no one around us could hear, she turned to me and said wistfully, "Och, Jim, we were so nervous last night, the way we ran off when we heard someone coming in the subway—"

She looked ready to shed a wee tear. I wasn't sure what she was saying, perhaps that it had all been futile and ridiculous, a missed opportunity for something wonderful. The working day passed uneventfully in this subdued sense of anti-climax, till it was going home time. We'd exchanged addresses; she said we should keep in touch, but nothing definite. And it was with a desperate cold sinking feeling that I watched her disappear in her green coat in the crowd through the swing doors at five for the last time, into the winter's night, home to her family.

I moped about for a while after that, Maureen constantly on my mind, but I heard nothing from her. I realised how difficult it must be for her, a hopeless situation really. I went to the cinema on my own, to be alone with my thoughts of her and feel weepy in the dark. Maybe I should have located a showing of Raquel Welch fending off pterodactyls in her bikini but it was Carol White in *Poor Cow* that brought Maureen vividly back to me and I did a very stupid thing after the film and wrote a letter to her telling her this and how much I missed her.

She wrote back to me at 5 Coolmore Green. I mustn't write to her again, she said; Graham had seen the letter and was suspicious now. Did she show it to him then, for some reason? I wondered. She didn't sound too cross really and said she would phone me soon when things had quietened down at home, '*Love, Maureen x*'.

CHAPTER 11

The Ministry of Truth

I finished at the Department in the March after Maureen's deparure and began a new career as a civil servant.

It was Maureen who had said of the Department, "This isn't much of a job for someone with your brains, Jim." I took her comment to heart and after she left I began looking round for something better. I enquired about journalism and got an interview with the editor of the *Belfast Telegraph*. A celebrated local character, he took the time to chat to me in his small office at the top of the *Telegraph* building on Royal Avenue. Feeling at ease with him, I talked glowingly of my love of books and writing, the trips to the island and so on. He listened interestedly, he seemed to like me, but then he told me I should give journalism a miss, that I was obviously enjoying a wonderful life exactly as I was and I'd be mad to throw it over for the slog of a newshound. Maybe it was a kindly brush-off, but at the time his words made real sense to me, we shook hands cordially and I went back down in the lift feeling relieved and grateful for the life I had now. Why change it, for goodness' sake?

But I'd lost patience with the Department and I was interested when Dad saw a vacancy advertised in the *Belfast News Letter* for a Work Study Officer at the Irish Spinning and Weaving Company on the Falls Road. It paid twice my current salary and "work study" was the up and coming thing, it seemed. I could do a Joe Lampton and move into the private sector—marry the mill owner's daughter; there was still room at t' top!

I got out of work for the interview on a foggy, freezing January morning. Alighting from the bus high on the Falls and turning down a side street, I was confronted by this monstrous, faded Victorian relic with its sinister high walls and long rows of dark windows looming out of the fog.

I fondly thought of the Department as Dickensian in a cosy fashion. The Irish Spinning and Weaving Company was something else, inhuman in its conception, one of Blake's "dark satanic mills". Entering the vestibule, wearing my fresh face and dark suit, I was greeted by the receptionist. Looking at her faded dark clothes and hair and the pinched little face, gentle as an angel, I imagined her the reincarnated spirit of some poor girl who had perished in an accident in the mill, mangled in the machinery. With an old-fashioned kind of deference that moved me, she showed me into the manager's office.

A polite, reserved little man, he outlined to me the duties of a time and motion work study officer. The wee millies will love me, I thought, snooping round after them with my stop-watch. But another part of me was drawn to the grotesque, weird setting of the old mill; being a part of it would be quite a story to tell.

I must have made a good impression or been the sole applicant, for the letter came a week or so later offering me the job. I'd dismissed it from my mind by then, however good a story it might make, and wrote back declining the kind offer due to a "change of circumstances".

It was back again gratefully to the safe routine of the Department. The *Telegraph* editor was right; I didn't know when I was well off. But again the feeling of relative contentment didn't last long. Essentially the work held no interest for me. I couldn't go on like this. And the dream of higher education had receded for the time being. So I applied for and was accepted into the civil service; bigger and more prestigious than the Corporation, it was the major regional white collar employer. I hoped there might be something there in the sheer size of it to interest me. And at least I would be working in the company of a lot of other young men and women not unlike myself.

The bus took you out to the eastern edge of the city. The white parliament building was striking and grandiose, neo-classical-imperialist, with a long approach through sleek, extensive grounds, past the statue of Sir Edward Carson gesticulating in a classic posture of heroic Unionist intransigence. And what a hero: he'd been allowed to remain Privy Counsellor while gun-running from Germany in 1914 for his illegal army of Ulster Volunteers, dedicated to blowing Irish Home Rule off the English statute book. There was the true spirit of Ulster Unionism for you; more a case of '*God save the Kaiser!*' when it suited them.

The ministry I'd been assigned to, Unemployment and Sickness, was tucked away in the woods in a wartime Nissen hut complex. You passed through the reception and the inner double doors on to the spinal long green, tea-smelling corridor that ran dimly away straight ahead of you as far as the eye could see. The loosening of my bowels that accompanied my progression up this long corridor every morning prompted me to dub the place the Ministry of Truth/Minitruth after Orwell.

There was a preliminary one-week training period at a building in the city centre. In the classes there I attended to the instructive bureaucratic drone for about a minute and turned off completely for the rest of the week. If they asked me a question, I hadn't a clue what they were talking about. I got by somehow; I looked intelligent and well-dressed. I got friendly with the chap next me, big Barney, who'd been a prison officer in England.

Then back at Stormont, start of the second week, the boss of the huts, McGovern, gave us his introductory talk. Now I sat up a bit, for McGovern was a character, Norn Iron style, a King of the Jimmies. An older, physically large man, he suffered with a heart condition, he told us, but as we soon found out, he suffered from no shortage of slabber.

McGovern had tricks up his sleeve to test the new recruits' attitudes. First there was an anti-Semitic rant. Hymie the Jew had come off the Liverpool boat in the early years of the century with everything he possessed on a handcart and gone on by fair means or foul to own the centre of Belfast. When McGovern finished his tirade we all sat there a bit stunned or maybe just indifferent; it wasn't altogether convincing somehow.

"Well, whadda yous think?"he barked.

"What about all the poor Jews?" I piped up contentiously. "There's loads of them in Manchester or down the East End of London. My sister told me; she's stayed in those places and all."

McGovern responded to my contention with a wee shrug and a studied obstinate silence. I was already guessing this was a game of some sort.

Then Damien, a Dungannon Catholic with piercing blue eyes, volunteered, "At least they don't stop you getting a drink on a Sunday."

Ouch! This was worse than anti-Semitism, it was hitting the Protestant state for a Protestant people, right below the belt.

"That's got no'hin' to do with it!" McGovern grumpily dismissed the upstart comment with the contempt it deserved.

Then he explained that he hadn't meant what he said about the Jews, who were in truth an honourable, hard-working people, an asset to the community; he was only testing us for any prejudices we might be harbouring. "Ye leave those at the door before ye set foot in this ministry. Okay?"

He went on to talk about the Stormont government's relationship with Westminster.

"'*Ach, yez are bein' subsidised!*'" he mimicked the supposed plebeian tones of the typical Irish nationalist opposition, forever sniping at loyal British Ulster. "So they say! But don't you believe it. What wi' one thing and another there's as much dough flowing back across the Irish Sea as iver comes this way. Just you remember that the next time they try to tell ye, '*Yez are bein' subsidised!*'" And he rolled his jowls in conclusive bulldog intransigence, the very image of the face on Carson's statue.

We were dispersed to various offices throughout the building for final on the job training before taking up our permanent posts. The offices were huge, anonymous areas, each with fifty or more clerks working cheek by jowl. Daylight filtered in the windows, through which were visible patches of dirty, blowy March sky, the lunatic lawn, and the neighbouring arms of the long black huts. The joined-up Nissen hut complex had been thrown up in the war and there was still the sense of a military operation being carried out here.

I was put with Gerry, an amiable slow, bearlike man who by coincidence was a neighbour of mine in Coolmore Green, though I had never laid eyes on him before, a middle-aged bachelor who lived in a flat with his widowed mother. He'd been a clerk in the RAF previously; there was a touch of the boys in blue about his short-back-and-sides and little clipped moustache. A dacent fella, he got by in a sort of easy-going daze, wedged fatly behind his desk, chain-smoking. The small blue eyes wore a glazed expression, his breath came stertorously, chesty from the lifeline of his fags.

"Get us a packet o' them animals, daughter, wud ye?" he'd hoarsely bid the chipmunk girl who sat at the desk facing us, if she was taking orders for the shop.

"Twenty *Embassy*?"

"Aye, here's a dollar." Drowsy with Benelyn, it was handy to refer to things like fags or Ministry forms, inanimate objects generally, as "animals".

"Oh Jim, do you know a Herbie Wise of Coolmore Green?" Gerry and the chipmunk enquired.

"Why yes, he's our next-door neighbour!" I said. We'd not spoken to the Wises for years, they were the low type.

Herbie Wise was one of Chipmunk's clients, it transpired, and he'd get abusive on the phone to her if there was any problem with his benefit payment.

"Do you know a Rosie Bonomo?" They showed me the letter, no address given, reporting Wise for working as a self-employed motor mechanic while claiming benefit.

Uh-oh! I recognised Dad's distinctive elegant handwriting; "Rosie Bonomo" was one of those names he'd collected on his travels and liked to trot out for the very sound of it. He disliked Wise for an insolent gutty, not somebody he cared to live next door to.

"No, I never heard of her," I said, colouring a little. Trust Dad!

Gerry took me through the complicated procedure for awarding benefits to claimants. It was a torturous process, all tied up in red tape, impenetrable to my brain. Regulations and forms led only to more regulations and forms, a Kafkaesque nightmare of bureaucracy. I never did get the hang of it.

As soon as I began dealing with the phone calls I heard the strange attitudes of some members of the public.

"Aye, yous'd pay me quick enough if I was one of the other side!" a man informed me darkly. Here was the very thing McGovern had referred to, the suggestion of prejudice on our part. I looked at the name on the claim form: it was neutral-sounding like a lot of names; it could have been either side complaining about the other.

"Oh, no!" I protested righteously.

"Aye, ye're young!" said the dark voice through the receiver, in a politer tone of resignation now.

I was transferred to another office, the other side of the spinal corridor, for a final week's training now before I went to my own desk with my own claimants. This time they put me with Effie, a middle-aged civil service spinster, plain as a pan loaf, with a flat up-country voice that matched the flat, faintly jaundiced expression of her brown cow eyes. The strong man-hands that might have milked a cow could clear a desk in the blink of an eye and she'd sit up, arms folded like the teacher's pet, waiting for the next in-post.

The sour-faced young male clerk at the facing desk, with greasy thinning hair, rat face, sneery little voice, would reach across and disarrange the neat row of Effie's sorted files between their khaki metal bookends at the top of her desk, and she'd straighten them again with brusque, darting hands, a strange childish performance by the pair of them.

Watchful and sharp, the woman was impatient with my beginner's tentativeness. Her impatience caused me to make more silly mistakes then and she'd snap at me again. The day was overcast and the khaki-shaded electric lights gleamed starkly on the desks and paperwork and parquet flooring, a relentless drabness. The clerks' expressionless faces were bloodless, yellow-tinged in the artificial light, like faces in a cancer ward.

By the end of the day I sat there in a boiling fury of resentment, ready to blow my top. I felt the place close around me like a trap, the regiments of clerks, the masses of forms. I felt that I had come to the worst moment of my life. Fight or flight. I wanted to curse the woman to her face and make a run for it, out the window and over the grass like a lunatic. Then I felt the warm trickle on my upper lip and saw the spots of scarlet down my shirt-front and on to the papers on my desk. I had to sit with my head back, hankie pressed to my nostrils, till the nosebleed stopped.

In the morning I told Mum and Dad I wasn't well and got him to phone into work and tell them I wouldn't be in. I stayed at home the rest of the week, reading mostly. It was the start of a malingering habit that persisted through my unhappy time in the civil service.

When I returned to work the following Monday it was to my permanent place in another office, my own desk, my own little sub-section where I would have the responsibility for my own group of claimants. Effie looked in to ask if I was better, she knew she had upset me, and I was appropriately curt with her, though not unimpressed that she should show some remorse.

So I started off at half-cock, inadequately trained, unsure of what I was doing. But at least I was sitting at my own desk now with nobody watching me. The clerks around me, Rob, a big Ballymena lad and Willie, a wizened Belfast midget, were decent and helpful but I was soon lost; the claims were seldom straightforward and I had a growing backlog of impenetrable queries in my bottom drawer, shoved away there out of sight, out of mind. When the anxious or irate, tearful or threatening phone calls came in begging for or demanding immediate payment and I could stall no longer, I took a deep breath and authorised payment anyway.

My desk was never clear, I was always behind, slaving away, head down, snowed under with claims. There were few distractions, next to no conversation worthy of the name. The highlight of my working day was the arrival at half-past-ten of the tea-trolley with its urns of tea and coffee and big buttered currant scones and again at three with cakes. People would read the *Mirror* or *Mail* for ten minutes over their tea or coffee and that was it, back to their claims. They were a reserved lot, one exception being a fellow across the office whose cynical face I recognised from my grammar school. Now a young married man but more like an overgrown schoolboy, he cultivated an eccentric boorish irreverence, banging files about, glaring round defiantly and exclaiming, "Knickers!" He liked to repeat the word with a sort of obsessional fetishistic relish. He had cut out a headline from the *Sun* and pasted it up triumphantly on the wall above his desk:

Knickers! Knickers! Knickers!

My office was situated at the farthest extremity from the front entrance of the building, a quarter-mile walk up the spinal corridor then a right turn just before the back exit. The only compensation to my twenty-year-old eyes was the sight of pretty girls and young women along the route; I'd never seen so many all under one roof. They had a certain Ministry look about them, attractive in a plain Jane way with their neat, reserved office clothes and hair; the sort of girl you might marry. One day I bumped into Margo, an attractive brunette I'd courted one night on the island. Awkward greetings were exchanged—we'd scarcely spoken before—then she was gone into the crowd and I never saw her again after that, such was the populous anonymity of the huts.

Some of the boys and girls at work were going steady with each other or engaged. It seemed you could score alright here at the Ministry. That was the answer really: someone to love. I envied these couples able to see each other at work against the terrible loneliness of the crowd. I told myself that when I'd settled in I could walk up to some nice girl and ask her for a date.

Then lo and behold, I got a phone call at the office from Maureen. I asked her to wait while I went and phoned her back from one of the call-boxes in the corridor. She'd got my number from somebody back at the Corporation Accounts Department. She was eating down the phone. She lived not far from where I was working now. I think it was the phone line that made her voice sound a bit flat and emotionless. I sounded very nervous. I cared for her still, a lot maybe, but there was such a darkness over the whole affair; we couldn't just be friends and it was impossible that we should be lovers. Neither of us suggested a meeting in the end and I never heard from her again.

In the lunch hour I ate an egg-and-onion roll from the shop and read at my desk, something solid from the bookcase at home, Flaubert, Gogol, Gorky. There was after all this other, finer world of literature that reached out to the beyond. Then it was time to step outside for a breath of the fresh spring air. A footpath took you round the grounds, past the smart new tower block that housed other ministries; I'd visited the restaurant on the top floor. Beyond it, the main road brought you to a halt and it was time to turn back. You felt a bit uncomfortable out of doors anyway, conspicuous in the windy openness under the moving spring sky; it was a relief to head back indoors, deep into the building to where you belonged at your own desk, with the tea-trolley coming at three.

But the first beautiful summery day arrived, with the girls on their lunch hour sunbathing on the grass in front of the tower block as I strolled past. A male voice called my name and I recognised Philip, the chap who had befriended me at the English night class. He came forward and shook my hand warmly, like a long-lost friend. There was that soapy gospel hall air about him, yet it was touching to see such a sincere, friendly face in this place of studied mass indifference. We had shared the dream of becoming teachers, as if it were some high noble calling. And I could hear how pleased he was with himself now as he told me he'd just got accepted at an English college of education, a Christian one, with his existing O-levels, and was starting there in September.

Hearing Philip's joy to be getting out of the civil service and becoming a student, I felt the old dream of higher education stir in me again and I knew I too would have to go to England, sooner or later; it was just a matter of time. It was liberating to think of it, to know there was this escape route. I wished Philip all the best and went off with a spring in my step. I was inspired, I too would be free; I'd be a student. I would teach. I would write!

I just let my feet carry me now. I didn't turn back at the main road this time but crossed over and then I was passing through the gates of the cemetery. On the other side of the high wall the workaday world fell away behind me, muted and distant. It was a vast old cemetery that swallowed you up. Strolling in the peaceful silence of the dead, I got absorbed in the names and dates on the crowded headstones, the old and young alike who'd been laid to their final rest here, the mystery of all those lives that had been and gone; it put everything into perspective.

I wandered a long way on down the cemetery road, far from the main road, with nobody else around. Bees droned in the hot, drowsy stillness, an intermittent lazy sound as they moved among the flowers on the graves. I observed the weightless mesmeric passage of richly-coloured butterflies. The grasshoppers' chorus throbbed from a hot green bank.

I came down to the bottom of the cemetery and there, suddenly and unexpectedly, on the other side of the fence, the open countryside spread itself before me. The patchwork of June fields lying bright and beautiful in the sunshine ran back to a white farmhouse nestling on the side of a green hill. A solitary cotton wool puff of cloud was poised high in the vivid blue sky directly above it. I stood there transfixed by the simple picturesque timeless beauty of the scene, feeling it enter me in waves of ecstatic sensation.

The subtle, delicate, half-formed impressions that rose in my mind then seemed rooted in vague subconscious memories of my country childhood and even to a time before that, to my farm-dwelling ancestors; I could feel their life close to the earth running in my veins still. Strange longings, an urge to transcendence, burst like stars in my breast. It was an overwhelming sense of the richness and mystery of existence.

I'd experienced these epiphanies throughout my life, starting in the sickbed of my Tyrone childhood as I lay watching the clouds sail past over the green faery hill beyond my window. After that they had come to me every now and then, always out of the blue: in a sun-shower in the street and a red sunset at the back of the houses; and as I got older, in the unconscious beauty in a girl's face and a golden evening on the English south coast—

The epiphanies came and went, you forgot about them in the long in-between times of arid worldly struggle. But imagine if there was a way of consciously cultivating these feelings of deeper meaning and beauty, to live primarily for transcendent ecstatic sensation. It was the root of the creative impulse, but why not take it beyond writing and painting and music and let it fill the whole of your life? Live by it like a fine religion of beauty, mysticism and poetry.

I felt inspired and transformed. I was running late for work; I'd wandered too far, lost in my thoughts. But that was good; this was the start of a new and better life, above things not under them. My legs carried me strong and confident now with fresh conviction and hope, back out through the cemetery gates, into the living world. The traffic belted heedlessly past; the ministries' tower block glittered in the sun. The industrial city spread itself before me. I had no fear of any of it now I had beauty on my side.

I knew who I was.

CHAPTER 12

Breaking Out

The summer of 68 was the last one we spent all together on the island. We had the two-week July holiday there; it was really something, like going back in time and being a native of the island. The weather blazed. It was another summer of love with the hippies in California; our transistor radio played the Beach Boys' *Darlin'*, the Mamas and the Papas' *I Saw Her Again Last Night* and the Flowerpot Men *Let's Go To San Francisco*. Well, we didn't need to; we had it all right here on our own Irish island, in the sun, gettin' back to the land, playin' our gui-tars and growin' our hair, us lads and some of the nicest girls you could ever hope to meet.

With the island season behind us for another year, on a golden Indian summer evening I alighted from the work bus in the city centre, on Donegall Avenue and bumped into Geoff on the crowded rush hour pavement. Hugh had brought Geoff over to the island a couple of times, that was all, but he'd been an instant smash hit with everybody and I felt we were close friends already.

"Jim! The very man I've been looking for!" he hailed me now. He looked different coming from work in his conservative dark business suit and polished black shoes, though with a raffish touch about his Paisley tie and pocket kerchief and the flop of long brown hair over his shirt collar. Geoff was a commercial artist which seemed an agreeable compromise between a steady desk job like mine and something a lot more creative; you didn't expect art to be more than a hobby.

Geoff had a warm, smiley way of focusing in on you, so you felt you really mattered. He said, "I was speaking to Malcolm at the Pound the other night and he tells me you and him have been talking about moving into a flat here in town?"

I nodded, "I think so, I'm not sure I can face another winter out in the sticks and the long commute across the city to work every day."

"Me neither, trekking in from Ballynahinch! Why don't the three of us look for a place together? Just imagine it, you and me and Malcolm in a nice wee pad of our own up around Fitzroy Avenue with all the students, the *Eg* and the *Bot* and Smokey Joe's and the Queen's hop!" He exclaimed ecstatically like that over the joys of life in Belfast; he was a born local patriot with an enthusiasm for place that was contagious.

Malcolm and I had only talked vaguely about getting a flat. It was easier on a small salary to go on living at home with your parents, but you got depressed with the growing realisation that here you were out of your teens now and your life was going nowhere. But in the few short minutes of that chance exchange with Geoff all doubt was swept away, I was nodding emphatically, "Yes, count me in, Geoff, it'll be great!" and I went on my way again, next bus, train, all fired up with excitement at the prospect of our flat. And now my horrible job didn't matter much any more; the flat would be liberation, independence, a decent social life. Now I would come into my own!

But would Mum and Dad be upset by my leaving home? Would they see it as a rejection of them? I was the youngest, the last one at home; now they'd be all on their own, growing old. Nervously over dinner that evening I told them I was thinking of moving into a flat in town with some mates, it didn't make sense for me to commute so far to work each day, but I'd still be back to see them a couple of days a week.

Only to be somewhat taken aback by the unbridled enthusiasm of their response, an uncritical, resounding "Yes!" to my imminent departure. Had I really been such a pain to have around them? Probably! I couldn't honestly blame them, and their attitude now neatly confirmed that it was definitely time for me to go. Immediately my relationship with them improved, moving into an entirely positive mode, just like great friends. They agreed with my suggestion that I should start calling them Edward and Sarah instead of Dad and Mum. Home had never been a happier place now that I was leaving it!

It took a while with one thing and another and we moved into the flat Geoff had found in Dunluce Avenue on Sunday the fourth of January, 1969, the last day of the Christmas break. Malcolm came to pick me up in his Minivan in the afternoon. I'd packed my little grey cardboard suitcase and brought my record player and record collection. Mum and Dad waved from the bay window as we drove off down Coolmore Green. It was only a removal of ten miles to the other side of Belfast, I was coming home for tea on Wednesday, but there was no doubting the significance of the occasion: two months' short of my twenty-first birthday I was finally leaving home.

Our breath smoked in the cold interior of the van; the heater was broken. The Sunday afternoon was very grey and still, Loughside frozen stiff as a corpse, scarcely a living soul out of doors as we manoeuvred round corners, out of the estate. Malcolm's army greatcoat covered him like a blanket and he'd grown a beard. He was quiet and unfathomable as ever but the adolescent bad moods had gone, he'd turned into a gentle grinner with a ready laugh, an advocate of "flower power".

We drove in silence mostly, along the Shore Road and in through the lunar reaches of the Rathcoole suburbs to the shut, grim sabbath streets of the town centre. Student land began at Shaftesbury Square with Lavery's Cobbles pub; it was dead up here too with the Christmas break but the terraced streets of student lets waited for the new term's invasion to begin and we would be part of the scene now! Up Lisburn Road, past the big new City hospital, we turned down the narrow Victorian street and parked a little way along.

Geoff answered the door of the small terraced house with its postage stamp of withered front garden. "What about yous!" he exclaimed, a traditional Belfast greeting, smiling broadly, indulgently from one to the other of us.

"We made it! We're here!"

"At last, can't believe it!"

Geoff looked completely at home already. The minute I laid eyes on him I knew I had done the right thing and that this was going to be fun. He always looked the part, the beatnik now, relaxed and unshaven, his long hair needing a wash, a big sloppy sweater that reached to the knees of his perfectly faded blue jeans.

We carried our stuff in, through the gloomy cold hallway running back to stairs that ascended into darkness. We had the ground floor flat, the door opening off the hall into the living room. A coal fire burning in the grate waved a welcome. An inner door led to the bedroom at the front overlooking the street; it was filled with a double bed and single bed, chest and wardrobe, with another fireplace.

"A family was living here before, a mother and two daughters," said Geoff. He stood warming his backside at the fire, twinkly blue-eyed and joking, "Leave the hall door open, lads, let in a bit of heat!"

He showed us the scullery with a small dining table occupying its narrow dark recess. The back door opened onto a little yard with the coal-house and toilet, and a door in the wall to the back entry. Above the high brick walls of the back alley the new sheer concrete and glass block of the hospital soared in the dead winter sky, like a monument to human suffering.

"No bath," said Geoff. "We can shower round the Students' Union."

He put the kettle on the gas ring for tea and soon we were drinking the hot brown liquid out of the chipped beakers, sitting round the fire that burned brighter as the afternoon light began to fail in the living room.

"Isn't this just great, our own wee pad!"

"That simple fact of having your own place makes up for any lack of home comforts."

"It's a wee bit bleak, right enough!"

"Ach, you don't notice it once you've got the fire going."

"We must embrace the bohemian life!"

When we had almost faded into the encroaching winter evening dark, Geoff clicked on a table lamp on a corner shelf by his armchair. A soft, shadowy light encompassed us, and the room looked almost beautiful. The sash window onto the backyard was a glassy block of night, dimly reflecting the room and our seated figures. The anonymous city was there right outside our window, dark and bitter with winter, but here inside we were warm and safe, friends together enjoying the craic around the fire.

Drinking nothing more than tea, we were loosening up, laughing together.

"It doesn't feel like a depressing Sunday night," I said. "You know that Sunday childhood sort of sadness: evensong followed by a Bovril drink, bed and prayers."

"Suicidal, you mean."

"With Monday morning looming," said Malcolm. "Monday: the worst word in the English language!"

"From now on every night is Saturday night!" said Geoff. "I declare it so! Now who's for the dance at the Floral Hall tonight?"

"Sure the girls will be waitin' for us!"

"Spot of grub first?"

"I'm starvin'! Forgot to eat today!" said Geoff.

I'd brought a cardboard box of Spar food Mum gave me and we set-to now opening tins and emptying them into saucepans: burgers in a rich gravy, baked beans, *Smash* instant mash potato. We wolfed it down in the dingy light and confined space at the scullery table. After we'd washed up Geoff shaved in the little mirror propped in the window then washed his long hair in the basin, one leg sticking up behind him.

"It itches if I don't wash it every day!" he said, towelling energetically. He went in the bedroom and emerged again shortly, transformed in a button-down collared cream shirt and red Paisley tie and dark trousers. He slipped on a stylish tan herringbone sports jacket and was ready for the dance. His scrubbed smooth face and clean, soft chestnut hair like a fox's pelt shone with an eagerness to be off to the excitement of night in the city.

Malcolm and I changed into smarter trousers and jackets, the rather faded ones we wore to work, not a patch on Geoff's fab gear. We piled into the Minivan and Malcolm drove us across the city to the Floral Hall on the hillside at Glengormley. I got off with some girl at the dance that night; the other lads struck lucky too. It seemed a good omen of the new, better life to come to us now. The dance didn't run late on a Sunday and we three lads were back in our cold new beds by midnight, Malcolm and I sharing the double. It was back to work in the morning.

"You're alive now, at least," I told myself as the bed began to warm up and I felt myself slipping towards sleep. It was all a big new adventure.

It was murder getting up in the morning in the polar region of the flat, negotiating the frozen linoleum wastes of the bedroom, braving the raw, ashy cold of the little flagstoned backyard with its lid of murky dawn sky, to the outdoor toilet. This was primitive. But we loved it!

We splashed the sleep from our eyes at the kitchen sink and in a jiffy we were fully dressed, big winter coats and woolly scarves, standing huddled round the cooker gulping down hot tea with a sense of camaraderie. Geoff wrapped his hands around his mug to warm his fingers and looked out with wide urchin eyes over the steaming rim like a Bisto kid. He brought a sort of creative flair to his every small action, taking a conscious, studied pleasure in it. Even the nasty cold shock of a back-to-work, post-Christmas Monday morning could be turned to a degree of satisfaction.

Out the door we piled into the Minivan; I crouched in the back and we flew off down Lisburn Road through the rush hour, important in our own transport, nipping round the buses at the stops, reaching the town centre in a few minutes, it seemed. Geoff and I got out at Donegall Square and crossed between the surging swirls of traffic to the island of City Hall, then moving in a reckless beeline, the only way to go, crossed the road on the far side by Robb's department store, dodging the great wheels of a heaving, heedless double-decker.

"Thought we was sent for there!" Geoff trumpeted in the Belfast parlance as we bounded to the safety of the far kerb and we laughed in the face of our mortality, as if drunk on the cold air and lead fumes of the new year's morning.

Here's me, I thought, *laughing on my way to work*! It was different now we were city boys, living right here in Belfast, part of the cheek and devilment its crowded anonymity permitted. Geoff worked in the centre; I caught the bus from Chichester Street.

On a bus going back up Lisburn Road at eventide I saw the famous policeman at Shaftesbury Square, the tall uniformed figure directing the convergent rush hour traffic like the conductor of an orchestra or maybe Charlie Chaplin, in a dazzling display of elaborate and complex hand signals. The effect was comical, though the officer's face was frozen in RUC grimness; it was too military and robotic a performance for my liking. Coming up to Christmas the motorists piled presents around him. Oh, but they loved their police in Norn Iron!

The flat was cold and untidy when we got back but we soon had it sorted, tidied and washed-up, fire lit, dinner on. I shopped on Lisburn Road: steak sausages, meat rissoles, chops, potatoes and bread. After tea we sat round the fire, cocooned in a sated warm contentment, chatting easily about our day, our legs in blue jeans stretched towards the friendly flames.

There was the sense of a truly wonderful new time in our lives, in our own place. It was good to be without TV; we would make our own entertainment here and there was the record player and the radio. Inspired by a record of Holst's Planets someone had picked up cheap, we started tuning into Radio 3 for classical music, finding it a marvellous balm to the nervous system and a deep joy to the heart at this tired, quiet end of the working day. There was a whole new meaning to life, couched in the friendship of the shared flat.

Later in the evening we sauntered along to the *Four in Hand* for a glass of beer. You went in a side door and upstairs to the long, narrow, wood-panelled bar, an open fire burning at one end, the way a proper old pub should be. And here I was, enjoying a drink with mates on a weekday night just a hundred yards from where I lived. I had escaped from the unsociability of Loughside, the bind of the train timetable and the dreary, lonely sort of sadness about being a young man still living with your ageing parents, however nice they might be.

It started with just the three of us in the flat but soon enough all the old gang were rolling up at our door as word of our whereabouts got around. And the flat became a home from home for all our friends, a comfortable refuge from the bleak winter streets.

Weekday nights were good, no night was wasted; there was the pub and Smokey Joe's café, a trip to the cinema to see Lindsay Anderson's *If* and dates with girls met at the dances. At the midweek student hop it was enchanting to find the Moody Blues there performing to the small midweek crowd, the magical *Nights in White Satin* in a dazzling white light show.

And the weekends were a glorious happening. We had a lie-in Saturday morning; it was a wonderful feeling waking up slowly in the shared bedroom, batting the craic to and fro between us. It was up in the bracing cold and into jeans and sweaters, lighting the fire and eating a cooked breakfast.

We went out free as students in the crisp winter's Saturday morning, into the Minivan and up through the tree-lined avenues to the laundrette and the Cash and Carry. We took a pleasure in all our little chores; it was part of our newfound independence. There was the buzz of student life all around us. Our breath steamed above the coils of our long woollen scarves in the frosty air. A lemon-pale sun shot its cold gleams through the mistiness and the black lacework of the bare trees in the long avenues of flats around the university.

Back at the flat we filled the kitchen cupboard with the tins and other cheap food we'd bought from Cash and Carry. Kettle on for afternoon cuppa, stoke up the fire. Then a sort of spell descended on the proceedings with the quiet, slow blue waning of the light at the windows, and you felt the deep, dark thrill of the oncoming Saturday night stirring in the pit of your stomach: the big booze-up and the Saturday dance at Queen's.

CHAPTER 13

Old Ruby Wine

In those first weeks in the flat there was a lot of drinking and chatting up the birds but then a settling down with not so much to prove. We got friendly with a local band, the Belfast Blues Brothers, who were playing on the fringe of the university festival. They came back to our flat after one gig and then came regularly. Paul, Brian, Bruce and Marty; it was they introduced us to the dubious pleasures of the Old Ruby Wine, bottled and sold by the Tohill Vino Company in Shaftesbury Square. Paul and Co had been enjoying it since their schooldays at Orangefield, drinking it up alleyways and under railway bridges. They were a year or two younger than us, still living with their parents and it was luxury now for them to come and drink their wine in the comfort of our flat.

Old Ruby came in a half-bottle size at 11s 3p, everyone had his own bottle and it was drunk straight from the bottle. The flat opaque bottle concealed a stomach-turning reddish-brown liquid, heavy and sweet and sticky like cough syrup, though less easy to swallow. But with perseverance you managed to get it down your gullet and keep it down, and soon enough you felt it beginning to do its wonderful work on you. All worry and doubt vanished miraculously; the fire-lit room grew brighter, the craic greater, your friends' faces dearer. It was like dying and waking up in heaven.

We sat in a circle round the fire, nursing our bottles on our laps between slugs. The Old Ruby Wine bound us in a fresh intimacy; we seemed to connect at some profound level. Every memorable phase in my life has a theme tune; for those Saturday nights in Dunluce Avenue in the early spring of 1969 it was the Peanut Butter Conspiracy's *Turn on a friend to the good life* from the compilation album *The Rock Machine Turns You On.* The album was filled with exquisite sixties' songs by Dylan, the Zombies, Blood, Sweat and Tears, Spirit and others, but *Good Life* with its eerie, ecstatic harmonies, tripping, up-beat rhythm and bubbling rock guitar, not to mention the lyric, seemed to precisely, uncannily fit my situation at that exact moment in time, the high of Saturday night sheer conviviality there in the cosy flat with the expanding group of cool new friends.

The solid presence of Paul, the drummer from the Blues Brothers, was central to these evenings. He was a medium-height, sturdy figure, with a heavy, beaky, John Lennon kind of face curtained by long, straight brown hair that he flicked back from his eyes. The deadpan challenge he presented to a hostile conventional world would readily break in a gap-toothed boyish grin. Things were alternately threatening or funny to him; he shook with laughter as the humour bubbled up out of a situation and overtook his impatience or anger with it.

Paul was eighteen, in his first year at the College of Art.

"I was going to go there," I told him.

"What happened then?"

"I never got it together somehow. I was going to night classes and ran out of steam. In the end I couldn't believe in myself as a painter. I tried for Stranmillis then and that fell through too, I'm one O-level short of the entrance requirement. So I'm stuck working in an office since I left school, four years ago."

"You poor sod!" Paul was genuinely concerned. "How do you put up with it, day in, day out?"

"God knows. I'm not even any good at being a clerk." I laughed at the patent absurdity of my situation.

"Can't you do something about it, man? What would you really like to do if you had the choice?"

"Write books, novels. I know that takes time but it's the only thing I really want to do."

Bruce, the rhythm guitarist, chimed in, "You and me, Jim, we're clerks, petty-bourgeois nonentities doomed to soul-less pen-pushing! Our only way out is the bottle or writing that novel we're always talking about. Hi, I'll bring my typewriter round Sunday afternoon and we'll have a go together! We could do a Waterhouse and Hall, write a kind of a Belfast *Billy Liar* maybe? We'll show the bastards what we can do!"

"That'd be great, Bruce. Two heads are better than one!"

Bruce—big lad, barrel chest swelling with indignation or *joie de vivre*, as the situation demanded, shaggy black curls, rosy schoolboy cheeks—was one of those larger than life characters that the Celtic nation produces, the life and soul of any company, gift of the gab, funny-clever, a travelling one man show. He could be superior and cutting to perceived enemies, or mean and direct, pugnacious, jutting his jaw with a defiant stare, but there was no real malice in him, it was just an act. He didn't need alcohol to let himself go either, though he could drink his fair share, becoming more and more expansive, till, all one big heart, he threw his arms round you in a bear-hug and told you straight to your face, man to man, "I love you, Jim mate!"

Bruce relished the sound of his own voice and the power his words gave him over any situation. His yarns were embroidered from everyday incidents, like the morning Malcolm gave him a lift to work in the Minivan:

"So we're driving up York Road in the rush hour and I catch sight of something out of the corner of my eye. I look over my shoulder and there's this wheel burling along the road beside us, overtaking us on the inside.

" 'Look!' says I. 'A wheel!'

"'Christ, that's mine!' says Malcolm. And helplessly we watch our missing wheel mount the pavement now, scattering pedestrians—"

Once he got going on some little incident Bruce could spin it out indefinitely, having everyone in stitches as he piled on the absurdities. Like any good yarn it was a mixture of exaggeration and half-truths but you believed every word of it because you wanted things to be like that, zany and ridiculous; it made life easier to bear.

With the drink taken Paul and Bruce quarrelled often, two pig-heads locked in a love-hate relationship.

" *'Leave me alone, dear, I'll be all right soon,'* " Bruce mocked Paul's bad mood, quoting the TV advert for women's "time of the month" medication.

"Ach, flip off, Bruce, ye big eejit!" Paul took the bait.

"It's tough being an art student, isn't it, dear?" said Bruce. "Shifting all that paint on canvas and having to work out the true meaning of life at the same time. Try livin' in the real world for a day. A proper day's work would kill ye, man!"

"You call what you do 'a proper day's work'?" Paul mocked bitterly. "Sellin' birdshite!" Bruce worked for an agricultural products company.

The insults were soon forgotten. The moods of a typical Saturday night on the Old Ruby Wine could move from mellow to joyful to crazy to an argument to a fight, but with no real damage done, just a drink-dulled Sumo-like struggle on the hearth-mat.

Everybody loved "wee Marty" Russell, the bass guitarist, another character and wit in the Belfast tradition. Marty was dapper and cute with neat long hair, like a pop star. Comfy in the armchair by the fire, nursing his bottle of Old Ruby, his lifeline, he was settled in for the night, slowly drinking himself into a coma. Gradually his ringing, mordant Belfast wit would dull and his words become confused and slurred, till his eyes crossed and then closed, his head slumped on his chest, still clutching the empty wine bottle.

He woke up later cursing and tottered to his feet, found the door and his way home somehow through the long dark streets of after-midnight south Belfast. He never came to the hops or showed any interest in meeting girls, though remarks he made indicated he was not lacking in heterosexual drive but accustomed to finding solitary relief for it. I thought the bottle he nursed on his lap was like a girlfriend to him, his wee Ruby.

Marty was a civil servant, like me; Brian the lead guitarist was another. I'd been watching Brian for some time before I eventually met him; I'd seen him playing in various bands around the town, wielding his red Les Paul electric guitar, with a following who gathered about the stage to admire his musicianship.

Brian worked in one of the ministries in the tower block. I'd seen him board the bus in the morning on the Newtownards Road, a stocky blond figure in a black jacket and grey trousers, and sit down just a few seats in front of me on the top deck, alone like me, looking out the window. He had a studious appearance, bespectacled, and looked older than his eighteen years. I liked Brian's music and the modest, gentle look of him and wanted to go and speak to him on the bus but I'd never summoned the nerve to do so.

I felt a kind of connection to Brian, as to a kindred spirit, another artist who had to earn his living working in an office; unlike the pampered, pretentious students who read their poems in the *Four in Hand*. I believed true art only came out of that grounding in reality; you couldn't buy it with a university education. Admittedly there was a touch of sour grapes on my part.

Time and circumstances had moved on and here we were now in my flat drinking together, the best of mates. In his cups Brian was responsive and good-humoured, his homely face creased in delighted laughter as the craic got going. He looked so comfortable there in his mustard cardigan with brown leather buttons, brown corduroy jeans, and his horn-rimmed glasses reflecting the firelight. He was unassuming in every way. He had acne and a facial tic but these only added to a winning vulnerability and warmth of character in his face.

"You like the blues?" he enquired, fingering my small collection of singles, LPs and EPs down by the record player. I had Howlin' Wolf, Buddy Guy and the Spencer Davis Group.

In his quiet, dedicated fashion, Brian had picked away on guitars in his bedroom through his schooldays, eventually playing at school dances at Orangefield and Annadale. Hearing Jimi Hendrix for the first time was a revelation to him. Sitting on a bench in Botanic Gardens one afternoon after school, smoking a joint, Jimi's head had appeared to him in a humongous hallucinatory bubble. After that there was no stopping Brian;

playing his guitar had taken on a mystical significance! He could play it with his teeth too, like Hendrix!

Yet Brian was no wild man. One of his ambitions in life, he said, was simply to marry and have children, to be a family man. I liked his gentle character; I was surprised once to see him in a tussle with Paul over what record to put on. Brian was the winner.

"He's such a stubborn wee bugger!" Paul complained breathlessly. "You wouldn't believe his strength!"

Everything was swinging, in the parlance of the day, till the Sunday morning the landlord sprang a surprise visit on us. Some of the Saturday night visitors had stayed over so there were bodies on the floor among the debris of the booze-up.

Nicholson the landlord was a curiously repellent character, creepy and vile. He called for the rent every Friday night. He was an unattractive, middle-aged country man, drab and dour in his long belted mac, always accompanied by his early-teenage daughter who observed the proceedings in silence.

Nicholson's presence, suspicious and malignant, killed stone dead the atmosphere in our happy home. A man of limited communication skills, he stood there among us in the charged silence in the sitting room, making small movements of his simian skull and breathing stertorously down his hairy nostrils as he flicked ugly, jaundiced, evil looks around him, reminding you it was his property and us in it. We always tidied up before he came, so what was the problem? Had a neighbour complained about noise?

At long, painful last he cleared his throat, a rusty bolt shot-to in a shitehouse door.

"Aye. So yous're lukkin' after the place? RIght. Mm-hm. Well now."

The hostile pregnant pauses between his miserly monosyllabic utterances stretched into hissing black holes of baleful silence, the bile rising in him like a black flood-tide. For the ten minutes or so he insisted on standing there, a dark shadow across our lives, the flat was no longer our home: it was his property and we were there on sufferance. We breathed a great sigh of relief when at last he'd pocketed our six pounds rent and continued on his greasy rounds.

That Sunday morning he arrived and served us with our week's notice. It was a rude awakening indeed. The following Saturday morning he was there to see us off. We'd found another flat just up the street a bit. Nicholson watched as we marched to and fro moving our bits and pieces.

"Out yous go! Donkeys is what yous are! A pack of dirty donkeys!" He kept repeating this like a mantra, as if relishing the debased metaphor and alliteration:

"Dir-ty donk-eys!"

The worst thing was shifting the hundredweight of coal my father had had delivered to the coal-shed at the back. We shovelled it into plastic shopping bags and cardboard boxes and humped it over the road and up the three flights to the new flat.

CHAPTER 14

Summer in the City

The flat at the top of the tall terraced house felt spacious, light and airy, lifting the heart after the cramped gloom in the ground floor of the small house we had occupied across the street. Two sash windows in the sitting room looked over the chimney pots towards the city centre and let in the afternoon sun. The street was tucked away out of sight far below; it was like looking out from the turret of a castle. Summer was a-coming in, with most of the students departing from the district. I felt the special magic of this first summer living in the city, like holding the world in the palm of your hand.

The summer magic brought Moira, my magic summer girl. There was a party at the flat of the art college girls down the street; I was drinking and showing off, trying to be clever and shocking. Turning my head at a pause in my performance, I was conscious of the dark girl sat next me on the divan in the crowded party room. A pair of dark eyes met mine; I couldn't be sure whether it was with a look of indifference or disdain.

"D'ye see enough then?" I said.

But even as the defensive, half-joking words left my lips, I was taking in the sweet face set in its frame of long, straight black hair and my very next words were, "Would you like to go on a date sometime?" I didn't care about their precipitate blunt awkwardness. And I was rewarded for my candour as she came straight back at me with a simple definite, "Yes."

I don't think we even kissed that night we met but a double date was arranged along with her blonde friend Marina and my friend Stuarty for the following day, the May bank holiday Sunday, a run to Helen's Bay.

Stuarty in his Fiat picked the girls up from the Limestone Road where they lived, and called for me at the flat around noon. It was a superb hot sunny day; we drove down through the peaceful Sunday city and out the County Down coast, hot and green with glimpses of shiny blue Lough. It was easy sitting quietly in the back with Moira, with no sense of strain, while Stuarty and Marina did all the talking in the front.

Helen's Bay was already busy when we got there. We found a space on the sand to spread our jackets. We'd not come for a swim; we paddled and lay in the sun. When Stuarty and Marina started courting, Moira and I went for a walk along the beach, holding hands. She was one of the best-looking girls I'd ever seen, with her shiny black mane and neat regular features. She was tall for a girl, "Five-foot-eight," she told me, "I can't wear high heels on dates." That was just an inch shorter than me. She wore navy needlecord jeans that complimented her slim, shapely figure.

When we reached a clear space on the beach she gripped my hand and pulled me after her, running along beside the waves. As we got our breath back at the farther end of the bay, lolling among some rocks, I stole a first kiss. With our lips pressed together, eyes closed, the sound of the waves and the children's cries went muffled and distant as if we'd been submerged in the sea.

"Race you back!" she said, pulling me to my feet.

She beat me the race back along the sand.

It was a really nice day out and Moira and I made a date for the middle of the week. She was waiting for me outside Robinson and Cleaver's, looking sensational in a simple short white dress that emphasised her lovely long legs and the fall of raven hair worn loose down her back. Then there was her personality, so easy and gentle, such a nice girl. It seemed at last I'd found someone worthy of the accolade of "my girl", capable of replacing Julie.

We sat on the top of the bus in the June evening, round City Hall and up to Shaftesbury Circus, heading for the flat. At the *Four in Hand* we both drank pints of Guinness and she challenged me to arm wrestling over the corner table where we sat tucked away. Her cheeks flushing prettily, black eyes glittering fierily, she beat me fair and square. That didn't bother me, I was never competitive; her tomboy streak was simple, fun and refreshing.

She worked in an office in town but moved in studenty folk club circles. She was something of a Julie Felix lookalike; it was a girl folk singer look of the time.

"I was born on a farm in Islandmagee,"she told me. "I spent my childhood there but when I was eleven Daddy died in a car accident. He was just turning on to the road at the end of our loanen. After that Mammy and I left the farm and moved to the house on Limestone Road. I went to the Girls' Model, left to start work at fifteen."

"Did you know Katie Burns at the Model?"

"Tubby Burns? Yes, I think everyone did. Life and soul of the party girl. Great craic!""

"It was Tubby broke my heart!"

"Oh yeah?"

"We went steady for six months when I was sixteen; she was one of my first girlfriends. I was heartbroken for a whole evening after she dumped me for someone older with a car. But I woke up the next day with this sense of overwhelming relief, like coming out of the dentist's. I was free! Though not for long; I met Julie soon after that, another girl from the Model. Now she was a nice girl, but she went to London. I was supposed to follow her there but I never did, I'm not sure why not."

"Julie Martin? I knew her to see. Fashion plate. I can just picture Julie up the King's Road in London."

"What about you, Moira? I daresay you've broken a few hearts?"

"Ach, away o' that with you. I went steady with Alistair for three years, he was a student at Stranmillis, came out top in his final year. Then one evening he said he'd something to tell me. He sounded so serious I thought it must be an engagement ring. But he told me it was over between us, there was a girl from Stran he'd fallen in love with. I couldn't speak for the rest of that evening, I mean literally, my throat seized up. He saw me home, asked me if I was going to be alright, very concerned and all. I nodded but I thought I was going off my rocker. I hurried indoors to do it in private."

"But you didn't go mad, obviously?"

"I was cut up alright."

"That's different. So was I with Tubby. It dents your pride, that's all. In truth you were never meant to stay with that person, they just happened along by chance and then became a bad habit. You should be grateful they ditched you; it means there's someone ten times better waiting for you round the next corner."

Moira looked a bit shocked by my words; you were meant to suffer for the rest of your life if someone ditched you. Maybe it was the difference between a boy and a girl. She gave me an arch look and said, "Jim, you are a character!"

She seemed to like me anyway. We walked back up Dunluce, holding hands in the broad daylight of the long evening and climbed the stairs to the flat. The others were out. The sun coming over the rooftops flooded the big sitting room with a golden light. We kicked off our shoes and courted on the single bed in the chimney breast corner. When I pulled the covers over us Moira exclaimed, "Oh Jim, your feet!"

She meant my sweaty black nylon socks. A wrestling match ensued; I pinned her wrists down on the bed and snatched kisses at the flushed, pretty wee face through the dishevelled strands of long black hair. I'd not had a girl before who wanted to play-fight like this, like your sister. I wasn't sure how much I wanted it either, I'd had something more serious in mind, but there was a light-hearted effect that wasn't a bad start to a relationship.

After just two weeks we moved house again. There were a lot of lets going after the exodus of students for the summer vacation and Geoff and Malcolm found a better place further up the Lisburn Road at Tate's Avenue, a whole terraced, three-bedroom house to ourselves. I had the slope-ceilinged attic room, which pleased me no end, two steep flights up, a cavernous whitewashed space with its single brass bed on casters looking small and isolated. I woke up islanded on the narrow bed on the cold ocean of linoleum. The skylight in the roof framed the changeable Belfast sky; you felt transcendent up here with the clouds, remote from the street. I lay on, wide awake, exulting in the bohemianism of it, like a Parisian garret. Here in the seclusion at the top of the Victorian house you could dream, write, paint. Though you lost something too, the companionship and craic of a shared bedroom. Comfort and privilege bred isolation and loneliness.

At the twelfth of July fortnight holiday period the other lads went off in cars to County Kerry. I was too content in my attic to move and I had Moira, my summer girl. We walked in the Botanic Gardens in the tranquillity of the mild summer's evening. A shower came, sweetening the grass and flowers. We sat in the wooden shelter with its walls carved with lovers' initials: *Skeetsie L Tara . . . Kelso L Mary O'R.*

I said, "If only I'd a penknife, I'd carve our names there inside a heart:, 'Jim L Moira, true'."

"Aw, that's nice," she said. "For posterity, like."

"We're a couple of city urchins, Moira; we belong to the streets and alleyways and the park."

"Long as this bench doesn't get too hard sittin' here. Hi, the rain's stopped."

"Where are we off to now then, wee-doll?"

"*I* fancy a Guiness!"

"C'mon then! Hi Moira, you 'n' me is quare pals, aren't we?"

"Aye surely, wee lad!"

We had a drink in the quiet of the *Four in Hand*, enjoying the curious peace of the city half-emptied for the July holiday. The stout went down a treat, black and silky, casting its warm spell on us. We sat there, a contented couple, glowing together.

"I've got it!" I said at last.

"What?"

"The meaning of life!"

"Oh yeah?" Moira was so grounded and unpretentious but she tolerated my metaphysical outbursts. "Go on, tell us then, wee lad!"

"It's all so simple really! That's the secret! It's you and me, right here, right now, together in this place in this exact moment in time."

"Okay," Moira nodded sympathetically. "And?"

"That's it, nothing else. That says it all! D'ye see?"

I expected her to pull a cute face or laugh at me but she turned to me, her dark eyes filled with the lovely respect a good woman feels for a man. "You know what, Jim, you really are something," she said earnestly. "You really are quite a person!"

It was great to be flattered like that by my lovely girl. Maybe I *was* special in some way then? I liked to think so, even if it was just to be the doomed writer in an attic. At least I had an attic now; that was significant. And Moira could be my muse.

The twelfth of July came. It was the date of Protestant King William of Orange's victory over Catholic King James at the Battle of the Boyne, 1690, an annual public holiday and celebration of Protestant Unionism. Everyone with any sense cleared out of town for this Orange Order jamboree with its crowds and noise, its superficial gaiety and darker undertones of aggression and madness. But this year, I thought, I didn't mind being here. I must take the opportunity of living in the middle of it to observe it, to understand it more. It was after all part of the culture, like it or not. Moira was coming over to see me in the evening; there would be solace in that anyway.

In the run-up to the Twelfth, in the side streets of grimy brick terraces you passed on the bus going to and from work, bonfires were being constructed, piled sky-high with pallets, boxes, old furniture and car tyres, ready for late on the eleventh night, when they would burn triumphantly across the city, the flames consuming the effigy of the Pope surmounting each bonfire. A charming old ritual indeed.

I woke high in my attic late on the Twelfth holiday morning to the flutey strains of the first Orange bands coming up the Lisburn Road on the long march to the hallowed Field at Finaghy where they all congregated. Some atavistic impulse, or socio-investigative function of my brain, I couldn't be sure which, made me hurry and get dressed and take myself up Tate's Avenue.

In the hot sunshine crowds of spectators lined the Lisburn Road, the bright banners of the Orange lodges fluttered past and the bands played rousingly, marching one after the other. The pageantry and carnival excitement sort of grabbed you, it was true.

Some of the spectators had brought armchairs out on to the pavement to sit and watch the lengthy procession in comfort, with their knitting and flasks of tea. Others watched from the grandstand of first floor windows above the street. Running gangs of young teenage girls, tan needlecord jeans tight across the curves of their hips, their feet squashed onto empty drinks' cans, clattered and whooped gleefully as they weaved along the pavement after the bands.

"Pictures of the Big Fella!" A man came by selling photo-portraits of the Reverend Ian Paisley, the hero of defiant Loyalism (another name for Unionism). The big bake of the bellowing bumpkin would be just the thing for your mantelpiece, I told myself.

The colourful procession flowed endlessly, stretching as far as the eye could see in both directions, in a great river of triumphalism. A sort of prize eejit, the drum major, walked in front of each band swinging the mace, a long baton he twirled expertly around his body and tossed high, high up into the dreamy blue summer air, catching it deftly on its descent, as, unbrokenly, jubilantly, he weaved and skipped along the middle of the road.

The bands with flute, bagpipes, accordion worked their repertoire of marching tunes: *The Sash My Father Wore, Dolly's Brae, The Protestant Boys, We'll fight for no surrender, The Billy Boys.* The warlike tribal blattering of the giant Lambeg drums pulsed remorselessly through it all, "like a boot kicking the Pope to hell", one southern Irish observer had characterised it.

Though, ironically, the Pope of 1690 had *backed* Protestant King Billy in Ireland as a means of cutting the Sun King Louis down to size. In the same vein, for further political-economic advantage, the hierarchy of the Catholic Church had gone on to consistently oppose the movement for Irish independence; indeed they had declared that hell was not hot enough for the Fenians!

Maybe then the loyalists should have teamed up with the Catholic hierarchy?

The gorgeous rippling silk banners, mostly depicting heroic King Billy on his white charger at the Boyne, were carried proudly aloft on their poles, the tassels held by small boys. Each banner bore the number and district of its LOL, Loyal Orange Lodge. They came from the Orange halls of every obscure corner of the six counties, as well as from over the border in the Irish Republic, Scotland, Lancashire and Canada.

The Orangemen in their dark suits and Orange sashes and white gloves, sweating manfully under bowler hats in the blazing sun, brought up the rear of each lodge, marching in long uniform rows. Their conservative dress and appearance of stiff-necked sobriety contrasted with the colour and noise of the bands, banners and spectators, reminding you that this was no joke, it was a serious, respectable and reverent affair. I spotted the tall, distinguished figure of the Prime Minister, Captain Terence O'Neill, marching with his lodge. He was the English-accented, officer and gentleman face of the new, less illiberal 1960s' Unionism that Paisley so vehemently opposed as the latest sell-out.

After a while the novelty wore off, the selection of stirring tunes seemed to fuse into a migraine but still the procession kept coming. I felt it tawdrier and more played-out by the minute and it was a relief then to go back to the empty, quiet cool of the house in Tate's Avenue and read Thomas Mann.

Moira came to me in the evening when the bands had gone. As we walked through the debris up Lisburn Road, she pulled a face and said, "It's just the worst day of the year, isn't it?"

"I tried getting into it a bit today," I admitted, "like the spectacle and fun of the thing for its own sake, the bands and banners and the pretty girls. It'd be a laugh except there's no fun in it really, it's just bigotry with pretensions to something grander than that. You have to feel sorry for the people there today, they're not all bad, just pawns in the old ruling class imperialist game, you know, *'Heome rule, Reome rule! God save the King!'*"

"Ulstah will feight and Ulstah will be reight!"

"Great accent, Moira*! Remembah the spirit of Londondreh! No surrendah!*"

"*Not an inch!*"

"Who'd want to be like Carson and Craig or Brookeborough, nothing but ruling class scum, when you've got all the real, freedom-loving Protestant leaders on the side of Ireland: Wolfe Tone and Robert Emmett, Parnell and Sir Roger Casement, wonderful enlightened, heroic men and true democrats, which means standing up for *all* the people, not privileges for the few. And we gave Ireland the great poet Yeats: we could be quoting his '*terrible beauty*' instead of Carson's crap. We have all that proud Protestant tradition of bringing everyone in Ireland together; why don't we hark back to that?"

"Maybe things are changing now with Catholics and Protestants coming together in the civil rights movement," said Moira.

"It's never really been about religion on the Irish side anyway. It's imperialism that shamelessly exploits religion as a divide-and-rule strategy. But it's 1969 and imperialism has had its day, here and everywhere else. Ireland was Britain's first colony and it'll likely be its last. Us Prods need to move with the times, put the 'superior' colonist mentality with its racism and bigotry behind us and stop making an enemy out of the rest of Ireland. It's we who need to open our eyes, see what is real and change our attitude."

"I couldn't agree more." Moira spoke out of that quiet wisdom of hers, nothing more really than an innate decency. "Sooner the better!"

We kept away from the pubs that night. A few friends dropped by the house, including Bruce who'd been in the thick of the celebrations on Sandy Row. Irish traditional music was more his thing but it was no trouble to him mixing in with the music and drinking of the loyalists on the Twelfth; to Bruce it was all about the craic, the whole craic and nothing but the craic.

Moira stayed that night, the two of us sharing the narrow bed in the attic. After she had dropped off to sleep I lay there awake for a long time savouring the darkness and silence, her sleeping head on my shoulder, the baby-faced moon keeking in at the skylight, the blessed peace of night after such a day.

We woke in the light of advanced morning, her skin warm and soft against mine, her long black tresses over the shared pillow. Oh, the glory of waking up with your girl beside you; a man's life didn't get any better than this! She turned her sleepy, sweet morning face to me and I kissed it. Little black eyes regarded me frankly out of the mass of black hair; anxiety furrowed her brow.

"What time is it?" she asked, alarmed.

"Eleven."

"Oh God, I have to go! Mammy's expecting me for lunch and she goes funny if I'm late."

She jumped out of bed and I got a good look at her getting dressed, lithe and fine in her skin, unself-conscious and practical as she snapped her body into bra and pants, tights, then more pants, red ones over the tights. *Two pairs of knickers!* I was discovering the secrets of woman, who was still a vast mystery to me.

My sex life had been a furtive, forbidden, mole-like activity carried on in the dark. This was only the second time I had spent all night with a girl. It was a joy to lie back on my pillow and watch Moira dressing in the morning light, so natural and everyday, lovely in an ordinary real way that was truly intimate. She put on her red dress, stepped into her shoes and went clattering down the steep wooden stairs to the toilet. I lay very still listening in fascination and wonder to the sounds of her ablutions.

This morning of July the 13th a summer wind mooched through the litter that piled the gutters after the Twelfth marches. There was a hollow feeling of exhaustion over the city, the holiday streets seedy and dead under a muggy overcast sky. We journeyed swiftly on buses that seemed put on just for the two of us, me and my girl, side by side on the top deck. We swept along York Street, under Gallaher's great steeple. We were a couple who'd spent the night together and were doing ordinary things together now in the clear light of another day. I had everything now in Moira, a real nice girlfriend at last. I kissed her goodbye and got down at the station for a visit to my parents'. It was just another stop or two to Moira's street. Everything seemed to fit now, the jigsaw pieces of my life coming together in a satisfying pretty picture.

CHAPTER 15

Exile

Work at the ministry continued apace, a ruthless fact of life, relentless and inescapable. I took the bus out to Stormont each morning, slouched in my window seat on the top deck staring out with a weird sort of fascination at the unfolding grey streets coming to bustling life around me, as if I were seeing the world for the first time. We went over the bridge into East Belfast, nosed out through the grimy brick channels, past the shirt factory and the Aerated Dough Company, and then it was the long straight road out to the farthest suburbs.

Always arriving a bit late, I hurried up the quarter-mile of corridor to my office at the rear of the building to sign in before the supervisor drew the red line of shame across the page at ten-past-nine. Anyone signing under the line was officially late. Increasingly that was me. Then it was back down the corridor to the wee shop for twenty Number 6 and a bottle of Coke and my lunchtime egg and onion roll. Back in the office, settled at my desk, I quenched my hangover thirst with gulps of the chilled, fizzy, sweet dark drink and smoked my first cigarette of the day, swigging and puffing as I started on the morning post piled high on my in-tray.

After a year there I had a different, friendlier crowd around me. On one side was Mike, a young married Englishman, ex-RAF, he'd kept the moustache, a mild, friendly man with a light, soft voice and an air of dreamy lethargy, with droopy eyelids and a dry, bored wit. He was struggling to give up the fags.

"Try a pipe, Mike," I suggested, though I'd never had much luck with one myself.

Mike shook his head. "I smoked a pipe for a while, Jimmy; it was more of a hobby than a habit: shavin' the baccy, fillin' the pipe, gettin' it goin' then tryin' to keep it lit." He grinned his vague, gentle grin at the ridiculous hard work of living.

Mike was hard up on a civil servant's salary with a family to keep; he'd borrow a couple of quid off me coming up to payday. He was thin, pallid, enervated, with not much of an appetite. The missus always packed him a big lunch, half a dozen rounds of sliced pan made into sandwiches. The sight of Mike's generous packed lunch, the caring wifely touch about it, moved my heart strangely; it struck me as beautiful and yet sad; it was the way I saw marriage when I was that age. Mike was soon full up and offering the rest of his sandwiches round, waving the neat parcel under your nose. Maybe the wife was trying to build him up with all that bread, put some energy into him.

"She's a redhead, Jimmy, with a fiery Irish temper," he said. I suspected his studied passivity could be maddening to a woman at times, but if she was fiery then it was better he should remain his calm self.

Lesley was on my other side, eighteen and straight out of school into the civil service, poor girl. My heart sank at first sight of her, glaring out of square hornrims through heavy curtains of long dark hair, her solid figure rooted oak-like behind her desk, ready for a lifetime's service. I thought, "Oh my God, typical civil servant in the making!" But then I heard her speak, an attractive soft, clear voice with a gently mocking humorous inflection and she had turned out a real pal and confidante.

Lesley hated Tony McCurt. A philandering married man in his mid-twenties, with a large chip on his shoulder, McCurt brought a coat-trailing menace to our quiet corner of the ministry. Sleekit, mouthy and abrasive, bumptious and arrogant by turns, you either steered clear of him or tried to humour him. Desk cursorily cleared, he loafed back in a characteristic pose of indifference, feet up on the desk, fag on. I watched him over the scuffed leather soles of his shoes, his ankles crossed, fag wagging in his lips as he talked, like something out of a gangster film. He had the gangster look, a face off the cover of a Bulldog Drummond novel, blue-shadowed, hollow-cheeked, cleft chin, the cruelty of the turned-down mouth and cold grey-blue eyes. He blew smoke-rings or fired provocative comments over his feet at random colleagues, "Ach, look at yous all, a bunch of shiny-arsed clerks!" and so on. "When are yous gonna stand up for yourselves?"

There were frequent complaints about his rudeness. Then Shirley the supervisor would twitchily confront him, entreating him to mend his ways.

"Do you hear me now, Tony?" She blinked defensively behind the magnifying lenses of her glasses like an agitated school prefect, her face and throat flushed with indignation. "I don't want to have to file a report on you, Tony, but you're leaving me with no other option, honestly now."

"Ach, report away all ye like, Shirley!"

"Right-t, that's it this time!" Shirley whirled on her toes and flounced off, heels clicking assertively over the parquet.

But all that ever happened was McCurt would be called in for a cosy chat with the chief and things would quieten down till the next eruption.

Rod in the office told me how McCurt, an open and notorious philanderer, had had another woman in his bed while his wife was giving birth to their youngest child. Now he was stepping out with an attractive curvy brunette from the department. She seemed a nice girl too; I wondered what she saw in him. He had a smile that crinkled and lit up his face boyishly, a kind of wolf cub charm and he could turn a honeyed teasing patter on a girl, together with a high pressure salesman's persistence. Clearly some girls didn't mind that he was a married man; perhaps it flattered them in a way.

McCurt chided me variously for a "long-haired git" or a "lazy bastard" but always affectionately, like a chivvying big brother. More importantly, he laughed at my jokes; they were a sort of defence mechanism. I realised I was well in with him when he invited me back to his house after work one evening. It was a comfortable journey in his recently acquired car. At the neat semi-detached property in Andersonstown I met his wife Phil and their two young children Aidan and Deirdre. Phil was nice but I picked up right away on the strain between the young married couple, a coolness or vacancy more than anything else.

"Jim and I are just popping over the road for a quick one," he told Phil.

The pub was a nice middle class one. The lounge bar's long window looked out over the city below. I was glad to come among Catholics though I wondered why Tony would bother with me; we had nothing in common beyond working in the same office. I suppose I had that certain wit and a shy quality that was unthreatening. I could listen attentively for a long time with a natural empathy subduing my own ego.

"Come back and have some tea with us," Tony said as we drained our glasses.

"Are you sure?" I could have done with going home; I felt nervous about sitting there in the frozen atmosphere between husband and wife. I wondered if he was using me as a buffer between them.

"Come on! You must be hungry!"

"Will Phil not mind?"

"Course not! C'mon, I'll drop ye down to Tate's Avenue after."

We walked back over the road, into the tidy, quiet, unhappy little house. Aidan and Deirdre were in bed now. Phil had a smile for me; I felt more relaxed then. She put out the tea of sausages and beans and bread and butter and we all sat down together.

"Where is it you're from, Jim?" she enquired.

"Loughside, near Carrickfergus. Sleepy wee dump. I moved to the Lisburn Road in January, flat-sharing, that's been a lot better."

She nodded and smiled, genuinely interested in me, I thought. "You don't miss the home comforts then?"

"Not a bit, it's just great living with mates and having all your friends visit. There's always something to do and everything right on your doorstep. I used to miss the last train to Loughside sometimes after a dance and have to walk the eight miles home."

"I've always been glad I live in the city," she nodded. "I'd cousins I used to stay with at Rathfrisland. It was great being in the country when you were kids, playing out in the fields, but then there was nothing for you there once you got into your teens."

As she talked I became aware how attractive Phil was, dark and slim, my type. I supposed she was two or three years older than me but that was no longer so significant after Maureen. I felt more at ease with a woman than a girl. The mature woman, the mother, was a kinder, better woman. I wouldn't mind a wife like Phil, I thought, having my children. You'd think you'd have everything then. What had gone wrong in this marriage? Why on earth would a man cheat on a woman like Phil? It was so sad really. Well, I thought, I'd love you if you were mine! The drinks on an empty stomach, the intense little trio of us around the tea-table with the attention focused on me, the strange attractive woman; it had all gone to my head. Was I being hopelessly drawn to another married woman?

"You'll come and have tea with us again, Jim?" she said warmly as I made my exit. I thought just having another person there must have been a welcome relief for both of them. McCurt had been uncharacteristically restrained and charming throughout.

"I'd love to. Thank you, it was delicious!"

I felt myself a little in love with Phil. Back in my truckle-bed in my attic in the dark, I tossed and turned for a long time, feverish with thoughts and images of the dark young Catholic mother whose husband no longer wanted her, up the road in Andersonstown.

The promising relationship with Moira fizzled out sadly as autumn came on. I'm not sure what went wrong but it was entirely my fault, I acted like a vandal and later I would kick myself for being so boorish and crass towards her; she was a lovely girl in every way and with her departure something beautiful had been lost in my life. The reality, I suppose, was that I wasn't ready for a permanent relationship at twenty-one. I was unsettled, I hated my job, and Geoff and I were talking about moving to London. Paul, who had flunked out of art college at the first year exams, had already gone over with a gang from the Club Bar.

The liberation of moving into my own place seemed to go wrong for me that autumn into winter. It started with losing Moira. Then some sort of devil got into me. The drink played its part of course, the smiler with a knife. There was a big office party one evening at Stormont Castle. McCurt brought Phil and picked up Rod and his girlfriend and me in his car on the way. I'd had a few drinks and was dancing with Phil. She was so easy to be with, so gracious and lovely. There was about her also the dark beauty and mystique of a young Catholic Irishwoman, that acted like a sort of spell on me.

On the way home afterwards Rod was in the front with McCurt driving and I was between the two women in the back. I was very conscious of Phil beside me there in the dark of the back seat and as the car pulled into Tate's Avenue I could no longer help myself and while there was still time I turned to Phil and kissed her full on the mouth. She responded affectionately. It was just one kiss, passionate and pure, a moment of heaven on earth. The car pulled up outside my house. I knew by the bristling set of McCurt's head and shoulders and the alarmed looks of the others that he was aware of what had happened but I was too drunk with a mixture of whiskey and the strange wild romance in my head to care. I stumbled away in to bed.

I woke for work with a worse than usual hangover and the events of the night before rushing at me accusingly. I knew I had done something awful in social terms but a part of me was glad I had done it. Phil had welcomed my lips on hers; she was a free human being after all, not some man's slave. I'd reminded her how desirable she was and she was getting her own back on Tony and teaching him a lesson.

At work Rod came over to my desk, all moral disapproval, "What were you doing last night kissing Phil?" He was a nice-looking young fellow with sandy hair and bulgy blue eyes that fixed me interrogatively. "After you got out of the car McCurt started shouting at Phil and saying, 'Just wait till I get my hands on that bastard Mitchell!'"

I was strangely confident. "Okay, I was drunk but I can't honestly tell you I feel sorry for what I did, Rod." The brief but ravishing embrace shared with my dark Rosaleen had been too wonderful to ever regret.

Rod seemed to soften then, nodding in understanding and saying, "What does he expect anyway, the way he treats that woman. He got a taste of his own medicine for once."

All I got from Tony was a dirty hurt look. His pride was dented a little, that was all, a hiccup in his emotional life. Soon he was coming to me asking if he could bring his new girlfriend to my room one evening while I was out and I could hardly say no; I'd put myself in debt to him, a sinners' pact.

I never saw Phil again. To have followed that up might have been justified given his ongoing contempt for her feelings but it was more than I could handle and I never heard from her. I hoped that at least my moment of moral weakness had reminded her of what a beautiful person she was.

I took up with an old girlfriend, Linda, I bumped into at the student hop. She'd been a beauty round town as a schoolgirl in her mid-teens, with her long blonde hair and the little hippy bells sewn on her bell-bottom jeans. Nineteen now, she worked in the imperial civil service and was rather overweight. She went roistering round in a girl-gang, all ex-Ballyclare High School, Duck and Dilly and Suzy and Kat. I was drawn now to a forthright, feisty quality about Linda. She had an attractive clear voice with an endearing lisp, a little hoarse from chain-smoking and she was as drunk as I was. I wondered if she was a bit hard and indifferent, the way extraverts can be, but then we were dancing and she was gazing adoringly up at me, a swooning fan as she declared, "Oh Jim, you looked just like Michelangelo's David then, the way the light caught the side of your face!"

She wasn't joking either, but she had drunk a lot. I wanted a girl who'd worship me straight out like this. Perhaps Moira had been a bit undemonstrative. My self-esteem must have been poor; I seemed to need the constant reassurance of a woman.

I made a date with Linda, just the two of us, midweek at the Cobbles where she usually drank. It was an exciting prospect having this legendary local lovely to myself. But as we sat there drinking pints in the lounge bar I could see there was something wrong with Linda now. She drank too much too fast and smoked too much; her nerves were in tatters, she talked incessantly—not so much boring as plain neurotic. She was someone who fitted more into a crowded, blaring dance hall or party, the kind of places I disliked most. She knew everybody in Belfast there was to know; I was quiet and reticent. What did she see in me anyway? Soon she was the worse for drink and telling me she loved me but already I could see it wasn't going to work.

We went back to the empty house in Tate's and got down to a court on the lumpy sofa with the lights out. She had such a nice face still, with lovely full lips; we kissed, but she was too highly strung to settle into a half-decent court, she squirmed about and kept my hands at bay, then suddenly it was, "Oh my God, Jim, Ah'm gonna be thick!" and a mad dash for the loo. I sat on alone in the dark listening to her chuntering away at the top of the stairs.

"Ah'm sowwy, Jim!" She came back white and tearful and I suddenly felt awful sorry for her and was hugging and gently consoling her. "You drank too much, wee girl! C'mon, baby, I'll walk you to the bus stop. The night air will make you feel better."

"Oh, Jim! I'm such a w'eck! I don't know what went w'ong with me. They uthed to thay I was the betht looking girl at the Maritime and look at me now!"

"You're still beautiful, Linda."

"Och, Jim, Ah'm fat! Ah'm a fwiggin' fat dwunk! No wonder you won't want me now!"

"Who said that? Of course I want you! Look, bring your gang round on Friday night, the lads will all be here and we'll have an impromptu wee party, what about that?"

That worked better, our small sitting room filling up and everyone talking; a bit of courting in the firelight later before the girls' last bus. These social evenings became a regular thing for a while. But Linda would drink till she passed out and I took up with Kat instead, little and dark and quiet, the opposite to Linda.

"Linda might wake up!" she protested feebly as I kissed the face off her. "She'd die if she saw me with you! I don't want to hurt my friend!"

"Och, you needn't worry, sure she's stocious again!" I insisted. "Look at her there, out for the count!"

I stuck it out at work safe in the knowledge now that I would be leaving soon. Geoff and I had made up our minds to move to London. He wanted to break into advertising over there; I would take any old job while I wrote my first novel, then I'd start teacher training at Goldsmith's in the autumn. It was all very exciting and hopeful, the promise of a fresh start with all the freedom and opportunity of the metropolis.

There was nothing for me in Ireland any more, only a job I detested and too much drinking—the two went together like ugly twins. Shirley the supervisor, commenting on the constant oversights in my work, asked me sympathetically if I was on drugs, meaning prescribed medication. She was a middle-aged civil service spinster but a good-natured woman with an endearing touch of the young girl in her soft freckled face. I couldn't honestly blame her or the civil service for my plight; my being there at all was just one ghastly great mistake.

Then I got a letter from personnel cancelling my annual pay rise and transferring me to a renewed probationary appointment at the Larne local office. That clinched it. Brendan Behan writes that a sign should be displayed over Larne harbour: *"Welcome to sunny Larne. The wages of sin is death."*

This development left me with effectively no choice but to hand in my notice. I felt grateful to the ministry in a way. I told them I was leaving the civil service and moving to London after Christmas and they agreed to let me stay on at Stormont till then.

I could stick out the remaining couple of months. After all, my colleagues were here on a life sentence. There were occasional blips in the servile monotony of the daily routine, odd little self-defeating rebellions. One lunch hour a crowd of us got stuck into pints of beer down the pub and rolled back to the office an hour late on the afternoon shift in a queer, futile little show of insurgence.

Shirley was waiting for us, all a-twitch. "Boys, Mr McGovern is waiting to see you," she informed us.

We trailed along to the head buck cat's office; nobody seemed too bothered that we were in trouble; there was a sort of strength in numbers and the drink taken. McCurt, always up for a spot of coat-trailing, was the ringleader, he'd been spouting politics down the pub and we'd lost track of time. Then there was Rod and Gerry and Joe and me; we were enjoying each other's company, the way you did when Catholic and Protestant mixed; it was like the vitality you get in mixed male and female company. I especially liked Joe Meehan, an easy-going, smiley, rumpled bachelor.

McGovern's jaw was hanging out like Carson's statue but he dealt fair and square with his errant clerks. Rod, the union rep, was telling McGovern we'd just got carried away talking down the pub and really not noticed the time. It was an unlikely enough yarn for the boss to have to swallow, but then Rod, insolent with the drink, had to go and add for good measure, "Sure it's no worse than your senior management lunches that have a habit of going on all afternoon."

McGovern's jaw thrust out like a fist but he controlled himself, cocking a quizzical eyebrow, well able for this wee shite of a clerk. "Are you telling me it was a working lunch yous were having then, Mr Swarbrick? Eh? Well, I'm very pleased to hear of such devotion to duty!"

We got off with a warning this time. No doubt it was a way of averting a proper clerks' uprising that might threaten to tear down the huts and topple Carson's statue.

Soon McGovern was having bigger problems. The auditors had uncovered a racket, a web of half a dozen of the younger clerks who'd been constructing false claims then posting out benefit payments to themselves, the entrepreneurial spirit in action.

The first clerk they'd caught at it was Timmins, a skinny wee Mod boy with a bush of curly mouse hair. It was said that a fit-to-be-tied McGovern had personally ejected him from the building, propelled by a toe up the backside. Then there was someone I was vaguely friendly with since we'd started at the same time, Dick, an English lad, son of a major at Lisburn army barracks. Dick had once taken me for a run in his little green sports car, very low to the ground and fast. He showed me the glossy flesh in a *Playboy* magazine he kept under the seat. He was certainly a lad, with a taste for the good life.

Now he came to me, blue-suited, lanky and fair, his complexion the colour of chalk, hands shaking. "Jim, they're saying all these terrible things about me, that I've been fiddling the claims. Now *you* know, Jim, don't you, I would never do a thing like that?"

I nodded my agreement to comfort him. I'd got myself in enough trouble here but it seemed nothing now compared to this with a possible custodial sentence hanging over it. I think Dick had gone into denial about it. His da, the Major, would kill him. And how would Dick ever get another half-decent job after this? You couldn't help feeling sorry for him and Timmins and the others. We earned so little yet were entrusted with large sums of money every day. It was like the banks, where some clerk regularly hit the headlines in the local papers, caught fiddling the accounts, and received a lengthy prison sentence.

"The real crooks in the City of London get away with far worse every day," was my conservative audit inspector father's verdict.

There was rioting in Derry and Belfast that August of 1969. Barricades sprang up at the entrances of the side streets where the bonfires had been. The same thing was happening in Catholic areas. It was all about loyalist resistance to the civil rights movement. When I got to work one morning a policeman was posted outside the entrance. It was the start of the troubles. The strangest atmosphere hung over the city, an almost palpable tension in the air. Then one evening at Tate's Avenue we heard the commotion in the near distance and stepping outside could see the smoke from buildings on fire in West Belfast.

We stayed safe in the house together, taking comfort in the companionable group of us. Our faces wore expressions of bewilderment, innocence and even a kind of amusement at the dramatic, almost surreal turn of events in our home town. We played the Beatles' White Album and Dylan's *Nashville Skyline*; this was our culture, not whatever madness was going on out there in the streets, or so we liked to imagine. We were young and comparatively privileged and had no real idea of the extent of the misery suffered by some of our fellow citizens.

The news reported nationalists fire-bombed out of their homes, fleeing to refugee camps across the border. The RUC and the B-specials, the sectarian part-time police, were accused of joining in the riots on the loyalist side. Grainne at work, who lived up the Falls, said her brother had got hold of a gun for their family's protection.

Then the British Army arrived in the province to keep order. A soldier was posted at the entry next our front door. Prime Minister Terence O'Neill came on local television to appeal in his urbane, patronising liberal fashion for calm and tolerance towards one's "Cethlic" neighbours, who might be unemployed and have large families but were still human beings after all. His attempts at mild progress in north-south cooperation had angered loyalists as a sell-out. Similarly they distrusted Harold Wilson's Labour government in London and resented the intervention of the British Army on the streets of Belfast and Derry as sympathetic to the besieged Catholics. A good question then as now is how loyal is a Loyalist and to whom exactly are they loyal apart from themselves?

Once the August 69 rioting had blown over life went on much as usual for us lads in the shabby comfort of the terraced house with our visitors and booze-ups. We also enjoyed the cosy back streets' culture around us, the chippie round the corner and the off-licence across the road which harboured an illegal after-hours and Sundays' drinking den in its back room.

The days dwindled down towards Christmas and our departure to London. In this final period in Belfast I hit a rock bottom. I had come to a miserable dead end between the awful job and the ultimately self-destructive escapist boozing. Finally I was brought to my knees, physically and metaphorically, and in this state, one hungover Sunday morning in bed in the attic, I found myself asking for guidance from above. I had been an agnostic for some years and even as I prayed now, the way I'd learnt to in childhood, I wondered if I were just wasting my time, but it seemed there was nowhere else to go. Then what a relief; in a flash, it seemed, I saw what I must do: learn to love again, *starting with myself—*

In a new wholeness of being I kept more sober and started writing every day. The isolation of my icy garret was perfect for this; I began to set down memories of my childhood and youth in an exercise book. I felt the immense satisfaction as the pages filled with my handwriting and grew in number each day. Writing was a celebration of life. I wanted to write directly from my own experience like this, creatively but with nothing false or contrived. Real life was too interesting to be bothered with bullshit.

I accompanied my new daily writing regime with a more focused and consistent literary reading habit after joining the local branch library on Lisburn Road. Geoff shared with me this clear new sense of creative purpose. In the bedroom below mine he was painting wonderful delicate abstract pictures. It was the start of something new, a precursor to the cultured bohemian existence we anticipated in London.

I was back for Sunday lunch with my parents at Coolmore Green, a weekly occasion, the roast in the oven, big fire in the hearth, the neat, fragrant pile of ironed clothes waiting on my old bed ready for me to take back for another week at work.

Dad spoke to me man to man, a relationship of equals that had developed since I'd moved away to my own place.

"And you'd give up your good job, Jim, and run off to London just like that?" There was concern rather than criticism in his voice. After all, I was making myself unemployed and homeless, at least temporarily.

"I would, Edward. There's plenty of work in offices over there in London and I can start teacher training next year. And of course there's my big brother Ned there to keep an eye on me!"

"Aye, he'd be the warm mark for you to be depending on. Though he's a great fellow with the strangers. Sure he hasn't learnt to look after himself yet at thirty-three years of age. I just hope that wee Coalisland lassie of his, wee Nora, is putting some sense into his curly head."

My sister Dorothy and her husband Big Bill arrived for lunch. They'd returned to live in Belfast after some years in London. Bill was a big, six-feet-four, gentle man, hooded sleepy eyes in a craggy Rugby player's face, a winning boyish grin. He looked smart in his club blazer and tie, crisp pressed flannels, proffering his

Embassy packet after the meal, the two of us smokers in the front room, our chairs facing the winter sunshine in the bay window overlooking the green. Bill talked in a relaxed, expansive fashion, with a great warm, gravelly Belfast charm.

"I never really took to London, to tell you the truth, Jim," he was saying. "I always felt like a foreigner there with the English, as if I could never really belong in the place. Though they were nice people really and funny enough, when a colleague in my office got a girl into trouble I was the one he chose to confide in."

It struck me, however, that Bill was a real Belfast man, born and bred, he belonged here in a way that I never could. He'd grown up there on the Donegall Road, like his parents and grandparents before him.

"You have real roots here, Bill," I told him. "We were a railway family, forever on the move from one town to the next, south to north, and west to east. I have no real sense of belonging in any one place, I mean except maybe Ireland as a whole."

Bill's story only confirmed in me the conviction that personal relationships were what mattered most wherever you went. The largeness and centrality of London drew me, the opportunities it presented, the social variety and culture it offered; all that was exciting and liberating. I had exhausted the potential of Belfast, there was nothing here for me any more and it was time to go.

I finished work at the Christmas break. The office organised a leaving card and collection for me. I was surprised by the staff's friendly messages on the card and their generosity, it ran contrary to the story I'd been telling myself that I was nothing and nobody in this place. I went round the desks saying goodbye. I was reminded that there were a few of them I had come to really like: Grainne, Rod, and a fanciable new girl from Carrick, Elaine, with short Mod blonde hair—alas, it was never to be, though I did write to her from London—no reply. And Joe Meehan: "You're going to be a writer?" he said. "You know, that's something I'd love to do, write a book."

I must have said something down the pub about my writing. "I'm going to try," I told Joe. This was getting better: *I was going to London to be a writer!* Well, why not? It was a good story.

The early December dark was closing in on the windows of the huts; it was cosy in the yellow-lit interior with the Christmas decorations up. Unbelievably I felt a pang of sadness to be leaving and worse still, *a sense of guilt*, as if I were betraying these people in some way.

We had a few days after Christmas prior to our departure. In the wintry sunshine Geoff and I took our unwanted clothes to the pawn shop on Sandy Row; a couple of quid each he paid us for the lot, it was hardly worth it, but we had to travel light and every penny counted.

I packed the one small suitcase, the grey cardboard one I used to take on holidays to my aunt and uncle in North Antrim; it still had the Ulster Transport Authority label on it, *Belfast to Portrush, August 1962*. Ah, that last steamy summer there with wee June in the hayloft! First love, ah! June had married at sixteen, I'd heard, with a couple of kids now. That girl didn't hang about!

Mum insisted on packing my electric blanket. We were booked on the Liverpool boat, night crossing, Tuesday 6th of January, 1970. I was one month short of my twenty-second birthday. It was one year since I'd moved out of my parents' house into the flat in Belfast. That had seemed such a big deal at the time and here I was now leaving Ireland, going away across the water to London. My old primary school teacher Michael Gibson drove me to the boat. I had character references from him and from Mark Moriarty, headmaster at the Belfast Royal School.

Geoff was all ear to ear grins and zany enthusiasm for our big adventure and we were off aboard the night ship, feeling the thrill of its stately progression, sure as fate, out along the docks and up the Belfast Lough in the winter dark. I ventured out on the windy deck to spot the lights of Loughside estate going past and think of my mum and dad there cosy by the fire and tele.

I had £60 in my wallet, a small fortune; a safety pin secured it in the inside breast pocket of my jacket. I had arranged temporary digs for us and the prospect of employment through the Emerald Staff Agency in Kilburn—Dad had spotted their ad in the *Belfast News Letter*. Everything was ordered and hopeful, it was a new decade, a new city, a fresh start.

"We must be passing the island soon!" said Geoff back in the yellow light and sickly warmth of the saloon and we went outside again to stand shivering in the blasting wind over the deck rail.

The ship was moving out into the Irish Sea, ploughing swiftly and powerfully through the furrowed, infinite dark heaving mass of water. We saw the lighthouse beam close by, stabbing the wild black darkness. Lighthouse Island! Then the indistinct shape of our island. It was strange to think of the little wooden house huddled there in its cove facing out to sea, its dark interior illuminated momentarily by each stroke of the lighthouse beam; the empty dark rooms filled with the ghosts of those carefree youthful years of friendship and carousal, guitars and girls around the crackling driftwood fire—.

PART TWO

A STRANGER ON THE EARTH

"I am a stranger on the earth—"
Vincent Van Gogh

CHAPTER 16

Snow, Kilburn

It was the 7th of January, 1970. The morning train from Liverpool whisked us south across the flat rural expanses of England with the sun dazzling on the patchy snow. Mid-morning, Geoff and I stood in the buffet car enjoying a beer in celebration of our journey to the glad new life in the big city. The warmth of the alcohol in our blood commingled with the winter sunbeams streaming through the carriage window to produce an inebriated sense of liberation and well-being. We wore big fixed grins, for here we were now, the months of planning come to fruition, our escape from the home town made good. London waited at the end of the line, a place big enough to accommodate our imagination, possibilities unlimited.

Out through the mighty portals of the great milling, echoing cavern of Euston station we took a taxi, as advised: "The Emerald Staff Agency, Kilburn High Road, please!" We were a couple of Irish lads arriving here like so many before us, gangs of us digging for gold in the streets.

The sunlit cold midday city streets, snow lining the gutters, opened out before us, bustling, racing, thrilling. We'd come to a real city here; Belfast was a village by comparison. Figures out on the pavement, glimpsed from the taxi window, seemed charged with significance; there was an aura of sophistication about them, they belonged here at the pulse of the world.

The Emerald Staff Agency was some way up the High Road, over a shoe shop. The man in the little office introduced himself as George White, a native of Cork. He had the soft, easy southern way about him, said to mask the shrewdness of the Cork man, and it was first things first: "Lunch time. There's a nice restaurant on up the High Road, before the railway bridge. I'll just let the landlady know you're here and you can drop off your cases. I'll tell her you've come over to work in the bank, she likes that." He dialled; an answering squawk issued from the receiver. He said, "Mrs Maloney? The Belfast boys for the bank are here. I'll send them on round to you. Thanks. Okay, men, and I'll see you back here at half-past-two."

The lodging house was just round the corner in a side street. Two terraced houses had been knocked through into one. It was Mr Maloney who came to the door, welcoming and polite, "Come in, boys." Gaunt, grey, stooping, his carpet slippers shuffled on the red tiles of the long narrow hallway and he called up the stairs, "They're here!"

Her squawk came from a room above, "Putt them in Tommy's room at the back!" She sounded just like my Auntie Kitty on the farm at Bushmills, calling down the stairs from her afternoon bed to Uncle Archie.

Our room was off the end of the hall, its sash window overlooking the backyard. Three single beds occupied most of the floor space. There were two small armchairs, one either side of the electric fire, a wardrobe in one corner of the chimney breast and a washstand in the other.

"These are your beds, together here, men," Maloney explained in his courteous Irish fashion. "Tommy's in the corner there. You won't see much of him, he's either working or sleeping. You'll need shillin's for the meter for the electric fire and the bath upstairs. The rent is five pounds a week payable in advance plus a week's deposit you'll get back when you leave. The price includes breakfast and dinner. We don't do lunch what with everyone out in the daytime. Dinner's from six to seven. Now here are your keys, front door and room. Is that all okay? Well, thank you, boys, I'll leave yous to it."

He bowed out deferentially, respectful of our white-collar status, I felt, and half-apologetic for the basic working men's lodgings he was providing for us. We shoved our cases away under our beds and stood there taking stock of the room for a minute. It was shut away from the sun, gloomy and chill. A faint metallic smell seemed connected to our room-mate Tommy.

"Good value anyway!" I exclaimed nervously; it certainly wasn't Cheyne Walk.

But Geoff didn't seem to mind. "Aye, full board for a fiver a week! How do they do it? Pack in the guests, I suppose. It'll give us a chance to look round for a flat of our own."

We walked up busy Kilburn High Road towards the iron railway bridge and saw the restaurant, green gingham curtains in the windows, matching tablecloths within, genteel and homely. The busy young waitress found us a table; the place was packed for lunch, humming with the energy of the city.

And here we were, enjoying our very first meal in London! It was a euphoric feeling; you had to pinch yourself to believe you were here. In my excitement I sent a fork flying; the waitress looked strained as she retrieved it from the floor and I felt like a clumsy oaf. It was good British fare, roast beef and two veg, apple pie and custard. We sat back afterwards sipping coffee, sated and glowing. We were housed and fed now; soon we'd have jobs, money coming in. It was all so easy and natural, everything on a plate.

Back at the Emerald Staff Agency George White pronounced, "Now, there is one thing I have to say to you, boys. The first thing you must do is get your hair cut. The companies we deal with just won't employ long-haired young men. That's the long and the short of it! Apart from that you'll have no problem finding work with your GCEs and previous experience."

We nodded faintly. We'd grown our hair for coming to London. This was a set-back!

George White looked at our application forms. "Now Geoff, you are looking to break into advertising here in London? Good. I have nothing on my books at the moment but I will make enquiries this afternoon. We will get there alright.

"Jim, you are looking to a future career in teaching but need to fill in till next autumn. That's no problem; there is so much work in offices. Is there anything that interests you particularly? Banking, the City? No. A small firm then? There are plenty of those here in North London . . ."

"Yes, maybe—"

We left it there, to call back in the morning and see what George had come up with.

Outside the afternoon was already growing dark, the sun extinguished by grey clouds, a bitter-cold evening coming on, our cold room waiting for us. Leaflets had been shoved through the front door advertising the Clancy Brothers at the Albert Hall. We fed the meter with shillings, drew our chairs up to the two-bar electric fire on the wall. Geoff had picked up an *Evening Standard* and was checking through the situations vacant, page after page of them in long, closely-printed columns.

"No wonder so many people live in London, all the work's here," he said.

I'd had enough of job talk for one day and was writing a letter home using the Basildon Bond hammered vellum blue writing pad and envelopes Mum had given me requesting, "Just a wee line to say 'arrived safely'."

It seemed the minute I set foot in London the writing bug got hold of me and I was scribbling away excitedly at my letter home, faithfully recording telling details such as "the second-hand book left on the mantelpiece, *Murder Gone Mad,* seems an ominous clue to the identity of our mystery room-mate Tommy!"

With the heat of the red electric bars on my shins, the armchair at my back, the pen moving swiftly across and down the writing paper, I was master of my own destiny. When you wrote about things you controlled them; you put yourself at the heart of living and everything became manageable and friendly.

The window had gone black, reflecting the bleak room in the dingy electric light. I said, "My shins are roasted sitting here but my back's cold!"

"I'm starvin' wi' the hunger!" said Geoff. "I can smell stew!"

Soon there came Mrs Maloney's unearthly shriek of "*Dinaaar!*"

Going through to the back of the house we were greeted by the high dancing flames of an open coal fire. The boarders sat crowded at long tables while Mrs Maloney and a couple of vigorous younger women bustled to and fro serving dinner.

Geoff and I were directed through another door into a smaller dining room occupied by a single long table with big navvies seated cheek by jowl around it. We were shown to the remaining two empty chairs together mid-table. We squeezed in uneasily among the big, surly, powerful-looking men, middle-aged to elderly, with their weather-beaten faces and large hands.

The meal was taken in a queer hostile silence interspersed with odd grumbles, you couldn't call it conversation. Over the table there hung an atmosphere of suppressed violence. They must have been exhausted from their day's labours out on the building sites. The effect was uncomfortable and intimidating. Even Geoff with his easy, sociable disposition, kept his head down; I caught a look of fear on his face. You wanted to hide your educated voice and soft hands.

However, we were hungry and didn't leave until we had eaten everything on offer. It was identical to the big meals I'd had at Aunt Kitty and Uncle Archie's farm on childhood holidays: the thin broth to start, the main course of stew, bowls of cabbage, turnip and potatoes; tinned fruit and custard for pudding, tea and biscuits to finish.

It was a relief, however, to finish eating and get out of there in one piece, away from the claustrophobic menace around the table.

"Heavy characters," said Geoff. "But plenty of grub, which was good."

"Room for a pint?" I enquired.

"Oh aye! One thing's certain, I'm not for staying in," he laughed, nodding at the desolate room. The fire had gone out, the meter empty.

"Kilburn, here we come!" I trumpeted. "Find a nice pub with an open fire and traditional Irish music maybe!"

"Maybe meet some nice wee Irish girls!" said Geoff.

"Aye, now you're talkin', fella! Hurry!"

Outside, the freezing cold penetrated our big winter coats. We walked down the High Road between the cold light of shut-up shop windows and the kerbside banks of dirty slush, looking for the bright, warm welcome of a nice pub. But each one we looked in on was uninviting, either a menacing shebeen or a stark cavern. There was a dead, midweek, midwinter feeling; too cold for the people to come out of their houses, apart from eejits like us. We plodded on, the dream of hot toddies and craic around an open fire rapidly receding.

It began to snow, big soft feathery flakes drifting down silently through the sodium light. Running out of steam then, just needing to be indoors, we landed up in a big renovated bar, a sort of palace to plastic modernity. The taped country-and-western playing promised some sort of life here but the only other customers were a gang of navvies playing cards quietly over in a corner. We got our tall cold glasses of the black and white stout and sat in another corner.

"More of the lads from the building sites over there," said Geoff. "They endure a miserable kind of bachelor existence."

"I never saw such a dour lot as the men round that dinner table tonight," I said. "Whatever happened to Irish craic?"

"Left it behind them in Ireland?"

With those words the depression struck at the two of us, simultaneously, like being hit with a stick. We sat there speechless, sinking in a black rising tide, our entire awareness narrowed to the bleakness of this single point in time, the exhaustion at the end of the long journey, the long day, the sudden overpowering sense of alienation and loneliness in the strange city, the empty, ugly barn of a pub with its lost, sad card-players and whiney music, the cold beds in the navvy house awaiting us.

Over the drinks on the table our eyes met, saying it all: *What on earth are we doing here?* Of course we didn't dare speak it, that would be the end. I had never seen Geoff, my cheerful mate, look like this before, so utterly crestfallen with the big sad saucer eyes of a lost boy.

Mistake! It was all a mistake, our coming here to London. Maybe it was just a nightmare and we'd wake up safely back in

Belfast where we belonged. Oh, if only. What foolishness, what vanity had led us here? Now everything was lost.

We drained our glasses joylessly, the sour chill of the stout making us shiver. There was only one thing for it.

"Early night?"

"Aye. We're exhausted. We'll feel better in the morning."

Outside the snow was falling thickly now, carpeting the pavement. But we felt none of the childlike excitement of it; rather it only added to the harshness and desolation of the late street so far from home, with the anonymous traffic swishing through, the sense of obscurity and loss.

The snow seemed to seal our wintry fate.

It was only half-nine but the lodging house was shrouded in the deep exhausted silence of sleep. Turning on the light in our room we saw the hump in the bed, the shaggy dark head on the pillow, Tommy, already fast asleep. His old-iron smell commingled with the residual warm, vinegary smell of chips, the greasy wrappings discarded in the bin.

We undressed quickly, silently, got in our pyjamas, light out and into bed. Past caring, I didn't bother even to brush my teeth. Shivering down between the icy nylon sheets I shut my eyes tight against the fact of my existence.

I could hear the even sleep-breathing of the other two but I lay there wide awake in the horrible enveloping darkness and silence of the strange house in the strange uncaring city.

The bedclothes were too light; I was cold. I remembered my electric blanket from home that Mum had packed in my case, sensible lady, but it was too late for me to think of that now. Eventually I sat up and reached out of bed for my overcoat on the chair and spread that over me on the bed. Then I ducked down under the bedclothes into the foetal position, the way I'd done as a school-child, only me and the dark down there, cocooned from reality.

Now visions of Home came to torment me. I could *feel* 5 Coolmore Green, the brightness, warmth and comfort of my parents' house. Then my thoughts turned in dreadful longing to the ease and familiarity of the life I had known in my home town, and one by one the dear faces of all my friends. I had to ask myself over and over again, in incredulous horror, what madness had brought me here to this cold bed in the great indifferent metropolis?

Homesickness. My mother had told me how she suffered it as a girl at boarding school in Dublin at the beginning of every school year. She spoke of it as a diagnosis, a proper illness, a disease you could catch, and now I understood what she meant; it ached through my brain and bones like rheumatism. Maybe there was a pill you could take for it?

When sleep came at last I dreamt I'd returned home, they'd taken me back in my old job on the Corporation, where I had been so happy without realising it at the time. I was sitting at my old sloping desk. I felt a supreme contentment now, knowing at last that this was where I truly belonged.

The dream was so vivid, so concrete and real, as dreams can be, that waking in the morning in the room in Kilburn was like the shock of a pitcher of cold water poured over my head. *"No! No! No!"* I wanted to cry out like a lunatic waking in an asylum.

It was Mrs Maloney's head round the door and her whispered wake-up call to Tommy that woke me. I sank back in despair, instantly wide awake. I thought Tommy must have gone back to sleep, then he heaved himself up with a groan of bedsprings, and sat on the side of the bed yawning and scratching his head for a minute. He dressed in the dark, very quickly, grunting as he bent to tie his bootlaces, and was gone out the door.

I lay on watching the darkness thinning in the room, the outline of the furniture materialising. I dozed off and was woken again by the electric light and Geoff's brisk morning movements. When I raised my head to acknowledge him, he grinned, "Good morning!" and sluicing himself at the washstand he sang in an Irish country voice, *"Gude marnin', gi-irl, an' how's the wor-ld with you-ou!"*

I said, "You're getting in form there for fratting with the culchies!"

"Sure am't I a culchie meself!" says he. "Ballynahinch born and bred."

"Did your ancestors follow Henry Joy to the gallows? Geoff, you're always so damn cheerful in the mornings. How do you do it?"

"Ach, *'get up outta that, ye impudent brat'*—!"

"*'And let Mr Maguire sit down!'* You know what, mate, I feel more Irish here than I ever did in Ireland!"

"I suppose you take it for granted there. Hey, smells like the full Irish cookin' in Ma Maloney's kitchen. I'm famished, so I am!"

"Ugh, think I'm gonna be sick!"

"Call yerself an Ulstermon and ye can't thole a gude fry in the mornin'?"

"I'll try," I said, sitting up and pulling on clothes. "Brrr! It'll take something to warm us up before we go out in the snow! I thought London was supposed to be warmer than Belfast."

The pain of homesickness had lifted with the darkness of night, leaving nothing worse than a dull ache, like a half-forgotten love affair. Geoff had a way of making himself at home in any surroundings. We might have been back in our flat in Dunluce Avenue a year ago, going through one of our morning comedy routines of bad songs and funny voices. Life goes on the same everywhere, the thought came to me comfortingly. At least I'd not ended up in Larne! Let's face it, that was the reality of the old life.

Mrs Maloney's big kitchen with its lovely penetrating warmth, the bright welcome of its hearth with the orange tongues of flame licking up the throat of the chimney, the smell of bacon frying, put the glad life of the God-given new day into you. There was plenty of room at the tables here around the fire, the navvies like Tommy gone for their early start. It was a good feeling too being served by the youngish woman helper with her full-bosomed, reassuring movements, the fresh look of the Irish countryside in her complexion, her brisk, capable hands bearing copious platters of steaming fries to place before us, pot of tea, rack of toast, butter and marmalade. With the sudden sense of well-being my appetite came back with a vengeance and I fell on the food ravenously, losing myself in the intense, immediate, deep comfort of feasting.

We sat back replete, lingering over a third cup of the hot sweet tea drunk close to the open fire. Most of the diners had gone now, only a pair of older navvies sitting together at the next table. A big old wireless was blarting away high in a corner; a news item about the latest war in Africa had got them going on imperialism.

"De same old story everywhere dey've been," one of them lamented in his fine brogue.

"Aye, take what dey want outta de place, den carve it up like a Christmas turkey."

"Den feck aff l'avin' de people at each udder's t'roats."

Geoff and I smiled at each other. I said, "Sounds a bit like the British in Ireland and all!"

Geoff was going for his haircut that morning. I wasn't; I thought I'd try the Labour Exchange instead of the Emerald Staff Agency. On our way out Mrs Maloney spoke to us. A small, grey, lame figure, she reminded me more than ever of Auntie Kitty.

"You're from the North," she said. "Protestants, are you? Well, nobody cares what you are over here. I have a couple from Belfast, Lily and Cedric, they're Protestants, been with me six months, they fit in the best. Cedric's a painter, he's been redecorating for me, Lily does some cleaning. They've been a great help to me altogether. How are you getting on with Mr White at the agency? I know there are good openings in the bank over here for young men like yourselves. Och, there's anny amount of jobs in London for those who are willing to work. I had one of the lodgers come to me the other day looking for a letter for the social security and him only just off the boat. Anyway, I wish you luck, boys and we'll see you for dinner tonight."

There was a good fall of snow in our side street, a Christmas card scene that gave you a fresh, beautiful feeling like a new birth. Our breath smoked and our cheeks glowed, like happy urchins at play in the snow-light.

The traffic ground away up and down the High Road, through the brown slush. The crisp air and unstoppable energy of the big city morning worked like a tonic on us. The homesickness was forgotten. In reality the world was at your feet here and. already I knew in my heart I had come here to stay.

"Oh, what a lovely accent!" the girl serving in the newsagent's cooed at me. "I can tell where you've come from!"

I smiled nervously at her, glad of her appreciation—I'd soon enough encounter its opposite—but suddenly lost for words I grabbed my change and scuttled away out the door, just wanting to fade in with the rest of the neutral workaday hordes. Oh dear, hope I didn't seem unfriendly! It struck me that I was now an ambassador for my country, for Ireland. Yes, the whole of Ireland, thirty-two counties!

At the Labour Exchange at Edgware Road the young woman clerk who interviewed me was very friendly too. What was all this stuff you heard about unfriendly Londoners and English? She saw I'd worked at the ministry in Belfast and said I could have a similar job right here in her office if I liked. I politely declined.

"Tired of big organisations?" she suggested. "Don't worry, I have another opening that might suit you better." She fished out the details. "It's a cosmetics firm at Hendon. You can do well with these small companies, rise to a senior managerial position in no time at all. Not like the civil service!"

I felt interested for a moment, imagining something small and cosy and personal, different to the anonymous treadmill of government offices. Somewhere my good looks, intelligence and natural Irish charm would be appreciated. I could really live the Joe Lampton dream now of room at the top. That was the way my mind worked at twenty-one, along the lines of my favourite novels and films. It could be Joe Lampton one day, Raskolnikov the next.

"Okay," I nodded. The pleasant, helpful woman made the phone call and arranged the interview: 11.15 at Hendon.

I had an hour or so to kill. I found a cheap café and sat over a coffee, looking out on busy Edgware Road. I was filled with the glory of the fresh start, the endless possibilities of the new life here in London. The barging traffic, the people on the street; I was part of something really big and kind of noble that truly fired my imagination. My hand itched for pen and paper. I must set-to faithfully recording the impressions and sensations that assailed you here at the centre of everything. If you were ever going to be a writer you would surely do it here.

I sat there a long time lost in a dream, an old habit of mine. Coming round slowly again I suddenly remembered the interview at Hendon and very casually decided not to go. It was, after all, just more of the same office life I had endured back in Belfast. It was time to break with that, to begin to live the creative life. I had no plan, I just knew I must do it, *now*. I stepped out on to the pavement of the hammering road and started walking, directionless. I moved in the living moment, free of encumbrances, past or future, just following my nose. Soon I was on a tube going to Trafalgar Square. I needed to be at the centre of things.

I emerged in the glittery, steely snow-light with the vaguely sinister impression of the large dark old buildings, Nelson so high on his column. I walked around, looked in at the National Gallery and browsed the bookshops on Charing Cross Road. The cash in my wallet would keep me going for now. When it ran out I'd wash dishes or something, I'd done that before. It occurred to me I might like to work in a bookshop, to read a lot and to write, they went together. I'd ask around the bookshops. I had come at last to the life I'd always longed for. Funny, you made things so difficult for yourself when it was all so simple really, just waiting here for you all the time.

CHAPTER 17

Hunger

After dinner that night—we kept our heads down and ate up quickly in the atmosphere of muted aggression around the long table of navvies—Geoff and I visited my brother Ned and his fiancée Nora at Willesden, just one stop north on the Bakerloo line. Out of the station you followed a long, cold, dispiriting road of narrow-fronted terraces curving away gradually forever, until you came to their number, 113.

Past dustbins, up a long garden path to the dark front door, the illuminated bell-tag for the ground floor back bore the names Mitchell and Devlin. That's my name, I thought; it seemed strange to see it here, so far from home. I felt shy suddenly and I pressed the bell reluctantly, scaring myself as I heard its rusty ring deep within the house. I waited there with a sick, lost, hopeless, dreary feeling, suddenly unsure of what I was doing here in London after all.

A light sprang up within and brisk clattering footfalls came up a long hallway, a shadow loomed in the narrow pane of frosted glass and the door flew open revealing the tall, dark figure of my elder brother.

"Come in, boys, quick! Jasus, it's could!" He ushered us over the drab linoleum wastes down the passage to one side of the stairs, into the small flat. Cosy heat enveloped us; there was a gas fire burning full on and a free-standing green dalek of a paraffin heater, the lovely warmth like home in Ireland; I was glad to be here just for that. There was a whiff of paraffin oil, residual aromatic dinner smells, sautéed onions and herbs, and somewhere behind it a cottagey dampness. The overall effect was very homely, like a piece of Ireland here in London.

Nora emerged from the kitchen at the back, a striking-looking young woman with long, straight, shiny black hair, large blue eyes and a proud aquiline face, like a Spanish dancer. I recalled her as having been somewhat withdrawn on a brief visit to our house in Loughside, but now she came forward to greet us warmly, all soft vibrant young womanhood, shining on us like the sun.

Just minutes ago there'd been no hope. Now the dark and cold and strangeness of the London night was banished in the warmth and hospitality of the young couple in the small flat.

"What brought you to London?" Ned asked then in his blunt cynical way, making you doubt your motives.

Why not? I said to myself but said aloud, "Oh, we'd both of us reached a dead end in Belfast. There was nothing for it but to move away and try something different."

"Some place bigger," said Geoff. "But not as far away as Canada or Australia!"

Ned was amused by our account of dinnertime in the navvy lodging house, the big steaming platefuls of stewed meat consumed in a baleful silence.

"Brings it all back to me," he said, "the digs in Camden Town when I first came over in 1956, Pat Fitzgerald and I working on the building sites. We'd get back from work shattered, ate an enormous feed of meat and spuds and turnip and cabbage and be fit for nothing after that. We'd get into bed then and read till our eyes closed."

Now Ned was an Art teacher in a boys' secondary school in Cricklewood.

"That one of your lads?" I asked, looking at a framed head and shoulders portrait of a black teenage boy hanging on the wall.

"Aye, Delroy. Good kid, happy to sit for me for ever, he was. They're nice lads, most of those I teach; the problem's just a handful of bad little buggers spoiling it for everyone else for as long as they can get away with it. They can't with me, but you should hear the Head, slimy liberal wanker; if there's trouble it's the teacher's fault every time, as far as he's concerned. Never 'the kids' as he refers to them in a hushed, reverent tone of voice, as if teaching them was some kind of a religion—you should hear the soft-voiced tosser. I'm permanently in his bad books since my colleague Taff Edwards and I decided to take matters into our own hands one day—"

"Show them your press cutting!" Nora laughed.

He fished in a drawer, produced the clipping from the local paper:

Mass caning at Cricklewood Boys' School

"A riot broke out in the dinner queue," Ned explained. "It was an us or them situation. I was lucky having Taff on dinner duty with me that day; he's a London Welsh Rugger boy, up from the Rhondda, somebody you can count on when the chips are down. Anyway, we got the canes and set to, restoring order."

Nora said, "We've had a brick through the front window of the house here, the old lady's flat at the front—they thought it was Ned's place."

"I'm a wreck!" Ned moaned. "I'm on tranquillisers to cope with teaching and I'm wheezy living in this damp hole. Can you smell it? We keep the heating on all the time but it still gets to you. Of course the bastardin' landlord won't lift a buckin' finger!"

The inside door of the water closet which I visited was papered with cuttings from socialist newspapers highlighting the outrageous goings-on of a capitalist system that was nothing more than legalised grand larceny. A revolutionary loo.

But soon Ned was talking light-heartedly again; his moods swung constantly. Now it was funny stories about the school with affectionate mimicry of cockney and Jamaican voices. He squirmed in his armchair with nervous energy, living the parts, crossing and uncrossing his sticklike legs with sudden vicious knee-jerks. Then suddenly he was up on his feet reaching for his overcoat.

"Time for a gargle!" he announced. "You coming, Nora?"

"I'll stay. Marking," she said, another teacher, French and Sociology.

"C'mon then, lads, we'll walk up to the Crown, Irish pub. Have you heard of it? It's in the song *McAlpine's Fusiliers*:

> 'The crack was good in Cricklewood,
> There was trouble at the Crown,
> There was bottles flying and babies crying
> And Paddies going to town . . . !'

"Aye, '*Paddies*'?"

"We can join in then!" said Geoff.

From the house we proceeded on up the road but its dread, frozen monotony was gone now; behind its windows were warm, lighted homes like the one we'd just left and every flying footstep keeping up with Ned's pace took us nearer the promised excitement of the Crown.

Soon we were crossing the Edgware Road to the great roadhouse, like a castle there. There was a dance in the hall at the back, girls glammed up heading in there. We stood with the men in the big public bar. Everyone was Irish. Later a folk group came on and sang Irish songs, one of them about James Connolly, the rebel leader of the 1916 Easter Rising.

"Look!" said Edward. "Your man coming: Blind Pugh!"

The blind man reached us, rattling his collection box. Edward dropped a silver coin in and the blind man moved on grimly, never a thank-you.

"Collecting for the victims of the troubles," said Ned. "I'd say he's a veteran of the struggle, that one, sight lost in action."

It was thrilling to stand there drinking in the London Irish crowd at the bar, out of the cold winter's night, and begin to feel a part of it all.

Geoff and I settled into a routine of job-hunting, going about our separate ways each morning, meeting up later. I walked for miles round the West End, registering with staff agencies, checking the situations vacant in the *Standard* as soon as it came out around midday. Geoff did the rounds of the advertising agencies; they seemed interested but there was nothing definite yet.

I hoped I might stumble into some unusual creative kind of dream job. I'd no idea what but surely anything was possible in London; maybe working for an enlightened small publisher of novels and poetry by unknown writers and they could publish me too. Failing that, I could work in a bookshop, reading the books or scribbling away at my novel in the lulls between customers. I hung round the bookshops on Charing Cross Road; I was thrilled to discover a whole secret side street of *magic* bookshops, shades of Yeats and Crowley, like a doorway to another secret world. But somehow I was too shy to ask any of them for a job.

I whiled away some hours at the National Gallery. I loved the massive dark old paintings with their vivid living faces and wondered about getting an attendant's job there. To be able to stand and stare at the paintings and the flow of life through the place would suit me better than being stuck in an office poring over ledgers. I definitely didn't want a career any more, like the ones I'd tried in Belfast. I wanted a mind uncluttered by the day's work, to be able to write when I went home in the evenings.

The snow didn't thaw, the grey days grew colder. Keeping the cold and hunger at bay often preoccupied me. My feet wouldn't warm up and I splashed out on a pair of fleece-lined shoes I'd been eyeing up in Lilley and Skinner's window on Kilburn High Road. But of course new shoes for tramping miles of streets daily turned out a bad idea; your feet swelled and the shoes began to pinch and I was soon crippled with blisters.

A ferocious, insatiable hunger gnawed at my guts all day. It was the cold weather and walking miles every day, and perhaps the hiatus of joblessness I occupied. I was conscious of my appetite as an unwelcome additional expense as I filled up between main meals with snacks of egg and chips and two slices washed down by tea in one of the greasy cayfs I favoured; then chocolate bars and crisps to keep me going on the street. Even after the copious dinner at the lodging house I was ready for takeaway chips again before bedtime. At times there were mad salivating cravings for sweets I hadn't eaten since childhood, like the thick pink and white bars of coconut icing—this on a Sunday night with all the shops shut, persuading Geoff to accompany me on a fruitless search for a sweetie shop in the desolate streets around the Elephant and Castle where we had been visiting friends from Belfast.

I wrote letters home to Ireland every day, to family and friends and some girls I had scarcely known there but sought to impress now. They were overlong letters dramatising my emigrant's plight, the grim lodging house and frozen streets and the fruitless search for work, oh God the hardship I was enduring!—while I sat back snug over an Espresso in *Patisserie Valerie* in Old Compton Street. I expressed myself freely in the letters, letting my thoughts range widely, luxuriating in this time I had found for such self-indulgence:

> *"So the questions is, wherein the meaning of this life? Is it time to dismiss the God of our fathers and embrace a brave new communism? Perhaps. But let this not be a merely political communism, for that is sterile and we ask more of life than our just rations as we enter this seventh decade of the twentieth century.*
>
> *"Yes, give us the necessities of life, shelter and warmth and nourishing food and good books, and let us be equal, class and creed, black and white, man and woman. But let it be on a spiritual level also, a kind of spiritual communism if you will, that is not only proper government and just laws, but is a thing rooted in our hearts and deeply felt and lived in each living moment, yea, rooted in our very soul, a religion of love that begins with the love of one's self and irradiates out to the rest of humanity, in every corner of the globe—"*

Dad wrote back faithfully—he was one of the great old letter-writers, the fine handwriting, the conscientious responses to every point you had raised, however silly, as above. I saved that pretentious-sounding stuff mainly for the old man. There were short missives, as she called them, from my mother's cheerful, stoical, self-contained little universe, and newsy letters from my sister Dorothy in Finaghy, and one or two of the old mates.

Only one of the girls I had favoured with a letter wrote back, and only once. Already you were out of sight, out of mind, as if you'd betrayed them in some way by moving away. It sent a lonely shiver through your chest. What girl would want to be just a pen-pal anyway? You felt the Belfast girls slip away from your reach now.

We finally came face to face with our room-mate Tommy on the Saturday morning. Till then he'd been a shadowy presence, asleep in the other bed when we got back, gone to work when we woke. Saturday morning at the Maloneys' brought a leisurely holiday atmosphere about the place, like a seaside boarding house. You felt it the minute you opened your eyes. The curtains were open, letting in snow-light and sunshine. Tommy stood at the basin in his singlet and trousers, tall and broad-shouldered, shaving in the small mirror.

"How are you, boys?" he greeted us in a lovely lilting west of Ireland brogue, soft like rain and sweet like peat-smoke. There was an immediate impression of extreme gentleness, the opposite to the sullen after-work crowd around our dinner table, who were older men who'd known harder lives, one supposed.

Tommy stood knotting a tie over his laundered white shirt, his scrubbed reflection looking back at us from the mirror: bright morning face, black curls, athletic build—a "fine-looking fellow" as the Irish say.

"You're from de Nort', boys? County Clare me," his voice flowed like clear mountain spring water. "Are yous likin' it over here? Ach, it's all right for a while. I'd like to get out of it one day. I'm saving up to go back to Ireland, start up on my own there."

You couldn't blame him; the way he said "County Clare" made it sound like heaven.

He reached into the wardrobe, jangling empty coat hangers; out came the waistcoat and jacket of the black suit, then the rolled umbrella. All he needed was a bowler to complete the city gent image. His mouth twisted in a knowing, boyish grin. "I'm off now to meet this woman of mine. Goodbye, boys!"

We were into our second week in London and I felt further away than ever from finding a job I might like. Meanwhile my money was dribbling away; soon I'd be broke. Geoff had already run out of funds but now he had the prospect of a job in an advertising firm in Charlotte Street; he was waiting to hear from them. Learning of his hardship, Mrs Maloney slipped him a fiver. "Och, you can pay me back after you start work," she said. "I know you're going to do well."

Desperate, I shut myself into the phone box outside Kilburn station with the morning *Standard*. It was crunch time; I would try anything. I penned a circle around every remote possibility, then, heart beating bravely, I began to dial.

"Male models required, high rates of pay, no experience necessary": but a voice informed me that *I* would be paying *them* for the initial training period.

"Sales staff required, big earning potential": commission only, the voice admitted, but refused to divulge over the phone what the product was.

My third call secured the guarantee of all the hours I could work distributing leaflets in central London but the rate of pay was pitifully low.

Running out of pennies, I crossed the road by the railway bridge to a sweetie shop and asked for change for the phone box. But the middle-aged woman behind the counter sent me packing with her sharp, "Aw'm sick of you people comin' in ere all day arskin' for chainge!"

The *"you people"* got me—I was no longer Jim—my first taste of racism, like a smack in the mouth. Back home we Prods were the racists, the British settlers looking down our noses on the Irish. Well, there you are, we were Irish too after all! Travel really did broaden the mind. I just stared stupidly back at the obnoxious woman and her young-bitch assistant behind the counter, cool as you please, both staring at me in blatant effrontery, as if I were a *thing*, one of *you people*, sort of subhuman. I turned away in disgust, I didn't have the words to challenge this kind of thing; there were no such words back then before Ken Livingstone. Rather, you needed to accept that the Irish really were awful, annoying foreign people who asked for *chainge* in shops all the time and only got the treatment they deserved.

A domestic cleaning agency offered me work straight away, over the phone; I could start in the morning. I just had to come into the office and register today. It was in a block on Charing Cross Road, a poky office on the ground floor back, Alsatian snoring in a heap, a pleasant young Polish woman asking me, "Are you an actor? We mostly get actors working for us. You work as many or as few hours as you like, when you like." She explained that they were four-hour sessions, morning or afternoon. The client paid you £2 a session; ten shillings (50p) of which went to the agency. The clients usually paid your fares and provided a meal although they were under no obligation to do so.

I agreed and she gave me my first job, an address in North London.

It was a relief to have the prospect of money coming in at last and there was a freedom that suited me in the casual nature of the work. Mrs Maloney approved. "Sure it's something to be going on with. Good for you, turning your hand to whatever's going!"

I was up bright and early in the morning with the other workers in the house; it was a long roundabout journey on the tube to Mill Hill East right up at the end of the Northern Line. I ate a good navvy's breakfast and cut up the High Road to Kilburn station. I'd never cleaned a house in my life but felt sure I'd manage somehow. I read James Leo Herlihy's *Midnight Cowboy* on the long ride. I still had to get used to the dummy-people on the tube pointedly ignoring one another. It felt rude at first but you were soon doing it yourself to fit in. It seemed that to speak to one of these strangers would be the most fearful impertinence.

Eventually the tube train emerged above ground, the winter sun shining on the red brick and green grass of the suburbs. I had charted my course carefully in the *London A-Z*; from Mill Hill East station I followed the footpath shown on the map that took me over countryside, down a lane between trees where grey squirrels capered—we didn't have squirrels in Ireland. Either side of me green fields stretched away flatly to the distant encircling rows of houses. There was no one else around. It was frosty and crisp in the bright sunshine, the last of the snow surviving along the ditches. It felt queer to be out in the country and still in London but I was enjoying it.

After a long walk I reached the houses, a maze of suburban semis. A friendly workman clipping a hedge pointed me the way up a cul-de-sac. Despite setting out from Kilburn in plenty of time, I arrived twenty minutes late, in a muck-sweat before I even started.

"Oh, you came along the old track," said the lady of the house when I explained it'd taken a long time. "My old regular cleaning lady used to come that way—Mrs Bugg, she came to me for years, till her legs gave up, arthritis, the poor old soul, crippled with it. So I've been having someone from the agency every week now. They usually send me Julian, do you know him? Dancer: wonderful graceful movements. You're an actor?"

"I'm a writer," I said. Why hide my light under a bushel?

"Oh." She didn't look so sure about that. Maybe I looked too young. "Well, we'll get started polishing the hall and steps."

It was an electric polisher. Machines scared me, they had a mind of their own. It started up with a terrific roar, pulling me after it, hanging on for dear life. Thinking of Julian, her dancer, I felt anything but graceful. Conscious of the lady's anxious critical stare, I managed somehow to guide the polisher over the tiled floor of the hall and the red doorsteps, though I couldn't see that my efforts made any difference. It was the same throughout the tidy little house that morning, the carpets I hoovered next, the loo on the half-landing, they were so clean already that my efforts left no visible impression; it was frustrating.

At eleven she called me into the kitchen table to a steaming mug of coffee. It was heavenly to sit down for a minute and drink it. The winter's morning sunshine poured into the small room. It was an ordered petty-bourgeois little house with a note of *"Coming home times"* pinned to the noticeboard. It made me think of my own mother, our chats over a cuppa by the fireside in Coolmore Green. Only this lady wasn't the chatty sort; she maintained a polite silent reserve. Soon she was dragging out the clanky bucket and rag-mop, signalling the end of my break. She followed close behind me through the house, checking on my progress. So there was never a moment's respite.

She kept me there till twenty-past-one to make up the time I was late. And the agency had phoned through my next job, in St John's Wood, for two o'clock. As I limped away down Squirrel Lane it seemed a very long time since I had come in the opposite direction that morning. My muscles were stiffening up and I had a grubby, sweaty feeling from my chores and the sensation that my pores had been impregnated with furniture polish and cleaning fluid. The way my knees wobbled dangerously at times made me think of Mrs Bugg the char who had come this way before me, a cripple now.

St John's Wood! Now there was a bit of London glamour after Mill Hill East. There was a gate in a high stone wall, a driveway, steps going up. The big door was opened by a good-looking housewife, in her thirties I guessed, impeccably dressed and well-mannered. She simply smiled graciously at my apology for being half an hour late, it was nothing, and showed me the stair cupboard where the hoover lived.

"Just run it right through the house if you would, please," she said charmingly, emanating warmth and distance at the same time somehow.

Again I failed to see what improvement the roaring, sucking, efficient machine made to the spotless carpets—fitted wall-to-wall salmon-pink on the spacious hallway and staircase with their manorial oak panelling. It looked as if they cleaned the houses for the cleaner coming so as not to look like dirty people. It was more relaxed here; this lady just disappeared and left me to get on with it. I took my time, pausing to admire the pictures lining the walls.

I went slowly round the bedrooms. Deep sash windows framed the sinuous black shapes of bare winter trees in the garden. The bedrooms were spruce and fragrant, like a display in a department store; no hint of human bodies polluting them. Oh and this was the master bedroom, *her* bedroom with the big, stately, glorious marital bed! Oh my! A typewriter was on a table placed before the window, a sheet of blank paper wound into its carriage. Oh maybe she was one of those chic English authoresses like Margaret Drabble or Penelope Mortimer. Now wouldn't that be something! We'd soon be talking about books and writing, it'd surprise and please her, the cleaner turning out to be a writer too!

She called me down to the kitchen in the basement for afternoon tea. Her two small boys were home from school in their posh little uniforms. She dealt effortlessly with the children, the mysterious, sweet little maternal smile never deserting her pretty face. Mother and sons took a tray upstairs leaving me in peace at the big pine kitchen table with the teapot and half a chocolate cake. It was the first food I'd had since my big breakfast in Kilburn and I fairly pigged into it. It was that lovely dark, heavy, sticky, creamy cake that left you feeling high and a bit nauseous.

The worst thing about this work was the way they didn't talk much to you. There was none of the homely chat of a Belfast housewife. Otherwise she seemed such a nice lady, the perfect wife and mother. It was the London way, I supposed, the same reserve you saw on the tube; not wanting to annoy each other. When I went back to the hoover after tea and started the ground floor rooms I found the pretty lady and her boys in a sitting room with the remnants of their afternoon tea. Everything about this house presented a picture of domestic bliss, calm and good-natured. There would be no voices raised harshly here, no bad manners from the children, nothing to wipe that fixed caring near-smile off their mother's nice face. Could it get boring? Could the beautiful house and wife and the nice boys be almost too much of a good thing, ultimately suffocatingly dull? Or was it just my interminable hovering with the hoover and the fatigue of being on my feet all day twisting my thoughts in an antisocial direction?

When I had got round all the carpets she let me go early and tipped me the tube fares, her smile sweetening. I saw she was a genteel, shy lady; a mature version of one or two girls I'd met of that sensitive disposition, like precious china dolls. She saw me out the door, watching me down the steps under the outside light. I was half in love with her by now. The big door closed discreetly behind me, the light was extinguished and the five o'clock January dusk engulfed me.

It was very dark under the big pavement trees of St John's Wood. Didn't Paul McCartney live round here? Fancy walking into him! I felt the glamour and magic of London touch me again; a city where you rubbed shoulders with legends and you yourself were a legend in the making.

I was tired-out and dirty, yet there was the satisfaction of a day's labours completed, the reassurance of cash-in-hand weighting my pocket. With the question of a career out of the way my needs were simple: I wanted to get back to the digs and eat like a horse, clean up, go out and and pour a few glasses of stout down my neck, then back early to bed and sleep like a navvy. The agency had phoned through my job for the morning.

Hampstead village in misty-lemony sunshine; the pub I had come to clean was near the station. It wasn't arty, just a common pub, a bit cramped and dark, with a hall out the back where folk singer Ralph McTell had played the night before, the poster said. Well, that was something anyway! They sent me to clean the toilets first, out in the little backyard. This made me swear under my breath as I scrubbed but as I was finishing the gent's the first customer came in to use the urinal, an ordinary older working man, who said, "You've done a good job here, mate—never seen this karzi lookin' so clean!" which made me feel proud and happy, a proper workman, although I suspected he was just being nice to a young fellow.

I had to sweep up the expanse of floorboards in the hall, hundreds of fag butts that had been dropped on it. The morning sun was shining through the high-up row of windows; I had the big golden space to myself. Mopping round, I whistled and felt the sense of liberation again. I was like Orwell; I'd chosen to be bottom of the heap. It seemed necessary and right that a budding writer should make this choice.

But when I was behind the bar in the lounge taking the call from the agency for my afternoon job the pub manageress swept in, peroxide beehive and flashing blue-winged glasses, screeching, "What's this? Personal phone calls? We pay you to work here!"

She angered me but the barman, a big, shy, gentle cockney told me, "Deon't worry, mate. She's all wright wreally. Barks worse bite. What can I get you to drink on the ahse?"

I sat in a dark corner of the bar and drank a glass of bitter before I left, washing away the morning's aftertaste of dust and suds. Emerging in the golden light and sharp air of the winding village street, I felt the alcohol going to my head, just sufficient for a warm mindlessness. I smelt the curry from the Indian restaurant across the lane. A sign in its window advertised a chicken curry lunch for six bob (30p). That was good value though still a chunk of my morning's wage of thirty bob (£1.50) but what the heck, I couldn't resist it.

The only customer, I felt absurdly privileged as the white-coated tubby, charming little Indian waiter came forward eagerly, escorted me to a window table and took my order. This is it alright, cosmopolitan sophistication, I told myself as I sat eating my chicken curry and looking out on the Hampstead village street.

When I had finished and was paying the bill, the waiter asked me, "Did you enjoy that, sir? Good, good! Come again! Thank you, sir and good day to you!"

I don't think I had ever been called "sir" in my life before. I liked it. The chap could see I was a gentleman, even covered in a morning's sweat and grime after cleaning out a pub. I left him a small tip and could just hear Dad say, "Aye, doin' the big fellow, like your brother, and you with nothing!"

Of course I'd made myself late now for the afternoon job down the line at Kentish Town. I felt dozy on the tube after the beer and curry, the afternoon a never-ending groan.

"Twenty-five after two. You vill make up thee time," the elderly lady greeted me in an East European accent. She was a sad bag of bones, balding, with skin the colour and texture of old parchment. She wore a pinafore with a pattern of small flowers on it.

She followed me round suspiciously while I pushed the hoover sluggishly through the barren rooms. The house was thirty years back in time, in the war, musty and gloomy, with horrible threadbare, vomit-coloured carpets and furniture. Bit spooky. To mitigate the boredom I fantasised that the old Polish woman was the ghost of a refugee killed here in the Blitz and that if you came back to this address tomorrow you'd find a new house standing here with new people living in it. It was a good yarn, though I frightened myself thinking it through and jumped when I heard her call out behind me, "Cup of tea for you!"

This was better. I drank it sitting at the table in the stone-flagged scullery, resting my aching feet, while she hovered gauntly about me with a supervisor's folded arms.

"Vat do you do ven you don't clean?" It was an attempt at conversation.

"I'm a writer!" I fired back at her; I was acquiring the blazing arrogance of the poor.

You'd think being a writer might interest someone but it was a conversation stopper with her. She glared at me a moment as if I'd confessed to being a pimp then turned her old face away in a gesture of disgust, or so I imagined; it was more likely to have been indifference.

"After tea break you give thee floor and cupboards here in kitchen a good vash. Bucket of hot sudsy vater and scrub hard is best way."

I slaved on till the last minute, a growing anger driving me close to smashing something. I felt used and dirty and limp like an old floor-rag. No fare money either when I left. I barged out rudely, without a goodbye, leaving her to the Blitz.

The next morning I woke up too tired and sore and cross to face another day's cleaning. I was expected in Golder's Green at nine. It was half-eight already. Well, they could clean up their own crap today.

I had a good vash at the basin and put on my smart office clothes. You were kidding yourself to imagine there was really any alternative to this. You had to face it, you were destined to be a clerk, at least for the time being. I took the tube to Trafalgar Square and walked up the Strand looking for staff agencies I'd not already registered with. In the first one I tried the young fellow there, not a lot older than myself, got annoyed as I shook my head and repeated "No" to the long list of awful dull job vacancies he read out. I think he took me for a work-shy longhair.

Then I found an agency across the street, its office tucked away at the top of the dark old block, very discreet and quiet, remote from the busy Strand below its deep old windows. It was another world, welcoming; they were different here, a smaller, more personal, sympathetic service, and arranged an interview for me at the BBC. Now this was *really* me and something to impress the folks back home!

I went over to Marylebone for the interview. They were really nice; it was working on BBC publications, the accounts side but, I told myself, maybe I'd be writing for them soon! They gave me the job straight off, to start the following Monday. I had fallen on my feet. The BBC! Those letters inspired absolute respect. Wait till I told them all back home!

CHAPTER 18

A New Life

Geoff had landed his dream job with a major advertising agency in Charlotte Street. That weekend we moved out of the lodging house and in with Paul and the Belfast drop-outs at Oval. Geoff and I shared the double bed in the small back bedroom with a hole in the window pane patched with newspaper. With fresh falls of snow that January it was very cold and we crept closer to one another for warmth in the night.

Jack, the first up, gave me a call at seven on the way out to his job cleaning offices. Geoff had another half-hour in bed. I braced myself for the chilling plunge to my clothes on the bedroom chair. Luminous snow-light filtered around the ragged curtains. I peeked through them at the night's fresh fall of snow, pristine on the backyard, the alleyway and the roofs of the condemned terraced streets beyond.

I splashed my face with cold water, combed the side parting into my long hair, donned my navy overcoat and the tartan scarf Lesley at the ministry had knitted me for going away, and I was off down the stairs through the kitchen and out the back door. Pat's hairdresser's occupied the ground floor front.

The snowy freshness outside was invigorating. I followed the tracks Jack had left down the path and along the alley to the side road. The council tower block flats opposite cast its big cold shadow. Turning the next corner on to the busy main road I was outside the parade of faded small shops that formed the ground floor of Roach Buildings. In the café there with the other workers I had my breakfast of tea and toast. The waitress was friendly; I was warmed through ready to start the day.

Straight along the road to Oval station. The thrill as you fell in with the streaming crowd and stepped out into space for the ride down on the long, rattling escalator, the gallery of framed adverts on the wall with their promise of glamour and sophistication flying past your face.

There was a grandeur and drama about the underground in the morning rush hour; you were part of an organism, swept along in a fantastic smooth-flowing river of ant-like industrious humanity, down the escalator and out along the subterranean platform. The electric rails vibrated like whip-cracks, there was a warning rumble and the tube-train burst out of the tunnel. The long carriages filled the crowded platform; the automatic doors gaped open impatiently. The carriages were packed solid; you squeezed in between the other bodies, got hold of a bar or strap to steady you; the automatic doors shut and with a jerk you were off, and this discomfort was part of the excitement, the drama: you were all aboard, hanging on for dear life, riding the unrelenting wheels of commerce, cheek by jowl with the pretty secretaries and sleek business men and all the other nondescript figures, a strange shared momentary intimacy between you all but with no communication. Individuals intent on your journey, you hurtled along the tunnels under the great metropolis at the clockwork pulse of civilisation.

I had the same couple standing near me on a succession of these morning tube journeys, a black man and a white woman, thirtyish, ordinary and poor-looking, their bodies pressed together, cuddling and kissing all the way, oblivious or defiant of the commuter crush around them. Never a word passed between the solemn couple, they might have been dumb. Between kisses she leant on his chest looking up adoringly into his face, he self-possessed and lordly in his male power. When her stop came she backed away from him in a sad, silent farewell, still staring into each other's eyes, and she raised her hand in a pathetic little wave, looking close to tears. The doors shut between them, the train jerked and they were wrenched apart, her staring sad, besotted face swallowed up in the platform crowd.

I walked from Oxford Circus to the office in Marylebone: up Regent Street, past the tall, grey, distinctive shape of Broadcasting House and into the quiet elegance of Regency terraces, Wimpole Street and Harley Street, feeling the famous names, their distinction, rub off on you; emerging on to the narrow village High Street. The office block was an insignificant-looking gaunt grey building, once a house perhaps. an outpost of head office further up the street. In the gloomy quiet within, an old-style cage lift hummed you up two floors to the accounts suite with its grey carpet, grey filing cabinets and desks that faced the tall windows framing rooftops and scraps of London sky.

I was in a small office at the back, high above the well of backyard enclosed by tall buildings. There was a cosy quietude here, remote from the bustle of the street. The atmosphere was friendly, the other clerks mostly young and cheerful. There was chat to lighten the routine; the tea-trolley came morning and afternoon. At lunchtime we went in a group up the road to the canteen where the menu included cheap options of faggots and pease pudding, spam or corn beef fritters, toad-in-the-hole, all new to my Irish palate.

After lunch I'd slip off to a good bookshop I'd discovered further up the street. Its interior was long and narrow with high book-lined walls, hushed like a church, with few other customers. The long-haired young man with an aristocratic look about him, who managed the shop, seemed happy for me to browse there interminably. Time, the office clerk's enemy, seemed to dissolve as I hovered by the literary fiction—new stylish paperback reprints of Malcolm Lowry and Patrick MacGill, I recall—sucking up the fresh print like a thirsty boy at a drinking fountain. My feet seemed to take root there, my body dissolved away, till I had left myself late and had to sprint back down the High Street to work.

Back to the ledger columns of debit, credit and balance, but the dream of literature was kept alive by those lunchtime visits to the bookshop and later the public library on Marylebone Road, the dream keeping me going through the slow grey office afternoons.

I got home in the dark and cold to Roach Buildings. An old ugly gas fire kept the dingy slum sitting room warm and cosy. Dinner, cooked in the greasy kitchen behind the hairdresser's on the ground floor, was carried up the stairs in steaming platefuls and eaten off our laps around the fire. The economical plain shared meal invariably consisted of boiled vegetables, moistened with a little butter, and filling up with bread and tea. I still had my bottomless appetite and ate the simple food ravenously, anxious that I might never satisfy my hunger.

After we'd washed up we sat round the fire with a satisfied tired feeling, reading. The only sound for long periods was the low hiss of the gas fire; there was no TV to wreck our peace. I sat in a corner of the shabby rust-coloured couch, leaning my reporter's notebook on the worn-shiny armrest and writing page after page with a swift assurance that I have never equalled since.

"What are you writing about?" they all wanted to know, amused and intrigued.

"It's a novel," I said, "about back home."

"When are we going to get to read it?" Paul enquired.

"Once I've finished this first part, about childhood."

Of course it was never-ending; I didn't want to leave anything out. I believe that, exiles all, they understood my writer's need to go back and hold a magnifying glass to memories, to recreate the past and save it for posterity or something. I was never precious about my writing; there'd been no ivory tower of university. I worked best just sitting round with the others with their rustling newspapers and desultory chat. Then writing wasn't such a solitary, heavy business. I believed the writer needed to be among his fellows, whoever they might be, at the heart of warm, companionable life, not stuck in any ivory tower. It was same as the way I'd felt about God and religion in my youth.

After flunking out of Belfast College of Art Paul had come over to London in the autumn with Bobby and Jack, fellow habitués of the Club Bar who were bored with their jobs as clerks at Mackie's Foundry. They roughed it in London to begin with, staying at a hostel in Drury Lane, working as porters and packers at Harrod's while they saved up the deposit to rent a flat.

Over here they were part of the growing hippy fraternity. The various visitors to the flat were all in that long-haired mould. There were the Dublin lads, outgoing, sociable and articulate, then the strange solitary types, older hippies like Jan, a Czech refugee, a gentle soul, and Jake who was avoiding the Vietnam War draft. Jake wandered mysteriously around London, sleeping on friends' floors. He presented a self-contained, compact figure in his combat jacket and jeans, no other visible possessions. He had a calm, biblical profile with his long fair hair, big beard and noble, wood-carved features. Because he spoke little I thought of him as some kind of intellectual saint at first, then I noticed his lips moving as he read *Melody Maker* and I wondered if he was just an imbecile. And I was shocked one night in the *Skinner's Arms* across the road when he turned on one of the barmen collecting up glasses and calling closing time and told him to "F— off!" The modest cockney lad backed off blushing, mortified, and I heard him tell the guvnor behind the bar what had happened. After that I couldn't help thinking, of Jake, so much for the great anti-war pacifist who nevertheless can treat an inoffensive waiter like dirt under his feet.

We cleared off back across the road to the flat. It was a Saturday night and we'd drunk a few pints. Back around the gas fire Jake rolled a joint. I felt the wildness of Saturday night in my blood and when the spliff got to me I sucked eagerly on it, drawing the pine-smelling smoke deep into my lungs. My head cleared and my mood lifted ecstatically, I was high! Another joint came round. Now I was beginning to see the Truth, the Meaning of Life that had always somehow eluded me before. I struggled to articulate it to the others:

"It's Spirit running through us—you and me and every living thing. It's the Spirit of love and peace and beauty and goodness and kindness and there can be no world worth living in without it. All we have to do is open our hearts and go with it—"

But suddenly I began to feel sick, as if I were choking on my own words. The joy of Spirit was swept away and the sense of an opposing malignant power nauseated and overwhelmed me. I broke out in a cold sweat; the room wheeled, once, twice, then continuously.

It felt like a long, long way to the bathroom as I staggered across the room, along the landing. I dropped on to my knees and embraced the cold whiteness of the toilet bowl like a lover and was horribly sick into it. Geoff came in behind me and fell on his knees beside me and was sick too. Between the excruciating bouts of retching and vomiting we knelt there like a couple of penitents around the throne, broken and contrite. It became a shared cathartic experience, as if we were vomiting up all the darkness of Blake's *London*.

In the spring Geoff and I moved to South Kensington, into a smart double bedsitter two floors up in Rosary Gardens, an imposing side street of fine tall redbrick terraces. Our shared room was small but well-organised, a single bed in two corners, Baby Belling cooker in a third. There was a built-in wardrobe and wall-to-wall deep-pile beige carpeting that extended throughout the house. A maid cleaned up weekly and changed the bedding. A little wrought iron balcony overlooked the quiet, elegant street.

South Kensington was affluent and trendy, another world from Kennington. The arrival of the hot summer weather brought a continental glamour to the district with drinkers crowding the pavements outside the smart pubs in the long evening light. Exotic cooking smells drifted from Italian, French and Asian restaurants. Exotic American hippies, men with pony-tails and orange satin flared pants, played Frisbee in the public gardens. It was truly cosmopolitan with a rich babble of foreign tongues.

I was lying sweating sleeplessly on my bed in the sultry summer dark, gone midnight, when a powerful-sounding car pulled up in the empty street below and sat with its engine running annoyingly. The car door slammed, stiletto heels clickety-clacked briskly over the pavement and a man's voice burst out very loud and clear in a torrent of emotional Italian, like a scene from an opera.

Then a man shouted down from a balcony across the street, the voice frightfully English and indignant this time, "I say, do you think you could be quiet down there? People are trying to sleep, you know!"

The car accelerated angrily away and I lay there smiling to myself in the dark at the little incident with its juxtaposition of national temperaments.

The Stanhope Arms pub on Gloucester Road was a friendly place where we drank with a mix of Londoners, northerners, Japanese girls and an elderly French lady. I got talking to a writer who drank there too, Mal Wibbley, gentle, bearded and solitary, writing in a little notebook he kept in his breast pocket, or reading something left wing like Castro's *Address from the Dock*. Mal worked as a book-keeper, saving up for periodic prolonged trips abroad. He offered me some good advice on writing: "Just write. Don't worry about anything else. Write every day. Serve your apprenticeship." I admired his workmanlike approach. I tended to see writing as a religion, the writer its high priest, raised up in its mystical glow.

My father died that July, 1970, aged seventy. He had been in poor health for long years, but it still came as a dreadful shock to me, a great tragedy in the small young world of Jim. The thought of my mother left on her own after all the years was the worst thing. Death seemed to me, at twenty-two, the hardest thing life had to offer.

Meeting with Ned helped. He kept grimly cheerful, the responsible big brother. We started drinking on the flight to Belfast, gin and tonics, then continued in the County Antrim pubs along the way home, so we were properly anaesthetised by the time we got to Loughside in the long summer's evening. I had dreaded this homecoming but was pleasantly surprised by the warm, supportive atmosphere being generated at the house in Coolmore Green, my sister Dorothy vivacious and homely, her husband Big Bill large and reassuring in his Belfast fashion. With their support my mother was putting a brave face on things, concerned for us as much as herself.

After the service in the Church of Ireland the funeral cortege proceeded along Shore Road, through Carrickfergus and out the Antrim coast. The wind dunted the car windows; sunlight gleamed through dirty tatters of clouds on to the white horses riding in on the bottle-green sea running away to Scotland. We turned on to the road that climbed to the county cemetery.

The vast graveyard spread across the hilltop overlooking the sea. The wind cut at us as we got out of the cars. White clouds parted biblically and the sun shone down on the lean, bespectacled figure of Reverend Jackson as he strode among the graves reading his prayer book. The wind raked his yellow hair, whipped at his long black and white vestments and moaned and whistled around the headstones. Here was the ultimate drama of life and death.

Our mother did not attend the burial and Dorothy stayed at home with her. I felt terribly alone as I stood in the cold wind with the small group around the freshly-dug grave. The depth of the hole waiting in the ground shocked me, it was so terribly deep and final. To think of poor Dad consigned forever to this impersonal spot, like a number on the bleak hilltop. I watched the coffin lowered gingerly down, down, till it rested there deep in the brown earth.

"Man that is born of a woman hath but a short time to live, and is full of misery. He cometh up and is cut down, like a flower; he fleeth as it were a shadow—"

Reverend Jackson's holy words fell clearly on my ears, charged with profound meaning, a poetry addressing the deeper human need to transcend our fate and recognise the higher, eternal purpose to our transient, troubled lives.

"Earth to earth, ashes to ashes, dust to dust."

As Reverend Jackson intoned the words of our father's final end, the gravedigger squatting on the edge of the hole dropped the lumps of dirt perfunctorily onto the coffin in the time-honoured ritual.

It was over. We turned away from the rasp of the shovel and the rattle of clay on the pine box, into the teeth of the wind on the hill above Belfast Lough.

Mr Gittings the BBC accountant, a Yorkshireman, had kindly told me to take as long as I liked off work, so I had the rest of the week at home with Mum and Dorothy and Ned. Nora joined us; she'd go in Mum's room at bedtime and sit by her bed, talking softly to her and calling her "Mother". We saw this as an Irish

Catholic kind of goodness, an authenticity of human warmth and deeper fellow-feeling. Mum wasn't sleeping much; she kept the light on all night and my old transistor radio tuned to Radio 2. Yet she was bearing up well—"She has shown great fortitude," said Dorothy—and I returned to England much reassured despite the wound I felt in my being, with no Dad any more.

Once I began to put the ineffable sadness of my father's death behind me and settle back into my London routine I felt the joy of the convalescent as I woke to the South Kensington morning, the summer sunshine flooding in the orange curtains on the French windows as you opened them to step out and sip a coffee on the little balcony overlooking the ruled elegance of the quiet street. Going to work on the tube you felt yourself an integral part of the swift, purposeful life of the great city. Above ground again you breezed up Regent Street between the tall buildings, leisurely and free, long-haired in an open-necked shirt in the bright sunshine, turning into the now familiar exclusive Regency terraces of Marylebone.

I liked my job at the Beeb, not the work itself keeping accounts again, but the relaxed atmosphere of the small office and the easy companionship of my colleagues—Dave and Clive, Mick and Marilyn, Jim and Derek, George Chan and Peter Shah—the undemanding rhythm of my days there that left me free to dream. There was time-killing chat and good-natured banter and the blessed rounds of the tea-trolley.

The messengers came and went with the post, freewheeling, long-haired young guys—"Save Mott the Hoople!" was their war cry that summer. The messengers brought all the latest news and gossip down from head office. There were lunch hour and after-work visits to the pub up the street. You really felt part of a working community.

I was happy to do all the overtime going, most evenings and all day Saturday. It saved me from the lingering sense of my bereavement in the narrow confines of our bedsitter. At 5pm we fetched in sausage sandwiches, bread and dripping and coffee in paper cups from the small Italian café next door on the corner of Marylebone Lane. The menu in the window advertised "*Chips with everything"*. The waiters hailed me as "El Cordobes!" the Beatle-haired Spanish bullfighter. I liked that!

It was easier to be at the office and lose myself in the long hours of undemanding work amongst agreeable people, and gratifying to feel your wallet stuffed with notes after payday. I found myself here again helping out some of the married men in the office with payday loans (no interest!), as I had done in Belfast. In the lunch hour I went down Oxford Street refurbishing my wardrobe. Out went the faded civil service suits and shirts I'd crossed the Irish Sea in, replaced by Lord John shirts in bold primary colours, a flared black jacket, green velvet loons I copied from the Frisbee hippies in the park. I was becoming a right little Beau Brummel.

In August a group of us went camping for the weekend in rural Essex. Dave's landlord in St John's Wood, an elderly tony lady called Jo, owned a country cottage at Little Baddow and invited us to camp in the field next to it. We hired a frame tent from a firm at Acton and a van to transport it in and there'd be a couple of small tents as well to accommodate our numbers.

It was a joy driving off into the country in the Saturday morning sunshine, out through the Essex suburbs from Mick's place in Hainault. Clive and I sat in the back of Mick's Cortina, his girl Angie beside him in the front passenger seat. Mick was a lanky, albino-fair, gentle working class lad, a neat Mod with his layered short hair and Ben Sherman shirts. His dad, a train driver, had died recently too. Angie was only sixteen, long brown hair and tight blue jeans; a loud, boisterous girl, hanging over the back of her seat gabbling uncontrollably and making eyes at us boys in the back seat, offering her large paper bag of the "swee'ies" she got free working in a sweetie factory.

We got to Little Baddow in the afternoon, turning into the lane at Jo's cottage a little way outside the village. The old lady emerged authoritatively and directed us into the field opposite where we could pitch the tents under some oak trees. Alighting from our vehicles it was hot and glaring in the great rural stillness, the grass decorated with sun-baked cakes of cow dung.

"Some refreshments for you!" Jo boomed benevolently and we repaired to her front lawn for lemonade and tea, biscuits and cake. We sat round in the sun and peace in the strange lovely old place in the heart of the country, tucking in like the Famous Five. Angie's shrieks of laughter pierced the rural solitude. Her friend Ann from the sweetie factory was a quiet, stolid little blonde; there were just the two girls, with six blokes.

The farmer from up the lane, whose land it was, stopped his Land Rover by the garden gate. "So these are our happy campers?" he barked. "Londoners, eh? No rebels among em, I hope?"

"All Commonwealth, Major!" Jo declared anxiously, as if unaware the man was joking. Clive was Australian, Philip Jamaican and I was Irish; the rest were Essex.

"Carry on!" cried the Major. "They can come up and see the new litter of piglets later!"

It took most of the afternoon to erect the big frame tent, struggling with the unwieldy poles, pegs and canvas on the hard dry ground under the merciless white void of burning sky. Then we walked up to the farm to view the tiny pink piglets suckling the line of teats on the underbelly of the vast sough stretched out across the pig-pen. Angie was ecstatic over the cute, funny, moving scene and I noticed the pleasure Mick took in her delight and how much he loved the girl.

A wash in Jo's bathroom with its damp country smell, a change of clothes, and we drove to the pub in a neighbouring village, Mick sounding his horn on the blind bends as we followed the twisting lane between its high hedges. We crossed a stone bridge and the pub was there above the river at the end of the village. Inside it was modernised, open plan and spacious with a juke box, dart board and a menu of meals-in-a-basket.

The evening passed in a slow, beery blur. I ate my chicken and chips in a basket. I avoided the darts, like all games, and moved around chatting to members of our party. The Essex crowd were nice, with a kind of humble quality I admired. Clive the Aussie was the oldest, a big, easy-going, humorous fellow. I found out he was really from Surrey, had sailed to Australia in his teens on the £10 scheme and driven trucks across the outback. Philip, from a well-off Jamaican family in Redbridge, was a big spoilt boy but lively good company, sociable and easy to talk to.

We were all tiddly by closing time. We stood around outside the pub for a while afterwards in the warm night, chatting with some of the local lads who had attached themselves to us. These were proper country boys, Essex style, with that decent, sociable, humble quality even more pronounced. They didn't seem to want to let us go. We could see the stars in the sky above, hear the river running below and smell the water and the night fields.

We got back to the tents around midnight in the dark field, finding our way by torchlight and lighting candles and oil lamps in the tents to get ready for bed. The two girls were sharing a small tent. I heard Angie call out to Mick with the lads in the other small tent, "G'night, Mick, lav!" and his reply, "G'night, dawlin'!"

A minute later our tent flap lifted and Angie crept in in her dressing gown and joined Clive in his sleeping bag.

"G'night, Mick, lav!" she called out again in a gratuitous kind of deceit and Mick's innocent response came again through the soft darkness in the field, "G'night!"

By the light of a low lamp left burning I could distinguish one bare female leg protruding from Clive's sleeping bag. I rolled over and crashed out.

On our way home on Sunday afternoon Mick was tearful. Philip whispered to me, "Clive's a right bastard going with Mick's girl like that!"

I nodded; what had happened was awful, but I couldn't help wondering whether, with the drink we'd taken, any of us blokes would have kicked Angie out of his sleeping bag. Such was the power a woman could wield over men. And boys cried too, boys got hurt.

We stopped off at a little sandy beach for a paddle and later to play football in a big sun-filled mown meadow along the way; I joined in the best I could, enjoying the location under the big blue sky. Philip invited me back to his home in Redbridge for a curry. His mother was a genteel, hospitable lady; his elder brother Rowland, a university student, was most unlike him, really cool and Afro-haired.

Philip said, "Jim here is a revolutionary like you," but big brother was giving nothing away; I waited in vain to hear all about the black struggle.

It was good to get back to the bedsit in Rosary Gardens, sunburnt, exhausted and filthy from the fields, and wallow in the bath before lying between cool, clean sheets.

In the autumn Geoff moved back to Belfast and I moved into a flat in Hornsey with Clive and Roy from work. It was a pleasant flat-sharing arrangement but with Geoff's departure I was bereft of a bosom buddy now and I was becoming conscious also of the need for a girl in my life. It was a lonely feeling. I'd dated a few girls in that first year in London, at the Oval and South Ken, and at work, but nothing had come of them. It was my own fault, I knew, the faint heart that never wins fair lady. They'd included one or two really nice intelligent girls I'd liked to have seen again, but I seemed incapable still of the effort required to take things further.

It was the summer of 1971. I was going up in the lift to the restaurant at head office and became conscious of the little dark girl standing next me in the confined space. Solemn round black eyes looked out of a soft childish face framed by neat, fashionably short black hair; slim legs descended from a short skirt. She sounded real cockney; she was telling the girl with her she'd been "stoned" the night before. I was sure she meant drunk, not high on weed; she wasn't the hippy type. I heard her blonde friend call her "Sharon."

Sharon had made a sort of impression on me. She was one of the comptometer girls and I noticed her about after that, her dark head, small regular features and neat, attractive figure, but she appeared oblivious of my existence. I had put her out of my thoughts till the office party at the BBC Club one Friday night. We had a room there with a bar and disco. The comptometer girls arrived in a big gang, they'd already been drinking, as had I, and there was little Sharon making a beeline for me, transfixing me with those solemn black eyes, and then we were dancing, clinging to each other and kissing without preamble.

So suddenly, out of the blue, here was all the affection I had been craving, a passionate forthright girl with no reservations or silly games to play. I stuck to her like glue, waiting anxiously when she was out of my sight for a minute at the loo, terrified I might lose her. But thank God she felt the same, hurrying back to my waiting arms, moulding herself to me.

"Comin' for a walk?" she said and led me outside. She took her shoes off, her feet in mauve tights dainty and strange on the hard London pavement. We strolled round the Langham in the soft grey summer's evening, two small figures holding hands, under towering Broadcasting House and the empty evening office blocks. An hour ago I had been on my own, nothing, nobody; now I walked hand in hand with my own girl in a glowing nimbus of togetherness. There was a shower of small summer rain; Sharon didn't flinch from it but lifted her soft little face sensuously to its caress, letting it refresh her skin and tickle her eyelashes.

"Your feet'll get wet," I said, my voice humble, in strange awe of her feminine power.

"Aoh, don't matter!" She had that earthy, natural, reckless quality.

A crowd of us came back to the flat in Hornsey afterwards and Sharon spent the night with me.

In the light of morning, beside me in the single bed, she was unexpectedly modest, covering her breasts with the sheet. Then she talked a bit.

"You from Norven Island? You a Proddy-dog or a Caffy-cat? Proper cockney, I am, born in the sound of Bow Bells, me granny told me!" I liked the idea of that, the sense of pride in her culture—my true cockney bird!

We had breakfast in the kitchen with my flatmate Roy and Sharon's friend Tracy from work. Afterwards as Sharon, neat as a pin again in her mauve suede skirt, helped me make my bed, our eyes met as we were smoothing the under-sheet, memories of the night before bubbled up and she drew me down on the side of the bed in the light of day.

I walked her to Turnpike Lane in the grey, close Saturday morning, shortcutting through the side streets. Passing a ground floor window we caught a glimpse of a big muscleman in his vest and underpants and she exclaimed, "Aoh, !ook at im, that's disgustin', that is!" She was a funny mixture of passion and propriety.

She told me she had a steady boyfriend. "Works on the Stock Exchange, drives an MGB," she boasted. My heart sank a little at this news but I didn't really feel jealous of some wee spiv; I was here with the real Sharon who seemed perfectly happy walking the back streets with her Irish poet.

Down in the busy station she threw her arms round my neck and we kissed goodbye, squeezing each other to death for a minute like real lovers parting. The escalators were waiting, running like a waterfall, and as she turned away from me to her descent I felt a rush of loneliness bring me close to tears. And she was gone, swept inexorably away downstream.

I walked back through the grey Saturday streets, across the railway footbridge and back to the lonely flat. That Saturday night on my own again was awful, Sunday went blankly on for ever. I clung to the memory of our time together, Sharon and I; the love we had shared for an evening, a night and a morning was very real, wasn't it? I couldn't wait to phone her at work on Monday morning and arrange our next date. But I had a funny ominous feeling it wasn't going to happen.

I dialled the extension for Comptometers. I was feverish with anticipation and very nervous, like a schoolboy asking for a first date. She came to the phone sounding flat and said she couldn't make it this week, though I could tell she wasn't against the idea of seeing me again sometime and we left it at that with nothing definite. I put the phone down and sighed, it didn't seem that hopeful what with her having a boyfriend already. Another disappointment. What did I see in her anyway? She was a bit young and not well educated. I was lonely and she'd given me pure unstinting feminine affection, which was everything to me just then.

Then a few weeks later, out of the blue, she turned up at the flat one evening after work with Roy and Tracy. The other couple disappeared into his room, leaving Sharon and I looking at each other in silence across the big sitting room with the evening sun shining in on us. She narrowed her black eyes at me in her solemn, rather severe way, almost glaring, but the light was in them too; colour suffused her cheeks, her eyes glittered in her hot face and in a moment she had crossed the ocean of the carpet and settled warmly on my lap.

Once again she disappeared from my life, for months this time. Roy hadn't seen Tracy either. In the autumn we heard they were pregnant, both of them—it wasn't us, it was more recent. Then one Friday night up the pub after work we saw them drinking in a corner with the other comptometer girls and the Scots girl Kirsty came over with a message from them. "Can Tracy and Sharon come to yours tonight, they want to know?" But by now I was with Flick, she was coming down from university to see me that evening, and Roy was engaged to another girl at the BBC.

Flick had come to work at the office that summer between school and university. I got on well with the student temps, who brought a fresh breath of freedom into our office world. Flick was an untidy-looking girl with glasses and bushy dark-fair hair; she impressed me as clever and funny and anarchic. Then one hot, sunny lunch hour a little crowd of us from the office were sitting in the small public garden behind the High Street, all squashed on to a bench together, and I was suddenly conscious of Flick, the messy schoolgirl, Beryl the Peril, as a young woman, squashed up beside me there, her legs crossed in scruffy black tights under a navy skirt like a school gym-slip and the hot sun burning into our laps. I felt a bit faint with a sudden rush of longing for a woman; the feeling continued to nag at me through the office afternoon.

When I asked her if she'd like to join me for a drink after work, just the two of us, she blushed to the roots of her hair and struggled to speak, then gave up the attempt and nodded her assent. We had our drinks in the upstairs bar of the mews pub round the corner. It felt awkward with her; away from the others she was tongue-tied and gauche. It was like taking some horrible spoilt child out for a treat and it all going wrong. At one point the barman had to come and ask her to take her feet down off a chair. Because of the awkwardness we both drank too much and somehow or other she had come back to the flat with me and we slept on my mattress dragged from the bedroom I shared with

Clive on to the sitting room floor. It was nothing like my night of passion with Sharon; we just cuddled a bit then fell asleep.

When I opened my eyes in the morning Flick was sitting up on her elbow watching my sleeping face with a doting, maternal sort of fondness, a loving look. She had slept in her bra and pants; the black tights and navy skirt and her blouse discarded on an armchair. The awkward schoolgirl shyness had gone, replaced by a womanly companionship. We dressed with no trace of embarrassment, and travelled into work together. Walking from the station across Wimpole Street and Harley Street in the morning sunshine and freshness, she stepped out with a new confident gait, her head held high, smiling softly. Beryl the Peril was dead.

Flick stayed over regularly at my place, sharing my mattress on the sitting room floor. Eventually she brought word from her mother. "She wants to meet 'this Irishman who's stealing her daughter away'!"

"Fair enough," I said. "Any time!" I had nothing to feel guilty about; I'd not seduced her daughter or anything.

"She's pleased you're Irish. She says there's no one better than a cultured Irishman."

"She's enlightened then. That's good." Though I wondered did her statement imply there were a lot of *un*cultured Irishmen? Kind of a back-handed compliment?

We went straight from work one day to the house in Tottenham, a narrow brick terrace back of Broad Lane. The parents had divorced; Flick told me how they'd had to give up their lovely big roomy house in an Islington square; the father had gone to live on his own. Life had been wonderful until the divorce.

Mrs Hartford, a primary school teacher, was a vivacious lady with an attractive dark Jewish look. Flick's Irish blood was on her father's side. Her young brother Stephen and older sister Janet had the mother's dark looks with really black straight hair; Flick was different, fairish, perhaps after the father.

"And what part of Ireland are you from?" Mrs Hartford enquired.

"County Antrim, near Belfast."

"Oh, the north! And what do you think about the situation over there? It seems to be going from bad to worse."

"Yes," I said. "Denying the Irish nationals in the six counties their civil rights for fifty years then beating them up when they objected to it wasn't enough for the imperialist cause, so now they've introduced internment: lock them up and throw away the key, maybe that'll do the trick!"

"How long is it all going to go on for? Do you see any solution, ever?"

"The two sides have got to agree to live together but it has to be as *equals*. The question is whether that is possible with partition and the gerrymandered Unionist majority in the Northern Ireland state. Sooner or later there will have to be an *all-Ireland* political *agreement* that *unites* rather than *divides* the Irish people."

Mrs Hartford's eyes were glazing over and then she had a bright idea. "Oh, give them more money! Give them all enough money and they'll soon settle down!"

"There's my mother's analysis of the situation," said Flick sharply. "Everything down to simple human greed in the end!"

Not wanting to get between mother and daughter, I said, "Well, it's true enough that every conflict has its roots in economics; there are always the haves and have-nots, that is what the class system and imperialism are all about."

"Okay, dinner!" Mrs Hartford was getting bored with Ireland. "Felicity, show Jim where to wash his hands."

We ate at the big table in the kitchen. The student lodger Ted joined us, an agreeable young northerner studying theology. The meal passed pleasantly enough but I noticed Flick was inclined to be short with her mother and her big sister Janet, another student, a plump, dreamy, smiling girl who seemed a gentle, harmless soul to me. The brother Stephen who Flick affectionately named "the Pig" was a dark, silent big lad of fifteen who watched me closely with, I imagined, something of the fascination I used to feel for my sister Dorothy's visiting boyfriends.

Afterwards Flick took me up to her room. We passed a big chest-high stack of paperbacks in a corner of the landing floor. "My sister's," said Flick disgustedly. "All bloody science-fiction, that's all she reads!. She's run out of space for them in her bedroom. She never goes out anywhere, possesses no social skills! She's doing a degree in *maths!* She's weird!"

Flick's room was the long, narrow back bedroom above the kitchen extension: her single bed along one wall, wardrobe and chest of drawers and bookcase along the other. The sash window above her desk framed the dirty brick steeple of the factory behind the houses; its phallic presence loomed there, darkening the evening sky. That industrial chimney over their backyard wall seemed to me a permanent visible reminder of how the broken Hartford family had come down in the world.

But in her own room Flick was relaxed and cheerful. I sat on her bed watching her tidy her things, stuffing her innumerable sweaters and pairs of jeans, her habitual garb, into drawers, clearing up books, slamming them down flat on the floor in a way that made me the book lover protest, "Hey, careful, you'll bust the spines!"

"*Possessions!*" she declared. "Who needs em?"

The sentiment rather impressed me. I was enjoying being there with her, the room felt so cosy and complete, her own bedsit within the family home. I'd never had that with my bedrooms, they were always just a place to sleep, chill sick-rooms in the daylight. Here I had the homely, warm feeling of sharing in a girl's world. I was grateful to be with Flick, to become part of this London family.

We passed that summer pleasantly together, popping in on her old school friends around North London, shopping on a Saturday afternoon. We'd take an early evening walk over the bridge on the Lea to the pub on the Marsh. Or more often, pick up a bottle of cheap Spanish wine from the off-licence on Broad Lane and drink it in her room, sitting on her bed as the lowering sun flared on the factory chimney. She walked me to the bus stop late, hanging dreamily on my arm. Waiting at the stop she buried her face in my chest, clinging to me, all tender and adoring. I was her first love.

In August she went off for two weeks camping in France on her own with a small tent. The postcards came most days, *"Missing you terribly."* After she'd got back her father died suddenly of a heart attack. Her mother gave her the key to the house in Waltham Cross, to go and see if there was anything there she'd like to salvage. We took the bus over there on a September Saturday afternoon, got down at the village and walked some way out of it along the blattering main road. The footpath ran out and we walked in single file, past the thistles that grew along the verge, with juddering great lorries bearing down on us, till we turned up a farm lane past dusty fields and pylons.

She'd joked about "my late lamented father" but I could see her sinking with every step on that demoralising walk. Her father's house was a barn conversion that stood among other farm buildings on a low hill. Flick was ominously silent as she turned the key in the door. Inside there was a big open-plan living room, rather bare. The table was set for a meal and there was a copy of *The Times* on it, the way he'd left it.

"What did he do?" I enquired, for something to say.

"He was a building contractor," she said. "In his younger days he was a trade union leader, he organised the national dustmen's strike."

"That was good."

"Well, not much to see, is there?" said Flick. I could see this visit had brought bitter memories of the upheaval and sadness of her fractured family life. Everything in her life had been good and generous and happy till then, with both parents in the big family home in Islington; then it had shrunk meanly, the man of the house with his forthright ways and the ready roll of banknotes he'd produce to kit them all out in duffel coats for the winter, that kind of thing—gone. And they were left with the endless female squabbling in the Tottenham terrace. She was bitter towards her mother, blaming her for their situation, I felt.

Walking away from the Marie Celeste-like scene of desertion and desolation, back along the grinding, murderous road, she strode ahead of me, careless of the proximity of the heavy traffic lumbering past, as if willing it to run her over.

It was Flick suggested I apply for a job as a library assistant. "Far more *you* than working in an accounts office. It'll be just like going to the library the way you do anyway, but getting paid for it. All the hippies from my school are working there now."

In October I started my new job at Westminster libraries and she started university up north. I saw her off on the late coach from Victoria with the other students and their families and boyfriends; it seemed such a depressing business to me. But I got a cheerful letter from her, she had settled in alright. She came back weekends and then I went up there. I was working in the library now and could finish at lunchtime Friday, take the northbound tube to the end of the line and hitch a ride from Staples Corner up the motorway.

Looking back, it was hellish, the long journey in winter, drenched or frozen as I waited for lifts, the six-hour drag up the spine of England. Towards the end of the journey the traffic diminished and coming off the motorway in the dark you had the sense of reaching a remote, cold northern realm, a stark landscape with gaunt stone houses looming up in the moonlight. At long, long last, I walked up the winding road to the brightly lit modern campus on the outskirts of the old town, lighting up the night sky.

I stayed in Flick's room in the halls of residence; it overlooked the space age ecumenical campus chapel. The other girls in her hall seemed nice, though Flick told me about an eruption of bitchery there, with a ganging up on one gentle, vulnerable girl.

"The ones doing the bullying are English literature students, you'd think they'd be more sensitive and enlightened," Flick complained.

I said, "Well, some of the Nazis were highly cultured people, weren't they? Didn't do much for them!"

The return journey to London on Sunday evening was another six hour trip. By the time I got dropped off on the North Circular the public transport had finished and I had a long walk to Hornsey through the sleeping London streets. I finally sank into my bed at one in the morning, half-dead.

Still, it was worth the hardship of those hitchhiking trips to avoid weekends on my own in the flat. I hated the idea of going back to my old solitary life; I'd got used to having a girlfriend. However, we inhabited different worlds now and the long-distance relationship soon began to deteriorate.

The Easter holiday in Ireland was the last straw. We went to my mother's in North Antrim; she had married again, at sixty, Dan Smith, a cousin and childhood sweetheart, and was living at his farm near Bushmills. Flick and my mother instinctively loathed one another. I put it down to Flick's aversion to the mother figure; she got on fine with my stepfather Dan and his little nephew Alex from over the road who'd drop by; she played with the small boy for hours. That impressed me but otherwise she was a pain. There was some light relief when we met up with Stuarty Rea for an evening in Ballycastle. There was a big crowd up from Belfast for Easter. Linda and her pals were there, she was as feisty and drunkenly gregarious as ever. I soon joined her in the state of inebriation and we ended up snogging in the backyard of the Antrim Arms. She told me she loved me still and I told her I loved her too; I meant it when I said it and asked her to come and live with me in London but oh, no, she said, she couldn't do that! Here was the tragedy of the exile, the girl you left behind. Still, to have some love and affection, even for a few hours, was a wonderful thing. Flick didn't care, there was no love lost between us; bizarrely she seemed rather taken with Linda's mad-girl persona and even started copying it.

It had been an excruciating holiday all round and I was glad to return to London. We got the mid-afternoon train from Coleraine only to find at Belfast that there were no taxis or buses from the station to take us to the boat. The city shut down after dark now; there were bombs going off right, left and centre after the Bloody Sunday shootings of civil rights marchers by the British Army, thirteen dead young bodies on the streets of Derry. That had taken the troubles on to a new horrific level with the feeling that terror reigned now.

"We'll have to walk, there's nothing else for it," I gulped. The prospect of a walk through dockland in the creepy dark that had closed like a lid over the city of troubles was hideous.

We were the only pedestrians abroad, lugging our cases through the dark between the lampposts down the long desolation of Corporation Street. The cars slunk past like killers; there was an almost palpable sense of menace and evil hanging over the dark, godforsaken streets.

The dingy glow of a dockland bar hinted at the continuation of normal life and as we passed the little pub the muted sounds of whorish revelry sounded weirdly from within.

I had a stitch in my side and my heart was banging in rhythm with the old cardboard suitcase against my leg. My worst fear was missing the boat and getting stranded there in the pitiless Belfast night along with the dead weight of Flick. The miserable holiday, the background of shootings and bombings, the breathless, hunted race for the boat: I didn't need any of this and I swore it would be a long time till I came back to the Northern Ireland state again, *if I ever did.*

The next day, safe upon the Liverpool shore, we hitched back to London. I recall the friendly, lively northern lorry driver singing the praises of Gilbert O'Sullivan playing on his cab radio. "He's great, this lad, he is the one!" Back in London Flick and I seemed to be an item still, somehow. It seemed easier to remain a couple, with whatever life you'd built up together, than to be back to square one on your own with nothing.

Flick went back to university at the end of the Easter break. It was then, after she'd gone and I'd been on my own a short while, that I began to experience a new strength of independence in myself. I shed my pathetic fear of being without a woman; it came as a real liberation, suddenly I had simply no need to go chasing after Flick or anyone else. I even looked forward to the weekend alone in the flat with my writing; there was at least a sort of dignity of self-direction about it. I put Flick out of my mind for good; busy with her university life she'd forget me too, it was easy. It was a great new strong, wholesome feeling to be my own man again.

It was the first weekend of my new independence, that Sunday in the springtime of 1972. I got up late as usual, got dressed, faded blue jeans and a green crew-neck pullover. I'd recently had a haircut and I was still clean-shaven. I breakfasted on bacon and eggs at the kitchen table, then shoved the dirty plate on to the communal pile of dirty dishes under the sink. Pouring a fresh cup of tea, I spread my exercise book open on the speckled red Formica table under the window that gave a first floor view of the girls' school behind us, deserted for the weekend. It was a dead grey Hornsey Sunday, nothing out there to distract me. I had taken up my tale of a County Antrim boyhood again, *Once Upon A Distant Shore.*

To have been born the unique person you are, to have lived your life as you did, was a marvel in itself, a magical thing. Writing it down, combining memory and imagination, you celebrated it and captured it for all time. It wasn't just you of course, it was all of life as it flowed through you. You were only a channel in the end, a conduit for experience. And the experiences chose you, not the other way round. As you wrote you felt the mystery behind the words and the mystery grew as your book progressed; that was the most powerful part of it. So I wrote swiftly with the cheap biro on the lined jotter, unself-consciously, taking a great satisfaction in filling up the pages. I was making a book, like Mark Twain, D.H.Lawrence, J.D.Salinger. It was an empowering Godlike process; between the covers of your book you re-created the world and made sense of it.

CHAPTER 19

The Girl on the Landing

I was reading in the sitting room when there was a knock on the door of our flat, about four on that Sunday afternoon after Easter. I opened the door and a lovely-looking dark-haired girl was standing there. In the momentary pause as our eyes met for the first time, before a word could pass between us, she gave a little backwards start and blinked as if she were seeing stars. I would never forget that classic boy-meets-girl moment. Then composing herself, she said, "Oh hello, we've just moved into the flat next door and can't get the geyser in the kitchen to light. We wondered could you help at all?"

Eager to oblige but ever a handless man, I called out to my flatmate Roy to bring the screwdriver and together we followed the figure of the girl with her long, thick, wavy black hair down her back, into the flat next door, down the long, narrow, dark hallway that ran parallel with ours, with three stairs descending halfway along, emerging into the iron daylight of the kitchen at the back where two other girls, her flatmates, were waiting. They smiled and laughed and pointed us to the dirty cream geyser on the scabby wall over the sink. Their flat was rather dingier than ours; it was cheaper.

I got Roy on the job fiddling with the contraption, unscrewing the casing. "Probably just clogged up," he said. The girls waited tense and giggly while he poked around in its ancient copper intestines, and I looked masterfully on, peering over his shoulder like a supervisor.

"They terrify me, those things," said the dark girl. "I always expect them to blow up in my face at any moment."

Roy blew on the wick, adjusted it. "Try it now." I was good with matches; I put a light to the wick: the little flame shot up, wavered and held. "That's it!"

The little chubby girl with long, straight chestnut hair over her shoulders, clapped and cried, "Yippee, now I can have a bath! It's in there next door behind the sink."

"Should be alright now," I said as Roy replaced the casing. "Any other problems at all? Oh, I'm Jim and he's Roy, by the way."

"Bridget," the dark girl introduced herself.

"Nicky," said the little round one.

"Jean!" She was tallish and dark-fair with wide-set, expressive, humorous eyes. Her quick frame seemed to tremble with a simmering mirth that regularly bubbled over into raucous laughter.

All three girls smiled and laughed continuously, as if the simple fact of human existence were a joke.

"The landlady told us about the nice boys from the BBC who live next door," said Jean, her shoulders shaking again, half-suppressing a laugh.

"Roy works there but I moved to the library last autumn," I explained. "You're students?"

"North London Poly, doing English."

"Oh, you'll get on well with Jim then, he likes students," said Roy and the girls all looked at me.

I said, "Yes, seems wherever I go I always end up hanging around with students."

Bridget said, "We're having a flat-warming tonight if you'd both like to come."

"That'd be great! We'll bring some beer," I said.

Back next door Roy said, "What about that Bridget then?" He was a Rugger boy, always up for it.

"They're all nice girls," I said nonchalantly. I was sure none of them wanted to be a Rugby player's girlfriend, they weren't the type.

Bridget rang our doorbell about seven to enquire, "Where's the off-licence?"

"Just five minutes down the road in "Crouch End," I said. "Hang on, we're going there too."

Roy and I walked up the street with her, on to Tottenham Lane. There was a pub opposite. "Fancy a drink first?" I said to Bridget.

"Okay," she said and Roy said he'd go on and get the beer for the party.

Bridget and I crossed the road to the pub. It was a plain little local; I'd never been there before. The front public bar we entered was quiet in the early evening. We took our beers to a corner table.

There was an intense quality about Bridget, as if she were a bit preoccupied or vaguely unhappy, though not with me, I thought. I was attracted to her but couldn't yet be sure she felt the same, though perhaps a little bit, so I held my emotions in check.

She said, "You're Irish?"

"Yes, Belfast," I said.

She said, "I'm Irish: McDonagh." She had an English RP voice but now I thought I could detect an Irish inflection there too. It was good news.

"McDonagh's a good name. I'm Mitchell. Both famous Irish patriot names! Whereabouts in Ireland are you from?"

"It was just holidays over there at my aunt's in Dubln when I was growing up; I'm from Surrey. Daddy would put my older sister Theresa and me on the boat train at Euston and Auntie May would be there to meet us off the ferry at Dun Laoghaire. I loved it over there. Auntie's housekeeper Ann would take us fishing for pinkeens in the Dodder. When I was older I got in trouble for making eyes at the butcher's boy in Dundrum. When he asked me for a date Auntie had to put her foot down!"

"Always plenty of craic down in Dublin," I said. "I have aunties and uncles there too and my favourite cousin Heather, madcap wild girl, though I haven't laid eyes on any of them for years."

"You lose touch," said Bridget sadly.

"You're studying English at the Poly, you said? Lucky!" I said, "I'd love to study literature. I only left the BBC to work in the library so I could read all the books all day."

"Why don't you apply for the Poly?" she said. "They'd take someone like you, mature student, like a shot."

I felt my heart lift at her confidence in me and the old dream of higher education, of freedom and enlightenment, take hold of me again. Having Bridget in the equation suddenly now added significantly to its appeal. Outside again, a little light-headed from the beer, we walked back down our street in the clear spring evening to the flat-warming. The double-fronted three-storey detached house I liked to think of as a "tenement" block stood at a right angle at the bottom of the hill, the last house in the street, facing up it. We went in the unlocked front door, up the dark stairway to the first floor. I'd known lonely, tormented times here, but with the arrival of the student girls now the dark old slum was magically lightened and transformed.

Through the door of their flat the music met us, Santana's *Black Magic Woman*. They seemed to be singing about Bridget. The party had gathered in the front room, Bridget's room. Roy was there with the beer from the off-licence. There were about half a dozen other guests from the girls' course, long-haired blokes and one quiet blonde girlfriend, all sitting round on the sofa and bed and floor in the spring evening light.

I felt immediately at ease in the company of students, the long hair and hippy music, a laid-back bohemian milieu. I managed to position myself on the end of the single bed close to Bridget who sat on the carpet with her back against the boarded-up fireplace, her arms encircling her raised knees. She was dressed in brown brushed denim jeans and a purple polo-neck. Nicky was next me on the bed; a beauty on either side of me!

"Oh, I'm so glad to get into this flat, away from home!" Bridget was saying. "My father and I just do not see eye to eye on a single thing! We just get on each other's nerves all the time. It started as soon as I was old enough for boyfriends. We were really close before that and then suddenly he turns into this tyrant: doesn't trust me any more, thinks no boy is good enough for me and anyway they're all only out for the one thing.

"One boy I dated brought me back a bit late from a party, the bus was delayed, and Daddy kicked him, literally, out the door. Then, you won't believe it, the poor boy got beaten up by skinheads down the end of our road! I have to laugh now thinking about it, it was all so awful!"

Nicky, on my other side, was charming and vivacious. She was a pretty girl too, her long, shiny chestnut hair enveloping her small plump figure that was neatly contained in a cheesecloth Indian smock and mauve trousers with little purple stars. She was warm and companionable, with a touch of the little girl, her eyes shining with wicked fun.

"You're Irish?" she was saying approvingly in her attractive light Brummy voice. "Ah, Seamus, sure you've got the smiling eyes! I'm a Celt too: Manx. Kennaugh, it's an old Manx name. We moved to Brum when I was small; we used to go back to the Isle on holidays. My heart's still back there with the Celts!"

Who was it to be then, Nicky or Bridget? I felt I had a chance with either of them. It was a lovely quandary. Nicky was fun and forward but maybe she reminded me too much of one of my failed first-loves, Katie Burns; while Bridget was different to any girl I'd ever met before, darker, more intense; I was drawn to a seriousness about her, a kind of maturity.

Towards the end of the little party Bridget asked, "Who's for coffee?"

"Would you like a hand?" I asked, bouncing to my feet. "Oh yes, please!" she said and I followed her down the long hallway to the kitchen. The hip pocket of her jeans was torn; she had perfect hips and walked with a proud womanly lilt, placing her feet down squarely on the floorboards with an unconscious rooted, strong physical self-assurance.

Down in the kitchen the activity of getting the coffee filled the pregnant silence between us. I was naturally shy and reticent until I got to know people, while she didn't care for small talk, but I could sense that she was glad of my physical presence there beside her spooning Nescafe and sugar into the dingy mugs.

Back in her room, Bridget was next me on the bed now. I kept turning my head to admire her profile, the lovable strong nose projecting from the long dark curtain of hair falling in natural ringlets, like a female laughing cavalier.

After coffee, with only Roy and me and the three girls left in the room, Bridget asked where she could get some cigarettes this time of night.

"There's a machine in the kebab restaurant on Turnpike Lane," I said. "About ten minutes' walk, I can take you there."

She pulled on a black shawl, shaking her long hair out over it, shouldered her handbag and we went out, stepping carefully down the unlit stairs. Out on the late, deserted Sunday night streets her clogs echoed between the rows of bedtime terraces. She walked with her head slightly lowered, her arms folded under the shawl, drawing it about her against the night chill. Getting into a rhythm together, we walked in a peaceful silence for the most part. We didn't touch yet but I felt that she was with me now. I talked a little about the neighbourhood, which was new to her, the pubs with "Railway" in their names, the handy Greek grocer's at the top of our street, the short cut via the waterworks to Alexander Palace.

"Such an ordinary ugly district really," I said, "but it's my manor, innit?"

"You make it sound interesting," she said, "and it looks alright to me, got character."

We crossed the footbridge at Hornsey station, the way dimly lit, metal plate clanking under our feet. The marshalling yards spread beneath us, a sheen of electric lights on the mesh of rails, the rolling stock stationary, bedded down for the night.

A block of council flats overlooking the track rose sheer, a glitter of lighted windows in the night sky. "How'd you like to live up there?" I asked, for something to say.

She shuddered, "No, thanks!"

I said, "It's the one thing I don't like in London, the high rise blocks, it just doesn't seem natural to me to be stuck away up in the sky like that."

"No: horrible!"

"I can see we agree on things!"

She laughed.

We went down the steps at the far side of the bridge into a dark back street, over the canal, past industrial premises, and crossed Wightman Road into the thoroughfare of Turnpike Lane with its shut small shops. The smell of kebab warmed the night air; in the restaurant window roasted lamb rotated on a spit. We passed inside, into the frenzied jangling gaiety of loud piped Greek music serenading the two long rows of empty red-clothed tables. We walked between the tables the length of the narrow, deep, glowing interior to the cigarette machine on the wall at the back. I felt clever bringing the girl on this obscure night journey to the gold packet of Benson and Hedges in its little drawer popping miraculously out of the machine.

When we got back her room was empty, the flat silent with the girls gone to bed. We sat down together on the green sofa under the green window curtains. The room felt big now with no one else in it. The heavy, dark, deathly silence of Sunday night enfolded the big house, but I had no thought of work in the morning; that seemed to exist in another world now.

"It's a nice room," I said feebly.

"I got the nicest room. Lucky," she said, her voice trailing off small.

I swallowed. We sat on, drowning in the silence. The moment had come. I must kiss her, she was waiting. Yet we were still so separate, such strangers, who'd only just met that day by pure chance. How could this be?

I turned my head and saw the pitiful look on her face. The slight remoteness, the self-containment had melted to a swooning kind of helplessness, begging to be saved from herself. I couldn't delay a moment longer; I went for her blindly now, a leap in the dark, fastening my mouth over hers like a famished leech, overwhelming her with my passion.

The sofa got uncomfortable; I said, "Shall we lie on the bed?"

"Yes, but you'll have to careful," she said. "I'll just go and get ready."

She went out to the bathroom. I undressed hurriedly, dived in between the cold sheets on the narrow single bed against the wall and lay there shivering feverishly, her Teddy bear beside me on the pillow. The old-looking child's cuddly toy, at once girlish and maternal, very feminine, touched a compassion in me, endearing its owner to me. From this angle on the bed, by the low shadowy light of the bedside lamp, the room appeared lofty and imposing with its high ceiling and plaster mouldings, and the elegant long drop of the heavy green curtains on the window. It felt like a stage set for a classical drama.

The door opened and Bridget swept in, the lovely heroine of the piece, long black ringlets and a flowery silk dressing gown. A look of fear passed over her face like cloud shadow, but blindly she let the gown slip away into a silky pool on the floor and she was quite naked, with a beautiful figure, her skin the colour of tallow in the soft light, her proud little face flushing with shame and courage, and nimbly she was in beside me. She turned off the bedside lamp and turned to me between the sheets. I felt the softness of her bosom against mine, her slim waist and the swell of her hip in the crook of my arm, and our lips met moistly in the dark, silent mystery of the London night.

I woke in the morning light filtering around the curtains, a green gloom like a woodland glade. The girl's face, half-lost in the luxuriance of her tousled dark hair over the shared white pillow, was strange to me now with its bruising of smudged eye-shadow and the heavy dark eyelids shut tight like some hibernating small animal. She stayed determinedly fast asleep as I slipped away out of her bed and the room.

The Monday morning had an unreal distanced quality; the night before was everything. I had no thought to spare for anything but the girl, going over and over our time together as if to convince myself it had really happened, that she had been mine for one night. Yet it was dreadful to think it might end there, like too many of the girls before her. And so my mood through all that long working day would constantly swing between euphoria and trepidation.

I got myself back next door, got dressed and out, on to the tube like a sleepwalker, popping up above ground again in the posh Westminster village where the library was situated, bursting in the back door ten minutes late as usual. More so than ever, I couldn't be bothered with the library that day in my overwrought condition. I kept sneaking off for a puff in the staff bog. It was situated oddly in a sort of cupboard in a corner between the fiction book stacks of the small branch library. You hunched there on the throne sucking your fag to a long hot red point. There was no window or other ventilation, so the smoke seeped out under the door into the library. Richards the snooty, buck-teethed librarian, a sad, crumpled, middle-aged bachelor, and Neil his spotty sidekick, twenty going on fifty, twitched their officious nostrils in disapproval but said nothing, just mentally chalking it up as a further instance of the fellow's unsuitability for the post, on top of being a hippy and ten minutes late every morning.

I couldn't eat that day. In the lunch hour I sat on a bench in the little graveyard where it was quiet enough for me to think uninterrupted thoughts of Bridget. I felt noble and godlike at moments, then frail with the fear of rejection. That a girl like Bridget should be mine, it was too good to be true! I settled into a kind of romantic wasting away process, suicidal-poetic, that brought a sort of fatalistic comfort. I was vaguely aware of springtime around me in the fresh green leaves on the churchyard trees and the riot of birdsong in the mild air.

It worried me that I was unable to call up any clear image of her face in my mind's eye. Wasn't that a bit strange, that you could sit there obsessing over a girl without a face? What if I didn't recognise her when we met again? Like, walked straight past her on the street? Or couldn't tell if it were she who answered their door? I was home at five that day, changing into my jeans. Oh good, I'd left my safari jacket in her room, the perfect excuse to go and knock on her door again. I stood there on the landing: now would we remember each other?

It was Bridget who answered my knock. Of course, now she was there in front of me, there was no mistaking the sweet pixie face with the frank regard of round green eyes that widened and glowed with a soft Irish kind of beauty and intelligence, while the cheekbones and lips contracted a little in empathy. Then a lovely warm smile spread over her face in greeting, with no hint of any reservation or the least embarrassment, and with an enormous sense of relief I knew it was going to be all right now, like the song of the day.

"Good timing!" she said, "We're just having a cup of tea."

I followed her down to the daylight in the kitchen. Jean and Nicky were sitting at the table under the window eating toasted teacakes. The homely gentility of the scene in the slum kitchen was reassuring. What a difference it made having girls in a house. The only man there, I felt a bit shy but they all made me so welcome.

"Had a nice day at the office?" Jean joked with her mischievous crooked grin and let rip a mocking laugh.

"The library, you mean," I said. "Afraid I wasn't in the mood for it today."

"Come to the Poly!" said Bridget. "You're wasted in that job."

Nicky said, "How do you stand it, all those hours, every day of your life?"

"The worst thing's getting yourself in there in the morning," I said. "Especially for the ten-hour shift, that feels like a year."

"At least you get to read the books, you said," said Bridget.

"That's the only compensation. I've worked my way halfway round the fiction stacks, just got to S for Singer: Isaac Bashevis. I'm back in Poland before the War. Magical!"

The conversation proceeded to life at the Poly; it seemed a wonderful relaxed, unpretentious institution. The girls all had plenty to say while I sat there drinking tea and listening. I loved the communal atmosphere in their kitchen; they were such jolly, unself-conscious, companionable girls.

Surreptitiously I drank in every detail of Bridget, she was so fine just sitting there in an armchair with her womanly composure, smiling and sipping tea, vivacious and easy now. She was dressed in a white shirt and black waistcoat and a black woollen skirt with big buttons down the front, her smooth bare knees like ivory crossed below the hem, long black woollen socks going down into scuffed clogs. She had a rash around her mouth and chin from my ardent kisses of the night before.

I was on my feet helping clear the dishes from the table when she came up behind me and caressed me over the hip pocket of my blue jeans. I must have a nice ass too! When I turned to her in a warm rush of gladness she looked up affectionately into my face then tippy-toed up and placed a kiss on my brow. It was an unexpected beautiful, tender moment. And I knew for sure now she felt the same about me.

I left the girls to get on with their Beowulf essay due at college; I was anxious not to impose on their hospitality, overstay my welcome. Back next door in my own flat I opened the fridge and looked at the bacon and eggs, my staple diet, and decided I still wasn't hungry. I'd not eaten anything since I met Bridget. There was no sign of my flatmates this evening. I'd no heart for my writing, its solitary, memory-fantasy world of ghosts and wishful thinking; what was it anyway compared to the reality of a flesh and blood woman? My phase of feeling comfortable in a self-sufficient, monkish solitude had been very short-lived indeed.

I got a glass tumbler and placed the open end of it against the partition wall and pressed my ear to the bottom of the glass, an eavesdropping trick I'd acquired as a lad, after a character in a Herlihy novel. Listening intently I caught wordless sounds of the girls' heedless raised voices and footfalls next door, far-off lonely echoes. Other voices, other rooms. It was an undignified waste of time. What now? I wandered up to our sitting room and turned on the TV in the light of the spring evening, sat staring unseeingly at the black and white screen while my thoughts turned endlessly on the girl next door. When would I see her again? Until that time my life was on hold.

Later there was a knock on our door. It was an unabashed smiling Bridget in her flowery silk dressing gown announcing, "I've come for coffee!"

"Come on through, I'll stick on the kettle!" It was good to feel we were both playing the same game: her move, my move. I was in a nervous kind of heaven.

"Oh, it's nice here!" she said as I showed her into the sitting room. The big light room with its fawn three-piece suite and matching carpet was a cut above flat 3, though I much preferred Bridget's bohemian boudoir.

I brought the mugs of instant coffee, put a match to the bronze gas fire. The tiny hissing flames mounted in its ugly grid as we made ourselves comfortable on the sofa.

"You got your Beowulf done?"

"Well, enough for one day or I'll go mad. I love Beowulf, hate writing essays. At least I've picked the right course this time. I had a term at Bristol doing French, that wasn't me at all, apart from some of the literature, Baudelaire, Rimbaud and Verlaine."

"It must be great reading them in the French."

"Yes, that bit was great, but it was all more about becoming a bilingual secretary ultimately. That's what my father had in mind for me. He was furious when I packed it in at the Christmas break. I got a job in London then started at the Poly in September. I love the course, Chaucer and Anglo-Saxon and Old Icelandic, and living in North London."

We sat and watched the TV for a bit, it helped fill in gaps in the conversation. Something in a programme made me come out with, "Sometimes I think the world would be a much better place if women were running it." It was a fairly original thought back then in 1972.

"Don't you believe it!" said Bridget. "More like hell, I'd say!"

"Oh, well, maybe you know something I don't," I conceded. It was auspicious at least that we both preferred the opposite sex; not a bad start to a relationship!

It was cosy there together on the settee by the fire as it grew dark outside. Bridget stared vacantly at the TV over the rim of her steaming coffee mug, sitting back very relaxed with her knees up, heels resting on the edge of the seat-cushion under her. I sat there in a growing yearning for her that focused on her dear little doll-like hands and exquisitely slender forearms and the marbly points of her knees protruding from the silky folds of the gown. Her bare feet were small, narrow and supple, almost prehensile. When I could no longer contain myself I put my arm round her and kissed her soft cheek. She turned her face to me, closing her eyes, and I kissed her lips.

We went next door to her room. The bedside lamp had been left on, its yellow light falling across the neat single bed with its white and black spread, the old orange Teddy bear on the pillow. The rest of the green room was in shadow, intimate and homely, sealed in by the long drop of the heavy closed green curtains. Bridget slipped off her clothing and got into bed in a seamless dancelike movement. She watched with a woman's smiling interest and frank amusement as I hopped about on the bedside rug removing my trousers, awkwardly, almost falling over. She looked ready to laugh out loud as I stood there finally naked before her. Yes, at these times we must look a sight to the opposite sex! But her mocking humour was tinged with real affection; after all we were designed for love. I clambered over her to lie next the wall, she switched off the lamp and we were safe in each other's arms again, warm and naked together in the cocoon of our lovemaking.

Afterwards she exclaimed, "Tea!" She put on a cute little-girl kind of voice.

"Tea?"

"Yes, fancy a cup?"

"Oh, yeah!"

"Teoast?"

"Mmm, yes, especially the way you say it, sounds a real scrummy treat!"

She rolled big eyes. "Teoast and wraspberry jam!"

"Violet Elizabeth, is it? Wasb'wy jam!"

"I'll scweam 'n' scweam if I don't get it, now!"

She clicked on the light. jumped out of bed and pulled on her dressing gown in a single fluid motion and stalked off down the landing, her bare heels striking the boards. It was midnight on her little red travel alarum clock. I should be asleep now for work in the morning, not up having a midnight feast! I lay back in a warm glow of male contentment.

Bridget's bedside lamp with its pleated yellow shade like a swirling dancer's pretty skirt and the base a round Mateus Rose wine bottle, shed a soft, shadowy light across the green bed-sitting room, making it a self-contained small, glowing world. Her own bits and pieces made the furnished room instantly homely and feminine: the Indian bedspread, a sheepskin rug before the fireplace and a squashy leather pouffe with a Celtic motif.

Looking down from the wall was a poster of Rousseau's *Innocence of Days*. A native woman crouched on big bare white thighs among hallucinatory-vivid green spears of jungle grass, a friendly-looking tiger prowling there as the woman contemplated her reflection in a mirror. I found myself studying the woman, a solitary, sensual creature rooted in wild nature, as if she might hold some clue to the mystery of Bridget.

Who came back shortly with a tray, steaming mugs of tea and golden slices of buttered toast evenly spread with raspberry jam.

"It's picture-squee!" I enthused. "Scarlet on the gold. It'd make a nice still life: *The Supper Tray.*"

"Do you paint then?"

"I have done. I will do again sometime. My brother's the painter of the family."

"What age are you anyway?" she asked, seriously.

"Twenty-four."

"Oh, that's good," she said, a thrilling note of respect in her voice. "My last boyfriend was twenty-four—actually he was my fiancé. I much prefer an older guy."

"You were engaged? I'm impressed!" It implied a degree of the maturity I preferred in a woman.

She said, "I got engaged at eighteen. I'll be twenty next month."

"So what happened to the fiancé?"

"Oh. Kevin—we both changed. He got awfully controlling of me. I wanted to be free to live the student life. In the end I gave him back his ring, both of us in floods of tears."

"You must have loved him?"

"It was more in love with being in love." She sighed. "What about you? Don't tell me you've been married or something, with kids."

"No, nothing like that at all. I was seeing a girl for a while there then she went to university up north. It was nothing really."

"Really?"

"Really and truly nothing."

"Look at the time. You have to get up for work in the morning. Sleepy-byes?"

"I'm not sleepy yet!"

"Oh dear, I see!"

I was woken in the morning by the sadistic yapping of the alarum clock. Our bodies were fast entwined, the way we'd fallen asleep the night before. Disentangling myself from Bridget's inert warm arms and legs was agony, a tearing away from heaven. I would have to become a student soon so we could lie in together.

CHAPTER 20

The Kiss of Life

"Well, you and Jean and Nicky have really livened the place up, that's for sure. I used to get back here after work and groan at the emptiness and boredom of it. I used to get quite depressed."

"Oh, po'r yo'! I suppose it was the proverbial loneliness of bedsitter land?"

"Yes, I've been through funny periods in London, ups and downs. Oh, there were friends and girlfriends from work, from the BBC. I quickly settled into the London life, I've loved it in so many ways, but sometimes there was this sense of something missing in my life."

"Perhaps you missed Ireland?"

"Oh, I always miss Ireland, at least the Ireland of my heart, with all the great youthful memories and wee Dana singing on the radio, '*Many Years Ago*', that'd bring sentimental tears to my exile's eyes. But the reality—lack of opportunity, the troubles getting worse—I've never missed that. No, London became my home the day I arrived here. Well, I had a first night of homesickness, but when I got up in the morning in the snow in Kilburn I felt like a new man and I knew I would never go back to Ireland. My father's death soon after I moved away affected me quite a bit and for a while I was inclined to mope around in my room too much."

"Poor you, that must have been horrid for you!"

I didn't tell Bridget about my premonition in that lonely time that a dark woman would come to the house and save me. Long dark hair fell down her back as she stretched her arms up around my neck to kiss me. She seemed to be Irish, maybe a nurse. The vision came back to me when Bridget mentioned she had planned a career in nursing then changed course when she got her A-level results. I didn't dare mention either that now I was getting happy images of Bridget on a sunlit lawn with our baby!

Several weeks passed; I had slept with Bridget every night since she moved into the house. I felt close to Jean and Nicky too; I valued female friendship and got on well with the other students who dropped by. Suddenly I was living the student bohemian life I had always dreamt of; I was a sort of honorary student and before long I would be a real one, I promised myself now.

The girls had an end of term party, the crowd from the Poly packing into Bridget's room in the light of the May evening. It was the first time I met Mervyn, his long bony figure seated cross-legged in the middle of the floor, holding court as he rolled a joint on the cover of *The Yes Album.* Very long sheer-falling brown hair framed the strange ageless wizardly face with its Frankenstein cliff of brow and the up-curving cleft chin trying to meet the downward curve of the great hook nose. He chain-smoked as he stared off into space through horn-rimmed glasses and talked continuously in a kind of student bedsitter stream of consciousness punctuated with hoarse laughter and exclamations of *"Far out!"* He was the supplier of dreams, of the marijuana and other mind-altering substances favoured by the students. Tonight he dispensed little squares of what looked like grey blotting paper that melted readily on the tongue and promised a twelve-hour hallucinogenic-spiritual "trip".

I was settling in comfortably with the student bodies draped around the smoke-filled room, the Doors on the record player, *You're Lost, Little Girl,* when Bridget, seated next me on her bed, began to get agitated. Then she turned to me and whispered, "I need to get out of here!"

Out in the street she said, "Sorry, I couldn't sit in that room another minute with all those people on top of us!"

"Shall we have a drink up the pub? That bar's always quiet early on."

We walked up the hill in the soft, clear evening light and crossed Tottenham Lane to the pub. We sat at the same corner table in the public bar with our glasses of bitter. The quiet ordinariness and anonymity of the working class bar was reassuring.

"Alright now?" I asked.

She nodded, "Think so! I couldn't breathe in that room."

We had not been there long when the bar began to fill up. As another influx of customers came through the door, I saw the look of alarm on Bridget's face and experienced my own first waves of anxiety.

"Getting a bit busy in here," I said. "Shall we go on somewhere?"

We drained our glasses and left. We laughed with relief to be outside under the spring evening sky. Yet it was unnerving here too on the street with a sense of everything at one remove, as if viewed through glass. We drifted along the pavement in no particular direction till looking up we saw the blue lamp of the police station. Panicking, we crossed back over Tottenham Lane and ducked down Cranford Way like fugitives.

The long, barren residential street dropped away under our marching feet, the facing rows of terraced houses parting before us, down, down into the valley bottom then steeply up ahead to high Hornsey Rise.

There was only one other person in sight in the vista of the street, a black girl walking up the hill towards us. She passed us on the pavement, a young teenage schoolgirl walking with a great easy roll of plump hips. She was sucking a sweet and the whites of her eyes and her strong white teeth showed in the soft ebony face as she swept past, oblivious of us. Bridget and I had to smile at one another then, the girl was so ordinary yet extraordinary.

That was like everything now. "Oh, look at the sunset!" said Bridget. The sky over Hornsey Rise was a weird preternatural shade of red.

"Looks like the Martians are coming!" I exclaimed. It didn't seem improbable.

We were two earth-children wandering in awe of creation. The street was long and pitiless like the road of life itself, but we faced it together. The fear lifted from us; Bridget linked my arm and we walked in a steady rhythm, talking in the soft, assured, intimate way of young lovers, making plans. In that moment I felt the decisive shift in our relationship from tentativeness to certainty.

She said, "Why don't you move in with me. What's the point in you paying for that flat any more, you're never there."

I felt the little leap of joy in my heart, as if I had been handed the world on a plate, all mine. "Oh Bridget, are you sure?"

"Yes, of course, it just makes sense."

The street bottomed out and then there was the steep ascent to Hornsey Rise. Into the flat evening silence a commotion was approaching, over the Rise. The milk float came sailing down the hill, a bizarre contraption that shook and rattled, moaned and wheezed and whined. We stared in awe as it dropped past us like a flying saucer.

"Oh my God!" exclaimed Bridget. "That frightened the life out of me!"

"It's like a cross between a horse and cart and a spaceship," I said.

We gained the summit of the hill where a small block of council flats stood in an open communal area of lawn. Under a tree a garden bench waited with a view over the valley below.

"A seat waiting here just for us!" said Bridget.

We sank down gratefully on the bench after our climb. The lights were coming on in the bowl of grey-blue twilight at our feet. At the bottom of the canyon to our one side was Hornsey station, the marshalling yard a tangle of shining rails. A movement of shunted rolling stock sent up a screech, a clanking and a groan. A snake of train with its row of lighted windows rumbled through the dusk away below.

In the silence after the train had passed we could hear a kind of dull commotion building close by. It was coming from inside the block of flats, raised angry voices that seemed to carry out through the brick walls. Then suddenly a first floor window was flung open and a large black lady leaned out and shouted at us. We couldn't hear what she was saying but it wasn't friendly; we supposed we must be trespassing here and we got up and moved on quickly, turning down a curving street over the hill.

"We're like naughty kids getting chased by the grown-ups!" said Bridget.

"I like that!" I said. "You'n' me's quare pals, Bridie McDonagh! Hi look, Harringay station! Shall we explore?"

We dropped down the long steep flight of wooden steps below the street.

It was an unmanned station, no passengers around either. Our footfalls resounded eerily along the dim ghostly platform under the fretted wooden roof. In the waiting room I lit an empty cigarette packet in the cold grate of the cast iron fireplace.

"Cosy!" I said as the flames rose briefly

"Creepy, dusty old joint. Too quiet!" Bridget shivered.

"Like the scene of one of those Victorian railway murders!"

"Oh, don't!"

I'd scared myself too. We hurried away, back up the steep board steps to the road. We *were* like children again, the small world of our neighbourhood filled with fresh adventures at every turn.

It was dark now.

"Cats!" said Bridget. "Look, they're everywhere!"

They slunk along garden walls, emerged from under parked cars, trotted across the road, their luminous round green eyes watchful and strangely knowing.

"But where are all the people?" I said. "Not a soul about! Maybe the cats have taken over?"

"Cat city!"

We dropped back down the hill to home.

As we approached our house Duncan came out the front door, peering out of his floppy hair, up and down the street, like a fugitive ready to make a run for it. He laughed when he saw us and spoke in his likeable Geordie, "Ah, Bridget and Jim! Bin for a wa'k? Ah'm tryin' tae get up the courage to go doon the sweetie shop!"

"We'll go with you!" said Bridget.

At the shop in Crouch End a bell tinkled as we entered. A man emerged from the back of the shop and positioned himself behind the counter, arms folded, deadpan, awaiting our order. Behind him the rows of tall glass sweetie jars rose to the ceiling; Duncan stood with his head back looking up at the jars, overwhelmed by choice. The doorbell rang behind us as more customers entered.

"Ahh—ahh—" went Duncan, scratching his head comically as the waves of tension mounted unbearably in the claustrophobic cramped space.

"Quaarter o' the humbugs, please!"he announced desperately.

Safely back on the street again with the paper bag of humbugs we laughed in relief. Somehow the smallest everyday actions had become an ordeal in a screamingly funny way. Life was like this for hippies!

We called in on the student Glyn on our way back, in a back street off the Broadway. He led us upstairs to the little attic room he inhabited on his own, where we listened by candlelight to Bo Hansson's *Lord of the Rings,* dreamlike Tolkien-themed instrumental music weaving fantasies in the air till you seemed to float away up around the walls and ceiling on it and out the skylight and up among the stars.

Glyn was a dark Welsh wizard, silent and secretive behind his long hair, beard and round glasses. There was no need to talk; the three of us drank tea and let the wizardly fantastic music flow through us. There was an ecstatic tenderness and fine spirituality in it that words would have spoilt; it was good to just sit there being the beautiful people, to imagine the world as gentle as us, with even a breath of disagreement no longer possible.

Back at our place it was all happening. The party had spread out from Bridget's room through the rest of the girls' flat and into mine next door. Each room, as we came to it, was the scene of a different pageant. In Jean's bedroom, the big middle one, the student Phil had used her poster paints to execute a psychedelic mural covering the whole of one wall, an enormous male hippy head smoking a joint. Phil stood back in paint-spattered jeans grinning and assessing his handiwork while Jean and the others cooed and gasped their appreciation. It certainly gave a facelift to the shabby room.

In Bridget's room Simon and Terry were strumming their guitars singing Neil Young *A Man Needs A Maid,* their performance building to a torturous intensity. Simon's wiry bush of wavy fair hair stood up as if he were on the receiving end of an electric shock; his face was hobgoblin-like, the brow elongated, wicked little blue eyes behind the square gold specs. Terry's strong white teeth gleamed in his beard like an animal in a bush. The big dark beard covered his chest like a biblical elder, his long, thick hair fell sheer to his waist. He was quaintly attired in the leather waistcoat and long boots of a storybook woodcutter. When their song was over he threw back his head and laughed a rumbling barrel-chested "Oh, ho, ho!" like a pantomime dwarf.

Jean came in with wide, astonished young girl eyes and exclaimed, "Have you seen Nicky's room? It's full of people with shining golden hair!"

We wandered down the hallway and looked in from the doorway. The small bedroom was packed with people sitting on the bed and floor; a shimmering golden light came off their blonde heads, like a glimpse of some royal court of Faery.

Through to the kitchen, Nicky was presiding over a tea party, in her element, shining-faced, chattering and laughing as she wielded the big brown teapot, filling the proffered mugs. She had turned into a laughing peasant earth mother around a Manx cottage fire and acquired the look of the teapot, shiny, with the curved spout and the squat base.

Next door in my flat a group of "heads" were sitting round glued to the tele, mesmerised by the fleeting images from the black and white screen. The programme was *Rawhide*. I'd grown up on TV westerns including this one but never seen any of them like this before, the incidental theme music crashing and doom-laden, the American voices an inimical harsh gabble. A baddie swung round and snarled into the camera, his rock-carved, bristled, monster face a caricature of evil. Everything was speeded up and sickening. I had to get out of there quick, away from the violence of the box in the corner.

Back in Bridget's room it was uncrowded and peaceful, the band Yes was on the record player, Fragile; the soulful, imaginative music filled the green glade of the room. I could have stayed there for ever, drifting on its moods, then Hilary came over and spoke quietly to me, "Bridget's looking for you. She's on the stairs."

We'd got separated in the party crowd a while back. I found her now, my love, sitting alone out on the dark communal stairway.

"Feeling lost," she said miserably.

"Let's get a breath of fresh air," I said and walked her down the stairs into the street. It was after midnight. We strolled a little way along from the door to be on our own and stood by the high wire fence of the girls' school, under the sodium night sky. There were the two of us and the universe.

The lamppost shone down on the lovely pale oval of her upturned sad little face in the mass of crinkly black hair. She had the sweet and tender romantic beauty of a fairy princess. The whole trip was a journey through the pages of fairy tales.

She laid her face against my chest; I thought she was crying. Then she mumbled something.

"What?" I said and she looked up at me with beautiful big pitiful moist eyes in the lovely soft face and said, "I love you."

I couldn't speak for a moment; it was as if I were dreaming, her three simple words everything I had ever wanted to hear. Then I spoke the brave noble words too, "I love you, my darling!" and we kissed and held each other tight there under the lamppost, two magical souls, the fairy princess and her prince, in the ordinary, sleeping city street.

Chapter 21

The Lovers

I didn't go to work at the library the following day; I got Bridget to ring them from a phone box and say I was sick. We were going to stay at her parents' in Surrey that night and go on to Paris the day after for the Whit bank holiday weekend. We packed small rucksacks for the journey, we were going to hitchhike, and I accompanied Bridget on the bus to Kentish Town, to her eleven o'clock lecture, her last one of the year.

What a liberation I felt that morning sitting next to Bridget among the other students high in the tiered desks of the lecture theatre listening to the pleasant young woman lecturer's "Introduction to Anglo-Saxon archaeology". Jean was there too, smiling over at me, and Duncan and the lads waved to me across the room. It felt so right, the pre-eminence of culture and the freedom to learn, a world of difference to the relentless, mindless servitude of work. I sat there indistinguishable from the other students, feeling that soon I too would be a bona fide student, that nothing could stop me this time.

After the lecture we had a drink and a sandwich in the basement bar of the Poly, then Bridget and I took the bus to Victoria. There was a great sense of excitement there on the teeming station concourse as we scanned the electronic timetable display boards, the two of us starting our weekend adventure together. Then window-seated in our train compartment, a cosy couple, we sailed over the rooftops and sunken grimy streets, and out past the four massive steeples of Battersea Power Station soaring in the pale blue spring sky.

Beyond Croydon the outlook grew greener and more suburban. We clipped along high on the embankment between the trees and braked for Burley Down.

"Here we are!"

"This is nice, Bridget," I said, "reminds me of Jordanstown in County Antrim where I'd like to have lived, all leafy and genteel."

As we walked down the station path to the road, the rumble of the train died away behind us and there was a hushed, remote feeling, like the heart of the country. The path sloped down between brambled banks to the road and a row of village shops. We went under the brick arch of the railway bridge and down long, silver birch-lined, silent avenues of detached, spacious houses and neat front gardens.

"A commuter land of order and respectability!" declared Bridget. "Even the birds in the trees in Burley sound middle class!"

"Well, it's nice and peaceful anyway," I said although the blank, deserted streets and the almost eerie quietude, the ghostly rustle of the breeze in the fresh spring foliage, unnerved me a little.

"Boring, you mean!" she retorted.

I said, "It's holy ground to me, Bridget McDonagh, the streets my love grew up in, walked to school each day. I wish I'd known you then, in your convent uniform."

"No, you don't! The uniform was frumpy and I was a bit of an ugly duckling at school, dumpy, with glasses."

"You were never ugly!"

"Here we are." I followed her through a gateway in a low stone wall. It was a good-sized mock-Tudor detached house. A rose bush twined itself around the front porch.

Her mother opened the door to us, a tall, handsome, well-dressed woman with her white hair piled high in a glamorous sort of bun. "Hello, darling!" she greeted her daughter sweetly.

The two women embraced, touchingly—I had never seen my sister and mother do that. Then turning to me the mother said, "How do you do, Jim!" and shook my hand warmly. It was all rather gracious and charming. I felt a bit of a provincial oaf there—silly, I know.

"We've been hearing all about you, Jim—the boy next door!" the mother smiled and laughed. "Now you come and sit down here in the front room and read the newspaper while I get on with the dinner. Would you like a cup of tea?"

The late afternoon sun shone into the big square golden room. I sat there on my own on the sofa sipping tea from a Willow Pattern cup and crunching a ginger snap. I flicked through the newspapers on the coffee table. Bridget was helping Mummy in the kitchen. I could hear the cheerful shouty feminine voices gossiping away as they banged pots and pans around. It could be lonely sometimes being a guy.

There were a couple of the Irish newspapers with the homely feeling of their smaller world, and the dreaded *Daily Telegraph*—I couldn't quite bring myself to stomach a dose of its invidious conservatism. Philip Callow had written of "the filthy microbe life" of newsprint, which pretty aptly summed up all the newspapers. That and what Henry Williamson called their "killing materialism". I pushed them away and sat back and admired the gilt-framed paintings of fresh yellow and blue Irish landscapes on the walls of the room. The rush hours' commuter trains passed regularly along the nearby railway embankment, an oddly soothing sound like a spring shower falling on the silver birches, then a rhythmical soft, fast beating away into the distance, like a jazz melody fading.

It was six when a middle-aged man breezed in the garden gate, floppy grey hair and grey suit, with the distinguished air of the professional man about him. The handsome face had a look of Bridget in the bone structure. I listened a little apprehensively as the front door burst open and he fussed through the hallway and into the kitchen, calling out in agitation to his wife. There followed a light bickering exchange between them; I could hear the firm, polite rebuttals of her rich, deep tones, not an inch given, and his higher, cracked, plaintive voice in a sort of controlled exasperation. It was nothing serious, just domestic trifles, tempered with cold "darlings".

I drank a sherry with the father in the front room while Bridget and the mother finished their preparations in the kitchen. Looking relaxed now in a tan polo shirt, brown twills and leather slippers, sitting up on a hard chair for his bad back, he said, he asked me about my job and I heard myself blabbing disingenuously about my deep desire to become a chartered librarian. Who was I fooling most, him or myself? I wanted to impress Bridget's parents as a suitor for their daughter.

It was a relief when Bridget stuck her dear head round the door with, "Dinner's ready!"

We followed her through to the dining room at the back. French windows overlooked a sunken lawn, tall trees at the bottom of the garden. The table was laid for four; Bridget's sisters and her brother were all away. The father put his reading glasses on and began to carve the roast chicken with great precision. There were starched white linen serviettes to match the tablecloth and crystal glasses for the wine, civilised little touches to turn a meal into a celebratory ritual.

"You're from Belfast, Jim?' said the father. "Things seem to be getting worse over there what with the extremists on both sides."

"Yes indeed, it's got really extremist since Bloody Sunday. It was an extremist act indeed when the British army, the putative 'peacekeeping force' opened fire on a civil rights march killing fourteen young people who'd done nothing wrong and it's caused a lot more extremism ever since, yes. When the troubles really get going *after* the peacekeeping force has gone in then it must be time to agree with the Beatle and say 'give Ireland back to the Irish'."

"What, a united Ireland with the Protestants and Catholics all together?" he queried in alarm, flushing a little as if I'd smacked his face with his rolled-up *Daily Telegraph*.

"Exactly! Simple, isn't it? We're not living in the seventeenth century any more."

"I'm from Dublin myself,' he said. "I came over to England during the war to work in construction. I was pro-active in politics here for some years, ran for the Liberals for Burley council, back when Jo Grimond was leader: a brilliant mind! I fear we may never see his like again.

"Ask me what I believe in and I'll tell you." Nobody was asking him but he let us have it anyway. "One word: Freedom! The free world, free enterprise, freedom of the press!" He was smiling now, kind of self-congratulatory, and as if it were all such fun; then he wagged an admonitory forefinger. "These are the values that must be upheld against Communists, Young Liberals and other extremists, trades union agitators and left wing mobs!"

Bridget gave him a sceptical look and spoke with a quiet sort of determination: "What about the other sort of extremism then? The right-wing kind?"

"Oh no, good gracious no, no, no, we don't want the Blackshirts marching down Holly Berry Avenue either! Ha, ha, ha!"

"Bet some of the neighbours round here wouldn't mind," said Bridget wickedly. "Like old Adolph next door, the secret policeman."

"Oh, old Bernie Mungbean's not such a bad fellow when you get to know him, his bark is much worse than his bite," said the father.

"He monitors potential subversives," Bridget explained, "shop stewards at Ford's and Aldermaston marchers and outspoken clergymen. Phone tapping and spying on them, that sort of thing. If you heard his views on society generally, considering he's a senior policeman, you'd think Hitler had won the war!"

"Well, I don't know," said the father. "'*Eternal vigilance*' as they say! Ha,ha! We must protect our freedoms from those who would undermine them. We are a parliamentary democracy, a mixed economy! That's why we are members of Nato, to help secure the shores of this archipelago of our United Kingdom. And now we have the Common Market to promote free enterprise across Western Europe! Britain is a nation of small shopkeepers when all is said and done. And don't get me wrong, I speak as a champion of free speech; I am unashamedly a Grimondite Liberal, consensus politics, social democrat moderate!" he declared boldly, the worse for two sherries and a glass of German sweet white wine. "My good wife here will disagree with me on some of those points but that's alright, she is a one nation, old colonial, old coaster, Empire Conservative—the backbone of this country!" He grinned in a gloating sort of idiocy with the surge of well-being he got from chewing on all the smug cliches.

Bridget, the devil in her green eyes now, piped up, "Well, Jim's a red flag Trotskyite Fourth Internationalist socialist revolutionary, aren't you, love?"

"A '*Librarians For Social Change*' activist, actually. Fighting for the rights of mothers to bring their pushchairs into the library! Power to the borrowers!" I tried to joke but the mother and father were staring very hard at me now, as if there might be some truth in Bridget's assertions, a link to the Kremlin perhaps. There was a momentary pause then the mother spoke firmly, "Who's for trifle? Or there is chocolate sponge cake with cream."

After the wine with dinner Bridget and I seemed to float to the pub in the suburban evening sunlight and birdsong, shortcutting along narrow paths between the high chestnut palings of the gardens, across the avenues, up over Durley Heights and down the other side to join the quiet back road past the station sidings and coal depot to the village.

It thrilled me to share with Bridget the scenes of her formative years, the magical intimacy of the streets she'd walked, the whole district imbued with her spirit, so that it became part of me too now, instantly familiar and dear, like coming home. I wanted to join up with the life she'd known before me, so I shared the whole of her life, as if I had always known her, that I might possess her completely! Ironically I saw it all in a romantic glow while she shunned the place as boring and irrelevant to the person she was now.

"You were having fun teasing your Daddy," I smiled. "Your Mummy and Daddy will think I am the most dreadful Marxist now, or something! Though it was funny, I have to admit!"

"Yeah. Poor man, he just rubs me up the wrong way with his endless *opinions!*"

"It's the influence of the media, I suppose? Tormenting everybody with its antisocial negativity and paranoia. My dad was the same, especially as he got older; used to drive me mad at times, much as I loved him."

"Oh yes, Daddy and I were really very close at one time," said Bridget. "I used to go with him to see Ireland playing at

Twickenham and once even, can you believe it, to hear Gerry Fitt speaking at a civil rights rally. That was all before the boyfriends came along of course; he couldn't cope with that!"

"By the way, did he ever get elected to Burley council? He didn't say."

"Oh no. He's too left wing for Burley! You know, when I was about seven, about 1959, a Communist family moved into the house opposite us and none of the other children in the street were allowed to play with their children. I remember thinking they must smell, although I never got close enough to them to tell!"

We strolled down to the Surrey village, hand in hand, in a glow of intimacy and had a quiet drink in the Station Hotel. We walked back with our arms round each other in the last long light of the peaceful spring evening, in the sensual dewy perfumes of cut grass and new garden flowers. The sunset flush of the sky had the Martian tinting of the night before; the strange magic of the trip still ran in our veins. We were warmly conscious of ourselves as a couple now, together and in love forever, two ordinary existences become one charmed vital life. We knew this was the greatest adventure and the true meaning of our lives. We could scarcely believe we should be so lucky, that we had been chosen for this great happiness.

In the morning we were off to Paris; now all our days would be an adventure, a joyful celebration of the life we shared together. That night we'd sleep at Burley, in separate beds for the first time since we met. As far as Bridget's parents were concerned we were going to a youth hostel with another couple, to same sex dormitories. But tucked in my wallet I had the address of Hotel Stella my brother had given me, where he and Nora had stayed in Paris.

We hitched down to Dover in the morning, a lift high in the snug capsule of the cab with a cheerful, chatty lorry driver who seemed glad of our company and enthused about his trips to the Continent and the joys of the French croissant; the English ones, he said, being "like something you'd jack up a lorry with."

The channel was overcast, grey and choppy; we ensconced ourselves in the ship's bar with the duty-free beer and fags. I told Bridget about my last visit to Paris:

"Nineteen-sixty-three, I was fifteen, with the school. We stayed in a vacated boarding school, an old grey building behind a high wall, with big long dormitories. There were girls from Liverpool in the one below ours. We dined in the basement—horse-meat on the menu was a novelty and tasted fine! The days were spent trooping round sightseeing; our party got photographed at the Arc de Triomphe with a gorgeous Italian starlet, don't remember her name, for *Le Figaro*.

"I recall the excitement queuing to see the Mona Lisa at the Louvre. There was the hit song about her by Conway Twitty then the disappointment seeing the painting, this ordinary-looking woman, we thought, no sex appeal! I'd heard it was all about the smiling eyes; great art isn't obvious, and I kept looking into her eyes for inspiration. The only other art I remember from the footsore blur of sightseeing is the ceiling paintings at Versailles and being told how all the ceiling artists went mad eventually. I always loved stories about artists going mad; it seemed you had to go mad sooner or later to be a true artist!

"Then one day we saw a drowned man pulled out of the Seine, looked like a long-haired beatnik. I thought that romantic, I pictured an artist reviled, starved and driven mad in his attic before throwing himself in the river. More likely he was just an alcoholic tramp who fell in the water.

"One evening there was a rumble of gunfire in the Champs Elysee where we were and we heard afterwards that one of the Saudi royal family had been assassinated on the steps of a hotel. That was exciting. It was the time of the uprising in Algeria; the letters OAS were daubed all over the city, the French opposition to the Algerian nationalists. Have you seen *The Battle of Algiers*?

"In the evenings we were allowed out unsupervised in the district around the school. Our teachers had warned us about Arab men and sure enough, at a fairground one evening, two young Arab men attached themselves to my mate Sam and me. They bought us Fantas and we all had a game of pinball in a café. They were nice, well-dressed, professional-looking young men, nothing sleazy-looking or sinister about them. The good-looking one attached himself to me, his ugly mate got Sam. Well, we were polite Irish lads so we gave them a game of pinball then excused ourselves and beat a hasty retreat back to the school.

"I got drunk for the first time in my life in Paris, with a crowd of the more advanced lads drinking the chilled French beer in a café one evening. Needless to say I got drunk. I loved the feeling of being liberated from all the painful shyness and self-consciousness of a withdrawn, chubby Elvis lookalike, fifteen-year-old schoolboy. I turned into a stand-up comedian; the wit just poured out of my mouth. I was brandishing a chair, acting out some yarn, holding forth, the thespian or hidden exhibitionist coming out in me. Everyone was laughing their heads off at me, clapping and cheering me on. I'd made it: suddenly I was the most popular boy on the trip: fame at last!

"Anyway, I was drunk every night after that for the rest of the holiday. The other thing I'd do when I was drunk was kiss everybody: the other lads, that is! I wasn't queer or anything, I just loved everybody and it seemed a French kind of thing to do and nobody seemed to mind. I never made contact with the Liverpool girls in the other dormitory though some of the lads dated them—I was too immature for that, still terrified of girls.

"A small group of us would sneak out in the middle of the night with our hangovers and parched mouths to drink chilled orange Fantas in the all-night café opposite the school. On our last night everybody got very drunk and ran riot in our dormitory. When a teacher from the school in the dormitory below came up to complain, Paul Ferris told him to eff off. Our teachers got back from a burlesque show, in the middle of it all and restored order. I'd not been involved in the riot, I was tucked up in bed. I heard Kipper, the English ex-fighter pilot who taught French, going round the cubicles with his slipper, enforcing order.

"On the way back home, on the train, there was an inquisition by the three masters in charge of the trip: Kipper, Taffy and Geordie. They had my name as one of the drinkers—I told them I had no part in the riot but admitted I had been drinking, thinking to impress them with my honesty, which proved a naive eejity thing for me to do. No one else admitted anything. So

Paul Ferris and I were made the scapegoats for the whole affair, up before the Head in his study when we got back to school. The Head went to our house to see my parents over it; he told them, 'Your son is not a bad boy, just easily led.' We had to apologise to the teachers in charge of the trip, that was all. My parents weren't angry or anything. Not until the next time I got into trouble at school. Anyway, that was Paris, 1963."

"Did you get in trouble a lot at school?"

"I just got caught a lot, that was all. Another time it was writing pornography in the back of a maths class. Brian Ritchie had started it and of course, being the literary type, I had to add my bit; there was sniggering and Jake the maths teacher descended on us. 'The Headmaster will be interested in yer taste in litrachur!' says Jake. It was pretty weak stuff but I was mortified at the idea of my mum hearing about it. I told Dad it was just a 'blue joke', he told those himself. Ritchie and I got six Saturday morning detentions for our efforts.

"Then that summer Stuarty Rea and I got done for setting fire to Bloody Bridge youth hostel—it was Stuarty did it and I was staying there with him. I knew nothing about it till we got to the bottom of the mountain, looked back and saw the smoke rising. Stuarty had chucked a lit cigarette butt on to his bunk as we were leaving. Funny thing for him to do but you do funny things at fifteen. We got suspended from the YHA for a year. My parents saw the letter. They must have wondered what was going wrong with their wee son: drunkard, pornographer, and now arsonist, all in one year.

"What about you at St Mary's? Were you a bad girl?"

"In the sixth form a group of us would skip games and slope off to someone's house to drink coffee and smoke cigarettes."

"I hated games too, it was any excuse to get out of Rugger practice. But in the sixth form it was no longer compulsory."

"That was enlightened."

"Yes, my mates and I spent that sixth form year between the Art room and Isibeal's coffee bar in the town. It was more like being a student than a schoolboy."

We disembarked at Calais in the late afternoon and headed for the Paris road, walking up a steep hill from the harbour, past little shuttered dark houses and a small café crowded with workmen drinking red wine. We came out on top at the signpost for Paris, a quiet road and fields stretching away with a desolate evening look about them under the grey sky.

"It's a lot of kilometres to Paris," I observed.

"All the cars off the ferry will have gone on by now," said Bridget.

But we got our first lift with an old farmer in a 2CV who drove us for forty kilometres or so. Then there were more short lifts, all local people travelling short distances. Bridget sat in the front next the drivers, conversing with them in her careful A-level French.

Ten o'clock, in the dark, it was raining and we sheltered under a tree by the roadside in some godforsaken spot not even halfway to Paris yet. Eventually headlamps approached, glistening on the rain through the blanketing darkness and a car pulled up, like a prayer answered.

The interior was comfortable, padded and leathery, the windscreen wipers going, cosy in our capsule as we cut on through the wet and dark. The middle-aged businessman type had an easy, direct, familiar manner. He spoke to us in French.

"Are you together?" he asked.

"Yes," we replied.

He said he would put us up at his house for the night; it was too late for us to continue to Paris. We could go on in the morning. We accepted his kind offer with thanks. Presently he pulled in at a little roadside café.

As we entered the dim, crowded little bar couples were dancing to a record of French accordion music, the women whirling delicately in their summery frocks. It felt like stepping out of the dark straight into the heart of French culture, with a natural gaiety that was timeless. Everyone turned to stare at us as we entered. But our driver was apparently well-known here. He ordered omelettes and beer for us and made a phone call home to warn his wife that they had guests for the night. Monsieur chatted with the crowd at the bar while we ate and drank in a corner, still attracting curious stares; we were newsworthy in this country place.

It was approaching midnight when we pulled into the drive of the detached house in the middle of a village. The large teenage son loomed silently in the doorway; behind him Madame hovered, tight-lipped, long-suffering you imagined, her matronly propriety at odds with her husband's impulsive, generous nature. We were shown smartly up to the small bedroom; the clean sheets in the comfy bed felt luxurious against our tired, stale bodies. We were exhausted, Bridget a little nervous as a guest in these strangers' house, but it was our first night together in France and we had to make love before we slept.

We were woken in the morning by Madame's knock on the bedroom door. The father and son had gone to work and school. She provided a breakfast of coffee and bread and jam and saw us out with no attempt at conversation. We turned along the village road in the fresh, clear morning and walked to the end of the houses, the pleasant roomy residences giving way to a row of peasant hovels and political posters stuck up on every available public wall space.

Two good lifts took us all the way to central Paris that morning: a gentle woman university teacher and a young couple with a baby, the man smoking a *Gitane* as he drove into the city with a Gallic assertiveness. Following my brother's sketch-map we took the Metro, emerging at the Comedie-Francaise, and walking up into the back streets behind it, a labyrinth of high-walled, narrow streets and little squares, cafes and cheap hotels. Hotel Stella was a gaunt, decaying building. The old woman at the reception had one room left, a room for three but still cheap. She gave us the key and pointed the way; it was up three flights of bare, worn wooden stairs, in the attic.

"Oh, Bridget, it's perfect!" I exclaimed. "I could write a novel here!"

It was quite spacious, simply furnished, a double bed and a single bed, one little window looking out across the Parisian rooftops, with the narrow street tucked away far below.

We went out to a corner shop and bought a long loaf, Camembert, smoked sausage, a bottle of water and incredibly cheap red wine in a plastic bottle, which we lunched on at the little table in our attic. Heavy with the wine afterwards, we lay on the bed and made love. The mattress was lumpy, the bedsprings groaning under the urgent movement of our bodies. After that we dozed a bit, then went out in the late afternoon to explore the district, stopping off for coffee at a pavement table where we could casually observe the flow of life of this strange, romantic city.

Conscious of our limited funds, we dined that night on the remnants of the lunchtime bread and cheese and sausage. Then we made love again on the humble bed under the sloping ceiling in the failing spring evening light from the little window. We took it very slowly this time, lingering on the sensations of our bodies conjoined as one, as if we might stay like this forever, Siamese twins.

"Oh, I love you!" said Bridget, looking up deeply into my eyes.

"I love you, my love!"

Afterwards she said, "This is what I always dreamt making love would be like."

"Your Taurus to my Aquarian: earthiness meets imagination, it's a potent mix. It's as if the universe is centred on our creaky bed here among the Paris rooftops."

Bridget laughed, "Is it worth coming all this way just to go to bed together?"

"To make love in a Parisian attic, yes, you can't get better than that. I wish we could stay here for ever. I'd wash dishes for a living, like Orwell."

"We could come and live in Paris after I finish at the Poly," she said. "I could teach in a language school."

"I could write here, for sure."

And one of those pipe dreams was born, to be discussed and planned endlessly but never realised because it was always too good to be true.

We had trips out, to see the Mona Lisa at the Louvre and climb the steps at Montmartre. American hippies were begging on the steps of the cathedral, "Give us a cigarette!"

They should have been kindred spirits but there was something dislikable about them, a rudeness and arrogance. "Playing at being poor," said Bridget.

Some of the other guests gathered in our room one late afternoon: a hip young Danish couple, a PhD student from London and Glenn, a sad American boy. Our love was a magnet to others, they were all our children; we'd never be one of those deadly boring exclusive couples.

We ate out in a restaurant on the last night. We hunted through the streets till we found a very cheap *prix fixe* menu in a little red restaurant run by Chinese: salad, steak, cheese and pudding. The red wine filling our senses, the drawn-out ecstatic moment by moment ritual of the simple tasty courses, the Paris night magic as darkness came down at the window, bound the pair of us, face to face over the candle burning on the small table, in a warm, rich glow of intimacy, a heightened spiritual state in which each word, each pause, each look, each breath in each slowly dropping moment was charged with meaning and the deep new love we felt for each other.

"Oh, Jim, this is so romantic!" she sighed.

"It's just like they say about Paris, the city of romance; it's a cliche but it's true. Maybe it's something they put in the wine!"

"We really love each other now, don't we?"

"Yes. I've never loved anyone before like I love you."

"Do you think you'll always love me, forever and ever?"

"I don't think it, my pet, I know it. Amen!"

CHAPTER 22

Summer and Autumn

After the end of year exams she went home to her parents' to do her holiday job nursing in a local old people's home. I stayed on in her room in the flat with Jean and Nicky who had work in London. I hated sleeping on my own again, albeit temporarily. I lay there in our bed wide awake at night, missing Bridget terribly and listening to the mice scampering on the landing. It frightened the two girls; one night they both came in my room with their bedclothes and slept on my floor. I put down mousetraps with cheese; in the morning the cheese had gone, with no sign of dead mice.

I was getting quite depressed but Bridget came to the rescue, travelling up early in the morning from Surrey on her days off, which she coordinated with mine at the library. I imagined her on the packed rush hour train to Victoria, a mysterious beauty with her secret passionate purpose there among the joyless deadpan commuters. She let herself in and was undressing as I opened my eyes. In a minute she was coming to me naked in the green morning gloom of the bedroom, then beside me in the bed, the length of her body pressing against mine, reassuring me of her love. Never a word passed between us till after we had made love.

Her family went away to Ireland for a week and I went to stay with her at Burley, commuting by rail to work in the library each day. Jean and Nicky came down on a Saturday and a few of

Bridget's old convent classmates called in. Dolores was a big dark, attractive Anglo-Indian girl, larger than life; she'd always been the wild one. Her steady boyfriend was away; she joked about him having an impractically oversized thing that was always getting in his way, "Not that I'm complaining about it!" she added with relish. "Oh Lord, I'm missing him!"

Moved by her friend's words, Bridget came to where I sat in an armchair and knelt on the floor between my knees, looking up at me, her eyes wide and shining with the pride she took in me there among her girl friends. "I'm lucky!" she said, "I've got *my* boyfriend right here beside me!"

Just the two of us again, we walked on the Downs in the quiet of the summer's evening up there under the sky as we followed the track over the grass. Woods covered the valley below, rooftops and chimneys and church steeples poking out of the treetops, everything fixed in the still golden light.

Walking back across the Downs we had a view all the way to the tall buildings of central London, then we were back on the mellow tree-lined avenues down the hill. The lowering sun shimmered through the leaves, fired bedroom windows and glowed on white gable ends. We dropped down the pathways like country lanes, until we turned into Bridget's avenue.

We entered the big empty silent twilight house and climbed the stairs together to Bridget's little front bedroom. It was a young girl's bedroom still, the single bed along one wall, bookcase with girls' classics against the other, the cream-painted chest of drawers and bedside table and the long narrow mirror on the wall. In the failing light and deep evening stillness of the small room with its window looking out into the treetops of the avenue, we undressed face to face, letting our clothes fall away softly around our feet. When I drew her into my arms, our bodies touching down their naked length, she trembled and closed her eyes, the lids dark and heavy, in a half-swoon.

"Oh my word, oh Jim!" she murmured.

I lay on the little narrow bed by the wall, my body stretched out long and thin and white in the evening gloom, while she knelt by the bedside kissing me. She was all obeisant soft curves and long dark hair hanging down in abandon. Then she was above me, looking down into my eyes with a curious wide-eyed, soft candour of calm love and complete trust.

Back from holiday Mummy found a pair of my underpants in the wash, that I had missed somehow. Bridget overheard her telling her father about it, "And she's stopped going to church: she must be sleeping with Jim!"

Bridget handed me the clean little black pants, so easy to miss. "I told her you just came for the day and brought your laundry with you."

But it was dirty looks for me from Mummy for a while after that.

Bridget and a college friend Jane had, before I met Bridget, arranged a summer trip to Corfu together, cheap student flights and camping. The plan now was that Jane's boyfriend Freddie and I would motor down to Brindisi and meet the girls who'd cross to the heel of Italy by ferry. Then we'd tour back home up through Italy and France. When I went to book my leave at the library I was summarily informed that those dates were unavailable, already booked up by other staff. So I immediately tendered my resignation as from the first day of the holiday. I'd had enough of Richards and his sidekick Neil, the dull-fart bureaucratic petty snobs who'd never read a good book in their lives. Well, they could stick their bottles of glue and polythene covers and fines box; they certainly weren't going to stand between me and my girl. I'd have my week in the sun with Bridget and not even think about what I was going to do for a living until I got back. This was London where uncooperative bosses could shove their jobs.

During the girls' two-week absence in Corfu Freddie attached himself to me obsessively. He was there at the door every evening after work. You could hear him coming in his clogs; he had floppy mouse hair and a ferrety moustache; his eyes burned with a strange mix of humour and fanaticism. Jean and Nicky had gone on holiday to the Continent. I was Freddie's lifeline to the absent girlfriend Jane, whose going away on a trip without him had filled him with resentment, anxiety and jealousy.

"I get rough with my women sometimes," he told me darkly. He didn't like Jane being at college and hated students. He worked in publishing; there was talk of getting me in there too, all bullshit as it transpired.

We arrived at Brindisi in Freddie's purple Morris Minor at half-past-one in the morning. The dusty streets and white buildings were sound asleep. We located the youth hostel where the girls were sleeping after their ferry crossing the previous day. Past the hostel a dust road ran to the sea. We parked by the side of it. I got out for a pee in the long grass, the cicadas' chorus deafening in the hot darkness. Exhausted, we slept. We woke with the sun beating down on the car, got out and stretched our cramped, aching joints and walked back to the hostel.

As we approached the hostel the two girls emerged from it They were dressed in skimpy sun-wear, hair tied back, Jane a buxom redhead, Bridget very brown and smiling. I felt a little shy of her—did she love me still? Two weeks apart is a long time when you are in love. But she kissed me and took my hand to walk faithfully by my side, my girl, as close as if we'd never been apart at all.

We pitched the two small tents on a grassy spot above a little rocky bay and spread our towels on the grass next it to sunbathe. I stripped to my underpants, a little yellow slip that would double as swimming trunks. Bridget stretched out on her tummy in her black bikini; her skin was a golden brown on her back and the unconscious sensuous sprawl of her smooth rounded limbs. Soon I was kissing her, pressing up close to her. A passing Italian wolf-whistled us.

"Come in the tent?" I murmured.

Inside the bubble of the little blue tent we were instantly in a world of our own, oblivious of the busy morning sounds from the beach and the street. We quickly divested ourselves of our swimwear. Her breasts and hips freed from the bikini were a tender, milky white, curving softness, contrasting with her tanned skin. I was aching for her after our separation, the longest since we'd met, and she took me to her now in an access of devotion, paying homage to her man there in the small hot blue space with the hard Italian earth under the groundsheet beneath our knees. It was an ecstatic loving reunion; all our pent-up passion was spent in a few minutes but it made us whole again, a man and a woman together in eternity.

That moment of bliss in loving reunion in the blue bubble of our tent was the high point of the holiday. After that it was all downhill; we were stuck with another couple who were too self-absorbed and separate to provide any companionship, he obsessive and controlling of her, she under his malevolent spell with no life of her own, both to blame really. Bridget and I were only there, it seemed, to share the fuel costs, and his wretched twee little purple car was pissing oil.

I liked southern Italy: the warm-bath, pellucid green sea, the stone villages that seemed to grow out of the hillsides, the simple, cheap little restaurants that served pasta, parmesan and bread with carafes of red wine.

"We are the poor people," one humble waiter told us, "but we help one another."

We drove up over the stony high mountains, buzzing in a cloud of dust through remote villages, *Vota Communista* daubed on the walls, where happy children came running out to cheer on the funny little purple foreign car.

But the days soon blurred in the constant grinding, hectic push north up the west coast, leaving only senseless fleeting impressions of a country. The campsites were Spartan; Bridget didn't like sleeping in a tent. We got back one night on Mount Vesuvius and found our tent collapsed in a puddle after a rain storm. Too far gone to care, we crawled into it anyway.

There was a last final killing all-night push to Calais for the ferry. At one point Freddie was starting to nod off. I made myself stay awake to keep an eye on the bastard before he killed us all; it was the kind of thing he might do to get back at Jane for some imaginary infidelity. The sole purpose of my life at that point in time was to get back home in one piece and never have to be in Freddie and Jane's company again for the rest of my life.

On the morning crossing, afloat on a choppy glittering sea out of Calais, Jane came to us in tears on the windy deck. Her long red hair was wind-whipped across her tear-stained, freckled face. She was posh, a debutante or something and essentially a nice girl, it was a great shame she hadn't found a decent man worthy of her.

"I just don't understand what's wrong with Freddie!" she sobbed pitifully.

"Everything," was the answer to that though I didn't like to say it. We did our best to comfort her. You knew she'd go on putting up with his crap anyway. They were both to blame, the one answering some perverse atavistic need in the other.

I had no regrets about packing in the library. I was back home in the flat with Bridget and Jean and Nicky; I was free for a while. My needs were simple; I found possessions burdensome. I planned to do some writing. I liked the balance of the communal life of the flat around my intimate life with Bridget. This was the life I should be living. My hair had grown down to my shoulders; I had grown a beard at Bridget's suggestion. I liked my old fading clothes that fitted soft and comfortable on me as another layer of skin. Bridget and I were closer than ever. The little trials of the summer—the temporary separation, the underpants incident, packing in the library, the disastrous holiday—had only strengthened the physical-spiritual ties of the relationship.

Starting to run out of money, I remembered the cleaning agency. They had a job for me the very next day, in the morning at a house in Cockfosters. The tube took me way up to the end of the line. The house was a modest semi. The pleasant housewife explained that they'd had all the old carpeting up right through the house and she wanted the floorboards scrubbed before the new carpet was laid. She handed me the bucket of steaming sudsy water and the scrubbing brush, "Does the job properly," she said. "Mop just spreads the dirt around."

It was a Jewish house; I imagined they must be sticklers for hygiene or maybe it was part of their religion; I couldn't see the point in spotless floors if you were going to cover them with fitted carpet. Anyway, I set to, crawling backwards on all fours, scrubbing into the grain of the boards, dragging the bucket clanking after me. Soon my back and knees were aching. Two hours in—it might have been two days, two months—there was an elevenses' cuppa, just the drink, no nibbles. The lady asked if I could stay on in the afternoon independent of the agency, no commission to them, and I agreed, it was more money in my pocket.

The morning crawled on with me in a monotony of floorboards and scrubbing. Occasionally feet, shoes, ankles, legs in stockings or trousers passed within the restricted orbit of my vision. They were respectful of me and I wasn't put under any pressure to work quickly, but there was discomfort and boredom. It was the sort of mindless task that nevertheless requires just enough concentration to make it difficult to think of much else. The half-formed, repetitive, desperate thoughts that came to me were of pointlessness and absurdity, frustration and irritation.

One o'clock lunch: a slice of toast covered exactly in baked beans, washed down by a single cup of tea, they weren't going to overfeed me which was just as well perhaps if I were to drag myself round for another four hours.

I was halfway up the stairs, with the landing and bedrooms still to go. They dispensed with afternoon tea so I could finish half an hour earlier, at five o'clock. With four pound notes in my pocket—and only fifty pence commission for the morning due to the agency—I went hobbling off, crippled but rich, to Cockfosters station. I'd been on my knees for eight hours; it felt peculiar to be upright, more or less, able to look other people in the face again. I sat on the tube feeling sweaty and filthy, done in; but it'd be funny telling the others back at the flat about my awful day as I slaked my dusty throat with a glass of Bulmer's fine cider.

After a day of cleaning there was nothing for it but to don my smart jacket and try my luck with the job agencies. It always came back to this. I was a bit shocked when I entered my first agency and a woman jumped up from her desk and intercepted me at the door with, "I'm sorry but we can't register long-haired young men; the employers tell us they don't want them."

So much for swingin' London. But things had changed since I came to London in January 70; there was a recession on now, I'd heard. One thing for sure, I'd starve before I got my hair cut.

I was able to register with other agencies and there followed a few unsuccessful interviews. I could tell they didn't like the look of me. One accountant berated me for having worked only

in the public sector since leaving school; it showed a lack of the
entrepreneurial spirit, he suggested. They insulted you then shook
your hand and smiled as they dismissed you, as if it were a sort of
game you'd lost. They were the grey-suited money men, cold eyes
and white skin like fish, fat and indifferent behind their big desks.

Following a fruitless day's job-hunting, going home on the
top deck of the bus I saw a slogan roughly daubed in big uneven
white drippy letters on the gable end of a row of condemned
houses at Archway:

The Tygers of Wrath are Wiser than
the Horses of Instruction

I didn't know it was a William Blake proverb. I scarcely
understood the words but they seemed to strike at me on some
subliminal level, making my head light with a sense of revelation.

London never let you down for long. At a job agency at
Charing Cross some bright young go-getters, possibly impressed
by my school certificates and seven years of office work, said they
had, "Just the right thing for you, Jim: telephone sales—big, big
bucks!"

Of course no one would see you, so your hair didn't matter
and notwithstanding the Belfast accent, I was well-spoken.

"You'd be selling frozen chickens to the supermarkets, Jim.
How could you lose? With commission sky's the limit on earnings.
I'm talking really big bucks! They want you a s a p. Wouldn't you
like to earn a lot of money?"

"Well, yes!" Might as well get paid properly for making a
proper eejit of myself. At least it was different, and I was getting
desperate.

An hour later I was waiting in the reception at Frozchick of
Neasden, leafing through *Frozchick News*, the house journal,
which informed me that Frozchick sales were booming right
across the country. I saw my future: rapid promotion to director
of the Frozchick empire by age 30. Rolling in it! That'd show Mr
Fat Accountant and the rest of them!

The lanky, robotic, dark-suited sales manager who interviewed
me was impressed.

"Well, Jim, I believe you may be just the kind of person we are looking for here at Frozchick. But first you must pass the interview with our selection panel. They will fire questions at you. They will insult you, call you names. They will be testing your ability to work under pressure. Do you understand?"

"Yes."

"You will hear from us within the next few days. Be ready for the Frozchick challenge! And let me leave you with one thought: '*Frozchick is the future. The future is Frozchick*'. Okay?"

"Yes," I said, still trying to work this mantra out but suddenly it seemed I was made for life; they wouldn't have many applicants of my education and intelligence, I felt sure, and I'd done a lot of phoning at the BBC, chasing up debts successfully.

But that evening the doubt set in. Would I end up like that robotic manager, thinking, talking, living frozen chickens? And in bed that night I woke in a cold sweat from a nightmare of chickens, thousands of them, plucked and headless, chasing me down an endless corridor—

There was one other job offer going, an electrical engineering company at Chalk Farm, Records Clerk, £20 a week. It was the opposite to Frozchick, as low key and low paid as you could go; the manager had tried to persuade me that I was too good for the job. A telegram came from the agency with my appointment time for the Frozchick interview. With scarcely a thought I screwed it up and rang the engineering company instead. At least there was a common sense dignity, an integrity about their job. They said I could start on Monday.

Mrs Bloch the landlady dropped by unexpectedly one Sunday morning and found bodies strewn everywhere amidst the wreckage of a typical Saturday night. Mrs Bloch screamed when she caught sight of the psychedelic mural on Jean's wall. She gave the girls notice to quit right there and then.

"Such beautiful girls," she told Hilary who now occupied my old flat next door and added, lowering her voice confidentially, "but depraved!"

We soon found another flat, the other side of Crouch End, at the top of the hill. It was lighter, cleaner. Bridget and I occupied the biggest bedroom, at the front, high-ceilinged, white and spacious with big sash windows overlooking the quiet side street. A profusion of potted cacti had been left by the previous occupants of the room. The bed was two double mattresses laid one on top of the other on the floor, our heads under the window. There was a boarded-up fireplace with its high wooden mantelpiece intact. On the Saturday afternoon we arrived the autumn sun was shining into the big light room and with the great bed at its centre it seemed a heavenly nest for two. We stuck up Bridget's Rousseau and Mucha posters. Your own familiar pictures banished ugliness and made a place instant home. Elsewhere around the flat we all covered the walls with posters by Dali, Burne-Jones, Magritte, Blake and Escher.

I was first up and out of the flat each morning, stung awake by the little red alarum then slowly, agonisingly extricating myself from the warm knot of limbs, Bridget's clinging softness, her sleeping dark head on the pillow—everything that was nice—to lunge naked across the polar wastes of the big bedroom to my clothes on the chair, scrambling into shirt and underpants, a dark green V-necked woollen school jumper borrowed from Bridget and green cotton loons, high-waisted and skintight with wide flared bottoms, purchased for £2 in Oxford Street. I paid a quick visit to the icehouse of the toilet, happed myself up in my coat and tartan scarf and slipped out of the sleeping first floor flat without as much as a cup of tea inside me—Simon from the Poly had moved into the bed in the living room/diner.

Out in the frosty air I was glad of the protection of my plentiful long hair and beard. The long navy woollen overcoat from Belfast days hung shapeless and shabby on me now, my feet in scuffed desert boots. I crossed Crouch Hill and ducked along the path that ran above the disused railway cutting. I could fantasise a country walk here. There was a succession of lovely sunrises with a big orange-in-a-chip-shop sun burning off the morning mist and firing the autumn shades of red and gold of the cutting. The leaves crunched frostily under my desert boots. The hedgerow and fences were strung with a white lace of cobwebs. Amazingly you began to feel glad to be up, privileged to be alive in the new day.

I emerged by the bus stop on Crouch End Hill. It was bus to Archway, tube to Camden Town then a short walk over the railway bridge into the quiet back streets of Chalk Farm. The electrical engineering company was an anonymous long, single storey grey block; inside you entered a cavernous open plan office. We clerks occupied one farther corner of it. Phil Mangan got there early; smartly dressed in a light-grey suit, he'd be bustling about making coffee in his warm, homely Scots fashion. Jet black hair flopped over his forehead; he had a pale complexion and an aquiline, drawn, distinguished face. A middle-aged bachelor, he lived with a man friend and wrote for *Opera* magazine. I sat at a desk facing Len, tall, white-haired, elderly, ex-RAF, another bachelor, who smoked his way contentedly through the working day. The other records clerks were Sandra and Viv, two nice girls, and the Colonel, an octogenarian director of the company who'd taken on light clerical duties for something to do.

The manager occupied a smaller office behind glass partition walls; a quick, on the ball Yorkshireman, oiled black hair, black-framed glasses, ruddy complexion, he'd enquired in his blunt no-nonsense fashion why I was going for such a low paid menial job; I said it was to fill in before university then he was happy to employ me straight away, without a mention of my long hair—that was worth a pay increase in itself.

The busy times of the office day were first thing in the morning and last thing in the evening, when the engineers phoned in for their jobs and then to report back on them. The rest of the day was stretching out the paperwork generated by that, working with slow motion meticulousness, helped along by tea and coffee breaks, and I started buying *The Guardian* along with my *KitKat* morning snack. Somehow dipping into a newspaper at odd moments of the day was acceptable where reading a book was not. Or I'd write a letter to my mother or my sister in Ireland.

In the lunch hour I went out to a cayf where I bolted the inexpensive two course dinner in fifteen minutes flat then took a solitary ramble around the cold, dead winter side streets. A row of cider drinkers sat on the low wall of a public garden at Camden. One of them reared up alarmingly, blocking my path, squaring his shoulders and thrusting his terrifying ravaged face close up to mine, so I could smell the sour boozy breath.

"Help me! I am an alco-holic!" he appealed in a gasping croak. "I have to have a drink!"

His directness and honesty impressed me so much I dug out a silver coin for him.

"You are a gentleman, sir!"

They were still there, in the early dark as I hurried past after work. I took to crossing over the road to avoid them; my finances were very limited. Then an old ragged woman sprang from a shop doorway, intercepting me.

"Spare us a couple o' bob, son, wud ye? Ah can see ye've got a kind face." The Irish voice touched me; I pulled out a handful of coins, put a silver one in her outstretched palm, feeling virtuous.

"Och, c'mon, shur ye've plenny there!"she wheedled, her voice hardening. "Ye can afford more'n thot!"

And with another ten pence piece safe in her grasping claw she turned away rudely, looking for the next soft touch.

Sid and Arthur, two middle-aged technicians from down the other end of the big open plan office, like a warehouse, approached us conspiratorially one day. Sid was a gaunt figure, with a little grey moustache; he spoke in a slow, soft cockney, "Arfur and me's just s'yin' baht coloureds comin' to work here."

He looked across the office at the Indian girl who'd recently started, the only "coloured" in the place. She looked just out of school, a nice pretty girl with glasses and a shy smile. She had run off like a frightened rabbit when I hailed her in the tube station one evening.

"Sure we *know* Gita," said Phil.

"Yi but let one in and where's it gonna end?" Arthur was small and round with white hair and a squeaky voice. "It'll bring down our pay."

They weren't foul racists or anything; they were genuinely anxious for their own position. But I felt sorry for shy wee Gita over there and all of us looking at her and talking about her.

"Maybe we need a union to negotiate our pay," I suggested.

"Och, we dinnae want the union," said Phil mildly, "they'd stop our overtime!"

Absurdly perhaps, given the sluggish workload, we were doing a lot of overtime, two evenings and Saturday morning; it bumped our income up nearer to a living wage.

The Colonel weighed in now, "I say, there has been talk of bringing back the cat and, and you know, I mean I think they jolly well ought to!" He was such a cuddly old chap too. Clearly no one had told him that in truth there was only talk of penal reform.

Len didn't turn up one morning and they found him dead in his bedsitter in Camden. He was seventy. There was a brother in Liverpool, they thought. It was sad to me, to die alone in a London room like that, no family around you. The empty chair opposite made me uneasy, though soon I was busy for once that day doing Len's job as well as my own.

Then I was pleased to get Viv in his place, a dark-haired girl with glasses, intelligent. "I agree with what you said the other day, Jim, about needing the union here, though I don't think it'll ever happen, we're too small. Here look, I brought in a book you might like to read." It was John Reed, *Ten Days That Shook the World*. "About the Russian Revolution: it was amazing what happened back then."

The evenings drew in, dark and wintry. The only heating provided in the flat was a geriatric brown paraffin burner we kept in the living room-kitchen. We had a communal meal each evening: the menu included my curried vegetable Irish stew, Jean's liver risotto and Bridget's egg curry. After dinner we sat around; the girls did college work, we chatted, laughed and played records. Pink Floyd *Dark Side of the Moon* was a favourite that winter; for me it became a theme tune of London flat life. Not to be left out of the studying, I began A-level correspondence courses in English and Politics through "Wolsey Hall, Oxford". They even had a blazer, tie and badge and a shield if you wanted them.

Bridget and I would be in our bed by half-ten. Light out, burrowed down together in the warm dark cave of the bedclothes, we made love. The potent nightly ritual, the blissful, yearning moans climaxing in the cries of deliverance in the silence of the night, bound us ever closer, day to day, man to woman, woman to man.

After our lovemaking she'd curl up against me in a happy deep contentment and her voice sounded soft and reverent in my ear, intimate and thrilling in the secretive dark of the sleeping house.

"You're great, darling, the way you love me like that. I'm glad you're an older guy, a *man*. Not like the *boys* on my course; a girl could walk all over them! I can really look up to you and respect you. Do I please you too, love?"

"God yes, my darling! You're only just out of your teens but you're a mature woman already, Bridget. You're *all* woman. Not like the silly girls I met before. You give me all your love, holding nothing back. When we make love I *know* there's a God because He must have sent you specially to me out of all the eight million people in London."

"Oh Jim, shall we be married after I finish my degree?"

"That's the most beautiful idea I've ever heard of!"

"Then we can be together without hiding it from our families and all that nonsense sneaking around and pretending."

"It'll be lovely for us too, knowing we'll be together for ever."

"I love you so much, Jim."

"I love you, Brid, my wee wife!"

CHAPTER 23

East

In March I started a new job as a library assistant in East London. I set out from Crouch Hill on a wild, wet, typical spring day. They'd accepted me with my long hair; I wore a tie on my first day, with my black jacket, navy shirt and maroon needlecord flared jeans. I changed buses at Finsbury Park station with its socialist newspaper sellers and the walls fly-posted with pictures of the hunger-striking Irish prisoners the Price Sisters and Gerry Kelly, *'Force Feeding is Torture'*. It certainly wasn't easy being Irish. From here the bus took me East in a beeline across the North London map.

I sat at the front of the top deck looking eagerly out the window, a pioneer with the thrilling sense of new territory opening out before me. Blocks of redbrick council flats reared up on either side—Arnold Wesker had grown up in one of those flats—then gave way to Victorian terraces and rows of dusty-windowed small shops. A right turn and we were travelling due south now, past the public baths and the old Music Hall, under the railway bridge. I spotted the whitish walls of the town hall set back behind flowerbeds and benches; my stop was directly opposite it. I got down at the bleak, godforsaken spot by the high, sheer redbrick wall of the Salvation Army citadel. Lowering my head to the cold, gritty, blustering wind that blew up the tunnel of the long north-south thoroughfare of Mare Street, I walked in the clattering din of heavy traffic to the granite pillared portico of the Carnegie library on the corner.

The interior of the library was handsome and spacious, smelling pleasantly of polish and books. They showed me where to hang my coat in the basement and put me to my first task filing returned books off the trolley on to the shelves. The long high shelves were well-stocked with good hardback books. I paused to consider the photo of John Cowper Powys leaning on his walking stick on the back of *Maiden Castle* and read the first page. There were so many great writers still waiting to be discovered by me!

Readers were coming in after the doors opened and soon there was the controlled, bookish bustle of a large central library going on around me. When you weren't reading the time went very slowly. I was conscious of the interplay of sun and cloud at the windows above the book stacks, then the sky darkened over and the electric lights glowed from the high ceiling as a spring cloudburst beat around the walls of our snug, safe, civilised enclave of readers.

I had a walk out in the lunch hour, between the showers, turning off the busy main road, past a tower block and into the quiet side streets, faded Victorian terraces running back to a lonely green park. The uncanny desolation of the streets made me glad to get back inside to life and purpose.

I worked behind the big square counter of the lending library with a crowd of girl assistants; in the long moments of inactivity I couldn't help but be warmly conscious of their fine backsides in tailored slacks or tight skirts. I blushed when Joy, an aptly named smiling black girl, joked, "Hey Jim, keep, your eyes off the birds and on the books!"

Carolyn, with wavy black hair like Bridget's, struck up a friendly conversation with me. Her long, natural hair, caftan and beads signalled she was one of the hippy fraternity, as did my long hair and beard. The world felt a less lonely place with the shared sense of belonging to an exotic minority. Carolyn lived nearby with her boyfriend Richard, a disciple of Timothy Leary, she told me.

She had a brother who came in the library to see her. I was shelving books and felt a tap on my shoulder. I turned round and was looking at this little mad bloke. He'd mistaken me from behind for Carolyn's boyfriend Richard. Carolyn explained the situation afterwards, "That's my brother Allie. He's a junky. Sad. He lives with my mum."

I was put into the music library at the back, at the counter under the mezzanine, a cramped windowless space. I manned the counter while Miss McTaggart the Scots music librarian, a Moira Anderson (the Scots singer) lookalike, worked at her desk in the basement office. The music library, consisting of classical albums and a little jazz and folk, was terribly quiet. An hour would pass with no sign of a borrower. I was able to read a lot. Then suddenly Miss McTaggart would come round the corner and descend on me with her trademark bundle of newly processed Dietrich Fischer-Dieskau LPs, her long, petulant face, like a highly-strung racehorse and her bouncy high-heeled walk with the girlish White Heather Club swing of her kilt and neat shoulder-length brown hair.

The solitariness down the back under the mezzanine could get oppressive. Carolyn would pop in and see me whenever she could. I was grateful for her friendship. One morning she came over and said, "I've brought a j in with me, I thought we could smoke it in the lunch hour. I know a nice quiet little spot!"

"Sounds good!" I said though the idea made me nervous.

At one o'clock lunch we exited down the front steps under the pillared portico and turned left along the main street. It was one of the first summery days, warm sunshine and balmy breezes, new life and hope in the bustle of midday.

"Here!" We had hardly gone a hundred paces when she indicated the turning. "It's a little old Jewish cemetery tucked away behind the buildings. Me and one of the girls, she's left now, discovered it for sunbathing. Nobody else knows about it. There's never anyone here."

A decorative wrought iron gate opened into the little oasis of stillness and peace, contained by a high wall. We sat down together on a bench by the path. The little cemetery felt remote from the busy street, sheltered and hushed, roofed by a milky-blue sky and filled with the bright, warm midday sunshine, a scent of earth and the twittering of birds. Carolyn hoked in her handbag and produced the neatly rolled cigarette.

"It's Richard's home-grown," she said. "He wants to know what you think of it. Here, you can start it."

The joint was rolled with a menthol tobacco and tip, giving a cool, heady smoke. I exhaled and nodded my appreciation as I passed it to Carolyn. I hoped it wasn't strong; how would I cope with getting awfully stoned in the middle of the working day? What if a policeman walked in on us now, *"Ello, ello!"* It'd surely be the end of my library career! I was nervous and paranoid for a minute but soon happily indifferent to my fate.

Already things were going strangely suspended. The birdsong had become an amplified liquid flow between my ears. Carolyn sat next me staring at a fly perched on one of her kneecaps in the mauve tights she wore. She flicked the fly away and with a flick of her long dark hair turned her head to smile at me. She must have been feeling the same as me, the stoned strangeness, for she was smiling knowingly into my face, a big toothy, slightly crooked beam, warm as the sun on our laps. Her deep-set dark eyes crinkled and brimmed with fun; she seemed to be looking through my eyes right into my soul.

A sudden harsh gabbling voice made us jump. The old caretaker of the cemetery was standing there complaining. For a moment I thought he must be telling us off for trespassing, but no, he was confiding in us, in a diatribe directed against society at large, as far as you could make out his words: the carelessness and vandalism he saw everywhere he looked these days. He gesticulated towards the backs of the barracks-like flats beyond the cemetery wall, "Oh yes and our tribes is living there too!" he declaimed. "They're just the same! There is no respect any more!"

The old fellow shifted off, muttering away to himself. Laughing quietly at him to ourselves, Carolyn and I got up and left. It was so funny, the things that happened when you were stoned. You saw through the thin veneer of rationality to something essentially spirit. The life we took so seriously was indeed an illusion or delusion.

"Did you hear what he said?" I asked Carolyn. "He called us 'our tribes'! He thought we were Jewish too. Isn't that wonderful?"

"I am Jewish," said Carolyn a little bashfully. "Indian-Jewish."

"Oh Carolyn, that's wonderful!" I said. But I could see that she found my enthusiasm—it was based on my admiration of Jewish writers—a bit embarrassing.

Out on Mare Street clouds blotted out the sun and the wind blew cold and gritty again, chasing scraps of litter round our feet. The traffic charged past senselessly, with a fearful din like a military assault; it was back to reality. We crossed at the island and ascended the shallow flight of steps to the glass doors. In the library it was business as usual, the assistants at the long counters stamping out or checking in the books. I felt hopelessly at one remove from it all.

Back behind the music library counter I was having difficulty applying myself to even the few simple procedures required of me. My mind, carried away on flights of my imagination, refused to slot back into the necessary mechanical responses; I couldn't take anything seriously. Unfortunately there was a little rush on, borrowers on their lunch break in a hurry, coming at me with armfuls of records. I couldn't work out whether they were taking them out or bringing them back. I dithered hopelessly while an impatient queue built up.

Then into the midst of all this confusion came Miss McTaggart. I saw the not-unattractive horse face, long and bony, blanched with anger as she confronted her incompetent assistant—me, that was. But I just stared in fascination at the rattrap-like snapping of the wide thin pink-lipsticked mouth, in close-up, weirdly disembodied, like the Beckett play. I almost laughed in her face. I was seeing the world at one remove; nothing could touch me.

Infuriated by my obtuseness, she stamped her little foot in the stiletto heel, a little girl throwing a tantrum, and jabbing me aside with her bony elbow, proceeded to set to and deal with the impatient queue herself.

*　　*　　*

With the girls' exams over and the lease on the flat due to expire, Bridget set about seeking accommodation for the two of us.

"We need to do it on our own now, be a proper couple," she said.

I'd miss the others, I knew, but life moves on. Bridget was free to go flat-hunting in the daytime, while I was at work. To help things along she told prospective landlords we were a married couple, stuck a ring on her finger and got a character reference from an obliging lecturer at the Poly for "Mrs Bridget Mitchell". It took a time but then she found a place in Stoke Newington. We went together to the landlord's house at Stamford Hill to sign the contract.

Keva Mandelbaum opened the door of the modestly respectable little thirties-style terraced house and blinked uncomprehendingly at the young couple on his doorstep in the summer's evening light.

"Mr and Mrs Mitchell!" said Bridget.

"Oh! Oh! Yes of course! We thought it was the people collecting for the hungry children! Aw'm sorry! Come in, come in!"

He was an odd-looking middle-aged man, a heavy, rotund figure with a very large round head like a turnip. He wore the dark suit of an orthodox Jew but no side-locks and he was clean-shaven, with massive purplish jowls. Heavy glasses magnified his eyes with a wild childlike effect.

We sat in the living room, nervous on the sofa, acting the married couple, while Mrs Mandelbaum, a beautiful younger woman, warm and vivacious, with a northern accent, did her best to make us feel welcome.

"And this is my wife's cousin over from Melbourne," said Keva. A bearded, middle-aged Jewish man writing at the dining area table looked up friendly and cheerful and greeted us in a chirpy Aussie voice.

We stiffened as Keva read through our references, grunting and nodding, blinking in his perplexed fashion. The wife handed us cups of tea, her warm smile reassuring us that everything would be fine. Womanly goodness, kindness and caring, absolutely pure and genuine, poured from her lovely face.

"And what are you going to do when you get your degree?" she asked Bridget with kindly interest.

"Teach English probably," said Bridget.

"Oh, a teacher, like me!" said Mrs Mandelbaum. "I taught in a nursery school in Manchester where I lived until I got married. Now I have little ones of my own to keep me busy!"

Her eldest, a small boy with a strong look of his father, had been charging around with a mad, anarchic energy and now he was glowering at the visitors, vetting us from behind his father's chair. The Orthodox corkscrew sidelocks and shaved pate, indicating holiness, looked out of place on such a wee Dennis the Menace tearaway.

"Tolly, it's past your bedtime!" his mother said.

Tolly turned his face away from her, puffing out his fat cheeks and pouting in a gesture of obstinacy, and then continued his suspicious, demonic staring at the couple squirming on the sofa. It was as if he could see right through our subterfuge and would shout out and expose us at any moment, *"Liars!Liars!Liars!"*

All cleared with Keva at last, we signed the one-year lease and I wrote him a cheque for two weeks' rent.

"Thank you, thank you!" he said. "I call Thursday evening for the rent. If you get any problems that can't wait you can phone me but not on Friday night or Saturday when we have our Sabbath."

"I went to school with a lot of Jewish kids," I said. "My grammar school was in the Jewish district of Belfast."

Keva gave me a look. "Oh, *they* only call themselves Jews," he said dismissively, "but we don't consider them to be Jews at all."

The effect was intolerant and not a little rude. He didn't seem to think much of me either, probably disapproving of my long hair—ironic, considering Jewish side-locks and beards!—and preferred to address himself to Bridget. He told us about his tailor's business in Whitechapel and the changes affecting this. "All the Asians who have come in now. Big families of them, all working in the business. You can't compete."

"Thank you, thank you!" we mimicked him afterwards when we were out in the street again and we laughed and hugged each other with relief, the keys to our new home, our first place together, safely in my pocket!

Our first morning in the new flat was a Saturday; I was woken by Bridget's kisses and we made love in the new big double bed, as if to dispel the strangeness of the room. Lying there afterwards in each other's arms we slowly took in the details of the spacious, high-ceilinged bed-sitting room. The bed-head was in one corner of the chimney breast, the washstand in the other. There was a sofa under one window, a desk and chair by the other window. Two armchairs, one a rocking chair, stood before the boarded-up fireplace. The floor was strewn with our suitcases and the cardboard boxes and plastic bags containing our things that we had carried up the long, steep stairs from the taxi the night before. Too tired to unpack, we'd gone for a drink in *The Blackbirds* up the road then collapsed into bed.

"Help!" said Bridget in the morning light. "Where are we?"

I felt the same lonely shiver of strangeness. Yet we both knew it was right for us to branch out on our own; it was the next step in our life together as a couple.

She said, "It'll feel more like home once we get our things unpacked and put away."

She got up and picked her way naked through the chaos on the floor and bent down to fish her dressing gown out of her case. I lay on for a bit watching her perform her ablutions at the wash stand, so classically natural and feminine, like a painting. The two tall sash windows looked out on Manor Road. The 106 bus lurching past monstrously seemed to be coming through the wall but otherwise it was a quiet street.

We breakfasted in our kitchen-diner across the landing, at the back, a square orange room with the morning sun filling it. The deep sash window overlooked the long, unkempt rear garden running back to the high stone wall and big dense swaying trees of Abney Park Cemetery.

"It's amazing, these hidden-away green places you stumble upon where you'd never expect them, all over London," I said.

"You don't mind all those graves under your window? Bit creepy, I'd say!" Bridget shuddered.

After a trip to the High Street for some provisions we set to, putting our house in order. The gigantic old carved mahogany wardrobe that occupied most of one wall accommodated all our clothes comfortably. We stuck up our posters, Rousseau's wild woman, the elegant *Bieres de Muse,* and, really striking and impressive on the wall above our bed-head, the fiery red mystical Blake's *Ancient of Days.* We spread the sheepskin rug before the fireplace. The Indian blanket went on our bed, the Mateus Rose bottle lamp at our bedside. There was the leather pouffe and our small bookcase with Bridget's college books and my novels by Salinger, James Leo Herlihy and Bernard Malamud. The stereo we'd got Bridget for her twenty-first in May occupied the deep mantel-shelf along with our LP records: we were listening to David Crosby, Stephen Stills, Mahavishnu Orchestra, Spirit—. The music wove itself into the fabric of your life together; it was our theme music. The record player provided the focal point of the room; there was no TV, and no room for its blink and blather in the richly personal authentic world we inhabited: this was a happy state of affairs indeed.

By the mid-afternoon it was distinctively our place, our new home, comfortable and aesthetically pleasing. It was a touch that Bridget possessed, to turn anywhere into home. We sat back with mugs of tea, surveying our efforts with satisfaction. It was a big light room, shabbily grand with its faded gold-striped wallpaper and ornate plaster ceiling mouldings. Between the intermittent rushes of traffic from the road below, the house was deeply silent, sunk in its own timelessness. The overcast, muggy July Saturday afternoon hung suspended over the street; the big dark green dusty trees that lined it were very still.

"This is really something here," I said.

"You're glad you're here with me?" she said in her little girl doty-pet voice. "You won't get bored on your own with me?"

"Bored with you? Never!"

"You love me, don't you?" she smlled.

"How do you know?" I teased.

"The way you look at me."

"You can see right through me then. But do you love me too?"

"I love you—too much! The only other person I love as much as you is my mother."

"You can never love or be loved too much," I said. "It's the best thing there is."

We went out, locking our two rooms and descending the long flight of stairs with its burnished bannister rail. "The kind they slide down in comic strips," I said.

The dim of the cavernous hall was relieved by the glow of stained glass in the tall window over the stairs and the fanlight of the front door. The long run of hallway had a floor of small black and white checked tiles like a draughtboard. We exited, closing the big heavy black door with its hound's head knocker behind us. There was a neglected patch of front lawn and a cluster of dustbins just inside the privet hedge. We were on the corner of a long terrace of flat-fronted, yellow brick, three storey houses with the elegance of former days almost faded away from it, drab rooms to let and unkempt front gardens. A lane cut through to a factory at the back then the houses continued in another long terrace.

It was a short stroll to the High Street, passing under the dense plane trees in the sticky summer heat. The air was muggy, faintly rotten with an odour of drains and bins. On the corner at the end of the street a tower block of council flats reared up in the sky in concrete and brick and glass.

"We're East now," I said, "or next door to it. It's different, isn't it? More interesting somehow, more character."

"Older and poorer," said Bridget. "That lends character and atmosphere."

The West Indian and Jewish populations were in evidence. It was the heart of the old Jewish community, dark-suited Hasidic men with pallid, devout, bearded faces, corkscrew side-locks dangling from under their black hats, yet a brisk, businesslike air about them. The bewigged women struggled uncomplainingly with prams and kids. These were lives filled with purpose and humanity. It was good that people should be different; I simply liked looking at them, it was romantic to me.

We paused at the entrance to Abney Park Cemetery, the gates open on a vista of its mysterious depths, tombs half-buried among the trees and overgrown shrubbery.

"Like the set of a Hammer horror film!" Bridget proclaimed.

"Didn't Edgar Allan Poe go to school round here?"

"Oh no, don't tell me that!" She was terrified of horror stories.

Mervyn and Budgy called round that night. They'd recently moved into a flat together the other side of the High Street, a ten minutes' walk away. Mervyn had got a summer job on the parks. "Me and a bunch of grown men climbing trees, what a life!" he laughed, shaking his head.

"Beats being stuck behind a desk all day in Dagenham!" said Budgy. He was a clerk at Ford's. Mervyn and he hailed from the same small Devon town. Both of them sported waist-length hair and were dressed in granddad vests and brightly coloured cotton loon pants, yellow for Budgy, purple for Mervyn, their bare feet in open-toed sandals. Budgy cultivated a cheeky Cockney persona—his family had moved from London to Devon—with a comical, cunning look of the Artful Dodger; while Mervyn was the intellectual type, bespectacled and intense though given to zaniness and ready laughter. Together they formed the classic comedy duo of opposites.

Budgy explained, "Merv here was a brainy boy, passed the eleven-plus and went to the posh grammar school. He was headed straight for Oxbridge till he started turning on to dope in the fourth form, then all he wanted was to get out of his head all the time."

"Not all the time, just most of it. Anyway, I made it to the Poly."

"Better than stuck-up in Oxbridge," I said.

We'd bought cider, Dry Blackthorn in the tall bottle with the yellow label, and sat round sipping it and smoking in the evening cool of the comfortable, mellow room.

"And here's Moses!" Budgy stroked our slinking black cat that Bridget had acquired as a kitten in our previous flat, rather to my chagrin at the time, finding it a wee nuisance. "Hey Merv, we need a cat to make our place feel more like home and frighten off the mice and rats."

"Well, that's alright as long as you look after it, Budgy: see that it's fed and de-flead and change its litter tray and so on."

"He's very particular, our Mervyn," said Budgy. "Very domesticated: hand-washes his clothes and cooks like a dream. The woman that gets him will be lucky."

"Yeah, I wish she'd hurry up and show up, that's all," said Mervyn.

The evening sun keeked over the eaves and began to flood the room with its ruddy glow, setting Blake's *Ancient of Days* on fire. Bridget sat on the floor leaning her back against my knees, her long black hair over her shoulders that shook with her frequent happy laughter, her knees drawn up in the bunched skirts of her Indian dress. Her feminine spirit focused and lifted our small house-warming gathering. I felt so proud she was mine; I loved to share her company with the other lads. They must all have envied me so, yet there was such good feeling; that's the kind of couple we were, of the family of man, always ready to share our happiness with others.

The evening took on a lovely dreamlike quality. You felt the luxurious freedom of the weekend, the special glamour of Saturday night. The conversation was good-humoured yet tentative and gentle, tendrils of delicate new friendship reaching out to one another.

We were suddenly aware that the room had grown quite dark. Bridget turned on the bedside lamp and drew the curtains. She brought coffee. It was a magical room now in the light of the bedside lamp with its pirouetting lemon shade. The red Blake poster burned away over the bed, rich with the deeper spiritual meaning of life as it is revealed to the artist or saint. The long mirror on the big dark wardrobe door shone back light and depth and the mysterious mellow beauty of the old London room.

Now our little group had grown silent, feeling no necessity to talk. We leant back and closed our eyes, giving ourselves up to the pure sensation of the moment and the music, *Atom Heart Mother,* that flowed symphonically from the little rectangular speakers on the mantelpiece, out around the room and back. Like Blake's art, the music too contained the higher, transcendent logic of emotion and spirit. It fell away and rose again, growing in grandeur and drama, surging and breaking like the sea into fresh revelations, a sudden crystal clarity of vision so you opened your eyes wide and stared at one another in astonished flashes of enlightenment.

So the pattern of our new life together in our own place was soon established, a quietly, deeply satisfying time with a few friends dropping by and a new heightened sense of the intimacy we shared as a couple. At the centre of our life together was the act of love, the ritual of our lovemaking, the drama of our two naked bodies, man and woman, locked in physical-spiritual union on the big cushy bed under the flaming Blake poster. In the silence of the night, in the thrilling dark or by the low lamplight, golden on our skin, we existed purely for one another, in the intense, self-contained, ecstatic little world of our loving.

When it was daylight in the room, like a weekend afternoon, the ritual of love on the bed seemed heightened in the ordinary natural light on our skin in the middle of the living day. You took pause to slowly relish the smooth sweep of obeisant, strong, womanly back, with the sculptural tapering to the narrow waist and the superb globe of the hips, the fount of life, like holding the world between your hands. Outside the window the busy London streets and the whole living world seemed to radiate from the centre of the two naked figures, man and woman, kneeling together in worship of the love-force that drives the universe.

Bridget had a summer job with Jean in the civil service; so I found myself alone on my weekday off from the library. I'd got used to flat-sharing with students, with someone else around usually, so it felt strange at first being thrown back on my own resources, Bridget gone out to work, the big room in the tall old house all to myself; but I came to find a peace in the strangeness and solitariness. I took a pleasure in little inconsequential things, like the strange, muted, disparate sounds that drifted up faint and mysterious through the tall old rooming house in the dead quiet: ghostly creakings, wordless voices, odd bangs and thumps. From outside came the distant barking of dogs, the soughing of the wind in the big swaying trees of the cemetery, the commotion of a bus or lorry up Manor Road, rattling the windows. The house seemed to listen and be filled with the mystery of life.

I was conscious of the arc of the sun. In the morning it slanted in the tall narrow stained glass window in the gable end, glowing on the stairs and hall; by midday it brightly filled the kitchen-diner and by evening it had travelled over the roof and set on fire the large bed-sitting room.

The district was off the beaten track of tube stations and main roads; it felt set apart, full of a mysterious sense of history, deep-lying, layer upon layer. The time-forgotten avenues of faded tall houses with their spooky Gothic touches made a powerful impression on me. The Hasidim, a simple, devout people, blended into the general air of genteel impoverishment. From the top deck of the 106 bus you could see in the window of an upper room where Jewish men were gathered in prayer, heads nodding in devotion.

Friday evening we would peer from our landing down through the deep stair window at the ritual of the family meal in progress behind the ground floor gable window, the bearded pater familiar lighting the candles, the kids sat round, a glowing scene of perfect family togetherness and spiritual well-being.

There was the colourful side to Judaism: the big fur hats and tinselly sashes, the white prayer shawls worn under the sober dark suits. The most delightful sight was the noisy, anarchic fancy dress procession of Jewish children along the street below our window when Hanukkah came round.

There was more street entertainment when the strains of a flute drifted up to our open window from the hot, still afternoon street, a dreamy summery sound and we hurried to watch the Rastafarian go sauntering by below playing his flute, swaying his tall body in his colourful robes to the music. He seemed to follow a route on to Stamford Hill and Clapton.

Victor, a Jamaican, lived at the end of the landing above us, in a room at the back. On our first encounter with Victor he was cutting the overgrown grass in front of the house, toiling away with shears in the sun. A wiry, intense little man with a brisk, irascible, yet very friendly disposition, he paused in his labours to mop his brow with a hankie and welcome us to the house.

"That your black cat I've seen?" he enquired.

"Yes, that's Moses."

"I have some fish for Moses tonight."

Victor took to leaving treats of milk and snacks on our landing for Moses, who slept in the kitchen.

Every Sunday morning Victor had a group of friends back from his Pentecostal church for an hour or so. Gales of hearty, joyful laughter rang out from the small room at the back, making Bridget and I smile at each other. Sometimes after these gatherings Victor would leave a couple of cans of beer outside our door. The rest of the week he lived quiet as a London mouse; he worked long shifts at a factory in Dalston and ate alone in his room. You could see his light had gone out by nine.

I finally met Carolyn's boyfriend Richard of whom she had talked so much and who her brother had mistaken me for in back view in the library on occasion. Carolyn resembled Bridget in back view also, the type of long black hair, build and clothes. I went with Carolyn to their flat after work one evening; it was just ten minutes' walk from the library, a street down the back of dusty-willowed Clapton Pond, the site of the original village. There was a crumbling low garden wall and worn steps down to a basement. I followed her into the blinding underworld gloom. The smell of damp commingled with a distinctive piny herbal aroma. The walls were whitewashed; a short passage gave into the living room: a neatly-made white double bed occupied the greater part of it. The overriding impression was of uncluttered simplicity and order, very neat and clean. There was a refreshing coolness after the muggy streets; murky daylight penetrated from the pavement level with the window.

As my eyes adjusted to the subterranean gloom I was aware of the figure that seemed to lurk there like a creature in its lair. I saw the resemblance to myself that had confused Carolyn's brother, only Richard's black wavy hair was longer than mine, his beard fuller and his build wirier. He was dressed simply in a white T-shirt, faded blue jeans and sandals. He ignored me for a moment and stared morosely at Carolyn who had come over distinctly uneasy in his presence.

"Did you get the albums?" he fired at her.

She handed him the carrier bag of new LPs she'd requested at the music library. He looked them over with a studied, boyish enthusiasm.

"You can thank Jim for those," she said.

Richard looked up, acknowledging my presence for the first time. "I've got a list of more albums I want to order," he said, suddenly friendly, the thunder cloud on his brow clearing.

"Give us it then, that's what I'm there in the record library for," I said.

I wondered what it must be like for Richard here in the flat on his own all day—he didn't work. There was something of the caged animal about him, defensive and a bit intimidating, even to the measured stealth of his movements. Carolyn said he seldom went outside the door and saw nobody all day till she got back from work. He smoked his home-grown, listened to records, read the books she got him from the library by Timothy Leary, Carlos Castaneda and Ed Sanders. She told me she did the shopping, cooking and cleaning; Richard wouldn't touch "woman's work"!

"Cup of tea?" Carolyn offered drearily. She was a different person in her boyfriend's company, deflated somehow, her whole personality drooping in underdog resentment.

As she turned away to put the kettle on, Richard turned to me, man to man, tossing his dark wavy mane back from his eyes. "Wanna see the plants?"

"Yeah, Carolyn's been keeping me posted on their progress. The joint you sent in was really something," I said.

Richard's teeth gleamed happily in his beard. I had said the right thing anyway. He had handsome fine features behind the scowling mask of hard man pugnacity. I wanted to humour him, show him another, gentler way of being that was paradoxically far more empowering.

He led me into a secret little back passage, narrow and humid, filled with tall potted plants, stiff pale green leaves, under a Heath Robinson system of lighting he'd rigged up. Full of a boyish pride in his ingenuity, he talked earnestly and obsessively about the art of growing cannabis. I did my best to look impressed and fascinated; it was with relief that I heard Carolyn call, "Tea's ready!"

The awkward, hostile silence was resumed as the three of us sat round in the neat bed-sitting room with our mugs of Earl Grey. A joint went round. Richard got up and put an LP on the stereo, a powerful system with tall black speakers.

Into the sunken silence of the room came the sudden warning blast of a ship's siren, like a foghorn out on Belfast Lough. There was a pause with dark nautical washings and the more subdued and distant moans of ships' horns all around, mournful and desolate out on the dark waters, then a close-up, full-throttled, protracted ripping siren-blast.

As that died away to shorter, steady moaning blasts, persistent and mesmeric over the waters, the music was coming, the organ creeping up behind the sound effects, portentous, building with guitars and drums, louder, rising out of the flat, cold loneliness of darkness and water, ineffably sad, with a subtle ominous power like Fate. It was the most dramatic and awe-inspiring thing I'd ever heard.

We were out to sea now, ploughing through the waves and darkness, rolling with the ship. A sense of mission fired us, bright and hopeful, dark and doom-laden by turns, with the music swinging along in harmony now, steely guitar and wistful keyboard chords laid over the jungle beat of the drumming. Then fading, fading, off over the horizon, to eternity.

"Phew!" I exclaimed. "That was brilliant! What is it?"

Richard showed me the Steve Miller album, *Sailor*; we'd been listening to the opening track *Song For Our Ancestors*. The dramatic music seemed to forge a bond of some kind between the three of us in the room now and we sat on listening happily to the rest of the album with no need to speak.

Yet when the music was over the three of us seemed separate as ever, Richard dark and scowling, as if dropped back down to earth again, Carolyn miserable and crushed in the shadow of his brooding temperament.

Out of the blue Richard asked me, "What's goin' on over there in Ireland then with the shootings and bombings and the R.I.A. and all that?"

I said. "Just history working itself out, Richard. Colonialism and the inevitable resistance to it. Been going on for eight hundred years. Every century or so the Irish get fed up with it and start to hit back, until they get beaten down again."

"I'm Irish too," said Richard. "I'd go and live over there, right out in the country somewhere in a little cottage and drop a load of acid. That's the real revolution, the one inside your head, like Timothy Leary says. You know, that guy, he's had two thousand trips."

I smiled in a degree of sympathy though I couldn't think of anything worse than all those trips, like boiling your brains or something.

"Thanks anyway," I said, getting up to go. "That was great! It was good meeting you, Richard and I'll see you at work, Carolyn."

It was a relief to be out of that subterranean intensity and back up on the street again with kids playing and all the space of the sky over Clapton Pond.

"Richard liked you," Carolyn reported back to me at work next morning. "That makes a change; usually he can't stand the people I work with, the 'straights'."

"He's an interesting guy," I said.

CHAPTER 24

Blue Heaven

Autumn brought the return of the students to the city. Bridget finished her summer job at the tax office and started the final year of her English degree. I dug out and dusted off my correspondence course, determined to take the A-level English in the February examination.

The evenings drew in, it was turning to winter. Our only heating in the bed-sitting room was an old paraffin burner; we went out one frosty Saturday morning to the junk shop in Church Street and bought a four-bar electric fire with an imitation coal effect. It sat nicely in front of the boarded-up fireplace. With two sources of heat now, one at either end of the room, we were cosy. We drew the curtains against the early dark. The bedside lamp cast its warm, intimate glow across the fireside area. Bridget would get home first and have dinner ready when I came from my late shifts at the library. The kitchen-diner was unheated so we ate in front of the fire.

Weekday evenings were quiet. After dinner we studied for a while. It was a deeply peaceful, satisfying time. I discovered some pleasure in the study of Shakespeare's *Winter's Tale,* Chaucer with Bridget's help, and Robert Browning, a bit of a hippy with his spiritual predilection for *"good strong stupefying incense smoke".*

Later of an evening we brewed up some tea and put on a record. Spirit sang, *"Aren't you glad you're glad you're glad, baby?"*

They were speaking to us and yes, we were glad. Bridget sat on the floor with her back against my knees; we stared into the artificial flames of the electric fire.

"Tickle me!" she commanded, wiggling her shoulders in readiness. She couldn't get enough of having her back rubbed and stroked and scratched, like a cat.

After a while she came on my lap in the rocking chair, face to face, slipping her legs in the loose skirt through the gaps under its arms. As we rocked together she tossed her hair back, eyes closed in her rapt face, the tender music of love rising in her long full throat.

The family planning clinic advised her to take a break from the pill and she came back with a big bag of condoms for me to use instead. I had little experience of these gossamer rubber sheaths and the very first one I put on burst during intercourse. Then her period was late and she worried she might be pregnant. She located the nearest Catholic church to find some guidance and comfort in its prayers and ritual.

"There was a hippy couple like us there," she said after the mass, "so I didn't feel too out of it!"

"Yes, Catholics come in all sorts, don't they?" I said. "Like the name says."

"We'd have to have a fixed daily routine with a baby," she said in an alarming new tone of ordered practicality. "No more lying in bed half the morning! I'd like a little boy who looked like you, a wee Jimmy."

"Think I'd like a wee girl with your pretty face," I said, joining in the spirit of the thing. I loved the idea of Bridget having my baby, it was incredibly sexy and would be the fulfilment of our relationship—but preferably not right now. Still, I knew we would manage if we had to, though it scared me stiff if I thought too much about it.

We had quite convinced ourselves that parenthood was on the cards when her "visitor" came back at long last, and we were enormously relieved. After all that anxiety they gave her a Dutch cap which she had to insert carefully every night, a delicate, tricky operation she performed squatting in the middle of the floor.

An old pensioner, Reggie Barrell, lived alone in the back room at the top of the house. He'd stop and talk to anybody in the house who would listen. He wore a hearing aid but couldn't hear much anyway; he'd given up listening. He spoke in a flat monotone, in a rambling interminable monologue that kept you trapped with him on the stairs, landing or hall for protracted periods of time. Yet he was a decent, friendly old fellow and a part of you was glad to give him the time of day; what was all the hurry for anyway? He talked about his long years of service as an accountant at the Milk Marketing Board and his plans now to feed the starving in the Third World:

"Actually, I am engaged in an ongoing correspondence with Mister MacNamara, the President of the World Bank—"

How Reginald Barrell had come to end his days alone in a shabby bedsitter in Stoke Newington was something we wondered about. We had the feeling there was an estranged wife and family somewhere—once we heard him singing "*Happy birthday*" down the pay-phone in the hall. Had his family been unable to live with his magnificent obsession to feed the world? After a while we were inclined to avoid Reggie, hiding in our room as he paused outside the door to talk to Moses.

"Poor bloke!" said Bridget with her Catholic girl compassion. "He's lonely, that's all. It's just that you have other things to do and haven't got time to stand there talking all day."

"Listening, you mean. Yeah but you feel guilty," I said. "It's like we've got everything—each other and all our lives ahead of us—and he has lived and worked all those years and has nothing to show for it. Very sad."

"Well, Christmas is coming up soon; we can have him down for a drink," said Bridget. We felt better then.

We arranged it for the night before Christmas Eve. At seven I climbed the stairs to his room to tell him we were ready. There was the smell of boiled cauliflower on the high cold landing; a radio news programme was turned up very loud within.

"Come in!" Reggie greeted me. "Welcome to my humble abode!"

It was a big messy bed-sitting room, encompassing the kitchen; there was no homeliness about it at all.

"We're ready when you are, Mr Barrell," I smiled.

"Give me two minutes, my good sir, and I'll be with you!" He was fastening the gold cufflinks of a clean white shirt.

Back downstairs I told Bridget, "He's on his way," and winked. I felt conscious of the softly-lit, shining comfort and beauty of our room, a reflection of our shared love. "This is like paradise after his place," I said.

We had the sherry and glasses ready on the occasional table. I put *Lord of the Rings* on the stereo for gentle and calming background music.

The poor old chap entered the room beaming and spruce, all dressed up for the occasion in his blazer and club tie, a knifelike crease in his flannels. He bore small bowls of crisps and nuts.

"Oh thank you, Mr Barrell," said Bridget, showing him to an armchair near the fire. His scrubbed cheeks shone like red apples in the warm room. He paused, cocked an ear at the stereo.

"Twisty music!" he exclaimed, moving his arms and body to its subtle psychedelic rhythms.

He accepted a glass of sherry. We toasted "Happy Christmas!"

Settled in the armchair, glass of sherry in hand, ensconced in sociable warmth and comfort, with a captive audience, he launched into one of his monologues, scarcely touching his drink, as if there were no time to lose between the words that issued from his mouth, while the watery eyes wore a blank, inward expression. There was a sad irony in the contrast between his grandiose plans to save the world and the paucity of his own existence.

"Did I tell you about the letter I received from Robert MacNamara's office regarding my suggestions to him for the alleviation of hunger in the underdeveloped nations? Robert MacNamara, President of the World Bank, that is. He has taken note of my points, they say, although he is unable to act directly upon them at this present moment in time. You see, forty years with the Milk Marketing Board taught me certain invaluable economic lessons that could equally be applied on the global scale. It's simple mathematics really. Let me explain—"

The idea had been to enjoy a neighbourly Christmas drink, three-quarters of an hour or so. But somehow all sense of time was lost as the voice droned on interminably. It was eight o'clock and then it was nine.

He said, "That brings me to the ultimate question of how much life is valued here in our own country today: the Euthanasia Bill!—"

It was off to Bridget's family in Surrey on Christmas Eve. The light was failing as we walked from Burley Down station in the mid-afternoon. Christmas tree lights shone in the windows and from garden trees. Front window curtains were open on lighted, spacious, sumptuous-looking living rooms. Frost glittered tinselly on the pavement.

Bridget was attired in her heavy black ankle-length cloak and long boots, a red beret perched charmingly on the back of her black head. The mock-Tudor streets with their big garden pines were hushed and expectant with the sense of Christmas Eve, the retreat to the bosom of the family and the countdown to the magic midnight hour. The McDonaghs' front door was decorated with a holly wreath; there was a churchy *"Christmas Peace"* poster in the window.

Bridget's fifteen-year-old sister Carmel, a tallish, sweetly pretty girl, opened the door to us and we passed gratefully into the bright, luxurious, fitted-carpeted, centrally heated interior, a world of difference to the house in Stoke Newington.

Christmas Eve night was spent quietly here at Holly Berry Avenue, a simple, plain meal taken at the kitchen table with a glass of whisky afterwards if you wanted it. Bridget helped Mummy in the kitchen with the elaborate Christmas dinner preparations. Carmel, Theresa and young Peter went out with friends or retired to their own rooms. The old man breezed through intermittently with his brusque, waddling gait, offering drinks and wads of newsprint, his glorious "free press"—*aye, tell us another one!* I found myself left chatting with Auntie May, the maiden aunt doctor over from Dublin, by the coal fire burning in the sitting room, her highly-strung golden collie bitch lolling on the hearthrug at her feet.

"Waggle, Kelpie, waggle!" she'd say and the silly creature would roll on its back and waggle its paws in the air and look up at her with its soft, stupid eyes.

She knew my County Antrim, having worked at the Whiteabbey fever hospital in her younger days. "Ach, the people were great up there,' she declared. "Sure they'd give you the bit out of their mouths!"

"I'm glad you liked us," I said. "Funny, my parents, Protestants who came up from the South, used to say the northerners were a hard, miserable lot who'd give you nothing! My parents' attitude rubbed off on me a bit, I have to say."

I slept in Bridget's wee room, the scene of our summer passion. I was alone this time in the narrow bed against the wall. I had a browse in the bookcase, the books of my love's young girl days: *The Borrowers, The Lion, the Witch and the Wardrobe, The Secret Garden.* I loved her predilection for fantasy and mythology; it seemed part of her spirituality and mysterious beauty and refreshingly different to my kitchen sink school of literature.

I turned out the light and lay in the dark with the lamppost shining on the curtain, tired but wide awake, too excited to sleep, like a child. I heard them all going off to midnight mass and then returning a long time later, creeping to their beds. It was Christmas Day! The thought sent a thrill through me. Feeling no nearer to sleep, I got up and sat by the open window smoking and looking out through the bare branches of trees at the still, dark avenue, exulting in the heavy charged pregnant silence, feeling the strange, wonderful Christmas magic, the coming of the Saviour.

I opened my eyes in the morning feeling the blessing of this special day, Bridget waking me with a kiss and a cup of tea. Downstairs there were presents piled under the Christmas tree in a corner of the dining room; they were opened after breakfast with everyone sitting round, cries of appreciation and thank yous and kisses. I was moved that they'd got me presents, a Marks and Spencer's lamb's wool pullover and other bits and pieces. It was great to be made to feel part of this big family.

At one o'clock, with the roasting smells from the kitchen growing stronger, we assembled in the sitting room for pre-dinner drinks, toasting a Merry Christmas. I felt the gin and tonic go quickly to my head. The father, seated up on a hard chair for his back trouble, was sipping sherry and holding court in his self-satisfied plausible fashion.

"I'm middle of the road and proud of it!" he declared. "A liberal! I'm for the little fellow in a property-owning democracy, the mixed economy. This isn't Russia. We don't want the sinister figure of Wedgwood Benn and the Communist virus. No, you cannot better the achievement of our Western democracies. Let the market decide but have the safety net there if necessary. We must go forward now to the Common Market! *The Common Market!*"— this like a *Hallelujah!*— "The advanced white European economies must stand together in this post-colonial era—"

The barrage of journalistic clichés left you a bit breathless, as if you'd been worked over in a boxing ring without getting a single punch in; all I could think to say was, "He looks like quite a nice man to me."

"I beg your pardon, Jim?"

"Tony Benn. He's not 'Wedgwood' any more. I mean, he doesn't look at all sinister, does he? Quite handsome and kindly really! He cares about the ordinary poorer people in society, that's why the media hates him really."

That brought a flush of disapproval to the old man's face, as if I'd sworn in polite company, but he half-smiled and repeated his mantra, "Eternal vigilance, Jim, eternal vigilance!"

The rush of liberal cant was mercifully brought to an end with the call for "Dinner!"

In the dining room across the hall the long table was laid, with Christmas crackers by each place setting. French windows overlooked a sunken sparse winter garden, the heavy grey Christmas sky hanging above it. Inside we were cosy, we celebrated. The grub was passed through the hatch from the kitchen, steaming, piled-high, pale green serving dishes, until the table was crowded with the festive spread of turkey, ham, sausages, roast potatoes and parsnips, sprouts and gravy, bread sauce and redcurrant jelly.

Crystal glasses were filled with red and white wine. They said grace and crossed themselves, quickly in the Catholic fashion, before falling on the feast. The father had donned his cruddy old specs on a chain and with great pompous flourishes of steel began carving the huge roasted stuffed bird, piling the friable white breast and crackling or brown legs on to the plates. In an excited happy confusion the side dishes were served up till everyone's plate was full. Feasting and quaffing the wine, trying to follow the several conversations going on around the table at once, I had soon forgotten the annoyance of arid political passions in the sitting room and passed into a happy stupor of contentment in the moment.

After Christmas pudding the dinner was rounded off with brandy or port and chocolates and coffee and cigars. Crackers were pulled; we examined their plastic treasures, donned the coloured paper crowns and read out the corny jokes. The afternoon light was failing at the window, sealing us in in warmth and contentment. After the great communal chore of the washing up us youngsters set out on a walk to the Downs. Up on the high grassy open space we followed the track for a mile or so, till it grew rougher underfoot like a country lane and dark under big overarching trees that creaked and whispered in the gusts of wind.

"This is where the phantom coach and four has been sighted," said Theresa who loved anything other-worldly like that. She taught in a secondary school but was considering joining a religious order. She was a good-humoured girl, bright and outgoing, with a strong intellect, good to talk to. I'd had this immediate warm rapport with both of Bridget's sisters. Carmel, the youngest, was quiet, but with the same friendly directness and sense of fun. The three sisters were very different individuals, yet I felt this immediate connection to them all, through Bridget.

We emerged in a clearing in the trees and leant on the wall of an old stone bridge over a stream that tumbled into a wooded gorge with a quarry beyond. The lights of houses down on the Croydon road along the valley glimmered through the stripped limbs of the trees in the dusk. The mystery of this day of days seemed to deepen with the light.

Father Williams called after lunch on Boxing Day. It was a regular thing apparently, his annual visit at this time, unchanged in years. A fair, rosy, balding Englishman, gold rims glinting, he was tentative and self-effacing, apologising for his presence at this busy time, while Mrs McDonagh did her best to make him feel at home.

"You'll drink a cup of tea, Father Williams, with some of my mince pies?"

"Why, you know, Mrs McDonagh, how I look forward to your mince pies all year!"

He sipped the tea gingerly from the Willow Pattern cup and saucer, nibbled a mince pie primly. He spoke to me of his visits to the North of Ireland.

"I have friends there in the Alliance Party," he explained.

"Is there much support for the moderates over there?" McDonagh wanted to know.

"Well, we are only really getting started," Father Williams explained quietly. "We have a difficult job ahead of us but already the response has been most encouraging indeed. There's a Fund of Good Will among the People of the Province just waiting to be tapped. It's a question of breaking down the Fear and Mistrust that Exists Historically between the Two Communities. We have to Proceed Very Cautiously of course, make sure we Do Nothing without the Agreement of Both Sides."

"Do nothing at all in other words?" I snapped, unable to contain myself. "Maintain the status quo."

The priest blinked softly back at me and I felt a little sorry for the poor Englishman; at least he was trying, he wasn't just issuing self-righteous condemnations or washing his hands of the whole situation like the rest of them.

McDonagh said, "Oh no, we mustn't rush things, whatever we do!"

"Rush?" I queried. "It's been going on for eight hundred years, the same old hopeless colonial set-up."

Now there was a hasty change of subject from the Chair. "Well, tell me, Father Williams, what about Canon Gissing's ulcers? Has he sorted them yet?"

I went back to London a day or two ahead of Bridget to start work. After the evening meal the whole family gathered in the hall to see me off and suddenly I felt very moved. I felt a special closeness to Bridget's sisters with their gentle smiling sweetness and thoughtful candour, so communicative and personable.

McDonagh drove me to Burley station and waited on the platform with me to see me off. It was cold and I had the let-down lonely feeling of being cast out from the light and warmth of Christmas. Looking at Bridget's father, gone quiet and empty now off his soapbox, his face clenched and grey in the hard wind that blew down the platform, I suddenly missed my own dead father, the closeness and affection between us that had grown warmer in his last days, and the family life that was behind me now and gone for ever with his passing, and I only twenty-five, and tears came to my eyes.

CHAPTER 25

Hackney Days

I took the A-level English exam in February; it seemed to go alright. I saw myself as a student now in essence, filling in time till I could start my degree course. Then I'd wake up in the morning to another long working day and roundly curse the library as I wrenched myself out of bed, "Oh God, not another day in that place! I feel as if I'm already dead and buried!"

Bridget was up and dressed, looking fresh and relaxed, beautiful as ever.

"You look alive enough to me!" she smiled. Standing there naked and raving in the middle of the floor, I must have resembled the Cerne Abbas giant. You had to laugh.

As if in preparation for the student life my hair was down my back now and I was bearded like Che. At Dalston Junction one evening, coming from work, an old pensioner yelled after me, "Bring back army conscription!" More positively there were the frequent comments about my likeness to the Saviour. My South African dentist hummed *"Jesus Christ Superstar"* as he checked my teeth. Then one little workingman in the reference library approached me at the counter with big wonder-filled eyes and spoke to me in real awe, "Anyone ever told you you look like Him? Like Jesus."

On the evening shifts I was sent out to assist at one or other of the outlying branch libraries. Hackney Wick was the most desolate of these, especially on a winter's night, stuck out at the end of the bus route, a kind of tin shack overhung by grim council tower blocks. The small unmanned railway station there with the canal next to it would become the scene of one of the horrific "railway murders" of young women in the 1980s.

There were pathetically few readers at the Wick, maybe a woman changing her Mills and Boon romances. Sometimes a group of kids from the tower blocks wandered in looking for mischief. I tried to show them the children's corner but books meant nothing to them, like wee animals. I'd have to chase them out then they'd come and knock on the windows or throw stones at the tin roof.

Another outlying branch was a large decrepit building looming over a narrow street. It was weirdly gloomy and godforsaken, the interior dim and dusty, cavernous, with a lofty gallery. There were few borrowers on my evenings there. Smouf the librarian was an eccentric tramp-like man, his old clothes smelling of the Hackney grime and rain; a gaunt figure, lank-haired and pallid, with a gammy leg, who cycled everywhere on a big old bike with a basket, in his dirty mac and trousers' clips. Sometimes he'd while away the long empty hours firing his pellet gun in the shooting range he'd improvised in a dusty attic room off the gallery.

Near to the nine o'clock closing, he'd go hirpling crazily round the high gallery, straightening shelves and calling out instructions to me in a cracked, uncanny voice-from-above that echoed distortedly round the gloomy cavernous interior, so I'd have to look round desperately for its source.

Somehow or other, for I really wasn't much of a library assistant—more a reader-in-residence—I found myself promoted upstairs to assistant to the reference librarian Mr Nolan, a quiet, decent Communist, red tie, grey suit, who'd taken a shine to me. I also liked the assistant reference librarian Maurice, a pale, depressive Christian Socialist and pacifist, dedicated to his wife and daughters. But the other assistant, Douglas, was difficult, an odd bod with pebble glasses and a shaven head, who at twenty-eight still lived with his parents and assembled model battleships in his bedroom. He was officious and proprietorial around the library and liked to refer to the library stock as "*my books*". He swung between surprising odd moods of sunny mateyness and embarrassing hateful fits of foul temper, cursing the library and his fate.

I got to know the library users better up here where the feeling of timelessness and the wide selection of newspapers and magazines encouraged them to hang about and sometimes stop at the high counter for an enquiry or chat with the counter staff. They were mostly older men and often Jewish. Like Mr Marx, half-blind and nearly deaf, with his lists of long words. A small man bundled in a cloth cap and shapeless mac, he sidled round the end of the counter like a crab, peering for me, calling, "Ello, ello!" and I'd want to hide, there was something so irritating in his fussy, beetle-like insistence and shrill, "Can you help me with the meaning of some words? Can you look them up in the Random House for me?"

It had to be the big Random House dictionary for Mr Marx. He had a demanding, strident little voice, piping up out of a small beaky mouth in his pallid, flabby, formless face. Out came the grubby list of words in his big spidery writing, which he scrutinised with a little microscopic instrument pressed against the page. He nursed a warm, fresh bloomer loaf under the armpit of his grubby blue mac. He had difficulty then hearing what I was saying as I read out the definitions from the dictionary. The effect was maddening. Up close he smelt of the dirty Hackney rain on sweat-impregnated garments. It felt as if he was on top of me, crushing the breath out of me: "*C'mon, elp me, willya? Ah can't ear ya! Speak up willya? Wha'? Wha'? Aw cawnt ear ya proper! 'Presti-diga-tition', wozzit mean?*"

The squeak of heavy shoes announced the entrance of C. Levi, a burly figure in fawn gaberdine, with a large glaring head and big leathery creased bull neck under his cloth cap. He read the local *Gazette* in which he often had letters published attacking the new political fashion of "Women's Lib".

"They've not had to do the real hard dirty dangerous jobs like men do," he told me angrily over the counter in his Chapeltown, Leeds voice. "Like workin' in the foundries or dahn the mines. So wha' the hell are they moanin' abaht, equality and all that? Ask them to do the same work a man does and they'd soon change their tune!"

His colour deepened and his eyes burned and bulged with contemptuous fury. If I attempted to demur with some nice reasonable liberal point on the topic like, "I suppose not so many of us men have to do those real heavy jobs any more, you know," he would argue the bit out:

"But a lotta uz still do, lad! Uz working men. Maybe not the young shirkers as I call em. But *they* don't, the women don't! Oh no, no! They want owt for nowt, they do!" Aught for naught.

He was filled with the unshakeable obstinacy of his one man crusade. If you believed enough in something it took on its own truth, however perverse, and there was no arguing with it.

The local feminist Sally Shrapnel was also a regular in the reference library and a sparring partner of C. Levi's on the letters page of the *Gazette*. She was equally dislikable, supercilious with flat, disapproving eyes behind her glasses and a face that coloured angrily at nothing.

I looked up one evening and had to smile to myself at the sight of the pair of them waiting there at the counter for the *Gazette*; in truth they were two sides of the same coin. They can't have known each other by sight, they might as well have inhabited different planets, but the sparks were ready to fly when she pushed in front of him and I saw over her shoulder the habitual scowl on the man's big heavy face, the fat ears pricking out under the cloth cap, redden and contort in a snarl of suppressed homicidal fury.

To avert Murder in the Reference Library I had to act swiftly, with prestidigitation, passing the *Gazette* to C. Levi and turning a cute smile on Sally:

"*Time Out*, Ms Shrapnel?"

"No, but if I can't have the *Gazette* have you got *Spare Rib?*"

" I'm sorry; we don't do women's magazines."

"It's not women's magazines."

"It's just we don't get men requesting that title," I explained. "That's why it's classified a women's magazine."

C. Levi had backed off with his *Gazette*; in his place stood Mr Tatlock, a cuddly old man, snugly plump-bellied, scarf folded under his chins, cloth-capped, white hair behind his ears and a flowing white moustache. He brandished a walking stick and prodded the air dangerously with it to emphasise a political point.

"Try the Socialist Standard, daughter," he counselled Sally Shrapnel now, disastrously. "It's upstairs on the mezzanine shelves. I see to that every month. The Socialist Party of Great Britain, established 1904. I've been a member for fifty years. Say no to the reformist tricks of Leigh Burr-Parti and prepare for world revolution now!"

Sally Shrapnel darted a withering look at him—a revolution *with men*? And who's he calling "daughter?"—then turned and swept off with her long pink, cold-looking neb stuck in the air.

Len Silver, the one I'd named "the Mighty Midget" taught weightlifting classes although he must have been in his seventies, a diminutive muscleman, deep-chested, with that smart, clean-cut look of the fanatical body-builder, and big glasses, like a fly.

"Dahn at Shoreditch. I get the leader of the council and all the top-notchers comin' to me!"

He'd demonstrate press-ups to me, down on the floor as I craned over the counter, enjoying the zany inappropriateness of this performance in a public library.

"I could go on like this for ever!" he gasped.

Or he offered sound financial planning in his excitable squeaky gabble: "Listen! If you've *got* a nouse you can *get* a nouse! If you haven't *got* a nouse then you can't *get* a nouse! So *get a nouse!*"

Another fitness fiend, Sidney, an elderly midget with a baby face, soft and red and pitted like a strawberry, shorts and knobbly knees all year round, came in late in the evenings to study maps and chart his round-the-globe charity ride on a penny-farthing bike.

"Never bin done before. The problem is this area here, see. The Pacific. Ow do I get across it on the bike? Any ideas, young man?"

I scratched my head. "Going to be difficult, yeah!"

And there was Mr Reynolds, an artist and retired shopkeeper, with his gentlemanly mild, beaky, toothy face, nice snowy hair, respectable clothes, who spent his days travelling around London on his bus pass, sketching. It was a fixed daily routine, ending up at the reference library every evening, standing at the high counter for a chat.

He lived on his own in a council flat in Bethnal Green; he had never married. He was unfailingly equable, content in his solitary wanderings about the capital with his sketchbook; his art gave meaning to it all. He had a friend, another artist, a younger, middle-aged man, dark and shy like a small boy, a burly little bloke in a labourer's donkey jacket, overalls and boots.

"Bill here will tell you, he knows all about it." Something about politics, the workers, the class system, had come up in one of our little chats.

Bill smiled his shy smile, edging a bit closer.

"Bill knows the manual worker, don't you, Bill?" Bill nodded, looking pleased with himself at this attention. "He can tell you about the manual worker. Oh, yes! He'll tell you the same as me: *steer clear of the manual worker!*"

Bill nodded emphatically.

Geraghty, a fellow north Irishman, was another obsessive writer of letters to the *Gazette.* The cruelty of the British ruling class was his theme, as most recently evidenced in the internment camps of the Six Counties, *"methods of torture that would shame the ancient Chinese"* he wrote to the paper

I didn't necessarily disagree with that but as I got to know Geraghty a bit it did seem that the poor fellow was paranoid. Stocky and powerful, he had the cropped head and hunted belligerent look of the lunatic—sure enough, he'd been in Broadmoor, he told me. He dressed in a holy jumper and old grey flannels, bare feet in dirty gutties, and cycled round Hackney, racing the cars.

A bitterness consumed him. "Aye and I get harassment by the peelers, '*Go on ye fughin Irish queer!*' they tell me because Ah'm a bachelor!" And speaking of the Unionists of the Northern Ireland state, he said, "It was them turned the English against the darkies!"

"Irish queer" seemed an odd bit of name-calling; were we all gay stevedores now? And most Unionists had never laid eyes on a "darkie"; the nationalists were the "darkies" of the six counties. But it was interesting, the link between imbalance of the mind in a person and their country's history of persecution.

We saw quite a lot of our mate Budgy; as a couple we tended to attract stray dogs. He'd turn up at our place at all hours, unannounced. One morning he came in the kitchen window after walking through the cemetery and scaling the wall into our back garden, then climbing a drainpipe and crossing a conservatory roof. Another evening he arrived just as Bridget and I were getting going on the rocking chair. Then I got back from work one evening greeting Bridget by some silly pet name and Budgy jumped out from hiding behind a chair. That didn't bother me, I like being silly, but Bridget found it embarrassing and intrusive.

Budgy was certainly a character, consciously cultivating a Cockney zaniness. He made bizarre purchases at Ridley Road market on Saturdays: a giant bargain tin of spam; a horrible lifelike grinning sinister painted wooden puppet he named Charlie and practised his ventriloquism on. Then he got a kitten, Stan, a black, sturdy, wild little thing that clawed clothes and furnishings to shreds and shat everywhere but the litter tray.

Budgy's chinny grin, the matey cockney patter, the practical jokes, an innocent abroad: that was his bright cheerful side. But after a time a darker side emerged, bad mood swings, a bitterness that welled up inside him. Then he'd boot Stanley across the room or pick an argument in company. Sometimes students annoyed him, they could be so middle class and gormless. Budgy was "working class and proud of it". We were all going through a keen socialist phase, with the *Workers' Daily Press* delivered to our doors by local activists. It was liberating to dream of casting off the chains of capitalism and imperialism, of greed, exploitation and war. But it roused a kind of self-pity in Budgy, relating everything wrong with society back to all his personal grievances and he would become self-righteous and argumentative, tipping over into rudeness towards some of the other guests in our bed-sitting room.

"Now you're being irrational, Budgy," Bridget intervened calmly on one such occasion, lest we should end up with no friends. She'd had some practice at this kind of thing in dealing with her father's ideological obstinacy.

"Irrational? *I'm* being irrational?" Budgy let out a bleat of cynical laughter. "Me? You're all saying *they* don't realise what they're doing to the working class and I'm telling you they bloody well do, it's all been worked out in detail down to the last penny screwed out of the worker, can you not see that?"

"That's paranoia, not politics."

"Oh, paranoid am I now?"

"The capitalists haven't got the sense to plan it all as carefully as that, for goodness' sake, Budgy!"

Though with hindsight, Budgy may have been right.

At the same time he was turning away from the gentle highs of early-1970s marijuana to the harshness of whisky drunk neat from the bottle, *"the smiler with a knife"*. Drunk, he would launch into emotional binges, with everything spewing out: his parents' divorce, leaving school at sixteen to be a nurse in the loony bin like his father; the Devonshire girlfriend he'd worshiped, who mistreated and dumped him.

"We've all been through that, Budgy," I said, "the girlfriend or boyfriend who isn't right for you because you're both still too young for that kind of commitment and when it's over that's the best thing that could happen to you in reality. You're free then to meet the right girl or boy—it works both ways—when you're truly ready. Those early loves are transitional experiences, just part of growing up, that's all."

"But I loved her!" he insisted. "I'd have done anything for her!" Tears were streaming down his cheeks.

"Then let her go, if that's what she wanted!"

He had us all drunk on the firewater and all in tears as we collapsed into bed afterwards in the dark pit of depressive inebriation. Waking in the light of morning with a throbbing head you saw through it, how you'd been drawn into the illusory malignant world of drunken neurosis.

Budgy's next acquisition was a second-hand car. "Now I can take you and Bridge to the seaside! We can stay in my dad's chalet right on the beach!"

It was the Easter weekend. The three of us set off in the rundown Capri in the grey spring morning, out through the suburbs and on to the trunk road for Essex and the east coast. Budgy's driving was nervous and erratic but we got to the little seaside town by midday, still in one piece. The sun was breaking through the clouds over a glittery dark sea. The geriatric home where Budgy's dad worked loomed out on a promontory in the bay.

A back entrance, gloomy corridors and a cage lift took us up to his dad's apartment. His stepmother Sheila welcomed us, polite but reserved; all was not well in the marriage. Budgy's stepsister Alice, a wee girl of nine, came forward to greet him. Sheila served us a cooked meal at the table while a shower beat on the high windows and the gulls swooped and cried, like being on a liner out at sea. Alice told us about her travels with the drum majorettes.

As we finished eating, Budgy's dad appeared in his nurse's uniform. Budgy had talked a lot about him, he looked up to him as a sort of working class hero, an East End Communist. I saw a well-fed middle-aged man with a deadpan reserve and a way of speaking out of the corner of his mouth, his upper lip projecting slightly. Sheila kept away from him, in the kitchen; she was the nurse he'd left Budgy's mum for but now he had a young fancy woman on the side.

In an afternoon of sun, wind and showers Budgy showed us around the little Essex seaside town then we met up with his dad again in the pub at half-five. We stood at the bar in the small lounge. He had the fancy woman with him; she was young and high-spirited, hanging on his arm. He was smart in a good suit, slicked-back crinkly greying hair, a solid, well set-up middle-aged figure, almost distinguished-looking. He was in his element now, out on the town on a Saturday night, flashing his cash and ordering rounds of drinks, a g-and-t and a fag in one hand, the younger woman in the other.

"Town's full of bladdy Londoners down for the bank holiday," he was saying. "Oh, they're bad buggers. We get the bloody Krays' lot here an' all—the old mum has a caravan on the site. Half them villains ain't locked up yet. You'll see them down the clubhouse later, worse luck!"

The clubhouse served the chalets and caravan park; it was where we moved on to later for the cheap drink, late licensing hours and the "Saturday cabaret". The cavernous bar was busy. Budgy and I were at the bar ordering drinks when one of two men standing next us pointed to the leather pouch on Budgy's belt, a hippy fashion of the time, and said, "Zat one o' them Paddy-bombs you got on yor hip?"

It was a strange, vaguely intimidating remark that set the tone for the rest of the evening. When I went to the gent's a bit later I couldn't open the door; someone was holding it shut from the inside. After a few minutes the door opened and a group of men left. As I passed the cubicles I saw a man bent over the toilet bowl retching and spitting into it.

"Sawright," somebody was saying, "he fell over and hurt hisself, that's all! Fell over an urt isself, pore lad!"

I got a glimpse of the victim's bloodied mouth on the way back out, his teeth knocked in.

The atmosphere of incipient violence was almost palpable in the smoky, boozy air of the big noisy packed bar. Then suddenly a bottle smashed, instantly silencing the whole room. Two men confronted each other at the bar, one threatening the other with the broken bottle.

Then somebody stepped in, another gangster, "Eold it there, Frankie! E din mean nuffink, didja na, Bruce?"

Slowly the men backed off and immediately the great crowd-voice in the cavernous bar started up again at full volume. The moment of terror had passed; the drinking continued in a great release of tension as if nothing had happened at all. You knew not to ask any questions. As far as you were concerned nothing at all had happened, okay?

The centre of the floor was cleared for the cabaret. The music played and the dancer came on, a muscular black male who performed amazing acrobatic twists and leaps to the enthusiastic applause of the all-white audience.

Budgy, Bridget and I made our way to the chalet around midnight. It was one of a long row overlooking the beach, the waves washing up in the dark below our window. We emerged from the chalet in the hungover seedy overcast Sunday morning to view the sludge of green sea lapping the grey shale bank.

May time brought the warm weather and Bridget's finals. The student flat life went dead as they all swotted desperately to the finishing post. But it was a uniquely happy time for Bridget and me, just the two of us mostly, living in a quiet, deep contentment. She finished revising around nine each evening and we retired to the pub, strolling out hand in hand in the clear, soft light of the evenings lengthening to midsummer.

She wore her Indian dress and walked in her bare feet. Our long black hair hung down our backs. We were together in the knowledge now that we would be married in August and be together always. Every simple little detail of our walk to the pub in the mellow summer's evening seemed a manifestation of the wonder and joy we felt at this magic time in our lives. The level golden light glowed on the sun-warmed stone of a high old garden wall we walked beside. The soft evening breeze, like the breath of happiness, stirred in the new foliage of the trees and hedges along the quiet avenues. The sun flamed in a high window on Church Street. We walked in a living dream of the love we'd dreamt of all our lives.

Our route took us past the library that stood on the site of Edgar Allan Poe's old school, the setting of *William Wilson*. I'd worked in that library too, another cavernous, galleried interior, and felt the spell of the old master of mystery and imagination whose writing still touched my soul strangely. There was the church on the bend, with Clissold Park behind it, then the pub.

The working class local pub was quiet on these weekday nights; we took our beers to the same cosy corner table, obligingly empty and waiting for us. Every sip of beer, every quiet moment there seemed to bring us closer together in a kind of spell of the happy contentment of deep young love. The alcohol glowed in our veins, in calm and blissful sensations. The *Workers' Daily Press* sellers came through, the nice Greek girl Anna who had sold me my first copy and Bill, a very likeable, modest young man, Hackney born and bred, who'd beaten heroin addiction and made the Revolutionary Socialist Party his life instead. The world seemed a bright, hopeful place, reflecting the life Bridget and I had built together. We felt connected up to the force for spiritual progress that is embodied in socialism. Our love for each other went out to everyone around us and came back to us with interest. No capitalist could ever match such an investment.

We came away from the pub a little light-headed from the beer. It was a ghostly feeling back out on the narrow old high-walled street in the blue gloaming. The smell of frying carried on the warm night air; yellow light spilled from the chip shop; we got our takeaway of plaice and chips that we shared, eating it from the paper as we walked on home. We delighted in these simple common pleasures, a pint of bitter and fish 'n' chips. To go on to bed then and lie in each other's arms, what more could you want? Who needed pots of money? It couldn't buy you the one thing that matters which is love. We were rich in that. We felt our life together charmed and blessed in every way.

Bridget went home to Surrey for the month of July to help with the preparations for our wedding on the third of August.

I went to my wedding with the traditional hangover after an impromptu sort of stag night at the *Minstrel Boy* on Colney Hatch Lane. The lads turned up in the morning in their suits. I'd bought mine from Grant's of Croydon. The fashion of the day was wide lapels and flared trousers. We all had long hair that was somehow at odds with the suits. We travelled down to Surrey in two cars. Going through Croydon past the Fairfield Halls some jerk in a Merc drew level with us, wound down his window and started firing gags at us: *"Heard the one abaht the Awrishman?"*— What a daft country this realm, this England could be at times!

It was a wet day. In the Railway Hotel I managed to swallow a couple of whisky-and-gingers, hair of the dog and to see me through the ordeal of the wedding ceremony. The modern redbrick church, like a fire station, was frighteningly full inside.

There were a lot of people I didn't know, friends and family of the McDonaghs, some terrifying older women in huge hats. Ned and Nora were there, the only members of my family who were able to come. I took my seat at the front of the church, beside Budgy, my best man. I was glad of him now, a sincere friend in his own way and a lad, very much up for the public spectacle of a wedding.

The woman wedding singer at the back of the church gave a puissant performance of the *Ave Maria*. Then the organ struck up momentously, Wagner's *Bridal Chorus*. To hear it played at your own wedding, blasted out on a powerful organ, was something else, Earth-moving, the notes on the great pipes seeming to reach all the way up to heaven, sending shudders down my spine and threatening to blow the top of my head off.

I was conscious of Bridget coming down the aisle in her bridal white on the arm of her grey-haired, grey-suited pater. Her sisters Carmel and Theresa were the bridesmaids. During the long month back in the family home she'd been driven to her wits' end with the minutiae and stress of all the wedding preparations, feeling ready at times to call the whole operation off.

Budgy nudged me to my feet and we stood out in the aisle. Bridget drew alongside me. In the long white bridal gown she and Jean had made she was sylphlike and mysteriously beautiful. There was a sense of unreality; for a moment we seemed utter strangers, alien to one another, no longer Jim and Bridget even—

It was with such relief then that I saw the dear face smiling so sweetly at me from behind the veil under the wide-brimmed hat and in that tell-all tender moment we were reunited. She loved me still, all was well! I had to look away from her as tears filled my eyes, we were so fragile and vulnerable in that magical moment of life. It was such a delicate and wondrous thing, so ineffably sweetly beautiful, this love we shared that had brought us all the way to the altar.

We were two children of God joined in a love supreme and eternal, a state of shared being at once human and divine. Blake's angels—they had followed us from the bed-head in Manor Road to the suburban fire station church with its big-hatted matrons— hovered and shimmered all around us in joy and celebration.

ABOUT THE AUTHOR

John Kerr McMillan was born in Armagh in 1948, the youngest child of George, district audit inspector on the Great Northern Railway, and Meliora, daughter of the Rev John Kerr of Rathlin Island.

John grew up mainly in Tyrone and County Antrim. He was educated at Belfast Royal Academy and Bournemouth University and has worked as a clerk, library assistant and teacher. His writing is influenced by modern classic authors from D.H.Lawrence to J.D. Salinger.

John's previous novels, "On A Green Island"(2001) and "Summer in the Heart"(2011) won general critical acclaim. Philip Callow admired the "lovely lyricism and good writing which seems to come at you straight from the heart", while Edward Upward praised the "many marvellous episodes and descriptions that show John McMillan to be a born writer".

John lives in Somerset with his wife Fiona. They have two daughters, Siobhan, an actress, and Sinead, a musician. John is a regular visitor to Ireland where he grew up and London where he lived as a young man.